TRAPPED

PRAISE FOR THE IRON DRUID CHRONICLES

"This is the best urban/paranormal fantasy I have read years. Fast paced, funny, clever, and suitably mythic, is is urban fantasy for those worn out by werewolves id vampires. Fans of Jim Butcher, Harry Connolly, 'reg van Eekhout, Ben Aaronovitch, or Neil Gaiman's *merican Gods* will take great pleasure in Kevin iearne's *Hounded*. Highly recommended"
John Ottinger III, editor of *Grasping for the Wind*

"Atticus and his crew are a breath of fresh air!"
My Bookish Ways

"A truly entertaining series"
SFF World

"Kevin Hearne is quickly becoming one of my favourite authors . . . I highly recommend picking up the Iron Druid Chronicles"
Fantasybookcritic

"If you like urban fantasy that is fun and funny, then pick up *Hounded, Hexed,* and *Hammered.* If you like urban fantasy of great substance then you should pick up *Hounded, Hexed, Hammered,* and anything else Kevin Hearne puts out in the future. You'll not be disappo
Fi Mafia

TRAPPED

THE
IRON
DRUID
CHRONICLES

KEVIN HEARNE

www.orbitbooks.net

ORBIT

First published in Great Britain in 2012 by Orbit
Reprinted 2013

A CIP catalogue record for this book
is available from the British Library.

ISBN 978-0-356-50197-0

Printed and bound by CPI Group (UK) Ltd, Croydon, CR0 4YY

Papers used by Orbit are from well-managed forests
and other responsible sources.

MIX
Paper from
responsible sources
FSC® C104740

Orbit
An imprint of
Little, Brown Book Group
100 Victoria Embankment
London EC4Y 0DY

An Hachette UK Company
www.hachette.co.uk

www.orbitbooks.net

To those who have glimpsed divinity in beauty
or
to anyone who's ever had to think about baseball

Pronunciation Guide

If you're an old hand with the series, then you know that some of the Irish names can be challenging if you try to say them according to English spelling rules. Since I have a lot of Irish names in this book, I'm taking the opportunity to repeat some names that I haven't addressed since *Hounded*. As always, this guide is intended to help those who'd like to say everything correctly in their head. There is no requirement to do so, and I won't be annoyed if you pronounce things however you like—especially since these are presented largely in the Ulster dialect, and folks who speak in the Munster dialect would pronounce them differently anyway. You're supposed to have fun, dang it, so have fun whether you say these correctly or not! There won't be a test later.

Irish

Aenghus Óg = AN gus OHG (Epic douche. Dead now)
Brighid = BREE yit (First Among the Fae, her magical
    powers are rivaled only by those of the Morrigan)
Cnoc an Óir = KNOCK a NOR (Location on the plane of

Mag Mell; source of the healing hot springs. Literally means *gold hill*)

Creidhne = CRAY nya (One of the Three Craftsmen, specializes in bronze, brass, and gold)

Dubhlainn Óg = DOOV lin OHG

Emhain Ablach = Evan ah BLACH (That's a guttural *ch* that often gets left off and pronounced like an *ah*, as it does in the words *Fragarach* and *Moralltach*. Means Isle of Apples)

Fand = Fand (I know, right? What are the odds that you'd say it the way it's spelled? Daughter of Flidais, married to Manannan Mac Lir)

feeorin = FEY oh rin (A type of faery in Irish lore, which precedes the birth of George Lucas; bears absolutely no relation to the reptilian alien species in the *Star Wars* universe)

Fir Darrig = fir DAR ick (They're like Fir Bolgs but woodier)

Flidais = FLIH dish (Irish goddess of the hunt)

Fragarach = FRAG ah RAH (Legendary sword that can cut through any armor; the Answerer)

geancanach = gan CAN ah (Another type of faery)

Goibhniu = GUV new (One of the Three Craftsmen, specializing in smithing and brewing)

Granuaile = GRAWN ya wale (People ask me about this one a lot, so there you go)

Luchta = LOOKED ah (The *ch* is kind of a guttural job, but I'm approximating with a *k* sound here. One of the Three Craftsmen, specializing in woodcraft. He's sometimes referred to as Luchtaine in myth.)

Mag Mell = Mah Mell (One of the Irish planes of paradise; the really posh one)

Manannan Mac Lir = MAH nah non mac LEER (God of the sea and psychopomp to five planes of the afterlife, including Mag Mell and Emhain Ablach)

Moralltach = MORE ul TAH (Another legendary sword

with an enchantment of necrosis on it; one strike and you're toast. Means Great Fury)

Ogma = OG ma (First syllable rhymes with *log*. One of the Tuatha Dé Danann)

Scáthmhaide = SKAH wad jeh (Means Shadow Staff)

Siodhachan = SHE ya han (The real first name of Atticus given to him by his own dear mother)

Tír na nÓg = TEER na NOHG (Land of Youth. The primary Irish plane through which Druids shift to other planes.)

Tuatha Dé Danann = TWO ah day DAN an (The race o' people who were the first Druids and eventually became the gods of the pagan Irish)

Norse

Álfheim = ALF hame

Einherjar = EYNE her yar

Gjöll = Gyoll (Short *o* as in *not*)

Hugin = HYOO gin

Munin = MOO nin

Nidavellir = NIH da VETTL ir

Niflheim = NIV el HAME

Sigyn = SIG in (Hard *g*)

Skadi = SKAH dee (With a softish *d*)

Svartálfheim = SVART alf hame

Vir = VER

Yggdrasil = IG drah sil (World Tree)

Ylgr = ILL ger

Greco-Romans

Agrios = AG ree ohs (A Thracian horror)

Bacchant = BOCK ent (There are alternate pronunciations for these that are perfectly valid; this is just the one I prefer)

Bacchus = BOCK us

Oreios = oh RYE ohs (Brother to Agrios, another Thracian horror)

Polyphonte = polly FAWN tay (Learned what happens when you displease Aphrodite; mother to Agrios and Oreios)

Thracian = THRAY shen

YGGDRASIL

ALFHEIM VANAHEIM

ASGARD

NIDAVELLIR MIDGARD JOTUNHEIM

HELHEIM 11
9 10
8 MUSPELLHEIM
7
SVARTALFHEIM

and the Nine Realms of the Norse

The Rivers of   1. Svöl   2. Gunnthrá   3. Fjörm   4. Fimbulthul
Hvergelmir: 5. Sylgr   6. Slíd   7. Hríd   8. Ylgr
                9. Vír   10. Leiptr   11. Gjöll

Priscilla Spencer

Chapter 1

You know those spastic full-body twitches you get sometimes when you're almost asleep and your muscles want to play a practical joke on your brain? You startle wide awake and immediately get pissed at your nervous system, wondering what the hell *that* was all about. I've caught myself talking to it before: "Damn it, Dude"—yes, I call my nervous system Dude, and the Dude abides—"I was almost asleep, and now you've slain all the sheep I was gonna count."

What I felt as I walked on the Kaibab Plateau was kind of like that, except it was Gaia doing the spastic full-body twitch. It was more of an uncomfortable shudder that I felt through my tattoos, like when you step barefoot into the garage in winter and your nipples pucker up. But, as with those nervous muscle spasms, I got irritated about it and wondered what the hell was going on. And while I wasn't about to go to sleep, I was about to enjoy the culmination of twelve years of training an apprentice— and, save for the first few months of it and a harrowing episode halfway through, I'd conducted it all in peace. Granuaile was finally ready to become a full Druid, and we'd been searching for a place to bind her to the earth when I felt the tremor. I shot a question to the elemental, Kaibab, in the cocktail of feelings and images they use instead of language: //Confusion / Query: What was that?//

//Confusion / Uncertainty / Fear// came the reply. That chilled me. I'd never heard confusion from an elemental before. The fear, on the other hand, was perfectly normal: Despite their awesome power, elementals are afraid of almost everything, from placer mines to land developers to bark beetles. They can be real scaredy-cats sometimes. But they're never uncertain about what's going on with Gaia. Stopping in my tracks and causing Granuaile and Oberon to turn and look at me quizzically, I asked Kaibab what there was to fear.

//Plane across ocean / Early death / Burning / Burning / Burning//

Well, that confused me too. Kaibab wasn't talking about an airplane. He (or she, if Granuaile had been the one talking to the elemental) meant an entire plane of existence, a plane that was tied to earth somewhere on the other side of the globe. //Query: Which plane?//

//Name unknown / God from plane seeks you / Urgent / Query: Tell him location?//

//Query: Which god?//

The answer to that would tell me what plane was burning. There was a pause, during which time I stalled with Granuaile and Oberon. "Something's up with Kaibab. Hold on." They knew better than to interrupt, and they took this news as an invitation to be on their guard, which was wise. Anything worrisome to the avatar of the environment you currently occupy should rouse you to a caffeinated state of paranoia.

//God's name: Perun// Kaibab finally said.

Almost unconsciously, I sent //Shock// in reply, because it was truly my reaction. The Slavic plane of existence was burning, perhaps even dead? How? Why? I hoped Perun would have the answers. If he sought me in hopes that I had them, we'd both be disappointed. //Yes / Tell Perun location//

I'd also like to know how Perun even knew to ask for

me—did someone tell him I'd faked my death twelve years ago? There was another pause, during which I filled in Granuaile and Oberon. Thanks to Immortali-Tea, they hadn't aged any more than I had.

<Hey, isn't Perun that hairy guy you told me about, who can turn into an eagle?> Oberon asked.

Yep, that's the one.

<I've always wondered why he doesn't shill for shaving cream or razors with twenty-five ultrathin vibrating blades. He'd sure move a buttload of product.>

I don't know why, but perhaps you'll get a chance to ask him.

//He comes// Kaibab said. //Fast//

"Okay, incoming," I said out loud.

"Incoming what, Atticus?" Granuaile asked.

"Incoming thunder god. We should move near a tree and get ready to shift away to Tír na nÓg if necessary. And get the fulgurites out." Fulgurites would protect us from lightning strikes; Perun had given them to us when Granuaile was just starting her training, but we hadn't worn them for years, since all the thunder gods thought I was dead.

"You think Perun is going to take a shot at us?" Granuaile asked. She shrugged off her red backpack and unzipped the pouch containing the fulgurites.

"Well, no, but . . . maybe. I don't know what's going on, really. When in doubt, know your way out, I always say."

"I thought you always said, 'When in doubt, blame the dark elves.'"

"Well, yeah, that too."

<I don't think those are very practical solutions to doubt,> Oberon said. <They don't leave you feeling satisfied. "When in doubt, eat your neighbor's lunch" is better, because then you would at least be full.>

We stood in a meadow of bunch grass and clover.

The sky washed us in cerulean blue, and the sun kissed Granuaile's red hair with gold—mine too, I suppose. We had stopped dyeing our hair black because no one was looking for two redheads anymore. And after twelve uncomfortable years of being clean-shaven—my goatee had been distinguishable and damn difficult to dye—I was enjoying my new beard. Oberon looked as if he wanted to plop down and bask in the light for a while. Our backpacks were weighted down with camping gear that we'd bought at Peace Surplus in Flagstaff, but after Granuaile retrieved the fulgurites, we jogged over as best we could to the nearest stand of Ponderosa pine trees. I confirmed that there was a functioning tether to Tír na nÓg there and then looked up for signs of Perun's arrival.

Granuaile noticed and craned her neck upward. "What's up there, sensei?" she wondered aloud. "I don't see anything but sky."

"I'm looking for Perun. I'm assuming he's going to fly in. There, see?" I pointed to a dark streak in the northwestern sky trailed by lightning bolts. And, behind that, at a distance of perhaps five to ten miles—I couldn't tell from so far away—burned an orange ball of fire.

Granuaile squinted. "What's that thing that looks like the Phoenix Suns logo? Is that him?"

"No, Perun is in front of it, throwing all the lightning."

"Oh, so what is it? A meteor or a cherub or something?"

"Or something. It doesn't look friendly. That's not a warm, cozy hearth fire that you gather 'round with your friends to read some Longfellow while you toast s'mores. That's more like napalm with a heart of phosphorus and a side of hell sauce." The lightning and the fireball were turning in the sky and heading directly our way.

<Um. Hey, Atticus, think we should try that escape route just to make sure it works?> Oberon said.

I hear ya, buddy. I'm ready to scoot too. But let's see if we can talk to Perun first.

The sky darkened and boomed above, making everything shudder; Perun was traveling at supersonic speeds. He crashed into the meadow about fifty yards away from us, and large chunks of turf exploded around a newly formed crater. I felt the impact in my feet, and a wave of displaced air knocked me backward a bit. Before the turf could fall back to earth, a heavily muscled figure carpeted in hair bounded out of it toward us, panic writ large on his features.

"Atticus! We must flee this plane! Is not safe! Take me—save me!"

Normally thunder gods are not prone to panic. The ability to blast away problems tends to turn the jagged edges of fear into silly little pillows of insouciance. So when an utter badass like Perun looks as if he's about to soil himself, I hope I can be forgiven if I nearly shat kine—especially when the fireball *whoomped* into the crater Perun had just vacated and sucked all the oxygen out of my lungs.

Granuaile ducked and shrieked in surprise; Oberon whimpered. Perun was tossed through the air toward us like a stuntman in a Michael Bay film, but, upon rolling gracefully through the landing, he leapt back up, his legs churning toward us.

Behind Perun, the fire didn't spread but rather began to shrink and coalesce and . . . laugh. A high, thin, maniacal laugh, straight out of creepy cartoons. And the fire swirled, torus-like, around a figure twelve feet tall, until it gradually wicked out and left a lean giant with a narrow face standing fifty yards before us, his orange and yellow hair starting from his skull like a sunburst. The grin on his face wasn't the affable, friendly sort; it was more like the sociopathic rictus of the irretrievably, bugfuckeringly insane.

His eyes were the worst. They were melted around the edges, as if they'd been burned with acid, and where a normal person would have laugh lines or crow's-feet, he had bubbly pink scars and a nightmare of blistered tissue. The whites of his eyes were a red mist of broken blood vessels, but the irises were an ice blue frosted with madness. He blinked them savagely, as if he had soap in them or something, and soon I recognized it as a nervous tic, since his head jerked to the right at odd intervals and then continued to twitch uncertainly afterward, like a bobble-head doll.

"Go, my friend, go! We must flee!" Perun said, huffing as he reached us and putting one hand on my shoulder and another on the pine. Granuaile followed suit; she knew the drill, and so did Oberon, who reared up on his hind legs and leaned one paw against me and the other on the tree.

"Who in hell is that, Perun?" I said.

The giant laughed again and I shuddered involuntarily. His voice was smooth and fluffy, like marshmallow crème—if the crème also had shards of glass in it. But he had a thick Scandinavian accent to go with the nervous tic.

"This p-p-place—is M-Merrica, yes?"

A twitch, a stutter, *and* an English-language learner. He'd drive me insane just listening to him. "Yes," I replied.

"Hah? Who? Thppt! Raah!" He spat a fire loogie and shook his head violently. Perhaps this was more than a twitch. It might be full-blown Tourette's syndrome. Or it might be something else, as the signs all pointed to a highly unpleasant conclusion.

"Who gah, guh, gods here?" He giggled to himself after this, pleased that he'd managed to ask the question.

There was a disturbingly high squealing noise coming from his head, like the sound of fat screaming in a frying pan or air slowly leaking out of a balloon. The giant rested his hands on his knees and scrunched up his shoulders in an attempt to steady his noggin, but this had the unsettling effect of turning his flamelike hair to actual flames. The noise intensified.

"You are a god here," I said, taking an educated guess. I could have confirmed this by looking at him in the magical spectrum, but there was no need. There wasn't much else that Perun would fear. "But I don't know which one. Who are you?"

The giant threw back his head and roared in delight, clapping like a child and high-stepping as if I'd asked him if he wanted ice cream. My jaw dropped, and Granuaile muttered a bewildered "What the fuck?" which mirrored my own thoughts. What had happened to his mind?

Perun chucked me urgently on the shoulder. "Atticus, is Loki! He is free. We must go. Is smart thing to do."

"Gods below," I breathed, gooseflesh rising on my arms. I'd feared he was Loki once I saw the eyes, but I'd also clung to the hope that he was something a bit less apocalyptic, like an escaped military experiment along the lines of Sharktopus. Instead, Loki, the old Norse villain of the *Eddas*, whose release from captivity heralded the start of Ragnarok, was unbound and ready to paint the town batshit.

<Listen to the hairy guy, Atticus. Tall, scarred, and fiery there is stranger danger if I ever saw it.>

Perun and Oberon were right; the smart thing to do would be to leave. But the smarter thing to do would be to get Loki to leave too. I didn't want to scarper off and leave Kaibab at his mercy; I wanted Loki off this plane as quickly as possible. Time to lie to the god of lies.

"I am Eldhár," I called out to him in Old Norse. His

laughter, already dying out, choked off abruptly, and he focused those blue-and-blood eyes on me. The name was one I'd used before: It meant "flame hair" in Old Norse, and I'd employed it years ago when I'd gone to Asgard to steal a golden apple. "I am a construct of the dwarfs of Nidavellir." Tapping into my adrenaline and an older, more primitive part of my psyche, I smiled at the giant in the same disconcerting way he had smiled at us. "Glad am I that you are free, Loki, for that means your wife is free also, and I was built specifically to destroy her and all your spawn. I will behead the serpent. Eviscerate the wolf. And as for Hel: Even the queen of death can die." I laughed menacingly, hoped that it was convincing, and thought that would serve as a good exit line.

Without giving him a chance to respond, I pulled my center along the tether to Tír na nÓg, bringing Granuaile, Oberon, and Perun with me, shifting us safely away from earth and leaving Loki to consider how to address this new problem. Hopefully he'd return to the Norse plane and start asking questions—and hopefully the dwarfs had fire insurance.

I had plenty of questions for Perun—like how had Loki gained entrance to the Slavic plane, what was Hel up to now, and whether Fenris was still fettered—but foremost among them was finding out what idiot had thought it a good idea to teach an old god of mischief how to speak English.

Chapter 2

I didn't linger in Tír na nÓg but rather shifted us right away to an island in the middle of Third Cranberry Lake in Manitoba. It was one of my favorite escapes, covered with evergreens and rarely visited by humans.

I was breathing heavily even though I hadn't run anywhere yet. "It's too soon," I huffed. "He's not supposed to be going around burning things yet. We have a year left."

"What are you talking about?" Granuaile asked. She crossed one leg over the other and leaned on her staff.

"Perun will remember this," I said, catching his eye. "Remember when we were in Siberia and we ate that rabbit stew and told stories before we went to Asgard?"

"*Da*, I remember. I say, 'Next time, eat bear.'"

<I like the way this guy thinks.>

"Well, after dinner, Väinämöinen told us that story about the sea serpent. And I didn't say anything then, but there is this old time-bomb prophecy that the sirens spoke to Odysseus when he was tied to the mast—the only one that hasn't come true yet, and I thought the clock started ticking then. The prophecy goes like this: 'Thirteen years from the date a white beard sups on hares and talks of sea serpents, the world will burn.'"

"That's weird," Granuaile said.

"Is more than weird. Is unhappy stomach from spicy food. Is ass on fire," Perun asserted.

"*What?*" Granuaile cried, unused to Perun's attempts to be colorful in English.

Perun shrugged and tried again. "I mean is much discomfort. Ass on fire is very bad, yes?"

"Agreed," I said, "but those same sirens accurately predicted the rise of Genghis Khan, the American Revolution, and the bombing of Hiroshima. That pattern suggests they're talking about something bigger than a small fire, camp or ass or otherwise."

<That reminds me! I never did muster my horde on the Mongolian steppes.>

"You think my world is world of this prophecy?" Perun asked.

"No, I don't think the sirens would speak of planes other than this one. Plus we're a year too early. But that's what has me worried: The prophecies regarding Ragnarok aren't worth a damn anymore, yet it still might happen now that Loki's free. The sirens of Odysseus were always right, but maybe this time they're going to be wrong—or maybe just off by a year. I don't know. Killing the Norns screwed up everything. I suppose all I know is that there's a tsunami of shit heading toward a ten-dollar fan and we're standing on the fan. Jesus spoke to me of cataclysms, plural, and maybe we could avoid them if we got rid of both Loki and Hel, but who knows if Ganesha and his gang will let me pursue that now, because I promised I'd wait until—"

"Atticus," Granuaile said, touching me gently on the arm. "You've stopped making sense. Calm down."

"Right. Thanks. I need to slow down. You know what sucks about prophecies?"

"They never predict anything fun," Granuaile answered. "Just once I'd like to hear a prophet tell someone, 'Thou shalt win a bitchin' Camaro on a game show.'"

"Good point, but I was going to say that everybody has them. Prophets have been around as long as prostitutes."

<Often in the same bed, ba-doom-boom!>

"You can't figure out who to believe," I continued, "so you wind up treating all the prophets like Cassandras, but some of them really are correct. Hitting on the right one before their prophecy comes true, though—that's the trick. Worse odds than roulette."

"You hit women named Cassandra?" Perun said, frowning. "Is not right to hit women, even if name is ugly."

"What? Perun, I think you misunderstood."

"Oh." He looked crestfallen. "I am reminded many times. English is not best language for me."

"I speak Russian now, though it's not my best language either," Granuaile said. "We could switch to that if you'd like, if you would talk slowly and pronounce everything clearly."

Perun grinned. "*Da*, that would be wonderful!" We made the switch, and I tried to speak slowly for Granuaile's benefit.

"I've been thinking for a while now," I said, "that this prophecy about the world burning might be linked to Ragnarok, thanks to what we did in Asgard. That's why seeing Loki free is seriously disturbing. His release was always the trigger of Ragnarok in the old tales."

Granuaile frowned. "Yeah, but wasn't he supposed to ride a ship of the dead up to the Field of Vigrid, and it was a ship made of toenails or something?"

"He was," I said, nodding, "but nothing is going to go the way it was supposed to now. Regardless of any prophecies, a free Loki isn't a good thing for anyone. How'd he get to your plane, Perun?"

The great Russian god shrugged, his impressive personal thatching communicating the depths of his frustration.

"I don't know. I was in Alaska in the form of an eagle, eating a trout I'd just caught from a river, when I felt that something was wrong. I went to my plane and found Loki there, setting fire to everything. I threw lightning at him and he laughed. He was not hurt at all, and he said he was waiting for me."

"Why?" Granuaile asked.

"He was mad because I helped to kill Thor," Perun explained.

"But he hated Thor," I said.

"I know. He said that killing Thor himself became his dream during those years he was tied down under the great snake. Then he said, since I had taken away his dream, he would take away my people's dream. He left me a harvest of ashes."

"That's terrible," Granuaile said.

Perun nodded at her, grateful for the sympathy. "After that he said, 'You are like Thor, so I will kill you instead.' He attacked me, and he was very strong. Stronger than I thought he would be. I began to fear him, and I panicked. I asked the earth to find you."

That didn't quite compute. "You never heard that I died?"

Perun looked at me curiously. "When was this?" He poked me with a finger to make sure I was real. "You do not feel like a ghost."

"No, I mean I faked my death. You never heard about that?"

The thunder god shook his head. "I have been an eagle for too long, I think. I lost track of the years."

I knew what he meant; it was dangerous to spend too much time in animal form, because it became so easy to focus on the basic needs of survival and let all one's other cares drift away. And once those cares left, the memories began to drift away too, until even one's identity faded to oblivion and nothing remained but finding the day's meal in the forest. My archdruid had called it the "last shift." It was how Druids committed suicide.

"So you have no idea who set Loki free?"

Perun grimaced in regret. "He did not say. I knew nothing until I felt my world . . . burning."

Someone cleared his throat to my right. I turned to behold a faery—one of the flying kind, dressed up in the pompous green and silver livery of the Fae Court—hovering just out of throttling range. Gods below, how had he found me?

"Hail, Siodhachan Ó Suileabháin," he said, his voice redolent of scorn and aristocratic disgust, enunciated with such precision that one could hear capital letters, "the Supposedly Deceased. Brighid, First Among the Fae, summons you to an audience in her Court forthwith, there to answer Certain Questions, among which are Why are you still alive? and More Importantly, Why did you not inform Brighid of this Rather Important Fact?"

I briefly considered making this messenger disappear. I could shake his hand—or otherwise make contact with him—and, as a creature made of magic, he would crumble to ash from the cold iron in my aura. But then Brighid would know something had happened to him, and she'd send more after me. Whatever displeasure she currently felt would only grow if I made her wait too long. Still, this was an extraordinarily inconvenient time to ask me over for tea—or whipping, or whatever else she had in mind.

"I see. I am indisposed at the moment to attend the Fae Court. Will you bear her a message for me?"

"No. I am to bear you to the Court or nothing withal."

His tone—especially combined with Elizabethan

diction—finally annoyed me. Perhaps he needed to be reminded that I was not one of Brighid's subjects. "Do you truly have the power to bear me there?" I asked him. "Are you immune to cold iron, sir?"

His confident, supercilious manner withered, and he gulped. "No," he admitted.

"So this talk of bearing me hence is nothing more than bluster, yes?" I took a step toward him, and he back-winged. I gave him a thin smile.

"Yes," he said.

"Good," I said, and began to mock his affected accent and language. "It is most unfortunate that you may bear no messages back to your liege. Peradventure you may ask her a question, instead, the answer to which may speed my arrival thither. May I bring my companions—those you see here, including my hound—to Tír na nÓg under her personal aegis? I need a guarantee of safe conduct for us all to and from the Court. An affirmative answer will assure my immediate arrival."

"I will inquire."

"I will await her reply for five minutes only."

The faery nodded, said nothing, and touched the same tree we had used to shift here. He winked out of sight, shifting away, and I drew my sword.

"Spread yourselves and be on your guard," I said. "He may come back with friends. Or gods."

Oberon asked, <What if he comes back with snacks?>

Chapter 3

Granuaile didn't say anything, but I caught a tiny smile on her face as she palmed a throwing knife. I couldn't read her mind, but I could read her expression well enough: She was thinking, Finally, some action. After twelve years of training and sparring with no one but me, here was the possibility of a real scrap. She took cover behind a different tree and crouched down.

I hoped it wouldn't come to any sort of fight. This was precisely the crucial period when I'd lost my last apprentice, Cíbran—at the end of his training but before I could get him bound to the earth and give him access to magic. Granuaile had trained both her mind and body extremely well, but she wouldn't be able to survive the throw-downs I was used to fighting until she was able to speed herself up, boost her strength, and heal quickly using the magic of the earth.

Perun and I took up positions elsewhere, and Oberon lay down, sphinxlike, watching the tree bound to Tír na nÓg, ready to spring up and attack.

Stop wagging your tail. The movement will give away your position.

<But this is so exciting! I might get to pounce on a faery!>

Something much more powerful than a faery might

*come through there, so don't jump until you know what
you're jumping on, okay?*

<Okay, I'll wait until you say sic 'em.>

It was an excellent precaution, because the faery herald didn't return. Someone tapped me on the shoulder,
but when I whipped around, Moralltach at the ready, I
didn't see anyone. A soft snort of amusement was my
only clue that someone was actually there.

"Calm yourself and be at ease, Atticus," a woman's
voice said, and then Flidais, Irish goddess of the hunt,
dissolved the binding that granted her true invisibility.
"It's only me. I'm to escort you and your companions to
the Court. I am Brighid's guarantee no harm will befall
them in Tír na nÓg. Good enough?"

It was entirely satisfactory, even if Flidais wasn't
dressed in her customary fashion. She had made some
effort to appear courtly; usually she was dressed in her
hunting leathers, her bow and quiver were prominently
on display, and her red hair was frizzy and wildly
adorned with random bits of vegetation that could charitably be called camouflage. Now, however, she wore
a plain woven tunic, cream colored, with a band of
green embroidered knotwork around the neck and
down the sides, underneath either arm. This was belted
at the waist, and she wore a large knife there with a
handle wrought in polished malachite and mother-of-
pearl. I had never seen it before; it was either a recent
acquisition or something she wore only to Court. Her
hair had been recently washed and brushed, and the
flowers in it were clearly put there on purpose instead
of resting there accidentally. I noted privately that
when she was cleaned up like this, she looked quite a
bit like Granuaile. Instead of a skirt, Flidais wore loose
cotton pants—like those from a martial-arts uniform—
dyed brown to match her belt; she was barefoot. I suspected that the rest of the Tuatha Dé Danann would be

similarly dressed. The Celtic ideal for clothing was that it had to be easy to move in if you needed to fight and easy to take off if you wanted a quickie.

"Of course we'd be honored by your escort," I said. "But why did Brighid send you rather than her herald to fetch us?"

Flidais arched an eyebrow at me. "You were lying in wait for him, were you not? You and your friends out there? Brighid didn't want him to die."

"I wouldn't have killed him," I said.

Flidais shrugged a shoulder, a wry smirk on her face. "Perhaps not. It was safer to send me invisibly to prevent an accident," she said. She looked over my shoulder and called, "You can come out now; it's safe."

<Is this the lady we can't really trust because you never know what side she's on?> Oberon asked, rising from his position and trotting over to us.

Yes, but I'll keep it simple: Don't trust anyone except Granuaile and me.

<Okay. I sure won't trust Brighid. Remember how she set your kitchen on fire last year?>

That was almost twelve years ago, but, yes, I remember. Better stick next to me, buddy.

<Word.>

"Is this the same hound you had when last I saw you?" Flidais asked.

"It is."

"Hello again," Flidais said to Oberon. "Perhaps we will have occasion to hunt together soon." After a small pause, she frowned, because she had just tuned in to hear Oberon's thoughts in the same way I could.

"You forbade him to hunt with me?" A flash of temper sparked in her eyes.

"Forgive me, Flidais, but the last time we hunted with you, someone died. I'd rather avoid a second accident."

"You accuse me?" she growled.

Oh, I could. I could accuse her of *murder most foul, as in the best it is*, but I have done my own share of reddish work and I do my best to eschew hypocrisy.

"No. I forbid my hound to hunt with you. There is no accusation of any kind there." Flidais might have pursued the matter but was distracted by the large, hairy arrival of Perun.

"Is this faery?" he asked hopefully, speaking English. His eyes roved over Flidais and enjoyed the journey. He wasn't subtle. Flidais, for her part, gave Perun an appraisal that was not a whit less wanton. He was, undeniably, a mobile mountain of musk and virility, and Flidais was rather famous for her appetites. I introduced them to facilitate their mutual seduction; I didn't think either of them would have to work very hard at it.

As they continued their ocular foreplay, I spied Granuaile hanging back a bit, her face a grim mask. She'd met both Flidais and Brighid at the beginning of her training, and while she'd come to terms with the necessity of the *Baolach Cruatan*—the test of mettle—she didn't have fond memories of the event. Or of Flidais.

The goddess of the hunt didn't get so lost in Perun's eyes that she forgot why she had come. Speaking to me but still looking at the thunder god, she said, "I'll leave a marker for you to follow, Atticus. It'll take you to a tree directly outside the Fae Court. I know you're too paranoid to arrive without your sword drawn, but do try to be careful. I'll make sure the area is clear."

<Hopefully it won't be clear of edible foodstuffs.>

Some of this penetrated the almost visible cloud of lust hovering over Perun's head. "What? You are leaving?"

"We will have occasion to speak more . . . at length," Flidais promised. "Soon."

"Very soon!" Perun said.

Flidais nodded to Granuaile, acknowledging her existence but saying nothing. My apprentice responded in kind, and the goddess padded her way silently to the tree we'd all been watching. She winked at Perun as she laid her hand on it and shifted away.

"By axe and sky, she is fine woman!" Perun rumbled, and then a flash of white teeth under his beard made him appear young again. "Come! Let us go!"

"Rein in your nads for a moment, if you please, Perun," Granuaile said.

The thunder god's enthusiasm disappeared in a cloud of confusion. "What is nads?" he asked. "And why should I make it rain on them? Can you say this word in Russian?"

Granuaile ignored him and spoke to me. "Atticus, what's this going to be like? What should I watch out for?"

I sighed. "I'm afraid I don't have a helpful answer. You should watch out for everything. Though I've been to Tír na nÓg plenty of times, I haven't been to the Fae Court since before I met Airmid—which was before I stole Fragarach. It's been more than two thousand years and I was still in my normal human lifespan, so there's no telling what it looks like. The Tuatha Dé Danann—however many of them are there—will be in their true forms. But I imagine every faery you see will be wearing a glamour of some kind, so don't trust anything you see. Even the furnishings may be illusions, so don't sit on anything and don't feel secure just because you have your back to a wall."

<Will the food be real food?>

Probably not. "Oberon just brought up a good point," I said aloud. "Don't eat or drink anything while you're there. Accept no gifts, make no promises—don't even say that you *will* do something, because you'll be held to it. Words are binding in Tír na nÓg more than anywhere else. To be completely safe, if you're addressed or asked a question, tell them that I speak for you. Don't let them cajole or threaten you into answering on your own—they're trying to get you rattled so that you'll make a mistake. Also, don't get separated for any reason. You might see something attractive—don't take a closer look. If someone wants to tell you a secret, don't listen to it. There are those who would love to use any one of you as a hostage in order to control me, so don't give them the opportunity, all right?"

<Yeesh! I can see why you've been avoiding the place!>

As we returned to the tree that would take us back to Tír na nÓg, I searched for a token of Flidais's to follow to a certain point on that plane. It was a short-cut to follow within the realm; we'd shift to the same isolated spot in Tír na nÓg we'd used to get here, then hop over to the center, using her marker. I found said marker in the magical spectrum, a glowing green ribbon of knotwork that pulsed like a ready light.

"All right," I said. "Weapons free, mouths shut." I held on to my sword, Perun had his axe, and Granuaile held the blade of a throwing knife between her fingers.

We shifted to Tír na nÓg and found ourselves facing a small crowd of faeries on a field of heather. Simultaneous shouts of joy and dismay filled the air at our appearance, and pouches of gold or other tokens were exchanged in what was clearly a good-natured settling of debts.

"What are they doing?" Perun asked.

Flidais separated herself from the crowd and waved. "They were betting on whether you would show up with your weapons drawn or not. Come. Follow me."

I began to follow, but I moved slowly and kept my sword out. The downside to paranoia is that you occasionally become the target of sport like this, but the upside is that you stay alive.

The slow pace allowed us to wonder at the scenery

a bit. Apart from ordinary *sidhe*, who were difficult
to distinguish from humans at times, there were oak-
men, dancing feeorin, Fir Darrigs, *geancanach*, brownies, and a small delegation representing the Blue Men of
the Minch. Pixies flitted about excitedly, making snide
comments about us, no doubt, and causing small pockets of Fae to erupt in laughter wherever they paused to
whisper.

The sky above us was the precise shade of blue that
travel agencies want on all their promotional materials,
and I wondered, apropos of nothing, what its Pantone
number might be back on earth. Here it was the illusion
of perfection that Brighid wished to project: All was
well in Tír na nÓg, because how could it be otherwise
with such fabulous weather?

The Fae Court wasn't the stuffy European sort, of
course, with marble floors and gilt-framed portraits and
human accessories like fops and fools lying about. It
was, rather, this heather-kissed meadow in the middle
of a carefully tended grove. So when Flidais had led us
to "a tree directly outside the Fae Court," she meant a
tree on the edge of the meadow. Behind us lay the shade
of impressive oaks, and eyes in there were watching us,
I knew.

Judging by the sun's position, we were on the south-
ern edge of the Court; Flidais was leading us to the
northern edge, where there was a small hill—a hillock,
I suppose, a wee mound with hillish ambitions—upon
which sat Brighid's throne. I could tell she was there,
but the distance was great enough that I couldn't read
her expression, and in any case it was far enough away
that she didn't represent an immediate threat. The
crowd of faeries, however, which was parting to allow
us through, would soon be on either side of us and then
behind us, and I didn't like that so much.

"Flidais, please warn them to stay clear of my friends

and me. We may interpret sudden moves as threats and respond accordingly."

The goddess of the hunt stopped and turned to face us. "Do you truly feel we are so hostile?"

"I doubt Brighid is well disposed toward me right now. That is cause enough to be on our guard. The Fae take their cue from her; you know this."

Flidais smirked. "If Brighid wishes you harm, she'll deliver it herself, Druid. None of these would presume to steal her right."

"She has no rights regarding me." All the Fae within earshot gasped and went, "Oooooh," in expectation that I'd be paying for that comment soon.

"Do please tell her that to her face." Flidais turned to resume her walk to the throne and called back over her shoulder, "I can tell already that this is going to be an amusing audience."

<There's nothing amusing about a place where you can't eat or drink anything. I hope we don't have to stay long, Atticus.>

I have the same hope. I checked on Granuaile, and she gave me a short, tight-lipped nod to let me know she was okay. Perun was okay too—rather, he was hopelessly in lust with Flidais's backside. As long as she didn't go invisible on him, he'd probably be content.

Fae were flooding into the Court—or the meadow—attracted by gossip that had no doubt circulated on fluttering wings. A susurrus of excitement swelled from all sides, and our audience was quickly building to the proportions of a spectator sport.

A small formation of pixies, goaded by their friends or perhaps genuinely clueless about who I was and how I'd react to Fae flying at me, swooped in for a quick playful welcome dance over my head—or so I was informed afterward. There were seven of them one second, and two seconds later, after a couple of quick shooing motions above my noggin, there were only three left. The survivors, horrified by watching their companions disintegrate to ash in midair, stayed still enough for Perun to zap them with small fingers of lightning.

"Big mosquitoes here," he said, as a roar bellowed from the spectators on either side, who had seen the whole thing.

"Those weren't mosquitoes," Granuaile said, as Flidais whirled, a scowl on her face.

"What happened?" she asked.

"Pixies," I explained. "Maybe someone's trying to establish my bona fides."

Flidais raised her voice and spoke to the assembled Fae on either side. "I warned you he was the Iron Druid before he arrived," she said. "Molest him at your peril."

A three-note chorus split the air and sang menacingly, "And if the Iron Druid doesn't kill you, I will." It was Brighid's voice. In her aspect as the goddess of poetry, she could somehow hit three notes at the same time when she spoke—and if she wanted you to hear her clearly from seventy yards away in the middle of an angry mob, she could do that too. The effect was that she could speak once and you'd be told three times; it gave her an authority among magic users no one could match. She couldn't lie or tell half-truths when she spoke like that, so she didn't employ it often and she chose her words carefully when she did. "Let him approach undisturbed, or I will have your life."

Cowed, the mob of Fae quieted down and gave us a wider berth. Satisfied, Flidais turned and led us again toward the throne. It felt as if we were part of a very small parade, except everyone watching was sad because the flowers on the floats had wilted. The character of the buzz around us was not only muted now, it was resentful. Flidais was striding forward confidently, thinking that Brighid's very loud words and her presence

were enough to guarantee our safety, but I was still wary.
There were all sorts of Fae in the Court now, and some
of them were bound to be descendants of Aenghus Óg.
If those pixies had been sent by someone to confirm I
was truly the Iron Druid, that someone was still out
there. Honestly, I wouldn't put it past Brighid or Flidais
to have orchestrated it; I had supposedly been dead for
almost twelve years, so one way to make sure I wasn't
an impostor was to watch some Fae turn to ash at the
touch of my cold iron aura. And one of the best ways to
absolve herself of responsibility for any further attacks
would be to very publicly threaten everyone with death.
She'd follow through on the threat, of course; couldn't
have her agents blabbing at the last minute that she'd
sent them.

The Morrigan had told me after Aenghus Óg's death
that Brighid had conducted some sort of pogrom here
in Tír na nÓg; there had been a rebellion in his name,
lots of stockpiled magical weapons abruptly found
their way into angry hands, and a whole host of Fae
had died. Many—if not most—had been Aenghus Óg's
spawn, but I'm sure there were other factions represented as well. That meant tension among the Tuatha
Dé Danann—and I had caused all of it.

Well. Maybe not all of it. The Morrigan had her
tensions with just about everyone, but especially with
Brighid, and I had not caused that so much as exacer-
bated it. Regardless, I couldn't look for the same favor
in Court that I might have enjoyed in the past. I might
have even created some new enemies here, and until I
could verify who was content to let me live and who
would rather serve me a cold dish of revenge, suspi-
cion was the best policy.

The crowd of Fae ended abruptly about twenty yards
from Brighid's throne. It provided a nice little area for
subjects to feel small and weak during their audience. It

also provided some space, to either side, for some VIPs to sit and offer catty remarks or snide questions. To Brighid's right sat the Tuatha Dé Danann, and to her left sat representatives of the various Fae factions.

A quick glance at the Tuatha Dé Danann showed me that nearly all of them were present. Manannan Mac Lir, wrapped in his cloak of mists, winked at me from underneath his bushy black eyebrows. His wife, Fand, sat next to him, small and delicate and ethereally beautiful in a white sheath with the same sort of knotwork designs Flidais had embroidered around the neck; since she was Flidais's daughter, perhaps it was a family thing. There was a liquid grace to her, even when she sat still.

Ogma was there, tall and tanned and sporting a shaven head these days, along with two large gold hoops in his ears. He wore a golden torc around his neck and a kilt— nothing more. He'd always been a bit vain about his six-pack. His expression was one of polite interest, but you got the feeling it was a façade for his indifference. Next to him sat Goibhniu, the master smith and brewer who had made cold iron amulets for the Morrigan, Granuaile, and Oberon. Unlike Ogma, Goibhniu was riveted by the spectacle of an old Druid approaching Brighid with his friends. He sat on the edge of his seat, grinning with anticipation, his elbows resting on his knees and his hands clasped together between them. Brighid was his mother, and he was therefore probably one of the few people who thought it was funny to watch her get worked up. His brothers, Creidhne and Luchta, lounged next to him, quietly exchanging words and not even paying attention to our passing.

There was another row of seats behind them, and a couple of these were empty. One seat was presumably for Flidais, and I noted that the Morrigan was conspicuously absent.

While most of the Tuatha Dé Danann had dressed

modestly and with very little ornamentation, Brighid had gone out of her way to look like a model for a Frazetta painting. Conscious of how it set off her red hair, she wore a sheer green sleeve on her left arm, bound at the top of the biceps and at the wrist with a circlet of gold. She had a golden belly chain holding up another sheer cascade of cloth between her legs, but it highlighted rather than concealed what was there. Aside from these purely ornamental accoutrements, she was naked, the tattoos on her right side—among other bits—proudly on display. She also had two wolfhounds lying at her feet, their heads up and watching our approach closely. They were black hounds with glossy coats.

No commentary now, Oberon, I warned him. *Remember, she can hear you.*

I received the mental equivalent of a grunt in reply.

The last time I'd seen Brighid, she was similarly provocative. She'd asked me to be her consort, I refused, and then she tried to kill me when she found out I'd had sex with the Morrigan. Fragarach had helped me out of that fix, but I didn't have that sword to get me out of this. Brighid's eyes flicked down to Moralltach, so I sheathed it before getting any closer, thinking that might be a tad more diplomatic than pointing it at her.

Flidais halted before the wee knoll on which Brighid's throne sat. It was made of iron she'd forged herself; originally a master of copper and bronze, Brighid had made a special point of becoming proficient in the magic-repelling metal when the Milesians had brought it to Ireland long ago. They thought they'd driven the Tuatha Dé Danann "underground," but in fact they'd driven them to create a plane of magic, and so the Milesians were indirectly responsible for the birth of the vast panoply of magical "little folk" that plagued and blessed them and their descendants for generations afterward. Brighid's throne was a palpable symbol of who exactly was master of the Fae. It occurred to me, for the first time, that my cold iron aura *here*, in her place of power, was a challenge in itself. I had visibly mastered iron to a degree that she had not. And I could move around and stuff. Her throne just sat there. But judging by the hardness in her eyes, that particular issue was far down on her list of bones to pick with me.

"Majesty," Flidais said. "The Druid Siodhachan Ó Suileabháin, as you requested."

A tiny nod of dismissal gave Flidais permission to take her seat amongst the rest of the Tuatha Dé Danann. I found myself wondering with mad distraction who Perun was currently staring at. Would he follow Flidais to her seat or fix his eyes on Brighid's bare breasts?

Brighid quirked an eyebrow at me, waiting to see how I would address her. It was the first of many challenges, I knew. If I called her Majesty, it would acknowledge her as my sovereign and establish her as someone who could order me about. Taking a knee would also signal submission, and I wasn't about to do either of those things. Instead, I bowed quickly and courteously and said, "You wished for an audience, Brighid." Conditioned by my years in the United States, I almost blurted out, "What can I do for you?" That would have been disastrous. Instead, I coughed once to cover my mistake and confined myself to stating the obvious: "I am here."

"You delve quickly to the heart of the matter," she sneered. The triple voice was gone; only the alto register remained. "I was told you died twelve years ago."

"Whoever told you must have been mistaken."

"The Morrigan is never mistaken about deaths."

"Did she specifically say that I was dead?"

"Yes."

"She used my name?"

"Yes. She said the Druid Atticus O'Sullivan lay chopped

to pieces in the Arizona desert. This was corroborated by several thunder gods."

"Begging your pardon, Brighid, but that is not my name."

Brighid's eyes narrowed. "So I have been intentionally duped."

I did not ask forgiveness. I stuck to the facts. "It was a necessary deception, liberally applied to all. I did not wish to be pursued by the aforementioned thunder gods forever."

"Why not simply slay them, as you did Thor?"

"I never slew Thor. That was someone else. And since I returned Fragarach, I thought that was sufficient payment for a harmless subterfuge."

Brighid darted her eyes over to Manannan Mac Lir, who shrugged, obviously confused.

"Say that again, Druid," the goddess said.

"I never slew Thor."

"No. What was that about Fragarach?"

"I returned it. Via the Morrigan."

Brighid's eyes widened in fury. "The Morrigan!" she spat. "You gave Fragarach into the keeping of the Morrigan?"

"She promised to return it to Manannan Mac Lir," I explained.

"I remember my promises well, Siodhachan," a raspy voice chuckled from my left. The Morrigan stood there, naked save for an iron amulet around her neck, skin like cream in porcelain and hair darker than a mine shaft. Her eyes glowed red as she stared at Brighid, Fragarach cocked over her head and her taut body ready for battle. "I never told you *when* I would return it."

"*Cathéide!*" Brighid shouted, and she was suddenly transformed from barbarian princess to badass knight, covered from head to toe in magnificent armor she had made herself. It was one of the coolest bindings I'd ever seen.

I recognized the armor; she had made it specifically to counter Fragarach and be the immovable object to its unstoppable force. The armor came with a weapon: She hefted a massive bastard sword in her right hand and kindled a ball of flame in the gauntlet of her left, then set herself defensively on the hill next to her throne.

These two had hated each other for as long as I could remember, but I never thought they'd actually throw down. Maybe I just hoped it. But I never hoped I'd be in the way.

Chapter 4

A hush fell over the Court as the Morrigan and Brighid faced off. Perun could no longer contain his enthusiasm. After spending years as an eagle, within the past hour he'd been seriously flirted with, watched two goddesses appear starkers, then saw them prepare for battle. Joy in every syllable, he shouted, "Yes! I love Irish peoples!"

The Fae thought this funny and erupted in laughter behind us. The Tuatha Dé Danann, not so much—except the Morrigan. She chuckled and lowered Fragarach, but Brighid didn't budge.

"You may relax, Brighid," the Morrigan said, her red eyes cooling down to their normal dark brown. "I am not here for battle. I am here to fulfill a promise. You see that I have the Druid's sword. I've been holding it for a good while now." The tone of her voice made clear to everyone that she was enjoying the double entendre. The Morrigan's mouth twitched upward at the corners.

"The Druid is quite the swordsman. I'm sure you can imagine. Of course, imagining is all you'll ever be able to do."

I wanted to tell the Morrigan to shut up, but I didn't dare. She was dangerously close to revealing that she knew Brighid had offered herself to me. I'd promised Brighid never to tell anyone about it, but the Morrigan had guessed the truth. Brighid would probably not care about such distinctions if the Morrigan made it public now. She'd be humiliated in front of all Faerie and she'd want to char someone to a cinder as a result.

Brighid didn't move or say anything, and it was her best option. The Morrigan would hardly want to charge her when Brighid held the high ground; it didn't matter that the Morrigan was Chooser of the Slain—it wouldn't be fun. She'd be set on fire, for one thing. And taking a quick glance at the hill in the magical spectrum, I could see that said hill was warded extensively and prickling with defensive traps. You'd have to be insane to charge Brighid there, and the Morrigan wasn't; she was malevolent and petty and damn scary on a regular basis, but not insane.

She could see that Brighid was ignoring her gibes, so she resorted to outright mockery. "It's odd that a goddess of poetry should be at such a loss for words. Does this mean no one in the mortal world can remember their dirty limericks right now?"

"Return the sword as you promised and leave," Brighid said.

"There's an effort!" the Morrigan crowed. "You managed a line of pentameter." She rested the flat of the blade on top of her shoulder, holding it casually, the way a baseball player might while walking to the plate. With seeming indifference to Brighid, she strolled to her left toward Manannan Mac Lir. She knew Brighid wasn't going to move off her hill; she'd effectively trapped her there. If Brighid left, she'd surrender all her advantages in battle—and you needed every advantage you could get if you were going to cross swords with the Morrigan.

Manannan stood from his chair and waited, his hood up and his arms crossed underneath his cloak. The entire Court grew still and strained to hear whatever might be said, for Manannan did not speak often in public. The Morrigan paused in front of him and brought the blade down horizontally in her hands, holding it chest high in a clearly ritualistic way, reminiscent of the formal transfer of possession practiced in Japan.

"Manannan Mac Lir, I am here to return Fragarach to you as I promised the Druid Siodhachan Ó Suileabháin I would. Its original scabbard was lost long ago. Will you accept it?"

"I will," he said, disappointing everyone who was hoping for some more drama. I thought the Morrigan would have had a few more shenanigans up her—well, not up her sleeve. She didn't have a stitch on. But then I flicked my gaze over to Brighid and realized what the Morrigan was doing. Brighid still stood as if she expected the Morrigan to charge her at any second. The Morrigan's sudden appearance with the sword had goaded her into a defensive position, but now that the Chooser of the Slain was behaving in a completely nonaggressive and even polite manner, Brighid looked as if she had overreacted at best and like a frightened coward at worst.

The Morrigan placed Fragarach gently into Manannan's outstretched hands and said, "It is done." Then, without a farewell or even a backward glance at Brighid, she morphed into her crow form and flew into the grove surrounding the Court. She'd followed Brighid's curt instructions precisely, and now Brighid looked ungracious on top of everything else. The ball of flame still glowed redly in her gauntleted hand, and all eyes swiveled to her and registered that she was ready to fight a nonexistent threat. Realizing this, she muttered a couple of words, and the armor and ball of flame disappeared. To Perun's great delight, she was once again clad—if one could call it that—in nothing but wispy, transparent gauze.

She was seriously annoyed, however. Her eyes blazed

with a glowing blue light. "How long has she had Frag-arach?" she growled.

"About twelve years, I suppose. But I thought she'd returned it."

"And what of the amulet?"

I shrugged. "I'm sure she's been working on it, but you could see as well as I that it's not finished yet."

"The point," Brighid said, her eyes cooling while her voice took on three notes of creepy, "is that it will be finished someday. And I would rather that day never arrive." The unspoken bit we both understood was that Brighid did not want the Morrigan to be immune to fire-balls hurled by the goddess of fire, as I was.

The two black wolfhounds near the base of the hill had remained stationary and quiescent all through the Morrigan's visit; now they rose to their feet, bared their teeth, and growled. At me.

<Hey, that's rude,> Oberon said.

Stay silent for now, I told him.

"If you have naught but threats for me, Brighid, I will take my leave."

"You may leave when I allow it."

"We are none of your subjects, and you guaranteed us safe passage."

"True, but I did not specify how long it would take you to pass through."

I made a mental note to demand a fixed time period in any future negotiation with the Tuatha Dé Danann. Being duped twice by the same loophole in the space of a few minutes will drive a point home. *Now you can growl*, I told Oberon, and he did so with gusto.

"You and I had a conversation once, if you recall"— I raised my voice over the din of three growling hounds—"about the finer points of hospitality." She could take that one of two ways. She could remem-ber that I had completely outmaneuvered her, take it as a warning that I had similar plans laid now, and calm down. Or she could listen to her pride, already wounded by the Morrigan, and flare up. The building blue glow in her eyes pointed toward the second option, and my heart dropped as I realized I'd have to kill somebody to get out of here.

<This is awesome,> Oberon said. <If I wasn't already involved, I would totally want a bag of popcorn right now.>

Chapter 5

"BWAH-ha-ha!" someone laughed amongst the Tuatha Dé Danann. I darted a glance that way and saw everyone looking at Manannan Mac Lir, who had clapped a hand over his mouth. Flidais threw in a girlish titter, and then they all erupted—which gave everyone else permission to laugh as well, though they had no idea what they were laughing at. What had happened is that the Tuatha Dé Danann had "heard" Oberon's comment. My eyes slid back to Brighid, and her mouth was quirked upward on one side; as I watched, her hounds subsided and sat down. I told Oberon to lay off as well.

You might have just saved our bacon there, I added.

<You brought bacon for us?> Oberon asked, a hopeful note in his voice. <And I saved it? I am the Savior of Bacon! Atticus, I want you to introduce me from now on as "Oberon, Savior of Bacon.">

"Please explain, if you will," Brighid said in a much more cordial tone, "why you found it necessary to conceal your existence from me and the rest of the Tuatha Dé Danann."

"I needed some assurance that I would be undisturbed for a span of years, for I have been hard at work training an apprentice. You may remember her." I gestured over my shoulder. "Granuaile MacTiernan."

Brighid bestowed a nod of recognition, and I assumed Granuaile returned it. A murmur of appreciation rippled through the Tuatha Dé Danann. A new Druid would be most welcome.

"She is not yet bound to the earth," Brighid noted, seeing no tattoos on Granuaile's right arm.

"No, but she is ready. I was on my way to begin the process when we were interrupted."

"On your way where, if I may ask?"

"I was searching for an appropriate place in Arizona."

Brighid frowned. "You cannot bind a Druid to the earth in the New World."

That set me back on my heels a bit. "You can't?"

Brighid seemed as bemused as I was. "It may be done only in Europe. Only the Eurasian plate has agreed to participate in the ritual. I thought you knew this."

"No." I had never tried to bind an apprentice elsewhere—in truth, I had bound precious few apprentices to the earth in the first place. All three Druids of my "issue" were dead now. Two had been ambushed—or perhaps assassinated, shot in the back—and another had died in the civil war that resulted in the dissolution of the Carolingian Empire. I hadn't attempted to train anyone since the death of Cíbran, my last apprentice, in 997. And so it was no wonder I had never discovered this particular proviso to a Druid's binding, but it made sense. All levels of the earth, from elementals to plates to Gaia herself, must be involved, and the plates were notoriously loath to get involved in anything but their own slow movements and ceaseless grating against one another.

Manannan spoke up. "Brighid, if I may interject?" She waved at him to continue, and he rose to address me. He commanded everyone's rapt attention. "I cannot speak for all, but I hope I speak for many of the Tuatha Dé Danann when I say we welcome Granuaile MacTiernan to Druidry, and I, for one, would like to see you train many more apprentices. Druidry has been neglected far too long on the mortal plane." Emphatic nods among the Tuatha Dé Danann supported his statement.

"Thank you, Manannan, and all of you who agree," I said, and privately cursed myself for not taking note of who hadn't visually concurred. "If I could find such excellent apprentices as Granuaile, nothing would give me greater pleasure than to continue teaching. However, for me to accomplish this goal, I need to have a modicum of security. To that end, I humbly request that you keep my existence a secret, especially from the Olympians and the Norse."

Furtive glances warned me that I had made a troublesome request.

"If . . . that is possible?" I asked.

Flidais spoke up. "The Olympian Bacchus asked us to inform him if you ever showed your face here."

"Well, the Olympian Bacchus can go blow a goat." There was no love lost between us. I had called him a "petty god of grape and goblet" and derided him as a pale echo of Dionysus. All the Roman gods were; their worshippers had possessed so little imagination that they hadn't even moved them off Olympus. Two pantheons lived atop the same bald peak, albeit on different planes.

"Attempting to conceal it will strain our relationship with the Olympians," Brighid pointed out.

"Perhaps you do not have all the facts here. Bacchus does not want to know of my whereabouts so he can send me a skin of his best cabernet. He wants to kill me, nothing else. He has sworn to Jupiter that he will do so. You cannot strain our relationship any more than that. So do you want more Druids or not? If you do, then don't tell the immortal god of madness where to find me, and keep a close watch on your faeries."

"Regrettably, it may already be too late," Fand said,

in a liquid sort of lilt that perfectly matched her appearance. "I'm quite sure many of the Fae have already spread word of your audience here. Word will circulate quickly that you are back from the dead. Bacchus will hear of it sooner or later."

Three kinds of cat shit, Oberon.

<And an arrogant family of squirrels.>

There was nothing I could do about it now. "Speaking of people returning from a long absence," I said, "Loki, the Norse god of mischief, is walking the nine realms again. And he seems intent on burning others."

Brighid frowned. "Explain."

I waved a hand at the Russian thunder god looming behind me. "This is Perun, a Slavic god of the sky. Loki somehow gained access to his plane and burned it all. You could feel the plane dying on the earth. I tell you three times; Gaia shuddered beneath my feet. I do not know if Loki plans on attacking the Tuatha Dé Danann or the Fae, but considering the myriad paths to Tír na nÓg, I highly recommend taking steps to seal it off from intruders, keeping in mind that Loki has a reputation as a shape-shifter."

Brighid nodded. "I hear you three times, Siodhachan." She turned to her right and said, "Manannan. Ogma. Please see to our security and devise a plan to deal with Loki should he make his way here." She turned to her left and addressed the dignitaries there. "The Lords of Faerie and their respective hosts will assist you." They bowed in acquiescence and acknowledgment of the order. The hairstyles represented there, I thought, could start a revolution in Hollywood salons. I didn't know much about the Lords of Faerie and their hosts, other than that they didn't like me very much. I think that had something to do with the cold-iron-touch-of-death thing.

One of the lords cleared his throat to get Brighid's

permission to speak. He was dressed foppishly in an Elizabethan kit, cursed with the physique of an anorexic mannequin, and had half-lidded eyes that communicated his disdain for the universe. She looked at him and dipped her chin, giving him the green light to pontificate.

"Majesty, perhaps the shuddering of Gaia reported by the Iron Druid may explain some recent disturbing reports coming in from the rangers throughout Europe."

"Do share with us all," Brighid said.

"Most tethers to Europe from Tír na nÓg are now inoperable. The death of the Slavic plane may explain this."

"Begging your pardon," I said. "Are you saying that it's impossible to shift to Europe right now?"

The fop raised an eyebrow and sneered at me. "That is precisely what I am saying. Except for a small area in the south of Greece."

"The tethers for the rest of the world still work?" Brighid asked.

"Yes, Majesty."

"And the secret paths walked by the Fae?"

"Those still function admirably."

"So your theory is that the death of Perun's plane is causing this."

"It is a possibility."

"Where, precisely, in Greece may one still travel freely?" I asked.

"Anywhere in the vicinity of Mount Olympus."

I snorted. "An Olympian wants to kill me and the only place I can currently bind my apprentice to the earth is under the nose of the Olympians? Doesn't that seem odd to you?"

The faery shrugged indifferently. "The timing of the Slavic plane's destruction coincides with the beginning of the tether disturbance. I realize that correlation does not imply causation, but it is a plausible theory. Have you another to offer?"

I almost held back, but then thought better of it. I would never win the favor of any Fae host at this point, so I might as well enjoy myself and call it like I saw it. "I will offer the theory that you are an insufferable grundlebeard," I said, much to the amusement of the audience behind us, who were not of that particular lord's host. He'd always be called Lord Grundlebeard after this, and he knew it; his face burned red.

"Why is it that only the area around Olympus is free from this disturbance?" I asked, turning away from the Fae.

"It would make sense if you assume the Olympians are protecting their territory," Flidais said, rising from her chair to address the assembly. "I'm sure the dryads are under their protection. If the reverberations of Perun's plane are being felt worldwide, the Olympians would see it as their duty to prevent the creatures in their domain from suffering."

"Then why don't all the world's pantheons do the same?" I asked.

Flidais shrugged helplessly. "Perhaps they don't understand that there's a problem. Few depend on the earth for travel as we do, and they might be entirely unaware. And they might also be too weak to do anything about it, whereas the Olympians still retain a decent measure of their old power."

These were certainly possibilities. It would be as fallacious for me to assume that the world was out to get me as it would be for them to assume the world wasn't. In their favor was the timing: How could the Olympians have known an hour ago—in time to orchestrate something like this—that I was still around? I had to admit that, though it looked like a convenient trap for me, Flidais's theory held much more water. The Olympians were looking after their own.

"Brighid, though the news of my return has probably spread already, as Fand noted, will you neglect to tell Olympus, or to officially acknowledge my return, until such time as I can finish binding my apprentice to the earth?"

She tilted her head slightly to one side. "Why should I do this?"

"So that the world will have another Druid. One," I added with a wry smile, "who is perhaps not so annoying as myself." Self-deprecation is an enduring social lubricant and should be applied liberally in cases like these.

Brighid broke into a full grin. "For that, I would do much more." Her voice took on the three-note tone and she announced, "None of the Fae or the Tuatha Dé Danann are to speak of the Iron Druid's return until after his apprentice is bound to the earth. Transgressors will be severely punished."

I nodded my thanks instead of speaking it. "Will that be all, Brighid?"

"For now," she said. "Your audience was not without excitement. But Fragarach is returned and we have a new Druid to welcome." All was forgiven, then. At least in public. "Please inform us when she is successfully bound."

"I will," I said.

"Flidais will escort you wherever you wish."

A soft but excited *Da! Da!* escaped Perun's lips. As Flidais walked up to us, a coy smile on her lips for the thunder god, the assembled crowd began to murmur and discuss my audience. Flidais said the Tuatha Dé Danann all wanted to meet Granuaile; for them, she was the highlight of the day, for she represented something new. Watching them stand next to each other, I was struck again by how similar they looked—at least, when Flidais was all "cleaned up" like this. They were the same height, and their hair was quite nearly the same shade; Flidais's hair leaned perhaps a bit more toward auburn.

Granuaile had a slightly wild yet glazed look to her eyes, the look that graduates and brides get when they are congratulated by an endless train of well-wishers. Having your hand kissed by gods and your cheeks kissed by goddesses can set one's heart aflutter, but I think she bore it well. She didn't go all fangirl on anyone, but I suspect that's only because none of them bore the slightest resemblance to Nathan Fillion. I'd taken her to Comic Con about eight years ago and she got to meet him; when he shook her hand and said, "Charmed," she damn near swooned. Then she lost most of her language faculties.

"Am. Uh. I mean. Granuaile. That's me. Oh, gods! Hi. So handsome. You, and. Wow. Sorry! Can't breathe."

I got a lot of mileage out of that one.

Manannan invited her to his house for a pint of ale; Fand seconded the invitation and included the rest of our party and her mother, Flidais.

"Yes, of course, ye must all come," Manannan said. He looked expectantly at Granuaile, but she swung her gaze to me, which caused Manannan to raise a querying brow in my direction.

"I told them not to accept any food or drink while here," I explained.

"Ah!" The god of the sea nodded sagely. "A wise precaution. I should have thought to be more formal and observe the proper manners." He turned to Granuaile once more but addressed us all. "Granuaile and friends, I invite ye to enjoy my hospitality this day, expecting no favor in return and incurring no debts or obligations on your part. I keep a wholesome table." *Wholesome*, in this case, was the Fae equivalent of Certified Organic; it meant he personally guaranteed the food would be the simple sort, without any sort of bindings used before, during, or after its production.

"We will accept your hospitality for a couple of hours," I said, "and then we must leave to begin binding Granuaile to the earth."

Manannan grinned from behind his mustache. "Excellent. Please follow."

Carrying Fragarach in his left hand, he walked hand in hand with Fand to a tree on the border of the court and shifted somewhere. Flidais followed, then we found the binding marker he left behind and shifted to a tree outside a large castle set on a cliff overlooking the sea. In the "real" world, this castle was a poor stone hut, seemingly abandoned. Here in Tír na nÓg, it was an architectural wonder set on breathtakingly beautiful grounds. The famous hogs of Manannan Mac Lir—the ones that re-spawned after slaughter, providing him with eternal luscious bacon—snorted fatly in their pen and radiated decadence. Kine lowed in the distance, black-and-white Rorschach blots on a green field. Wolfhounds trotted around creamy pincushions of sheep. The scene was edged with golden highlights, a pastoral the likes of which Thomas Cole would have dreamed. Some faeries were visible here and there—the airborne and the grounded—and while they looked at us curiously, none approached. The three members of the Tuatha Dé Danann were waiting for us and smiled a welcome, beckoning us inside. Manannan delivered Fragarach into the hands of a sleek servant who was no doubt the human form of a selkie. She bowed to him and bore it into the castle ahead of us.

Fand dismissed most of the faeries in the castle immediately, "for their comfort and yours," she said to me. When I had last been a guest at Manannan's estate,

I wasn't known as the Iron Druid, and the Fae rather liked me. Circumstances were much different now, and, as such, we were treated to the singular privilege of being served by Manannan and Fand in the kitchen. It smelled of apples, and when I remarked upon this they mentioned a cider press through a door in the rear. They set out a platter of fruit, cheese, and bread, then poured us each a flagon of ale and toasted our health. They gave Oberon a ham bone with plenty of meat left on it.

<Please tell me it's okay to eat this. It smells so good,> Oberon said.

Yes, it's okay.

Oberon set his ears back and reared up on his hind legs playfully. <Have at thee, Hamlet!> he said, and pawed at it a couple of times before chomping down and trotting off to enjoy it elsewhere.

Manannan and Fand wanted to learn more about Granuaile since she was shortly to be a full Druid, so they encouraged her to talk about herself. Flidais and Perun quickly lost interest, however, and began conducting a hushed conversation of their own, every murmur vibrating with the frisson of sexual tension.

Before long, Granuaile was talking directly to Fand. The god of the sea had apparently been waiting for this development, because Manannan jerked his head at me to repair to another room, where there was an open window looking out on his sheep pasture.

"Fly with me down there for a moment?" he asked, pointing.

It was unusual, but it seemed a harmless request, so I shrugged. "Sure." We stripped and shifted to our bird forms; he was a great shearwater and I a great horned owl. Manannan took his cloak of mists with him in his talons. We leapt from the window and coasted down to the sheep, where we shifted back to human. Manannan quickly shook out his cloak and used it, enveloping us entirely in mist. Then he bound the air around us so that no sound could travel out of a bubble around our heads.

"Faeries and enchantments everywhere up there," he explained with a jerk of his head toward the castle, "and some o' them are quite talented at remaining inconspicuous while they eavesdrop. I just wanted to have a word with ye that wouldn't be overheard, and I didn't want our lips read either."

"Okay," I said, though his preamble made me curious and more than a little nervous.

"It's not only Bacchus who wants to see ye dead," he explained, "or who might suspect you're still alive. There was an envoy from the Svartálfar a couple o' years back, asking if ye might be alive after all."

"Well, I suppose it had to happen someday," I said, and sighed. "I actually have cause to blame the dark elves."

"Blame them for what?"

I shrugged. "Whatever vexes me at any given moment. They have been my universal scapegoat for ages. The truth of the matter is I don't know much about them."

One of the stranger developments of modern times is that more people have heard of dark elves today than at any other time in human history. This is almost entirely due to the twin influences of role-playing and fantasy-based video games. Or perhaps more credit is due to the artists who depicted them visually with dark skin and fantastic white hair; they had impossibly magical manes, as if they'd found some eldritch concoction in the deeps that gave them +5 flowing locks.

Even literature got it wrong. There are only a couple of passing references to dark elves in Sturluson's *Prose Edda*, but they're a bit confusing since they seem to conflate the dark elves with dwarfs. I have often wondered how much of that was intentional; in my mind it's impossible to make such a mistake. They didn't look a damn bit alike, if my sources were correct.

To be fair, Snorri Sturluson had priorities other than filling in the history of the dark elves. He wanted to preserve his country's myths and culture without upsetting the Christian authorities of the time. He had to stretch like Mr. Fantastic to make the Norse gods descendants of the Trojans—and thus, to the Christians, not really gods at all, merely heroes—and he probably couldn't figure out a way to explain the dark elves satisfactorily. Then again, I wouldn't be surprised to learn that the Svartálfar had paid him a visit while he was writing the *Edda* and encouraged him to elide their existence all he wanted—perhaps more than he wanted.

The reason that there is so little information about dark elves is that they tend to keep to themselves, and, in truth, from what little I have heard, this is rather kind of them. Any interaction they have with humans tends to ruin the humans' day.

"I know a bit about them," Manannan said. "I got the short version o' their history from one o' the Álfar."

"The Álfar spoke to you? Why?"

"This was some time ago. I had the story from a treasure hunter who wanted my help in locating wrecks at the bottom o' the Irish Sea. Since he wanted a map, I asked him for a map in kind. I never could figure out where the nine realms were located on the World Tree, so he gave me a map that he swore was truth and told me a story about how the Svartálfar were born. Would ye like to hear it?"

"Yes, I would—and I'd love to see the map as well. If the dark elves are actively searching for me, I'd prefer to be armed with as much knowledge as possible."

"That is wise, especially where fighting them is concerned."

"Why so?"

"Patience, Siodhachan. I'll tell all, even as he told it to me."

Ages ago, even before the Tuatha Dé Danann had come to Ireland, the king of the Álfar—for there was only one kind of elf back then—commissioned a map of the Nine Realms of Yggdrasil. Asgard, Álfheim, and Vanaheim at the top were well known, but less was known of the six lower realms. The lowest three, in particular, were almost complete mysteries. Niflheim was a land of ice, and it was within that realm that Hel reigned over the moaning, inglorious dead; Muspellheim was a land of flames, where Surtr and the fire jötnar lived, awaiting the day of Ragnarok, when they could burn the whole of creation; but there was another land, both between and underneath them, subterranean and dark, beyond the jaws of the great wyrm Nidhogg, that did not even have a name, and no one knew what waited there in the black silence.

The largest party of Álfar was sent to explore this land, and none returned. All other parties returned and the map grew into an atlas, yet the king was displeased by the loss of the last crew. Another party, half again as large, was sent to seek them after forty years, but they did not return either. Ailing and old, this king—whose name has been purposefully forgotten by the Álfar—sent out a series of single adventurers. They were told not to explore but rather to discover the fates of their forebears and report back.

The answer to the mystery came three years later. Five strange beings appeared at the court of the Álfar king. Dressed in robes of a white material that looked like silk yet shimmered so that other colors reflected from its surface, they very nearly sparkled when they moved.

The beings appeared to be elves, except that instead

of the light flesh and light-blond hair of the Álfar, this company had skin of obsidian. Each had a single queue of jet-black hair growing from the very top of his head, bunched together in places with silver circlets and falling down to the waist. Their eyes were green and abnormally large. They carried weapons unlike any the Álfar had seen, longish curved daggers that were not quite fit to be called swords, crafted not of iron or bronze but of some dark material; hilt, blade, and guard were all made of the same inky substance.

Approaching the throne, the strangers bowed but did not kneel to the king. He demanded to know who they were.

The one in the middle answered: "We bring greetings from Svartálfheim, the ninth realm of Yggdrasil."

"What do you say? Explain."

They were descendants of the first party he'd sent to the subterranean world, the entrance to which lies between the Ylgr and Vir rivers, and they had come to tell him and all Álfar that it was named Svartálfheim.

"You're elves, then!" the king cried. "My subjects!"

"No, not your subjects. The sons of your former subjects."

The king was not pleased by this show of independence but not inclined to argue the point. He was not sure he wanted them for subjects, for in his eyes they were strange.

"How came you to look thus?"

"We were given the *Gjor at Reykr*, the Gift of Smoke. We are now Svartálfar, as you are Ljósálfar." This was the first time the distinction was made between the two races.

"What nonsense is this?" the king demanded.

"Svartálfheim is nothing like Álfheim. The caverns have changed us. We are no longer like you. But, for the sake of our former kinship, we would have ties with you so that both our kingdoms may flourish."

"Both our kingdoms?" the king spluttered. His face grew red and he stood from his throne. "You have some king other than I?"

"Of course. You are Ljósálfar, not Svartálfar. We would not suggest that one of us lead your people."

"And that is as it should be! But you owe me your allegiance! I funded your expedition! I supported the families left behind!" Thinking of this, the king decided they should be his subjects after all. "And, despite your dark skin, you are Álfar! Acknowledge me as your sovereign!"

"Our sovereign is in Svartálfheim. We are but ambassadors of his goodwill."

"Goodwill would be acknowledging your rightful king. If I am not your sovereign, then you and your ancestors are deserters and traitors."

The five Svartálfar stiffened. "We are none such," one of the other dark elves said. He was not the spokesman, but none of his companions bristled at his interruption. "We are a different people now, as your senses must clearly report. We acknowledge our debt to you and will gladly repay your generosity. But we will not subject ourselves to your rule when you are none of our own."

Perhaps a less prideful king would have found the strength to negotiate from this point. Perhaps the dark elves had said enough to provoke any king beyond all endurance. Regardless of might-have-beens, the king of the Álfar roared for his champions to take the dark elves and throw them in his dungeon.

"We wish all here to remember that we did not begin the violence and that we offered to pay our debts to the Álfar," the spokesman called loudly. "You cannot prevail against our martial art, *Sigr af Reykr*. Send to Svartálfheim when your new king wishes to talk in peace."

It was an odd thing to say, since they had yet to move, but the reason for it became clear shortly. When the Álfar champions tried to seize them, the Svartálfar became incorporeal, their white robes falling to the ground and their silver hair ties clinking after them, as something like coal dust bloomed where they had stood. Their strange knives did not fall to the ground but transformed with them. The dark elves became solid again outside the ring of champions, naked, holding those wicked curved blades, as black as their bodies. They could have slain all the Álfar then with a twitch of their wrists. Instead, they waited for the champions to turn, and this time the champions tried to use their weapons. Swords and axes swung at the dark elves but swished through nothing but black mist. Four clouds swirled back out of reach, but one wove sinuously through the air toward the king. The spokesman for the Svartálfar became solid at the bottom of the steps leading to the king's throne, black knife in his left hand.

"Your orders gave our people life," he said, "but we will let no one order us into submission. Rethink your orders and let us talk peaceably, or else you and you alone will suffer for overreaching."

"Slay them all!" the king ordered, and his bodyguards rushed down to meet the threat.

The dark elf waited until their weapons were descending upon him, then he turned into a plume of curling smoke and rose up the steps toward the king. Seeing this, the king drew his sword. His bodyguards would not recover and reach him in time. He swiped at the tendrils of smoke, to no effect. Long wisps of it entered his mouth, and he coughed once before he died.

The dark elf solidified with his right arm down the king's throat. He yanked hard and tore free the king's jaw and unmoored his throat from his spine. The gush

of blood showered the elf in gore, but he turned to mist
again and the blood fell like rain as the king's corpse
tumbled down the stairs to meet his bodyguards, a silent
testimonial to their utter failure. This, then, was *Sigr af
Reykr*, Victory from Smoke.

The stunned court of the Álfar noticed two things as
the Svartálfar retreated: One, the dark elves never kept
their incorporeal form for more than five seconds—they
always solidified for at least a full second before dis-
solving again to mist—and, two, they could be killed.
The latter was discovered just before the Svartálfar ex-
ited the audience chamber. An archer, high on the bal-
cony surrounding the court, had been closely observing
the changes and movements of the dark elves. It was
he who realized their smoke form could last no longer
than five seconds. He nocked an arrow and carefully
followed the movements of a single dark elf. Once the
villain turned to smoke, the archer counted to five and
released his arrow at the center of the mist when it was
but ten paces from the door. The dark elf became flesh
a split second before the arrow lanced into the space
between his shoulder and neck, spearing his vitals and
ending his life.

He collapsed before the door and the champions bore
down on him, stabbing him again and again for surety,
but in all likelihood he was already dead. Within seconds the body began to crumble in on itself, smoke rose
from the corpse, and inside of a minute all that was left
was carbon mixed with fluid, a wet puddle of tar with
the archer's arrow in the middle of it. The blade, too,
dissolved into the mess.

From that day to this, the Svartálfar and Ljósálfar
have hated each other. The dark elves have held peace-
ful if rather tense talks with the Æsir and Vanir, and
they have traded well with the dwarfs of Nidavellir and
with the denizens of Jötunheim. On Midgard, as you

might imagine, they have found employment as assassins. But in Álfheim they are forever attacked on sight for their unforgivable treason and regicide.

When Manannan fell silent, I prompted him to continue. "Go on," I said.

"That's it."

"What? That can't be it!"

"That's all I was told. I can tell ye it's more than most people know about them."

"There has to be more though. Centuries of war and rivers of elfin blood, battles that lasted for three months—come on!"

The sea god shook his head. "No. The Álfar despise the Svartálfar as traitors but refuse to go to war on their own kind. Between you and me, I think they fear entering Svartálfheim and being corrupted in the same way. The turning-to-mist trick seems like a fabulous plus, but they make awfully messy corpses. The Álfar think it unwholesome somehow and a high price to pay to exterminate traitors who are otherwise doin' no harm to the realm."

"Which realm?"

"I misspoke. No harm to Álfheim."

"Yeah. Tell me more about that trick of theirs. What is the 'Gift of Smoke,' precisely?"

Manannan shrugged. "Some kind of mutagen."

"Hey, look at you busting out the modern words!"

He scowled at me. "Not all o' the Tuatha Dé Danann believe the mortals have nothin' to offer us."

"I'm of your mind, Manannan, and have been for a long time. I approve. No one knows what this mutagen might be?"

"Theories abound, but the Svartálfar refuse to discuss it and no one has delved deep enough into their realm to see it. They meet envoys and conduct trade in a couple o' large chambers not far down from that dark stair they built. What's going on deeper inside, no one knows."

"Sounds like North Korea. Can't believe one of the Álfar told you this though. It wasn't exactly flattering to their king."

Manannan nodded. "They are nothing if not an honest people."

"So if this story is true, it means the dark elves aren't inherently evil."

"No. They are a proud people and will not hesitate to kill, but they seek no lands beyond their own and have no wish to dominate others."

"You'd never know it from the way people talk about them, myself included. I mean, I'm not going to stop thinking they're creepy as hell—because if your body turns to tar, you're fucking creepy, right?—but I'm frankly shocked to hear they don't want to destroy us all. They need to get a good PR guy."

"What's a PR guy?"

"They're kind of like the old Greek sophists who played with words until you believed up was down. PR guys get paid to make people believe that a pile of shit is an investment in soil fertility. Professional liars."

"Ah!" Manannan's expression lit with comprehension. "They are politicians?"

"No, they're smarter and less pretty. They advise politicians."

"Oh. Well, I thought ye should know the dark elves are seeking ye."

"I appreciate the thought. It is bizarre. Two years ago, you say? I wonder what set them sniffing after my trail."

"I wondered that myself, lad. Hoped ye might have an answer."

I had a possible answer; thanks to a certain rendezvous six years ago, three of the Norse gods knew I was alive. One of them could have let slip the truth, intentionally or not. But since I had no way of knowing, I just shook my head. "No. But it's one more enemy to watch out for. I'd love to see that map of the nine realms."

"I'll get ye a copy."

"You are kind. Might you have a place in the castle where I could perform a divination in private?"

"What sort?" Manannan asked. Some of the old Druidic divination rituals could be messy, what with sacrificing animals and all. I had never favored those methods: Truth stained with blood is not so savory as truth arrived at without the forfeit of life.

"Just wands," I reassured him.

"Oh, sure." He waved a hand dismissively. "Not a problem."

"There's one other matter we should speak of. That hairy Russian god doesn't have a home anymore, and he's being pursued by Loki. Do you think the Tuatha Dé Danann might grant him asylum here for a time?"

Manannan grunted and smirked. "I feel certain Flidais will grant him nearly anything right now. It's fine with me, if ye vouch for his character."

"I do."

"Then I can't see too many objections if he has our support. I'll send a faery to Brighid right away." He dispelled the binding of the air around us, gathered up his cloak of mists, and we shifted back to birds before flying up to the tower. In our human skin again, we got dressed, I retrieved my pack, and Manannan showed me to a room where I could perform a divination. It was a spare chamber—a guest bedroom—decorated in burgundy and gold. I withdrew my wands from my pack and selected five at random while focusing on my question: Where and when could I best bind Granuaile to the earth? I cast the wands on the floor in front of me and interpreted the pattern they made; diplomatically, in the company of others, I would call the result less than sat-isfactory. Since I was doing this in private, however, I winced and cursed as I might if someone were to pluck out my short 'n' curlies with a pair of tweezers.

I performed several more castings, refining my ques-tion and eking out every wee drab of vague meaning from the wands. The depressing conclusion was that there was not going to be any better time or place than at the base of Olympus in the near future. Whatever it was that had disrupted all the tethers to Tír na nÓg in Europe would remain in effect for an unconsciona-bly long time, and every minute wasted now was an-other minute Granuaile would spend unable to defend herself—at least from anyone stronger or faster than a human. The problem was that she and I were going to start running into plenty of such beings; Brighid's gag order aside, I knew very well that word was spreading even now: That bloody Druid was still alive.

Chapter 6

Oddly enough, Manannan's news about the dark elves relaxed me somewhat. I didn't have to wonder anymore: Everyone really *was* out to get me. Still, after we bade our hosts farewell and shouldered our packs once more, with Flidais and Perun tagging along, I felt confident enough to show Granuaile a few highlights of Tír na nÓg before we shifted back to earth.

"The land of eternal summer is also the land of the dead, but fortunately the dead tend to keep to themselves."

"How do you mean?"

"Well, you know how you can attract senior citizens to certain communities by offering shuffleboard courts and bingo nights? Plop down an IHOP nearby for them to lounge in during the daytime?"

Granuaile looked lost. "What?"

"Have you ever been to an IHOP on a weekday morning, when everyone else is at work?"

"No," Granuaile admitted.

"Well, that's where all the senior citizens go. Or they go to a Village Inn or a Denny's or whatever. It's because, once you hit sixty or thereabouts, you don't ever want to make your own pancakes again."

"You're over sixty," Granuaile pointed out.

"And I never make pancakes. I go to IHOP with all the other old people."

<It's true! He only makes omelets and—damn. I keep forgetting she can't hear me yet.>

"But I don't want to make my own pancakes *now*," Granuaile said. "Does that mean I'll start wanting to make them when I'm old?"

"I don't know. The point I was trying to make is that part of Tír na nÓg is very attractive to dead people."

"What's so attractive about it?"

"Mostly the lack of living people. They don't like being reminded that they're all dead. And there might be a pancake buffet. Twenty-four-hour keno. Concerts featuring Elvis impersonators. That sort of thing."

<Do they sing "Suspicious Minds" in the white high-collared jumpsuit?>

Always.

"You're making Tír na nÓg sound like Las Vegas," Granuaile said.

"Well, it might be. Because what happens in the land of the dead stays in the land of the dead. I simply don't know and I'm not anxious to find out. Manannan and the Morrigan won't tell you anything if you ask them either. They won't even say how they decide who comes here and who goes to Mag Mell or the other Irish planes. It might not be their decision. But the point is, there is plenty of real estate left over for the living. And for the Fae and other curiosities. Check this out. I mean, in a minute." I gestured to an oak in front of us. "Put your hands here and get ready to go."

"How do you know where you're going?" Granuaile asked.

"Can't really explain until you're bound and you can see things in the magical spectrum," I said. "But, basically, every destination has its own unique sequence of knots. Think of it like airport codes back on earth."

"Do I have to memorize them all?"

"Not unless you want to hate your life. The ones

on earth are based on coordinates. Tír na nÓg is odd, though, as you might expect. You kind of need to know where you're going or else you'll appear in the middle of an ogre orgy or something horrific like that. We're going to a popular destination here—there will be plenty of Fae around, but Flidais and Perun will follow."

<Are you sure about that? Because I'm fairly certain they're hoping we'll leave them behind.>

I cast a glance behind us and saw that Perun was now carrying Flidais, supporting her buttocks with his hands as she wrapped her legs around his waist and locked them behind his back. They were playing tonsil hockey already and making soft, muffled moans. Granuaile followed my gaze and flinched.

"Ew. How did she even find his mouth behind all that hair?" she wondered aloud.

"Honestly, I'm surprised at how much restraint they've shown so far. I expected them to slip off to a room in the castle somewhere. I don't care at this point if we ditch them. Do you?"

My apprentice shook her head. "No, I think that would actually be good. I don't want to listen to them."

<They kind of sound like those chefs on TV when they taste their own food at the end of their shows. You know what I mean?>

Foodgasms, yeah.

<Excellent word! I'll have to remember that.>

We shifted to a well-traveled riverbank in Tír na nÓg, and I smiled as Granuaile gasped and dove for cover, while Oberon began to bark loudly.

Heh. Calm down, buddy, it won't get us.

<Oh. Warn a hound next time, will you?>

"Oh, my God! Is that a *dragon?*" Granuaile said, peeking from behind the trunk of the ancient tree we'd used to shift.

"Yep."

"Like, for reals? It's not a wax replica or something like that?"

"No, it's very much for reals."

"Then how come it's hanging in the air there and not moving?"

"It *is* moving. It's just in a slower timestream. Welcome to the Time Islands, the source of all those stories about how time moves differently in Faerie than in the mortal world."

We stood on the bank of a river not quite as wide as the Mississippi but doing very well for itself. In the middle, stretching both upriver and down, islands of various sizes displayed rather interesting vignettes. One of the more stunning was the huge golden dragon floating only thirty yards in front of us. Its wings were outspread and beating slowly downward against the air, its jaws open and presumably hissing. An egg warmed in the sand of the island beach beneath it.

"Can it see us?"

"Nope. We're a blur to it—sort of like mist—since we're in a faster timestream. See those islands there?" I pointed downriver to some nebulous shapes. "They're moving even faster than we are. To anyone standing there looking at us right now, we're either moving very slowly or as good as frozen, like that dragon seems to be frozen to us."

"So that dragon thinks it's flying in its normal timestream?"

"Yep. Eventually, if it keeps going in the same direction, it will bust out of there. That will be an exciting day for the Fae, if they let it happen. About a thousand years ago—the last time I checked—the claws of its hind legs were still touching the sand. She's launching an attack, you see, defending her egg."

"Defending it from what?"

"Whatever asshole faery decided to go bag it centu-

ries ago. Maybe it was one of the Tuatha Dé Danann
who brought it here, I don't know. Somebody wanted
to show off."

Granuaile cocked her head to one side. "Isn't that
what you're doing right now, sensei?"

"What? Well, no," I said. "This is definitely somebody else's show. I just thought you might like it. Don't
you think it's cool and neato-schmeato and stuff?"

"Oh, yes. I do." She fluttered her eyelashes at me. "Is
there anything else you'd like to show me?"

"There's someone upriver you might recognize," I
said. "It's not that far. Keep your eyes open as we go."
I pointed up into the canopy, where several pairs of eyes
were already watching us. Pixies and other flying varieties
of Fae hovered or perched in the tree above us.

"Right," Granuaile said, her tone businesslike. She
hefted her staff in her hand. At my suggestion, which
she accepted readily at the time, she had affixed iron
caps to either end. The Fae would see that and know
that messing with her came with a certain amount of
risk. "Ready."

We hiked upriver along the bank by ourselves; as
Oberon had predicted, Flidais and Perun had not followed us and were no doubt engaged in heated, hirsute
carnality in Manannan's field.

I asked Oberon to take point; Granuaile was next,
and I brought up the rear. Oberon had my permission
to treat anything that didn't look human as hostile, provided they wouldn't get out of our way first.

*Give them a warning growl and a commanding bark,
at least, before you destroy them,* I said.

<Oh, I like how you phrased that, like their destruc-
tion is inevitable. Thanks.>

Well, it is inevitable. You're like a Terminator hound.

<Are you sure you want to use that analogy? Because if
I'm the Terminator, that would make you Skynet and the

enemy of Sarah Connor, and you've always had that thing for Linda Hamilton.>

Oh. Right. I take it back.

<If you're going to compare me to a Hollywood badass, then I want to be Jules from *Pulp Fiction*. He was Super Fly TNT! He was the Guns of the Navarone!>

Whoa, there. You're forgetting something. Jules didn't eat pork. That means no bacon or sausage.

<Auggh! Inconceivable! I take it back!>

I think you're a badass in your own right, buddy.

<Really? You don't think those hounds of Brighid's were badder?>

Nah. They were all for show. I bet she never takes them hunting. And they weren't very bright. Brighid hasn't taught them to talk the way I taught you. I touched their minds briefly while we were at Court. All they know are a few basic commands and a few random words.

<What words?>

Food. Potty. Bitches.

<Ha-ha! Well, wait. Maybe I shouldn't laugh. If you think about it, that's pretty Zen. Or maybe something even more significant. You know, Atticus, that might be like a holy trinity for canines.>

Don't you think that including bitches in the trinity is sexist? You need to think about it from their perspective, too, if you're trying to come up with some sort of universal canine dogma, heh-heh.

<Me? Dogmatic? Perish the thought! But you have a point: I should probably recast it in terms of general sexual behavior. Humping, perhaps, would be a good catchall phrase to describe our basic needs. And then, you know what? I could make the trinity alliterative. Ham, humping, and the holy hydrant!>

Are you setting yourself up as the prophet of a new religion?

<Why not? I hear there's money in it.>

What do you need money for? I give you everything you need.

<I could refute that easily by pointing out that there is, in fact, no poodle bitch trotting along beside me now, but let's see if you'll give me this: Will you type out my holy writ if I dictate it to you?>

Sure. What's this religion going to be called?

<Poochism.>

And the name of the holy writ I will be typing for you?

<The Dead Flea Scrolls: A Sirius Prophecy.>

Granuaile's voice interrupted our plans to revolutionize canine belief systems. "Is that an airplane?" she asked, pointing ahead to a long, narrow strip of an island. A twin-engine metal airplane hung suspended above it, a trail of smoke coming from the left engine, and it appeared to be headed for what might be charitably called a rough landing on the island.

"Yep. That's a Lockheed Model 10 Electra."

"No. Wait. There's a pilot in there?"

"None other than the famous aviatrix herself."

"Shut up. You're telling me Amelia Earhart is in that plane? Alive?"

"Until she crashes, yeah. She might survive the crash; we don't know. Hasn't happened yet. But generally airplane crashes don't leave many survivors."

"You have Amelia Earhart alive and you're casually speculating on whether she will survive a crash? Atticus, we have to save her!"

"How? Think about the problem. Once you enter that timestream, you'll be moving as slowly as she is. You can't prevent the crash. No one can."

"But that's horrible! Prolonging the moment of her death—"

"For her, nothing is prolonged. It's still the last few seconds before she crashes."

Granuaile clenched and unclenched her fist several

times before she spoke again. "Gah! What's the point, then? Why is she here? Do the Fae enjoy watching people die in slow motion?"

"No, that's not it at all," I said, puzzled that she didn't see the miracle here. "She's inspirational, Granuaile. A strong, brave woman like Amelia—well, the world could use a few million more of her."

Granuaile paused to consider, an angry set to her jaw at first, but after a moment it relaxed into regret and she shed a tear for Amelia. She wiped it away impatiently. "So is that what you have up and down this river? Bits and pieces of history?"

"That's exactly it. Some of it is accidental—lots of those missing ships from the Bermuda Triangle wind up here—and some of it is purposeful, like Amelia. Here we preserve what otherwise would have disappeared forever."

"Have you preserved anything here?"

"No, too dangerous for me to keep coming back here when Aenghus Óg was around. Too tricky to retrieve things anyway."

She frowned. "I thought you said you couldn't retrieve things. Don't you slow down when you try to access them?"

"Think of those arcade games you see in restaurants and grocery stores, where a hook comes down and epically fails to snatch the plushie. They use hooks on really long staffs. As long as the majority of the staff remains in this timestream, it won't slow down. It just moves superfast in the slow stream, which means you need to be careful about touching objects—they're easily breakable. And that illustrates the point about why we can't save Amelia: If we tried to yank her out of her plane, we'd break her neck or snap her spine."

"Okay. I think I've seen enough. Can we go?" Her words were clipped, annoyed.

This hadn't gone the way I'd imagined. When I was first shown the Time Islands by my archdruid, I'd been filled with wonder. So had all my previous apprentices. Granuaile, however, had become upset. Occasionally this happened: Modern values and the ancient ones I grew up with were radically different, and sometimes I misjudged rather badly what was cool and what was repulsive.

"Sure," I said, walking over to the nearest tree. We needed to talk about this, but there was no need to do it in front of the many faeries in the canopy, who no doubt were eavesdropping on our conversation. Not wanting to take Lord Grundlebeard at his word, I placed my hand on the trunk and attempted to find the tether to one of my favorite spots in Gaul—or, rather, France. It wasn't there. Nor were any other of my accustomed destinations in Europe. Resigned, I searched all available points to which we could shift and chose a tree in the eastern foothills of Mount Olympus. I pulled us through to that spot and half-crouched, listening and scanning the area, expecting trouble. When nothing like trouble presented itself, I straightened and enjoyed the view below us.

"Well, here we are," I said, gazing down at a town of seven thousand souls, orange-tiled roofs, and white buildings in a cushion of green; beyond it, the blue flag of Poseidon's sea stretched to the horizon, where it met a lighter sky. We were underneath the canopy of a pine; most of the trees here were pine, cedar, or fir. Olympus loomed behind us, and the path to the summit was visible nearby.

"Where is here?" Granuaile asked.

<And is it dinnertime?>

"That is Litochoro, Greece. 'City of the Gods,' if you want to buy the tourist name. Lots of people come through here. We need to find a place off the beaten path where we can safely get to work on your binding. When we need supplies, we'll come down to this town to get them."

"All right," Granuaile said. "Lead the way."

I led the way, picking a careful path between trees and staying on the south side of the trail. I was heading for the course of a natural wash in the foothills; there would be some runoff there for water and plenty of deadwood for fuel. Oberon kept pace beside me instead of zipping off through the forest to sniff that tree or mark that bush.

<Atticus?> Oberon said.

Yeah?

<I consider myself a fairly discerning student of human intonation, and, as such, I feel it is my duty to inform you that Granuaile sounds unhappy.>

I know she is, buddy. I'm not sure why, but I'm going to find out tonight once we make camp. Now is not the time to press her. She might not know precisely why. The hike will give her time to mull things over.

<You are wise.>

Not really. A wise man wouldn't have irritated her in the first place. Do us a favor?

<Sure.>

Scout ahead a little bit, but not too far—make sure you can hear us. We're looking for a good place to make camp, but it has to have little to no evidence of human traffic, and we need a thornbush.

<Aren't the good places to camp usually the ones without thornbushes?>

Usually. This is a special case, however.

<Okay. You're the one with the snacks, I guess.> Oberon trotted ahead, his nose low to the ground, searching for spoor. Granuaile and I hiked behind him in silence, keeping our meager human senses alert for any sign that we might not be bushwhacking alone.

Normally I am not the sort to indiscriminately whack bushes. The undergrowth grew thicker, however, as we climbed the slope and strayed ever farther from the path, until there was no space between the brambles. We had to push our way through what turned out to be rather thorny bushes indeed. I could almost feel Granuaile's mood worsening behind me as scratches appeared on our arms, and occasional punctures through our jeans made us curse. My own mood was beginning to sour as well.

"Can't you ask the earth to clear a path for us through this stuff?" Granuaile finally asked.

"I could," I admitted, "but that sort of thing might draw the wrong kind of attention here."

"Whose attention?"

"The Olympians. Both sets. We're in their territory now, and it's not just them we need to worry about— it's all those nymphs and dryads and the entire mythological zoo that the Greeks dreamed up and the Romans ripped off. If I take off my sandals and start drawing on the elemental here, it's a fair bet the Greco–Romans will be tipped off that someone's using magic in their backyard. I haven't completely given up on my paranoia yet. I want us stationary and isolated if possible before I take any risks."

The two of us silently fumed as we waded and picked our way through a sea of uncomfortable thorns and woody branches. After a half hour of this, Oberon's voice in my head was a welcome relief.

<Hey, Atticus. Look up. See that vulture?>

A broad black wingspan sailed overhead, moving from my right to left, angling toward a steep hillside.

I see it.

<Watch where it goes.>

Normally, vultures alight in trees or they alight on the ground next to something dead; they are not cave dwellers. But this vulture sailed right into a sizable cave entrance up on the hillside, and I could plainly see that there were thornbushes nearby.

How'd you spot this?

<I saw him fly out earlier. At first I thought it was a bat, because that's what flies out of caves, but he's weird. He circled around once and went right back in. So there you go. Kind of high up, but it's a cave.>

Yeah. And probably up for grabs too. Either that's a nest or there's something dead in there. We can probably use it either way.

I pointed the cave out to Granuaile and said we should go check it out. She merely nodded in reply and followed me in grim silence.

It's funny how when someone is Not Talking to You their every movement speaks volumes. Granuaile had little holsters on either hip, each with three flat, leaf-bladed throwing knives nestled on top of one another. She could throw them accurately with either hand to finish off opponents or take them out to begin with; her staff was more of a defensive weapon, meant to disarm or trip rather than deliver lethal blows to someone in heavy armor. Her knives made a soft clinking sound with every step she took, though I hadn't heard them before. Perhaps I simply hadn't noticed. Now, however, they communicated her burning desire to draw one and toss it between my shoulder blades.

Negotiating the hill was tiresome, and the clinking of the knives soon tapped out a different message: *This had better be worth it.*

We were joined by Oberon, who was panting happily, his tongue lolling out. The forest was full of wonderful smells to him.

"Hi, Oberon!" Granuaile said, stopping to pet him. "Are you having a good time?"

<Tell Clever Girl I said it's a beautiful day,> he re-

plied, using his nickname for Granuaile. He called her that about half the time, having developed a fine appreciation for her habit of sparring with me verbally as much as physically. <And just about everything in the forest is terrified of me, so I feel like quite the apex predator right now.>

I repeated this for Granuaile's sake and she laughed.

"You are certainly top dog," she said to him.

<Atticus, have I told you before that I approve of your apprentice?>

Yep. Every time she strokes your ego.

That light feeling evaporated after a few minutes as Oberon wandered sideways to investigate a rustling noise. The accusatory clinking of Granuaile's throwing knives resumed behind me, and I began to wonder when she would say something. Since we were by ourselves she couldn't be waiting for a private moment, so I had to conclude that she was waiting for something else. I would simply have to wait along with her.

Oberon halted abruptly as we approached the mouth of the cave; he laid his ears back flat against his head and grumbled softly in his throat.

<Atticus, something about that cave doesn't smell right.>

I stopped hiking and so did Granuaile. She didn't have to ask what was going on; she could tell Oberon was talking to me.

What's wrong with it?

<Well, I should be smelling a nasty bird and dead stuff, and I do. Except I also smell a human. And a bear.>

A human and a bear? That makes no sense. Unless the human is wearing a bearskin.

<It's kind of warm for that.>

Maybe it's a bearskin rug.

<In a cave?>

Well, let's go check it out. Cautiously.

I drew Moralltach as silently as I could from its scabbard and knew that Granuaile would be readying a knife and her staff behind me. I crept forward, the soft noises my feet made in the gravelly hillside unnaturally loud to my ears. I heard some scratching ahead and the soft, dry rasp of a bird's throat.

My sword crested the lip of the cave's mouth first, and I paused to see if anything wished to attack the bare blade. When nothing did, I risked a peek.

Two black eyes glared at me over a sharp beak. Oberon's vulture was perhaps ten yards away, standing in a pile of bones and rotting tissue and watching me. There wasn't anything suggestive of a nest; it was more of a mess hall, with an emphasis on the mess. It wasn't convenient to water and it reeked, but it would work if we cleaned it out. The high ceiling was kind of a bonus. We had to convince the current resident to leave first.

"It's just the vulture," I said. "Come on up, but watch out for the beak."

Vultures have no strength in their talons to speak of, because their prey typically doesn't try to run away from them. Their beaks, on the other hand, are perfect for piercing skin. Strangely, the vulture showed no signs of alarm when I advanced to the lip of the cave. Even when Granuaile hauled herself up, I didn't see a threatening display of the wings. The bird continued to stare as if it expected us to drop dead and provide it with lunch.

It was when Oberon appeared that the vulture finally showed signs of alarm—and also showed signs of not being a vulture.

Oberon barked and growled, showing his teeth, the hair on the back of his neck raised. <Atticus, that thing is a thing!>

What?

<It's not normal!>

As we watched, the vulture screeched, spread its wings, and grew—but not into a nastier vulture. It morphed into something else entirely. The neck thickened, the beak became a snout, and fur replaced feathers. Stubby vulture legs became stubby human legs, but what roared at us from the top half—

<Gah! It's a great big bear!>

"Gods damn the Greeks and their unholy hybrid monsters!" I muttered, then addressed the creature in Greek. "Are you a talking bear-man or just hungry?"

The bear roared again and Oberon tried to bark louder, but then the creature spoke in a malicious rumble: "I am Agrios of Thrace, son of Polyphonte. Who are you?"

I was tempted to tell him "nobody," but I wasn't Odysseus and he wasn't Polyphemus.

"I am Atticus of . . . Attica," I replied. Saying anything else would be meaningless to him. His myth was coming back to me. This fellow had been turned into a vulture by Hermes and Ares long ago; his mother and brother, because they were the "kind of nice" Thracian abominations, were only turned to owls. Agrios was the loathsome one. He'd been spawned because his mother, Polyphonte, had managed to tick off Aphrodite, so the goddess of love made her couple with a bear, and *rawr*, Agrios and Oreios were born.

"Aren't you supposed to stay a vulture?" I asked.

"I was taught how to transform by Thracian witches. I served them for a time, until I opened their bellies and ate them. Olympus has forgotten me. As long as I don't hunt the puny mortals and take only that which is given me, I am left alone. It has been many years since I was sent a sacrifice. Who sent you?"

"Whoa. Hold on. We're not sacrifices. We're just out looking for the handsomest caves in Greece and thought this was a likely one."

I shot some quick instructions to Oberon: *When we*

fight, circle round behind him and bite him on the back of the hams.

<Got it.>

"You *like* my cave?" Agrios said, idly scratching his belly in confusion.

"Oh, yeah. Love what you've done with the carrion. Most people don't think of using carrion as an accent for their décor, but I think you've stumbled onto something special here. It's trendsetting."

Granuaile whispered to me in Russian, "What are you doing?"

"Knives only. Do not engage him," I whispered back in the same language.

The Thracian groused, "If you are so interested in décor, why do you come with a sword and a giant dog who growls at me?"

I shrugged. "Sometimes people in caves are impolite. But I can tell you are civilized."

The bear threw back its head and laughed an ursine laugh.

"Knife to the throat now," I told Granuaile, and she had thrown it before I finished the sentence.

Go, I told Oberon, and he charged around the creature's side. I charged too, straight toward the outraged roar as the knife sank into his throat. I didn't want him lumbering after Granuaile. Her staff would be of little use against such brute strength in close quarters, and her knives, however accurately thrown, were probably not enough to bring him down. Bear hide is tough, and the layers of fat serve as a sort of biological Kevlar.

When Agrios lowered his head and charged me, Oberon was behind him. Instead of biting the creature in the back of the thigh, Oberon caught an ankle and yanked, stretching Agrios out until he did a face-plant in front of me. The fall drove Granuaile's knife deeper into his throat and left me an ideal opportunity to take a free strike. I hacked down with Moralltach, expecting to end it there, but he rolled out of the way in a very human move and tore free of Oberon's jaws. He ignored the hound and me and launched himself after Granuaile, who had nothing but wee irritating needles and a staff that he'd treat like a toothpick. I didn't have an angle to cut him off in time.

Oberon was faster than I was, and he snagged the guy by the ankle again. It didn't halt his charge, but it slowed him down a bit, giving Granuaile a chance to toss another knife. It hit right between his eyes but didn't penetrate into the skull and mess with his brain. Roaring, Agrios lunged at her again, dragging Oberon with him, but Granuaile twisted away and chose to tumble down the hillside, out of his claws' range. That helped me, because now I could swing Moralltach without worrying about clipping her; the enchantment on its blade would spread necrosis through friend as easily as foe. Diving toward the creature before he could follow my apprentice downhill, I thrust Moralltach desperately at his side and managed to open a shallow groove in his flank. He bellowed and yanked his leg free of Oberon's jaws again, trailing tendons and flesh. He wanted Granuaile more than anything. Using the three limbs that Oberon hadn't savaged, Agrios grunted and leapt in a frantic attempt to break free of us. Victory erupted from his muzzle as he fell over the lip of the cave, but it cut off with a surprised yip once he landed on the steep hillside. Moralltach's necrotic enchantment had reached his heart, and he could no longer control his fall—or, indeed, anything at all. He rolled in a growing billow of dust down to the bottom, a blackened ruin. Granuaile, who'd found the trunk of a young tree to cling to, watched him in horror.

"Well, go, team!" I said, trying to distract from the fact that he'd been much faster in action than I'd anticipated. "Is everyone all right?"

<I'm fine,> Oberon said.

Granuaile was staring at the corpse splayed at the bottom of the hill. "I didn't know they were all real. I mean, the gods I knew about, but the mythological creatures too?" She tore her eyes free and looked up at me for an answer.

"Well, the Greeks' more than anyone else. Their tales keep getting told and reinforced."

"So the manticore? Bellerophon? The chimera? Pegasus? They were all real?"

"Oh, heck, yeah. They had much more press than this guy did."

Granuaile shook her head. "Please tell me I won't be bound to the earth here."

"No. We'll find someplace else."

"Then let's go. Now." She turned and began to pick her way gingerly down the hillside. I resheathed Moralltach, vowing to clean the blade as soon as I could.

<I didn't think her mood could get any worse, but obviously I was wrong,> Oberon said.

I know. We need to find a safe place for her to yell at me.

<This place is safe now.>

Yeah, but it stinks, see.

<So we need to find a safe and fragrant place for her to yell at you.>

Yeah.

<On it, boss! Follow me between the hills.>

I caught up with Granuaile at the bottom of the hill and flashed a grin at her. She gestured for me to lead the way and said nothing, a bleak expression on her face. I resumed picking a thorny path through overgrown bushes. There was no peace in the valley because there was no peace between us.

And so of course the bloody Norse chose that moment to swoop in and make everything worse.

<Atticus, I think we're being stalked by the ghost of Alfred Hitchcock. First it was a vulture, and now two giant ravens are coming our way.>

Where? I looked up and saw that most of my view was obscured by scraggly trees.

<That way. Um . . . the direction Santa Claus comes from.>

North? I turned to my right and saw the ravens after a moment. They were huge and familiar. They were Hugin and Munin, Odin's ravens. Hugin was new; I'd killed the first one in Asgard years ago, but Odin had eventually hatched a replacement—or rather, Munin had. As they circled nearer, a rainbow arced down from the sky and terminated a few feet from us. I wasn't surprised there was no pot of gold, but I was faintly disappointed anyway.

A serene woman floated—or, rather, seemed to float— down the rainbow to meet us. Her long blond hair, gently curling, blew softly in the wind, and a dress of muted oranges and reds completely concealed her feet. The dress was tied underneath the bust and billowed some- what, giving her a disturbing resemblance to a Dalek as she moved. Still, her bearing spoke of peace and quiet strength, and the tiny smile on her face made it up to her blue eyes once she reached the end of the rainbow and stepped onto the earth.

"Well met, Druids," she said.

"Indeed. A good day to you, Frigg," I said. Granu- aile's eyes were only slightly widened as I introduced her to Odin's wife.

"I'm honored," Granuaile said. She tried to curtsy but remembered too late that she wasn't wearing a dress to do it properly, so her gesture turned into a sort of awk- ward bow with a flourish.

"As am I," Frigg said. She turned her gaze back to me. "Odin sent me to visit you."

I squinted up at the sky. Hugin and Munin circled

overhead but didn't look as if they had any intention of landing.

My adversarial relationship with the Norse had been blessed with a truce about six years ago when I returned Odin's spear and admitted that I owed them something for the slaughter I'd brought to their door.

A blood price was mentioned, but it wasn't my blood they wanted. As ever, Odin was concerned most with preventing or delaying the onset of Ragnarok, and he recognized that I could be instrumental in addressing those concerns. I had agreed to help if I could, since I had been the idiot who'd kicked off the apocalypse by slaying the Norns, crippling Odin, and aiding Leif Helgarson in his quest to slay Thor.

That didn't mean everything between us was now Kool and the Gang. Frigg was simply better than any other surviving member of the Norse pantheon at concealing her urge to kill me.

"I expect you've heard something about Loki?" I said.

"We have heard and seen much," she said. "May we speak for a time?"

"Sure."

"Good. Events are moving toward the cusp of disaster, and we need to make our move soon if we want to avoid the worst."

I steeled myself for unpleasant news. Regardless of what Loki had been up to, I was at least partially responsible for setting events in motion. Frigg reminded me of this immediately.

Shortly after your raid on Asgard twelve years ago, Hel realized she could freely travel the nine planes of Yggdrasil, for that had been forbidden her until then. When Odin had cast her into Niflheim long ago and given her control of the nine realms, her authority extended to only the old and infirm and those unfortunate enough not to be called to Valhalla or Fólkvangr. She could never leave her frozen land on her own, not without the Norns telling Odin and him casting her down again.

Once freed, she spent much more time on Midgard than we'd originally thought. Odin missed much while he was recuperating, and Hel took advantage of this. She returned to Niflheim with several conclusions, no doubt, one of them being that she needed to learn English, the new dominant language, just as many of the Æsir did some centuries before. We can infer she thought it best that Loki learn it as well, for she sent a shade, one gifted with speech, to teach him the language. We had guards posted at the entrance to Loki's cave, of course, but they could do nothing to stop the shade. Seeing that it could not possibly set Loki free, and seeing also that it was providing him a welcome distraction from his captivity, we let the shade remain. However, we increased the guard at the cave—fifty Einherjar, outfitted and trained in the use of modern weapons—and also installed some . . . observers inside. These were sort of like Odin's ravens.

We began to receive reports that Hel was building forges in her realm and trading for raw materials from the Svartálfar. The dwarfs, bless them, refused to do so. Hel had learned from her time in Midgard that swords and shields would not be enough to carry the day. About nine years ago she started to manufacture weapons in earnest and to train her *draugar* in their use. She now has a massive army of soldiers with automatic weapons, who cannot be killed unless their heads are destroyed or struck off from their bodies.

Odin has been preparing the Einherjar to meet them, but even with modern body armor, they are at a disadvantage. The dwarfs have chosen to cast their lots with ours and have likewise been making preparation for the final battle. They have new transports and weapons unlike any I have seen.

According to our estimates, Hel could have begun Ragnarok during the past year with a fair chance of success, especially once Surtr and the sons of Muspell got involved. With no Thor to meet Jörmungandr, and no one to stop Fenris, her victory seemed assured—at least on paper.

What has prevented her seems to be a psychological inability to proceed without her father, Loki. She could have the world for her own right now, she could lay waste to Midgard and shape it howsoever she wills, but instead she craves his favor.

Some days ago, she made her move. She brought two thousand armed *draugar* to the cave against our fifty Einherjar. She stepped over their honorable corpses and entered the cave, wearing the form of a bent old woman.

Sigyn, Loki's wife, recognized her and demanded that she leave.

"You have no cause to be here!" she cried. "Is not Niflheim enough for you?"

Hel ignored her and spoke in her sepulchral voice to Loki, as the snake dripped its venom into the bowl Sigyn held above his face.

"Father," she rasped, "we can leave this place today and win Ragnarok. The old prophecies are null. The Norns are dead. Heimdall, who was fated to slay you, is dead. Freyr is dead. Týr and Vidar are dead. Even mighty Thor is dead, and my army is ready."

The god of mischief did not stir until he heard the name of the thunder god. "What?" Loki said. "You say Thor is dead? How?"

She told him of your party's invasion of Asgard and how you surprised us with defeat. She named your party:

the werewolf, the vampire, the alchemist, the Druid, the wizard, and the thunder god.

"What thunder god?" Loki wanted to know.

"Perun. The Slavic god. He has disappeared."

"But he is not dead?"

"I do not know, Father," she said. "He may be dead."

"I know how to find out," Loki said, grinning in such a way as he had not for centuries. "Set me free, daughter."

"Father, I cannot unbind you. Only you can do this. But I can make you do it sooner rather than later."

"How?"

"Answer me first: Do you still love this cow?" Hel jutted her chin toward Sigyn, who had protected Loki as best she could from the snake's dire venom all these years. But she was not Hel's mother. Loki's monstrous children were all borne by a giantess.

"Her?" Loki sneered. "No, I hate her. She has neither killed the snake nor erected a roof over my head, despite my pleading that she do so. She is thoughtless, worthless."

"And so I set you free," Hel said. She sloughed off her human visage and appeared in her true form, sprouting like an unwholesome weed to the roof of the cave. She pulled the wicked knife, Famine, from its scabbard in her exposed rib cage and plunged it into the neck of the faithful Sigyn.

Loki's wife gurgled her last breath, and the bowl of caustic venom toppled full into Loki's face. He screamed and writhed violently, and still the snake dripped on, under the goddess Skadi's command to continue. Loki jerked and pulled at his restraints, and the earth shook underneath Hel's feet. He cursed her. He swore vengeance upon her. And then, as the venom continued to eat at his eyes and chew at the substance of his flesh, he begged her for mercy.

But Hel had none. Mercy was an empty room in her

heart, where nothing at all was sacred and no living creature, not even her father, could cry so piteously as to make her take heed.

Loki bucked and howled as the venom bore deeper. He thrashed and shouted his defiance. The earth trembled more violently, and this grew and grew until his bonds were finally snapped and he was set free. Blood and tears streamed down his purpling cheeks, and he seized the snake that had tormented him so and burned it alive in his hands, his fire returned to him now that he was unbound. No freedom had ever been bought with so much agony, and he vowed it would be avenged sevenfold, beginning with the Slavic thunder god.

We do not know why he focused on Perun rather than on the vampire who killed Thor; perhaps it was because he was a target of convenience. Loki knew that the entrance to the Slavic plane lay hidden somewhere in the Ural Mountains, and it was to these he flew upon first leaving his cave.

He left Hel behind, without thanks, bereft of approval, and with no signal that she should begin Ragnarok. Unable to follow him, she returned to her realm, sullen and uncertain, to await further word from her father.

"And that is why we must strike now and slay Fenris," Frigg finished, clearly angling for the non sequitur of the year.

"I beg your pardon?" I said.

"We must demoralize Hel and prevent her from launching an attack on Asgard. Odin has decided that the best way to do that is to slay Fenris."

"Well, that's nice, but we can do it a bit later."

"Now is the perfect time."

"I disagree. Vehemently."

Frigg's eyes clouded, and the ravens above squawked. "You swore you would help us. You swore to render what aid you could in place of a blood price."

"And render it I shall. But not right now. I have an apprentice to bind to the earth, and until she's bound, I'm not doing anything else."

Frigg shifted her eyes to Granuaile and pursed her lips in dislike, realizing that my apprentice was an obstacle to her goals. "Bring her along, then," she said.

"No way." I shook my head to emphasize the point. "She isn't ready yet. After she's bound she could actually be helpful and may choose, of her own free will, to give us her help. But right now she's a liability and a potential hostage."

I flattened my hand and used it as an impromptu shade against the sun as I searched out Odin's ravens. I called out to them to make sure the mind they represented heard me.

"If my apprentice falls victim to an 'accident,' Odin, I won't help you at all, you hear me? Just be patient a while longer."

"And if Ragnarok begins while we are being patient?" Frigg asked.

"I'll take on Jörmungandr myself if it does," I said. "That's how confident I am that it won't happen, okay? I think we have a year left." At least, I hoped we did.

"Based on what information?"

"I'll keep that to myself. But nothing is changed here, Frigg. I will keep my word as soon as my apprentice is bound."

Frigg had nothing nice to say, so she didn't say anything. She nodded curtly and turned her back on us, floating up the rainbow into the northern sky. The ravens followed her.

I hoped that after this encounter Granuaile would be more willing to talk, but my optimistic expression was immediately crushed when she shook her head at me and scowled.

"A liability and a hostage, Atticus?" she said. "Really?"

<Fall to your knees and grovel. Now!>

"Well—"

<Nope. Fall!>

"I put two knives in that bear thing and distracted it while you missed," she said, "but *I'm* a liability?"

"Look, Granuaile, against human opponents, I'd say you could take just about anyone," I said. "But Frigg was talking about messing around with the supernatural, and you're not in that power class yet. You will be soon."

"So a vulture that turns into a bear-human hybrid isn't supernatural?"

<Lie down and offer your throat. No, wait, that's how dogs submit. I know! Give her your wallet!>

"Yes, it is, Granuaile, and you handled it superbly, no doubt. But right now you can't heal yourself if you get wounded. You can't speed up or cast camouflage or take advantage of any of the spells I regularly use to stay alive. I would very much like to make sure you stay alive, so I hope you'll forgive my poor choice of words. I wanted Frigg to go away, that's all."

She gazed at me, her disbelief every bit as plain as her disapproval, but she had no more desire to wrangle over it. She turned her back on me, leaving me unforgiven, and we trudged westward toward Olympus without speaking a word to each other.

A hot hour's hike up the valley finally brought us good news from Oberon.

<Atticus, I think I found a place!>

You did? Where?

<I can see you from here.>

I looked around me and saw nothing but more trees, stubborn undergrowth, and a few stretches of bare rock wall ahead, where the mountain fell precipitously into the wash. I could hear it running with winter snowmelt but couldn't see it yet.

I don't see you, I told Oberon.

\<That's the kind of place you want, right?\>

It is indeed.

\<Keep heading toward the water. I'll direct you when you get closer.\>

After I gave Granuaile some encouragement that we were near a possible campsite, we shoved our way through the brush to the water's edge. It was a narrow, rocky stream, easily jumped in some places but running fast.

Can you still see us? I asked Oberon.

\<Sure can. You're looking for a good place to cross that torrential sluice of doom. That was an excellent example of both hyperbole and assonance, by the way, for which I deserve a turkey leg and a long brush by a tall person with soft hands.\>

Where do we go from here?

\<Upstream. I'm on a ledge on the other side. There's a pine tree here and some thorn, but behind it there's a cave in the side of the mountain.\>

I looked in that direction and saw the place he was talking about—I saw the tree on the ledge, anyway. *Awesome. Any animal tracks or other sign in there?*

\<Yeah, but they're years old.\>

Is the cave deep enough for us to lie down, tall enough to stand?

\<It's definitely deep enough. You might have to watch your head, but I think you can walk for most of it.\>

The difficulty we faced getting up to the ledge only made it more attractive to me once we finally arrived; there was very little chance we'd be disturbed by any humans in a place like this—few people are trailblazers anymore, when it's so much safer and easier to follow the trails already blazed.

We hopped the stream about thirty yards past the tree, then struggled our way up to the ledge. Oberon waited at the mouth of the cave, wagging his tail. The entrance was completely choked with brush, but it was spacious inside.

How did you ever think to look for this? I asked Oberon.

<I didn't think of it, to be honest. Finding it was a happy accident. You see, there was a squirrel on that pine tree, giving me some lip as I was passing down by the stream. He said some bawdy things about my mom—>

Oberon, come on.

<Well, all right, I don't know what he said, but he definitely had an attitude, just like all squirrels, and he deserved to be chased up to the top and kept there for a while. I wouldn't have come up here otherwise.>

Well, this is perfect. We owe that squirrel for leading you here.

<Wait a second! How come the squirrel gets all the credit?>

I was thinking he'd get all the credit and you'd get all the sausage.

<Oh! That sounds completely fair, Atticus; I really can't argue with that.>

"We're going to camp here, then?" Granuaile asked, peering into the cave and breaking the silence.

"Maybe," I said. "Let me scope this out first." Using the magic stored in my bear charm, I triggered my faerie specs and looked for any indication that there was a magical booby trap here or an alarm that would go off if I drew power from the earth. This cave could be the favorite spot of a cyclops or a nymph or something spookier than an old monster like Agrios. It took a while to check thoroughly; any magic performed by the Greeks wouldn't look like the Celtic bindings of my own work. I found nothing. The ceiling of the cave wasn't blackened by the smoke of ancient fires, which corroborated my growing belief that we were the first humans to set eyes on this cave in centuries—perhaps the first humans ever.

"It looks good," I said, shrugging off the straps of my pack. "This might work out perfectly."

"Okay," Granuaile said, extricating herself from her pack and setting it down with a relieved sigh.

"Oberon, I'll need you to scout all possible approaches to the cave. We can see pretty well down below, but we need to know what's behind us. Would you mind?"

<Not at all. Am I allowed to hunt?>

"Don't hunt yet. Scout all you want, but let's just establish what's normal for the area so we can spot any intruders later."

<Okay. But I'm bagging something before we leave or I'm a pug with the muscle tone of French bread.>

"Agreed."

Oberon turned and disappeared with a swish of his tail through the brush. Granuaile began to unpack in brooding silence.

Backpacking is different when you can cast night vision. Items like flashlights and lamps and oil are unnecessary. We had plenty of food—mostly soup mixes and jerky and dried fruit. It was a nutritionally deficient diet, but it was only for a few months, with resupply available at a tolerable distance in Litochoro. Water and wood for fuel were plentiful. The large pine tree would help diffuse the smoke from our cook fires.

Granuaile was yanking goodies out of her pack with increasing force and tossing, then throwing, them down on the ground. She was working herself up for something; the whistle on the old pressure cooker was about to go off.

"Fire away whenever you're ready," I said quietly.

She did not appear to hear. She still had a few more items to yank out and slam down, and I approved. Violent unpacking should never be interrupted or unfinished.

"Those weren't gods!" she finally exploded.

"I beg your pardon?"

"I mean the Tuatha Dé Danann. Frigg was fine. But I expected something a bit nobler from the Irish, you know? Not a festival of pettiness and gamesmanship and freezing people in time, staring at them morbidly before they die. Why should I pray to them?"

"That's an excellent question. You don't have to."

Her expression, full of challenge, morphed into confusion. "I don't?"

"No, of course not."

"I thought all the Druids worshipped the Tuatha Dé Danann."

"They do." I smiled wryly. "But that's because I'm the only Druid right now."

"No, I meant . . . in history. When there were more of you around."

"It varied a bit. The Druids on the continent tended to like Cernunnos, for example, more than those of us who came from Ireland. The Wild Hunt was bigger on the mainland too. There was no central doctrine for all the Celts."

"So I can worship who I want? Or not at all?"

"Of course. Gaia doesn't give a damn who you worship; when the Tuatha Dé Danann became the first Druids, you can bet they didn't worship themselves. You're going to be bound to the earth, Granuaile, not to a religion. You can dress like a pirate on Fridays and worship the Flying Spaghetti Monster if you want. Gaia won't care as long as you protect her."

"Oh." Granuaile settled back on her haunches but

then gave that up and carefully arranged her legs in the lotus position. She rested her hands lightly on her knees, kept her back straight, and fixed her eyes on mine. I recognized the posture; she was about to argue with me.

"Please explain why you continue to worship the Tuatha Dé Danann when you have no need to do so and you are clearly aware they are flawed beings."

I settled myself so that my posture mirrored hers before answering.

"Your question assumes that gods must necessarily be perfect. That is a prejudice of monotheism. People of pagan faiths are not upset by gods that reflect human foibles. In fact, it's rather comforting."

"I grant you the prejudice, but the question remains. If you are not required to worship them—if you retain all magical powers regardless of your faith or lack thereof—why do you persist?"

"I'm in it for the afterlife, same as anyone else."

She frowned. "Are you throwing some sort of pagan Pascal's Wager at me?"

"Catch!"

"Thpppt."

"Don't be so dismissive. Where is the downside to spending eternity in Mag Mell, or even in Tír na nÓg? Both are beautiful places."

"So are most versions of paradise."

"Hence the reason I encourage you to believe what you wish. The heaven of the Pastafarians is supposed to have beer volcanoes, which sounds like a fantastic idea to me. Imagine eruptions of a mellow chocolaty stout. There might be all-you-can-eat hot wings."

Granuaile's tone turned accusatory. "You've been training me in the rituals of your faith for twelve years and allowing me to believe that worshipping the Tuatha Dé Danann was bound up with being a Druid."

"For me, it is. My own prejudice. I apologize for the omission."

"They were once merely Druids, you say. The Tuatha Dé Danann."

"Yes. But they were skilled in their own magic even before that."

"How did they become gods? What powers did they accrue when they did?"

"They became gods once people worshipped them as such. They became vessels for Celtic faith, tuning forks for our yearnings, keepers of our hopes and prayers. And the powers they gained were those assigned to them by worshippers. Manannan Mac Lir was not a psychopomp until people thought he was; he was only a Druid with some extra powers in the sea."

"So why don't cult leaders achieve godhood?"

"Because they're megalomaniacs drenched in douche juice."

"But so was Thor, right? And let's not forget that there was certainly no shortage of douchebaggery in Tír na nÓg today. I'm asking seriously. Some cult leaders inspire fervent devotion in their followers. Shouldn't they gain godlike powers?"

"No, because they all die in thirty to fifty years and their cult dies with them. Godhead transcends generations and requires the concerted belief of a large number of people."

"How does your belief in Manannan Mac Lir as a psychopomp give him the powers of one?"

"Figuring that out is one of the reasons I'm hanging around. I think the Large Hadron Collider might yield some clues."

"You're talking about particle physics now?"

"Yep. They're slowly discovering why we have more matter than antimatter in the universe. Smash a proton, and you don't get simple matter and antimatter. Some particles degrade and change very quickly."

"Change into what?"

"Damn it, Jim, I'm a Druid, not a physicist!"

Granuaile rolled her eyes at the allusion. "I understand, but what's the connection with godlike powers?"

"The connection is that there are clearly some powers and processes in the universe we simply don't understand yet. They are ineffable—for now. I don't know how it's possible for Gaia to have a magical nature. And the Tuatha Dé Danann cannot tell you how, precisely, they gained the powers of gods on top of the powers of Druids. But they can tell you they didn't always possess them. Some grew slowly, and some were discovered abruptly. And it's no different with any other gang of gods. Some of them have bought into their own origin myths, which is distilled shite on its face—the world can't have been created in hundreds of different ways— but the smart ones will tell you they're not sure how they got the gig they got and they don't remember creating humanity, much less the world. For most of space and time, they weren't there; and then, one day, they were, complete with a small but hopefully growing collection of praying humans."

Granuaile slumped and let her lotus position tumble apart. Her face was sad and haunted.

"What's the matter?"

"Nobody has the answer, do they?" she asked quietly.

"No. I'm sorry."

Chapter 7

Oberon returned from scouting and declared the area safe for now. <Safe for us, I mean. Not safe for rodents. They're all chittering out their last will and testaments.>

I took my sandals off and said hello to the Olympian elemental. I'd never found one so happy to hear from me—and they're happy as a rule. The emotions flooded up from the sole of my foot and made me smile.

//Many many welcomes / Bounteous joy and harmony / Wishes of good health and pleasure// she said. By prior arrangement, Granuaile and I had agreed to call her Olympia rather than Olympus.

//Harmony// I replied. //We are happy to be here//

//Query: We?//

//Druid brings apprentice / Ready to be bound to the earth//

If elementals could pee from excitement, Olympia would have done so when she heard that. I had to weather a torrent of gushing before I could interject a request.

//Please conceal our presence here from all gods and other beings// I said. //Privacy needed to bind apprentice//

//Privacy assured// Olympia answered. //Will steer animals and gods away//

I laid my right hand on Oberon's back. //This animal is my friend// I explained. //Please let him do as he wishes//

//Dog is Druidfriend// she agreed. //Piece of self coming / To talk to apprentice//

A small white marble—actually made of smooth, cloudy marble—appeared between my toes. I picked it up and presented it to Granuaile so that she would be able to speak to Olympia. She smiled as she closed her fist around it and introduced herself. Her expression was always beatific when she spoke with elementals. I wondered if my face still held that same sense of peace and joy after two thousand years.

Introductions complete and satisfied that my magical tracks would be covered, I let Oberon take us for a walk around the cave's neighborhood. I went barefoot and asked the earth to ease the way for us, including Oberon, while we were in the area. The thick undergrowth—including thornbushes—moved aside to let us pass and then closed behind us so that we could move freely, while anyone else would have to fight their way through, as we had the first time. Oberon was establishing a patrol route for the area that couldn't be readily seen from the cave entrance, showing me that the easiest way for someone to approach us without much warning would be upstream to the west. There was a flat stretch where the stream slowed and widened, creating some pools deep enough to swim in. It was a popular watering hole for deer, judging by the tracks. Oberon would no doubt hunt here.

Speaking aloud so Granuaile could hear my side of the conversation, I told Oberon, "We're going to hike into town to grab supplies to make some snares, so that we can hopefully add some variety to our diet. We'll be staying the night and coming back in the morning."

<Well, can't I stay here and hunt?>

"No, we need you to come along so that we'll look cool. Without you, we'll look like stupid foreigners."

<Oh, yeah, I forgot. Irish wolfhounds are the ultimate accessory for humans.>

"You'll have plenty of time to hunt when we return. Like, three months."

Oberon's tail wagged. <Great lakes of gravy! That sounds like a long time! Is it?>

"It's longer than I've ever given you before."

<Wow! Wait. What's the catch?>

"The catch is, if you don't catch anything you have to eat jerky. It's either fresh tender meat or dried, tough, and salted."

<A stark choice! And yet a challenge worthy of the noble wolfhound.>

"Careful with that ego. You could knock somebody over. Let's go."

We stopped back at the cave to pick up our packs, now empty and ready to be refilled with additional supplies. Making our way down was much easier with Olympia smoothing the way for us. By the time the trail led us to town, we had no trouble looking like we'd been hiking all day. I placed a call to my attorney, Hal Hauk, and had him wire some money to us from the States. We found a restaurant with dog-friendly patio seating and shoved down some gyros and spanakopita. Oberon approved.

<I like this country. I can eat in the open with you guys, and the meat is good. What's that white stuff you're putting on it? It's not horseradish, is it?>

Tzatziki sauce. It's a cucumber–yogurt concoction.

<Can I try a little?>

Sure. I slathered a bit on a piece of gyro meat and fed it to him. He ate it noisily, his tongue flapping around as he tried to taste his food instead of inhaling it.

<Eh. It's not terrible or anything, but it cools down

the temperature and mutes the flavors of the meat. I'll take mine plain.>

We relaxed and spoke of Granuaile's upcoming binding as the sun set. There was a decent sporting goods store in the small town catering to the many tourists who wished to hike Olympus, and we planned on visiting it shortly before closing time. We extended our supper into something of a feast, reasoning that we wouldn't have the opportunity to eat like this again for quite some time.

Half an hour before closing time and a bit besotted with a fine bottle of pinot noir, we walked the two blocks to the sporting goods store. Oberon spotted a park nearby full of people walking their dogs, so I cast camouflage on him, gave him my best wishes, and told him to listen for my call.

The store had aisles of cooking pots and meals in silvery pouches, along with plenty of shoes that were designed to look like they could vault boulders without the assistance of feet inside them. And the tents! My goodness, tent architecture has come a long way since the old days. But we were looking for simple materials like wire and wire cutters or, failing that, string and scissors with which to make some snares for squirrels, rabbits, and the like. There would be no problem finding enough branches to hold tension for the springs.

Thanks to the influence of Olympia and perhaps the wine, Granuaile was now in a very good mood, and it was impossible not to love life when she smiled so often.

My own smile evaporated when I saw the pale spooky bastard eyeing her from the next aisle over. He didn't have enough sun on his skin to qualify as a hiker; what was he doing in here?

I flipped on my faerie specs and suppressed a shudder

when I saw the dull gray aura of a vampire about his head, with an ember of red in the center.

Taking a calculated risk that he would be unable to understand Old Irish, I spoke in it to Granuaile. There is no word for *vampire* in that language, so I said, "Do not look up, but there is a walking dead man in the next aisle, staring at you. He is stalking us. You, actually. Do not look him in the eyes for any reason. Your iron talisman will not prevent you from being charmed."

"What are you going to do?" she asked in the same language.

"Chat with him. Remain here and keep your eyes down. Say something in a cheerful tone of voice to me now and smile."

"Okay, just leave me here all alone, then!" she said joyfully. I moved away from her, down the aisle, and then turned around an endcap of handheld beer coolers to walk up the aisle in which the vampire stood. His eyes flicked to me, a shadow of nervous worry in them, but he quickly returned to pretending to look at water purification tablets. I muttered bindings under my breath that would increase my speed and strength for as long as the magic stored in my bear charm lasted.

The vampire was dressed in a white linen shirt over blue jeans and expensive running shoes. I noticed with some amusement that he had stayed away from the aisle where they sold wooden tent stakes.

Stopping a few feet away and facing him squarely, I greeted him in Greek.

"Good evening," he said, his eyes furtively landing on my face and then whipping back to products he couldn't possibly want to buy. I continued to stare at him and he said, "I don't work here, if you have a question."

"Oh, I have a question, all right. You see, I'm sort of

new in town and could use a little help finding someone you might know."

He stopped pretending to shop and turned to face me. "Do I know you?"

"No, but I'm sure you know the gentleman for whom I'm looking. He's a vampire who sometimes goes by the name of Theophilus."

I expected the expression of shock—widened eyes, a droop at the corners of the mouth. The attempt to charm me was also expected. His mouth pressed into a thin line of determination and his eyes narrowed. I grinned at him, protected by my cold iron aura.

"You can't charm me, sorry. But would you be so kind as to direct me to Theophilus? We need to talk, he and I."

This was the bit where I expected him to sling a question at me. "Who are you?" was my best bet, but "Why do you want to talk to Theophilus?" would have been reasonable, or even "Did you say something about a vampire a second ago?" What I got instead was an all-out attack, complete with kitty hissing and an attempt to tear out my throat.

Since I'd been braced for it and was already juiced up, I didn't go down to the ground, but I did back up quite a bit, until I had his arms locked in mine.

I had added a new charm to my necklace in response to my last encounter with a vampire, when I quite nearly died because I couldn't finish speaking the unbinding. Until now I hadn't had an opportunity to test it. A mental command would trigger a proxy unbinding of a target vampire. I'd figured that, like all my charms, it would take years to perfect. I triggered it now and was surprised to see the vampire flinch and become afflicted with existential horror—like the moment when you're sitting in the hot tub with friends, some of whom are amazingly sexy, and a squirming sensation in your bowels means your diarrhea has come back. It wasn't success, but it was better than nothing. I began to speak the unbinding aloud.

This lad wasn't as strong as Zdenik, the vampire who'd nearly snuffed me. Zdenik had been nearly as old as I was, and my magic had drained rapidly trying to hold him off. This vampire was probably only a few hundred years old, and I could tell he was beginning to think it would have been far safer to simply talk to me. He abruptly changed tactics and decided to disengage. I held on to him, my fingers digging firmly into his arms. I couldn't let him get away to prey on humans for a thousand years. He tried to use my strength against me, lunging back in for another attack since I was pulling on his arms, and I did release one arm to block access to my throat. Almost finished. He sank his fangs into the meat of my forearm, thinking perhaps he would simply drain me the slow way, but that was fine—it would be far too slow to do him any good. I stepped back, allowing him to think he had an advantage, and his free arm clutched at me to keep me from escaping. He was hooked now, but I paid a price when I finished the unbinding.

Some vampires sort of melt when they're unbound and they simply splash on the floor. This guy exploded, showering my immediate vicinity and me in blood and gore. I looked fairly guilty, in other words, of a particularly heinous murder.

"Eww," Granuaile commented from her vantage point. She was untouched by a single drop of blood. "I ducked," she explained.

The lone store employee began to curse steadily and hysterically in Greek, his eyes the size of Ping-Pong balls. He had a cell phone out and was shouting into it as he ran from the store, escaping what he clearly thought was certain death.

"We have a problem," I said.

"Ya think?"

"That didn't go the way I thought it would."

"I should hope not, because that would be pretty sick. You're completely covered in viscera."

I turned off my speed and strength bindings and said, "I'm camouflaging us. Help me find the surveillance systems. We need to destroy all record of what happened."

"Right. Except for that pool of goo on the floor."

"Yes. They can make of that what they will. I just don't want them to watch the video and conclude I did something magical—or conclude he was a vampire."

"Okay. We have all we need, right?" She held up a small basket full of the supplies we'd come for.

"Yep." I cast camouflage on her, and as she faded from view she said she would check the back of the store.

"I'll check behind the register," I said, casting camouflage on myself. That drained my bear charm down to dangerous levels. I wouldn't be able to maintain this for long.

I found a few monitors behind the register, but they were using a feed generated somewhere else.

"Back here, sensei!" Granuaile called. I followed the sound of her voice to the rear of the store, where there was a sign marked EMPLOYEES ONLY in Greek and English on a locked door. I bound the tumblers into the unlocked position and opened it. Inside were even more monitors and a black console with a tangle of cables snaking in and out of it.

"That's our baby. Looks like a disc system similar to the one I had at Third Eye way back when."

Granuaile pressed a few buttons and got several discs to eject. Searching her shopping basket with my fingers, I took out a pair of wire clippers and cut through all the cables in the back of the console. The monitors turned to snow as I did so.

"We'd better be sure this has no hard-drive backup," I said. "We should smoosh it."

"Aw, yeah, rage against the machine! Let's do this!" I heard Granuaile shuffle backward and pictured her brandishing her staff. I threw the console down hard, rattling the case, but once the iron tip of Granuaile's staff descended upon it, there was a significant dent.

"Again," I suggested.

The console acquired two more dents in quick succession.

"Hold off," I said. "Let me jump on it a few times."

"Go."

I did a gleeful mosh—or was it a skank?—upon the top, which did little to it but did manage to make me feel better.

"It's bolted together fairly well. Let's just take it with us and dump it into the pond in the park."

"Good idea," Granuaile agreed. Sirens could be heard approaching. "I think we should exit quickly."

"Yes, let's."

Using the last dregs of my magic, I camouflaged the security console and the discs Granuaile had removed from it, and then I carried the console out of the store under my arm while Granuaile carried the discs out in her handbasket. The police screeched to a halt in the street and leapt out of their vehicles, square bodies emphasized by swaths of body armor and contrasted with cylindrical weapons of one kind or another. They utterly failed to see us as they surrounded the store; we slipped between them and jogged to Enikkea Park. There I called to Oberon, who found me easily by following the smell of blood. He'd been all alone for some time, since the dog walkers had all gone home once the sun went down. He'd entertained himself by sniffing around and chasing wee critters. I dissolved all camouflage and tossed the console into a square pond with a fountain in the middle of it. Granuaile snapped all the discs in half and threw them in as well.

"Did I miss something there?" Granuaile said. "You asked him about a vampire named Theophilus and he attacked?"

"Yep, you heard it all."

"Who's Theophilus?"

"Leif told me about him before we raided Asgard. He's supposedly the oldest vampire living. Unliving. Whatever."

"Do you think that was him?"

"No, not a chance. Theophilus would have been able to overpower me."

"Then why are you looking for him?"

"I want to ask him if he knows anything about the old Roman pogrom against Druids. If he didn't have anything to do with it directly, he surely knew who did. Leif thought that Theophilus spent part of every year in Greece; naturally every other vampire in Greece would be well aware of his territory."

"So you never intended to kill that vampire?"

"Oh, no, I intended to kill him. Just not so publicly, and only after I'd gotten something useful out of him."

"I'd say you got something useful. He wouldn't have attacked unless he had something to protect. Theophilus is alive and around here somewhere."

I nodded. "Good thinking. But it's an unfortunate development all around; he's going to know there's a Druid nearby, because only Druids can do that to vampires. Are you sure you didn't get tagged by any of the blood?"

"I'm not sure about my back, but I didn't feel anything," she said. She turned around and looked over her shoulder at me. "Can you see any?"

She appeared clean. "Nope. That's excellent, because we still need a carrier for the tattoo ink. I have the ink itself ready to go, but I need you to sally forth and get a couple bottles of ethyl alcohol. Failing that, some strong vodka." I gave her a wad of euros. "Oberon and I will wait here. Perhaps I'll take a quick dunk to get the worst of the blood off."

"Be back as soon as I can, sensei," she said, and then jogged toward town.

I waded into the pool and began to splash my face and arms. There was no one around to object to a quick bath, so I didn't try to be subtle about it.

<This is weird. I feel like I should be telling you a story right now,> Oberon said. Usually I told him stories while he bathed.

Well, why don't you? It's about time you told me a story.

<Where am I supposed to get my stories? I'm the only hound who knows language well enough to tell them.>

I think you just answered your own question. You have to make them up.

<Fine. There once was a Doberman named Jean-Claude Van Hamme—>

Wait, nobody would name their dog that!

<Whose story is this?>

Yours, I conceded.

<Thank you. Because of your rude interruption, I will never tell you about the exciting adventures of Jean-Claude Van Hamme, but I will tell you a different story, one that I have been working on for a while, if you promise not to interrupt. Do you promise?

I promise. I'm sorry for interrupting.

<Very well. Brace yourself for a tragedy. It has lost bones, lost balls, a profound waste of sausage, and everything.>

I can't wait! And I wasn't kidding. If I had a tail to wag, I would have wagged it.

<Here it is, then . . . >

Oberon's story, a mystery after the style of Sherlock Holmes, was called "The Purloined Poodle." It featured a canine sleuth named Ishmael (a Weimaraner) and his trusty assistant, Starbuck (a Boston terrier), who foiled a nefarious plot set in motion by Abe Froman, the Sausage King of Chicago.

Oh, Oberon, that was a wonderful mystery! I said when he finished. *Bravo!*

<I think it should be *Sir* Oberon. Arthur Conan Doyle got a knighthood for stories like that, so I think I should get one too.>

I doubt the queen will knight you. She's a bit stuffy about that sort of thing. But I can make you a Druidic knight if you wish.

<You can?>

Sure!

<Gravy! Sir Oberon the . . . um, I need a majestic adjective here.>

Sir Oberon the Scruffy!

<I think not. I said *majestic*, as in noble, awesome, godlike, et cetera.>

Sir Oberon the Modest!

Refreshed and feeling far less icky, I waded out of the fountain and checked to see how well I'd done. My cotton shirt was a lost cause; I'd need an industrial-strength cleanser to salvage it, and it wasn't worth the trouble. I stripped it off and threw it on the grass, where I unbound the entire thing and let its component molecules mingle with the landscape. There would be no evidence for a forensic pathologist to find.

Granuaile returned shortly thereafter with two bottles of ethyl alcohol in her pack.

"We can get a hotel room if you want, but it's probably best to get out of town. Feel like hiking back with night vision?"

She did. "I want to get started as soon as possible," Granuaile said. "Ever since Laksha told me what you really were, I've wanted this. Let's go."

Chapter 8

Some moments are pregnant with epiphany.

The moment just before you take your first successful bike ride. That bit where the lights go out at your very first concert and people scream because other people who play rock and roll are walking onstage. The doubtful glare at a shiny can seconds before you chug it, choke on it, and realize that you're a beer snob after all. That moment, sometime after the honeymoon is over, when it dawns on you that the honeymoon really *is* over and marriage will require a bit of work. And then that moment before your first child is born. They are the moments during which we are briefly, acutely, conscious that our lives will be changed forever . . . in the next moment.

Granuaile was having one of those moments. Her muscles were tense and she was holding her breath, because I held her right heel cupped in my left hand and pointed a sharp thorn at the sole of her foot with my other hand. Said thorn was hardened and sharpened and still attached to a living thornbush, which was of course in contact with the earth and thus with Gaia. The ink was ground lapis lazuli, mined in Colorado, mixed with alcohol.

Both of us were in a trancelike fugue, though only I was in contact with Gaia; Granuaile was being helped by Olympia, via the marble clutched tightly in her hand. We would pause occasionally to eat and sleep and keep our bodies functioning, but, once established, the connection with Gaia would have to stay open for three months. We'd be extremely vulnerable and less-than-sterling conversationalists.

Oberon understood this. It was to be a long, lonely time for him. And he also understood that, should it be warranted, he would snap us out of it, whether Granuaile was completely bound or not.

I hadn't told Granuaile what would happen when I first pierced her sole with the thorn and the consciousness of Gaia rushed in. There were no words to prepare someone for that. So I simply jabbed her where Gaia said I should, then held on as she spasmed, screamed, and passed out.

Chapter 9

Druids are trained to multitask and maximize their mental capacity. They're encouraged both to think big thoughts and think several different ones at the same time. But no one's mind is capable of keeping up with Gaia's. A single human brain cannot contain the mind of the world. That's why Granuaile shut down when flooded with the consciousness of Gaia. I had done the same thing. Everyone does. But no one ever forgets the scope of the power there, the breadth of the love or the depth of the pain glimpsed in the second before oblivion saved them from insanity.

With Granuaile unconscious, I could continue to tattoo the sole of her foot, which would have otherwise been quite problematic. The number of nerves there makes it difficult to proceed—reflexes are tough to work around.

There were no designs marked on Granuaile's foot; the shape of Gaia's binding came directly from her, which I saw in the magical spectrum as a green overlay on Granuaile's skin. The pattern looked like a Celtic wreath; it was similar to the loop on the back of my hand, except there was no triskele design in the center of it. This was an inhibitor loop, a sort of filter that would allow Granuaile to feel Gaia's presence and speak with her while remaining conscious. Until the loop was completed, she wouldn't wake up. Ever. It was the one portion of the ritual that absolutely could not be interrupted, so I worked steadily for five straight hours until it was finished. I checked it carefully and then asked Gaia if it looked satisfactory.

//Good// she said. //Give her to me//

Though Granuaile's foot was still bloody and raw, I set it down flat against the earth of the cave. She gasped and sat up, her eyes wide.

//Welcome child// Gaia cooed, for I heard everything she said through my own tattoos. //A strong Druid you will be//

Granuaile gaped and looked panicked.

"Speak as you would to an elemental," I told her. "Your emotions and thoughts will make sense to her."

//Infinite gratitude// Granuaile's feelings said. //I feel blessed//

//We are all blessed child//

Tears sprang out of Granuaile's eyes and ran down her cheeks. I knew precisely how she felt, and my vision blurred as my own eyes filled with tears.

"Thank you, Atticus," she said. "It was worth the wait. I would have waited a hundred years for this."

"You're welcome," I replied, "but you may have thanked me too soon. There's no more get-out-of-pain-free cards after this. You'll feel every stab from now on."

"It's okay," she said, lying down again and nodding. "It's totally okay. I know what it's for, and it's worth it."

"All right," I said. "Do you want to continue or wait a few minutes?"

"Continue," she said.

"Let me know when you want a break, then."

She didn't need many breaks. She handled it much better than I had, in fact, though I neglected to mention it. The bit around the ankle was dodgy—it's a sensitive area—but we proceeded smoothly through days and weeks until we reached mid-thigh. The borders on either side of the entire band allowed her to draw on the earth's magic; this was a fail-safe in case any part of the tattoo was damaged, but it also meant any part of her right side could draw if she was wearing shoes. The knots on the inside of the band, meanwhile, changed as they rose, allowing her to perform different bindings. The first ones allowed her to bind her sight to the magical spectrum and to cast night vision. Each of these contained riders, like those in contracts, that allowed her to cast bindings on others besides herself.

After that came the knots that allowed her to supplement her own energy with that of the earth, so she could increase her strength and speed as well as run or fight for long periods of time without tiring. These bindings could also be cast on other people.

I was about to begin the next sequence when Oberon's insistent voice broke through my trance.

<Atticus? Atticus, I'm really sorry, but I think we have a problem. This isn't normal. Someone's out here with us.>

Chapter 10

Unwilling to pull myself entirely out of the trance, I paused, dropped the thorn, and spoke to him. *How do you know?*

<Well, there's a freshly butchered T-bone here. Expertly carved, some delicious marbling in the meat, looks like corn-fed Angus. And you just don't see those dropped casually on the ground in the Olympian wilderness. Especially on my patrol route. And it can't have been here for long, or some other animal would have already snarfed it. So that means—>

Somebody's out there. You're right. Damn it five thousand ways. Judging by where I am in the tattoos, it's only been about three weeks. And you know you shouldn't eat that meat, right?

<Hey, I've seen my share of heist movies. They always poison the dog. And you took great pleasure in pointing that out, I might add.>

It was all training for this particular moment, see? You're alive instead of dead like those dogs in the movies.

<Thanks, Atticus. What should I do?>

Can you see any tracks? Smell anything besides the meat?

<No, and that has me worried. What if my nose is turning human?>

It's not turning human. You can still smell the meat.

<Yeah, and it smells delicious.>

Don't touch it, Oberon. Don't even lick it. It's poisoned for sure. Look, I'm going to come out there and see if I can spot any clues. Stay there, keep a sharp ear and nose out, and let me know if you sense anything.

<Okay.>

And stop staring at the meat. Look around for who put it there.

<Aw! Wait! How did you know?>

Canine Psychology 101. Seriously, don't look at it. Look for the dastardly villain.

<Gah! It's so hard to tear my gaze free! It must have a tractor beam!>

Oberon. It's dead meat. You are stronger than other dogs. Look away.

<I can't! It's got me! Atticus, it's got me!>

Oberon! Watch out for the cows raining down from the sky!

<Where? Oh. You tricked me!>

Don't look back at the meat! Look around for who might have dropped it.

<Whew. Okay. That was scary. Hurry up, I'm creeped out now.>

I'll be there as soon as I can.

I made apologies to Gaia and Granuaile. Anybody with the heart to poison a dog would have the heart to do us harm as well, and we couldn't ignore it. //Pause necessary / Will continue binding later//

"Atticus? What's going on?"

"Someone's out there. They dropped a T-bone in Oberon's path, and it's a good bet that it's poisoned. We need to take care of this before we continue. Find your knives and strap them on."

"We *can* continue? We *will* continue? I'm just check-ing," she said as she found her knife holsters and at-tached them to her belt.

"Yes to both. You're going to cast your first magic before I go." I tossed aside my backpack, looking for Moralltach. It was still where I'd stashed it, and I slung the scabbard on the strap over my back.

"I can do that without the binding being complete?"

"Yeah. Everything I've done so far is complete in itself. The inhibitor loop on the bottom of your foot worked immediately. Same for these other bits." I fetched her staff and returned to where she was sitting. Granuaile seemed disoriented by the sudden change in plans—and perhaps a bit dizzy, because her leg was still swollen and oozing blood. I offered her a hand up and she took it. Pulling her to her feet, I said, "Cast the binding for magical sight."

"Okay, but how?"

"What do you mean, how? Did you forget the words? I made you do all those drills for nothing?"

"No, but . . ."

"Say the words, see the knots, and be the hand that ties them. The power is there now."

Granuaile didn't have any charms to cast bindings via mental commands. She'd have to speak everything until she could craft her own charms. And so she began, in a halting voice, disbelief in her eyes that she could make this happen. I triggered my charm so I could watch it: When she finished the final phrase that energized the binding and drew power from the earth, I saw the white glow of magic flow up from the cave floor and illuminate her tattoos underneath the skin, and I heard her gasp as her eyes saw much more than they were used to seeing. She put out her hands, suddenly unbalanced. Magical vertigo—sensory overload.

"Sensei? This isn't . . . oh, shit."

I stepped closer to make sure she didn't fall. "Search for the outlines of things."

"This isn't like looking through your eyes. It's too much."

"I know. You need to ignore the gossamer threads of all the bindings around you. If it's below your feet, block it out; you don't need to see all the bindings there. You have to train yourself to ignore the sensory input of these peripheral bindings, the way freeway drivers ignore billboards and speed limits and so on. You understand?"

"Uh . . . yeah? I think? Whoa."

"When you're driving, you don't focus on everything at once, but you have peripheral awareness of it, right? You focus on what you need to at any given moment, whether it's the car in front of you, the jackass in the lifted truck passing you, or the sirens behind you, whatever. Everything exists, everything is there, but you don't have to see it all at once. Does that help? You don't have to see all the bindings you're seeing right now. Just focus on the outlines of the physical stuff you saw before."

"Yeah, well, the bushes don't give me much of an outline, sensei, because they're fucking bushy."

"Here," I said, thrusting her staff into her hands. "That should be a simple enough shape to focus on."

"No, because I see the oil from my fingers and the wood cells and—what is that thing? Is it some sort of bug larvae living in my staff?"

"Bring it up close to your eyes. Focus on the shape. There's a big censor bar across your vision. That's all you see, only the outline."

"Oh. Wait, that helped."

"Good. Now keep your vision in that mode, if you will, when you lower the staff. See outlines instead of everything."

She slowly lowered the staff and sighed in relief when the mass of bindings didn't blind her with light.

"Okay," she said, putting one end of the staff on the

ground and smiling at me. "This is just a little bit awesome. I've cast my first Druidic binding."

"Congratulations. I need you to cast two more before I can leave."

The smile disappeared. "Leave?"

"To check on Oberon, remember? We're not alone."

"Oh, yeah."

"Cast the bindings to increase your strength and speed. I don't care which one you do first."

<Atticus, it's super-spooky here. All the animals are quiet.>

Coming soon, buddy. Almost ready.

I cast the same two bindings on myself. She cast speed first, and once she was done she grinned. "I so want to spar with you now."

I was so proud of her and I wanted to hug her rather than spar, but then I'd have to start thinking about baseball, and this wasn't a good time for that.

"Keep that in mind. If I move quickly now, does that mess up your vision?"

"No, I can still see the outlines. I can see the surface features, too, without getting overwhelmed. It's like everything has this soft glow around it, and if I don't focus on the glow I'll be fine."

"Excellent. That's exactly what you want. Now, I don't know who's out there. It might be a magic user. When I come back, I should look like this. If you see me plus something else—two different outlines, in other words—it's not me. It's something else, casting a glamour. Whack him. Or her. Or it."

"So that's why you want me to have magical vision on—"

"For positive ID. Right. Be back as soon as I can. Vigilance!"

Casting camouflage on myself, I eased out of the cave and past the thornbushes to descend to the stream.

Which way from the cave, Oberon?

<West. I'm just south of the stream, where the watering hole is.>

The watering hole was the outer limit of the range where I could still hear him in my mind. I began to mince his way, trying to keep quiet and scan the area for movement. *And you haven't seen anything in all this time?*

<Nope.>

You're not staring at the meat again, are you?

<No, I swear. I'm not letting that tractor beam get hold of me again.>

And you haven't heard or smelled anything?

<No. The fact that I'm not hearing anything is a bad sign.>

Yes. Okay, I'm on my way, trying to move quickly but also quietly. I'm having the bushes move apart for me where necessary. I'm in camouflage.

I didn't hear anything either, except for the soft sounds of my own footfalls on the ground. Oberon was right. This was unnaturally quiet. Five minutes' determined march through the growth brought me to the watering hole. Nothing moved except for the water in the stream.

Walking south from there, it was less than a minute before I came upon Oberon and the steak.

<Atticus, is that you? I hear something coming.>

Yes. It's me. I dissolved my camouflage so he could see me. Oberon's tail wagged.

<Saint Lassie be praised!>

I examined the steak. Clearly it had been carefully placed. There was no dirt on the sides or top, as there would be if it had tumbled haphazardly from someone's grasp. It was discolored in several places, more than would be expected by simple exposure to air; there were subtle shadings of red that Oberon's canine eyes wouldn't have picked up. Something had been sprinkled on it. What the poison was didn't matter to me. What puzzled me was Oberon's insistence that he'd seen no tracks nearby. I had doubted that because I figured he'd simply been blind to anything except the steak, but there truly were no tracks here except his and mine. That led me to several unsavory conclusions.

It probably wasn't a deity; a deity wouldn't have silenced all the creatures. Still, it was something with the ability to manipulate the earth like a Druid—or it wasn't touching the earth at all. Something that could fly.

"We have to get back to Granuaile," I said. "Right now!"

That's when I got an arrow in the back.

Chapter 11

I should probably back up a wee bit. As I was telling Oberon we needed to return to the cave, his ears pricked up and he looked into the distance behind my right side. And then, saying nothing more than <Atticus!>, he leapt at me, knocking me down. As a result—due to the fall—the arrow intended for the middle of my back hit me high in the left shoulder, scraping along the top of the blade. When I hit the ground, the impact drove it all the way through and nearly stabbed Oberon, who landed on top of me.

I cast camouflage on us almost by instinct, then belatedly remembered as another shaft whizzed overhead that I should camouflage the bloody arrow sticking out of me too.

<I saw something move up in the trees back there and it wasn't a bird.>

Go, Oberon! See if you can circle around and flank them.

<Got it.> He bounded away and I struggled to my feet. The shock was wearing off and I was beginning to feel the pain. I triggered my healing charm, drew Moralltach, and looked about me for enemies.

I didn't have far to look. A squad of five yewmen, spread in a skirmish line, approached from the direction of the watering hole, bronze leaf swords raised high over their right shoulders, advancing as samurai would through the brush. Their tiny dark eyes searched for me—and found me. They could see through my camouflage.

Though only three feet tall, they were terrifying creatures, knotted and gnarled with anger, sprung from the boughs of the enchanted guardian trees in the Morrigan's Fen. They were the Morrigan's answer to many of the Tuatha Dé Danann, for while they were living, they weren't animals and thus weren't subject to Flidais's control; Moralltach meant nothing to them, for they were not made of flesh, and Aenghus Óg's old sword would not affect them except in the way any normal blade would—which wasn't much. I'd be better off with an axe. Someone had done their homework to send them against me.

In Druidic circles, yew was the harbinger of death, an omen of ill news, and this, coupled with the fact that they were the Morrigan's creatures, meant that even among the Fae the yewmen were feared; they were creatures that made goblins wake up sweating in the night. They served the Morrigan for a hundred years, guarding the Fen—which was really her stronghold as the Fae Court was Brighid's—itching for a fight and never getting one, until she let them go to Tír na nÓg, where they became eager mercenaries.

I had little to no hope that the Morrigan would appear to defend me now. She'd made it clear some years ago that she depended on me to take care of myself, despite her vow to prevent my death by violent means.

Oberon, they have swords and they know how to use them. I don't want you engaging them. What they don't have are bows and arrows. See if you can find the archer and tell me where he is.

<Okay.>

These lads didn't fly, and that arrow had come from a

higher angle than they could conceivably achieve. Whoever had dropped that steak wasn't a yewman, and he
was out there ready to take a potshot at me; that's why
I bothered to keep my camouflage on.

Their stances gave me an idea—they were providing
such lovely targets. I created a binding of like-to-like,
so that their bronze blades abruptly bound together on
either side of the one in the middle. The effect was amusing, because the yewmen didn't want to let go. They
were yanked by their swords toward the lad in the center, and once he was holding not only his sword but four
other yewmen with their swords bound to his, he had a
bit of trouble, and the whole mess of them fell in a heap
to the ground.

I thought of binding the yewmen together in the same
way, except that I was afraid of what would happen if
I tried. These were the Morrigan's creatures and would
hardly be effective against the Tuatha Dé Danann if they
could be bound like any other piece of wood. Rumor had
it that the Morrigan had prepared for that—perhaps it
was a rumor she'd spread herself. Still, it would be silly
to allow her yewmen to be bound and unbound by their
bark; they had to have protection. Olympia, however,
might be able to help me. The yewmen were never intended to walk on this plane; they were the boogeymen
of the Faerie lands, but to Olympia they were simply
odd trees.

//Druid found trees / Unnatural movement / Query:
Help root / Bring harmony?//

//Exclamation! / Unnatural movement! / Trees must
root / Grow / Nourish / Harmony//

The yewmen did not have vocal cords. It was part
of their mystique, playing the silent, implacable killer.
But if they could have roared in frustration, they would
have. Wherever their bodies touched the ground, roots
sprouted and clutched handfuls of earth, grabbing Greek

real estate like foreclosure vultures. Swords forgotten, they tried to pull away and even leap away from one another and the earth, but Olympia was determined to make them feel at home. They were immobilized inside a minute, save for their arms and heads, a new miniature grove among the undergrowth. In the pursuit of harmony, Olympia would work steadily on the Morrigan's enchantments until the yewmen were nothing but trees again. In the meantime, they were acutely aware of what had been done to them and who was responsible. I jogged past them, grinning, and their black eyes held bloody promises as they followed my progress.

"Heh! Fuck yew," I said.

The arrow in my shoulder bounced awkwardly before me. Had I not shut down the pain, it would no doubt be giving me all kinds of trouble. I concentrated on the shaft of the arrow—a hollow aluminum one, I noted—and unbound its molecules near the exit point until it crumbled away like a wafer cookie.

It occurred to me that I should have been so calm and rational about the arrow Ullr shot into me in Asgard, but once that fight began, little was calm or rational.

Have you found the bowman yet? I asked Oberon as I approached the pond.

<No, I haven't spotted him. I think I heard him, though. He's around somewhere in the canopy.>

He's neutralized for the moment, since he can't see us; let's go back to the cave and help Granuaile. It's a more defensible position anyway.

<Okay.>

As Oberon turned from wherever he was and picked up his pace, I heard his footfalls—tiny pads, soft pantings, the occasional rustle. I could get a vague fix on him based on that. As I tried to spy where he was moving, an arrow lanced down out of the canopy and thudded into the earth next to the stream, just below the pond.

<Hey! That was close!>

Top speed back to the cave, Oberon! Our assassin must have camouflage of his own. There was no way I could get to him up in the canopy with only a sword. I needed one of Granuaile's throwing knives. Or five.

Oberon dove into the bushes and sinuously wove between them, his passage clearly marked by the wake of quaking branches and leaves. If the assassin remained where he was, the angle for a shot was increasingly poor; his arrow would turn awry as soon as it hit the undergrowth. To get a good shot at Oberon now, he'd have to fly out and shoot straight down.

I took a slightly different path and offered much the same target; movement could be tracked by the bushes moving out of my way, but I kept low and there would be no clear shot unless the shooter moved from his current position.

Oberon would get to the cave first.

Don't barrel into the cave announcing your presence. You will sneak in there like a Celtic ninja. Don't pant.

<You know that's like me telling you not to sweat, right?>

I know, but try to keep a lid on it until I get there.

<Do Celtic ninjas have to wear pajamas?>

No, silly! Celts always freeball it.

<Okay, good. Just making sure.>

No arrows whistled by me on the way to the cave. Oberon wasn't attacked either. Part of me was relieved, but another part was worried about where the assassin was.

A steady stream of cursing and percussive knocks greeted my ears once I got to the cave. Granuaile was under attack.

She was cornered by a faery assassin—the kind of faery with wings. At the moment he wasn't flying, because the cave didn't have sufficient room. He was casting a glamour and protesting loudly in the visible spectrum that she was doing him wrong and he meant no harm, while in truth he was trying to stab her with a wicked pair of silver knives. Granuaile wasn't falling for it; she was fending him off by fighting against the outline of his true form. The iron caps on the end of her staff—probably only an eighth of an inch thick—weren't hurting him. He was armored with hardened leather and she hadn't touched his skin yet. I wondered how long the fight had been going on; she seemed to be holding her own fairly well, but the fact remained that she was playing defense and she didn't have much room to back up.

I told Oberon, *Bark your head off to distract him, but don't engage. What you see isn't what he looks like. I'll take him out.*

<Okay. Tell me when.>

Now.

Oberon can sound deadly when he wishes. His loud, abrupt arrival startled the assassin, causing the faery to step back and take his eyes off Granuaile for a second. That was a critical error. Her staff whipped low, and she swept his feet out from under him. He landed hard on his backside, crying out because it probably hurt his wings. Before he could flip up and away, I stomped on his left wrist, dissolved my camouflage except for the arrow in my shoulder, and pointed Moralltach at the space between his eyes.

"Drop your knives," I said. "Now."

"Why should I? I'm dead anyway." Granuaile had moved to pin his right arm down as well.

"Because if you do, I pledge to report to Tír na nÓg that you died honorably. If you do not, I will take your body back and report that you died a coward, casting shame on your family."

"Your word?" he asked.

"You have my word that I will report you honorable if you drop your weapons and answer my questions."

He dropped his knives. "There is no shame in falling to the Iron Druid. My name is Dubhlainn Óg of Shannon Heath. Make it quick."

"I will. Who sent you here?"

"I was paid by the Svartálfar of the Norse."

"What? You can't blame this on the dark elves. How did you find us here?"

"The dark elves are paying me, as they paid everyone here today. They are spending significant money on your head. But it is also true that someone in Tír na nÓg betrayed your location. I was informed anonymously."

"Informed how, precisely?"

"In writing. A note delivered by a pixie. It said to search the woods near Litochoro. I found the dog first and used him to draw you out."

There was much there to think about. "Am I the target, or is Granuaile?"

"The contract specifies either or both, with a bonus to be paid for both. The apprentice, however, is the softer target."

"Ass malt," Granuaile muttered, and in so doing managed to ruin one of the few charms of the 1950s for me.

"You say the dark elves are paying others. Who are they paying?"

The assassin shrugged with his eyebrows. "They are paying faeries. They are paying their own kind. Beyond that, I do not know."

"Who among the dark elves wants us dead?"

"I cannot say. Assassination is a business of intermediaries."

Not for the first time, I wished I had Fragarach instead of Moralltach in my hand. I might not get any better answers out of this faery, but at least I could be sure that they were truthful.

"How many in your band?"

"Aside from myself, there's a pod of yewmen and their shifter." The yewmen were incapable of shifting planes by themselves, a wise precaution of the Morrigan's. The shifter must have been the one with the bow.

"Dubhlainn Óg of Shannon Heath, may Manannan see you safely home," I said to him. I flicked my eyes to Granuaile. "Would the soft target like to do the honors?"

Without answering, she crunched the iron cap of her staff into the faery's forehead. He grunted once, stiffened, and crumbled to ash.

"We cannot stay here," I said.

"I know."

"Are you injured?"

"No. Feeling pretty good, actually." She flashed a grin. "I kicked a little bit of ass."

"Yes, congratulations. You did well to track his movements through the glamour. But whose blood is that on your arm?"

A crinkle appeared between Granuaile's eyes. "Where?" She looked first at her right arm and then at her left, which she had curled around her staff. One end of the staff rested on the ground, and she was leaning on it a bit, hand above the elbow. That's where she saw what I saw. A trail of blood from the outside of her wrist wove down to her elbow, where it dripped. "Huh. He must have nicked me. I didn't even feel it."

"Not a good sign. These guys probably favor poison." Even as I said it, Granuaile's knees buckled and she dropped to the cave floor, her confidence replaced by confusion. Her staff tumbled out of nerveless fingers.

Her expression filled with a dollop of panic, and I think it was safe to say that mine did as well. "Poison?" she said. "I hope it wasn't iocane powder."

"Hopefully not. But probably potent if he was gun-

ning for us. Speak to Olympia about it and ask her to
heal you. She'll probably be happy to do it. And look—
there's more on your leg. Quite a lot."

Granuaile looked down at the outside of her left calf,
where the assassin had more than nicked her. There was
a deep gash, and for her to be unaware meant either he
was using some sort of numbing agent or she had some
really amazing adrenaline.

"Oh, shit, I don't even feel it—right. Same solution."
She closed her eyes and spoke to Olympia, while I did
my best to look unconcerned. Forcing myself away from
her side as she concentrated, I began to gather our supplies.

<We're leaving now?> Oberon asked.

*As soon as we can. This place isn't safe anymore. If one
group of assassins was told to look here, then another
was probably told the same. Speaking of which, would
you mind keeping an eye on the wee valley? There's still
one out there, and I don't want to be surprised again.*

<All right.> Oberon turned to the cave entrance and
wriggled between the bushes to give himself a commanding view up and downstream.

And don't forget to look up. He's a flier.

<Okay. But honestly, Atticus, I think you should invent
a ranged weapon for me to use in situations like this.>

*If I did, you would just use it on squirrels. Is it all
clear out there?*

<Yes. I don't see anything.>

Granuaile raised her head and opened her eyes.

"You were right, sensei. A numbing agent and a neu-
rotoxin. Olympia spotted it and broke it down, though.
Now I can feel where he got me."

"He was waiting for you to fall down like that so he
could finish you. Can you move again?"

"Yeah," she said, waggling her fingers, "I think so."

"Good to hear. Pull this arrow out of my back, will you?"

"What? I didn't even see that!"

"Had it camouflaged." Despite having the pain under control, I winced when she yanked it out. There simply wasn't anything comfortable about the feeling. "Thanks," I said, and began to close up the wound. "Pack your things. We have to get out of the area before we have more assassins than we can deal with."

Leaning her staff against the wall of the cave, she moved to comply, albeit with a slight limp. "Where will we go?"

"Back to Tír na nÓg for a brief while. Someone there is not only helping assassins find us, but they're colluding for some reason with the dark elves. It's a mystery worth investigating."

"When will we continue my binding?"

"As soon as we can. Believe me, I want it over with as much as you do."

Chapter 12

I have seen children play a game of tag in which they can't be tagged if they're touching "base," which may be a tree, or an old tire, or any other object. It is a safe zone—a place where one can catch his breath and maybe throw a taunt or two at whoever is "it."

Irish base is the plane of Mag Mell. There is no discord allowed. Fae assassins would not dare defile it. One can relax there, heal there, and even practice the damnable art of diplomacy if so inclined. That is where I took Granuaile and Oberon once we shifted away from Olympus. I created a tether to Tír na nÓg first using the tree in front of the cave—it would be senseless to try to hike back, wounded as we were and under the eye of a flying sniper—and once we shifted to Tír na nÓg, I pulled us a bit farther along the tether to Mag Mell.

The blood on our bodies startled and angered some of the Fae nymphs at the hot springs of Cnoc an Óir at first, but when we made it clear it had been shed elsewhere and we had come only to heal, they were polite, even solicitous, and asked how they could help. I asked them to take messages to Goibhniu and Manannan Mac Lir in Tír na nÓg, imploring them to visit me at the springs on a matter of some urgency. Bless them, they sent two nymphs straightaway, and the rest of them offered carved soaps and bandages and invited us to soak in the restorative hot springs.

The grounds around the springs were lined with spongy turf; verdant hedges grown for the sake of privacy separated individual soaking pools. There were larger pools available for parties of two or more, and it was into one of these that Oberon and I eased. Granuaile was led to a single pool nearby but well out of sight.

<Explain to me again why you are unable to stand the sight of her unclothed,> Oberon said, as I stripped and stepped gingerly into the pool.

It isn't that I can't stand the sight. The problem is that part of me would stand very tall. And it wouldn't matter how much I thought about baseball either. Hmm. Maybe I should try thinking of a geriatric hockey game. Very cold and lots of broken hips. That might work.

Oberon snorted. <Human mating habits are stupid.>

I'm trying not to get in the habit with her, Oberon.

<But you want to.>

No, I don't. Well, I do, but you see, I can't, and . . . it's complicated.

<No, it's stupid.>

I sighed. *Maybe you're right.*

<You know I'm right. Dogs are much smarter about this. Bitch comes into heat, the Marvin Gaye song plays, puppies in nine weeks. Leaves more time for playing and napping when you're not worrying about all the things humans worry about after sex. I swear you spend more time worrying about it than doing it.>

A nymph approached but kept a safe distance, then informed me that Goibhniu was on his way. I thanked her and she left.

Brewers are craftsmen to be envied, and Goibhniu is one of the finest. His daily work is easily tested and tasted, and unlike, say, one of those people who greet you in a soulless big box store, he can point to the produce of his labor and say, "There. I made that." These days he has a taproom next to his smithy (for he is also an extremely accomplished blacksmith), and he is often found behind the bar, pulling pints for people and grinning as he serves up his latest creation. I have always liked him. Then again, it's difficult to dislike a man who takes pleasure in giving away free beer.

"Siodhachan!" he bellowed good-naturedly, striding toward me across the turf. He was dressed in a simple brown tunic with white knotwork and a cream-colored belt. He carried a big dark bottle in each hand. His arms were thrown wide, giving the impression that he wished to hug me with beer—a poster boy for the idea that Beer Is Love. "Good to see you outside the bloody Fae Court! You simply must try a draught of my latest." He sat down cross-legged at the edge of my pool and popped off the top of one bottle with his thumb and a subtle unbinding. He handed it to me and then opened the other. "I call it my Bagpipe Porter. A steady note of sonorous malt with top notes of clove and vanilla dancing a jig along the sides o' your tongue."

"Good health and harmony," I said, raising my bottle to him. He clinked the neck and echoed me, then we enjoyed a few delicious swallows. "Magnificent," I told him.

"Yes, isn't it?" Goibhniu smirked at his own narcissism. "If only there were a bard to catalog all the fine beers I've made. Alas!" He stopped mocking himself and turned serious. "But I've been summoned with a note of urgency. What is the matter?"

"Someone in Tír na nÓg is after us. Granuaile's binding was interrupted by a group of Fae assassins—yewmen and some lesser Fae."

"No! Is she all right?"

"Healing. A pool or two that way." I hooked a thumb to my left. Goibhniu frowned, his eyes flicking down to my shoulder.

"I see the remains of a wound there, if I'm not mistaken," he said.

There was little visible beyond a pink puckering now, but among Druids that was telltale enough. "Aye. Arrow from ambush."

"Whoever did it will ne'er get another drink from me," he said.

"That is just and thoughtful of you," I said. "But I wondered if perhaps you and your brother might be up for a bit of a challenge."

"Which brother?"

"Luchta."

"A challenge, ye say?" Goibhniu's eyes glinted. "Haven't had one o' those in some time."

"We haven't had a new Druid in some time either," I said. "I was thinking perhaps the occasion should be marked by a new Fae weapon."

The corners of Goibhniu's mouth drooped. "Not another sword?"

"No, your brother Luchta will do the bulk of it. Granuaile prefers the staff. Not the wizard's sort, but the fighting sort. A quarterstaff. Can you craft it in such a way that one end is inlaid with iron to strike against the Fae and the other inlaid with silver to dissuade werewolves and their ilk?"

The smith's expression lit up. "Ah! That would be something new! It must be both light and strong, of course, specially bound to resist shattering and splintering. Working the metal into either end must serve both functionally and aesthetically to deserve the Fae name."

"I daresay it would be a challenge for both of you. There are no templates for such craft."

"I think you are right, Siodhachan!"

"Add such enchantments as you think are fit and meet, and it will be a legendary weapon the likes of which the world has never seen."

"Indeed! It has been too long since the Tuatha Dé Danann have crafted something worthy of legend." He shot me a wry grin. "Aside from my ales, of course."

"Of course."

Goibhniu pounded the rest of his porter at an alarming rate and then wiped a wee bit of foam off his upper lip. "I must discuss this with Luchta immediately." He got up and brushed dirt off his breeches.

"Wait. Shouldn't we discuss payment?"

"Ha! Is not the challenge payment enough? And considering how much trouble you tend to get in whenever you show your face in public, I imagine your apprentice will do the same; thus she will bring me fame for ages to come. Nay, Siodhachan, it's entertainment and sops for my ego that I lack, not money, so I think you've paid me—and I daresay my brother—well already in the bargain. We will work on it forthwith!"

<Nay and forthwith? I think this guy needs to drink more responsibly.>

I bade Goibhniu farewell and another nymph appeared, very sorrowful, with what she thought was very bad news. "Manannan Mac Lir is not to be found at the moment. He is in the ocean somewhere but is due to return soon. His wife, Fand, invites you to their home to wait."

"Excellent. I think we will do that." I smiled at her to indicate my gratitude.

<Forthwith?>

Indeed. Feel like barking at Granuaile to let her know we're leaving?

Feeling better and much refreshed, we shifted back to Tír na nÓg to visit Manannan. Fand was waiting for us outside the doors. When she saw Granuaile's limp, she said, "You poor children! Do come in and tell me all about it!"

"If you don't mind terribly, we'd rather not relive it," I said.

Fand looked bemused, then embarrassed. "Oh, but of course! Let's get you fed and rested until Manannan returns."

She led us into the kitchen and nattered on about what everyone had been saying after our audience, while she fried some bacon made from the famous hogs. "It's the bacon of eternal youth," she said, smiling at Granuaile as she served her a plate. "Should heal you right up and taste sinful."

Granuaile's jaw dropped at the four slices of bacon draped on a blue ceramic plate that looked one of a kind. It wasn't just the bacon: She knew her knots well enough now to read that the white knotwork around the edge was a blessing of good health to anyone who ate from the plate.

"I . . ."

"Yes, dear?"

Granuaile said nothing more.

"She's a bit overwhelmed," I said.

"I understand."

Fand also had sausage links made from the same hogs, so she fried a pan full of those for Oberon and placed them on a plate for him.

<Great Lord Sirius, Atticus, this is the best sausage ever! Manannan could rule the world with this sausage. Why, he could probably even teach a rottweiler manners with sausage like this.>

That good, huh?

<This is the Sausage of Great Price.>

It's free, Oberon.

<I know. That's a great price!>

Rather than argue the semantics of *great* with him, I laughed inwardly and enjoyed my own plate of bacon and bread.

Fand was a gracious hostess, and thoughts of how unlike her mother she was caused me to inquire, "How
does your mother these days?"

"Oh." Fand blushed. "She's still besotted by that
thunder god you brought with you."

"Perun is still here?"

"Aye. He's been granted a sort of asylum. He's welcome to stay on the plane as long as he wishes, but once
he leaves, he cannot return without invitation. He is not
anxious to return to earth, I hear, since Loki is after
him—and since my mother is being so . . . hospitable."

I diplomatically ignored that bit. Fand was clearly
embarrassed by her mother's legendary libido. "Has no
one spotted Loki?" I asked.

"No. He's either hidden himself well or he's on the
Norse planes somewhere."

A faery cleared his throat at the entrance to the kitchen
and bowed when we turned. "M'lord Manannan has returned."

"Excellent," Fand said. "Please let him know where
we are."

Another bow and scrape and he was gone. Manannan
must have been close behind him, for he entered almost
as soon as the faery disappeared, a scowl on his face.

"What's this?" he said without greeting us, eyeing
Granuaile's bare arm. His hair was wet and he carried a
harpoon in his right hand. It was etched with knotwork,
so it was probably a named weapon. He had been hunting in the sea. "Siodhachan, I thought you were binding
her to the earth."

"I was, but we were interrupted," I said.

"Interrupted?"

Before he could ask by whom, I said, "I wonder if
we might have a private word, Manannan?" The sea
god's eyes flicked to his wife and back to us, and then
he nodded.

"Of course."

It wasn't Fand I was worried about but rather her faeries. I bowed to the lady of the castle. "Fand, your hospitality remains legendary. Please excuse us."

"You are welcome anytime," she replied.

We followed Manannan to a room of slate and glass. Granuaile's limp was already disappearing, thanks to the springs of Mag Mell, the bacon of youth, and the plate of good health. A faery ducked out just as we entered, saying the fire had been laid. The hearth glowed warmly in contrast to the cold appointments of the room. Shelves of bluish gray stone lined the walls, and on these rested books bound in leather and various objets d'art. There was an enormous pearl couched on the tongue of an open oyster shell, softly glowing with reflected firelight. Four golden high-backed armchairs with dark blue cushions waited in front of the hearth for us to be seated, and Oberon leapt onto one, considering himself an equal participant in the coming conversation.

<The faeries jumped me too, Atticus, so I should get to sit in a comfy chair.>

Manannan raised an eyebrow at Oberon's behavior but made no comment. His eyes turned to the door and lost focus—or, rather, refocused in the magical spectrum. He mumbled a binding and sealed us in; no one outside the room would be able to hear us. Unless . . .

I turned on my faerie specs to see what the faeries might have been up to in here. I trusted Manannan implicitly, but he lived in a castle full of the Fae and he wasn't around often to watch them. Scanning the bookshelves, I saw something interesting on the oyster shell—subtle but barely discernible against the natural shimmer of the shell. Bindings. Unfamiliar ones.

"Manannan?"

"Hmm?"

"What are these bindings over here?" I pointed at the shell. He stepped closer and peered at them, frowning.

"I'm not sure. It's not my work, I can tell you. It might be harmless, but I don't like strange bindings in me own library. Especially when I want privacy."

He unbound the knots and they fizzled away, leaving only the shell behind.

"We should look for more," I suggested. "I want to be sure no one else hears what we have to say."

"That bad, eh?"

"Aye."

"It might be better for us to leave the castle entirely, then," Granuaile said. "Shift to somewhere isolated on earth, where we won't be overheard."

"I know just the place," Manannan said. "Not another word until we're there."

We followed him out of the castle in silence to a tethered tree, and then we shifted, following his lead, to Emhain Ablach, the Isle of Apples. I'd never been to this particular Irish plane, but it was impossible to mistake it for anything else, with the ocean behind us and an orchard in front of us.

"All right, what is it?" Manannan asked.

"Pie!" Granuaile said, delighted with the scent filling her nostrils.

<Yeah, but it's a fruit pie. If you want me to get excited, take me to the doggie promised land, the Land of Canine. Instead of milk and honey, there's steak and kidney.>

"Pie is the problem?" The Irish god of the sea looked lost.

"No, that's not the problem," I clarified. "Manannan, we were set upon by a band of assassins on Mount Olympus."

"A band?"

"Yewmen and some others. They meant to kill us.

They poisoned a steak and left it for my hound. They interrupted the binding of my apprentice. And they're working with the Svartálfar."

We recounted the whole harrowing tale and watched storms form on Manannan's face.

"Ye can be sure I will investigate," he said.

"That is kind of you," I replied. "But mightn't you have any ideas now about who's responsible?"

Manannan sighed. "Ye haven't been keeping up with the Court, that's sure," he said. "These days it could be almost any faery ye point to."

I frowned. "Am I that out of favor?"

"I'm afraid ye are. And ye did yourself no favors a while back with your audience. Now that Aenghus Óg is dead and most of his lot have been cleared out, Brighid is living in brickshittin' fear of a coup attempt by the Morrigan"—he suddenly balled his fist under my nose and shook it, his blue eyes promising pain—"and I'll crush your scrotum if ye ever suggest I said that, am I clear?"

I gulped. "Very well. I shan't speak a word of it."

His fist returned to his side. "Good. Now, what ye have to understand is, there are plenty of Fae in Brighid's camp that count ye on the side of the Morrigan because they can't count ye on the side of Brighid. They have half the brains of a pickled herring, we all know it, and so ye can imagine how their fancies are runnin' away with what little sense they have. To their way of thinkin', eliminating *you* means eliminating the growing threat of the Morrigan. They figure she'll never finish that amulet on her own. Will she?"

I shrugged. "I haven't shown her the last part of the process. That doesn't mean she needs to be shown. She knows the theory. She could finish it without me."

"Huh. Well, regardless, the Pickled Herring—can we call 'em that?—think they're going to score major

points with Brighid if they can do anything to thwart
the Morrigan. They're probably right, if we're honest.
But o' course none o' them would have the spine to
act directly against the battle crow. Wave and tide, I
don't think *I* would have the spine t'do that! So they've
decided you're a tad easier to kill. Nothin' personal,
y'see. It's not your fault that your life is in the way of
their personal ambition."

"Silly of me to be offended, then."

"Right. Now, there is one way I can think of to get the
Pickled Herring off yer back for good."

"What's that?"

"Ye could become Brighid's consort."

"No way!" Granuaile, who'd been silently enjoying
the smells of pie and cider up to this point and petting
Oberon, clapped her hand over her mouth as Manannan and I turned to her.

"Sorry," she said in a tiny voice. "Did I say that out
loud?"

"She's right, Manannan," I said. "That's not a viable
option."

<What I said earlier about human mating habits.>

"It isn't?" He looked as if he was going to ask why
not but then changed his mind. He shrugged. "Ah, well.
We'll have to do everything the Old Irish way, I suppose."

"Aye. And speaking of fighting, I have another matter
to discuss. Now that my existence is somewhat known
again, would it be possible to exchange Moralltach for
Fragarach?"

Manannan's mouth formed a tiny black hole of surprise before he cleared his throat to mask it. "Well. That
kind of thing takes some thinkin' over. . . ."

I didn't want that. Someone would talk him out of it.
"Moralltach is the sword that killed Thor. Its fame has

grown more than Fragarach's. You'll score bushels of points with the bloodthirsty lot."

"Hmm. It's good to have them on your side, no doubt," Manannan said.

"I can guarantee I'll make life more interesting with Fragarach."

Manannan Mac Lir smirked. "Now, that's a compelling argument, that is. All right. I'm not lookin' forward to what Brighid will say when she finds out, but damn if it isn't me own sword to do with as I please. A plague on these Pickled Herring, anyway. Follow me back. We'll exchange 'em and be done. Don't say a word while you're in Tír na nÓg, lad. Whoever's listening in on me won't realize we made the switch for days. Then go get your apprentice bound properly."

I beamed at him. "You're my favorite sea god, you know."

"Aw, get your nose out of me arse. Just make life interestin' as ye promised."

Chapter 13

Once I shifted away from Tír na nÓg with Fragarach in my scabbard, I found it difficult not to grin like a geek at a Trekkie convention.

I had it back. After twelve long years, I had it *back*. Gifted to me this time by one of the Tuatha Dé Danann, not stolen from them!

Giddy euphoria seized me and I shivered with it. A squee welled up in my throat because I felt cool again—impossibly, inhumanly cool, like Laurence Fucking Fishburne—but I suppressed it savagely; if I squeed out loud, all the cool would be gone.

"Why are you shaking?" Granuaile asked. "Are you cold?"

"Oh. No. Um, excess energy. Excitement to get started again." To calm myself, I told Granuaile about the odd origins of the dark elves and how we'd have to fight them if it ever came to that. Keep moving, flank attacks, and, damn it, keep your mouth shut.

"What about your nose or your ears?"

"I don't think that would work for them. They become flesh and blood once they solidify; the bones of the skull would slice right through their arm. If they're willing to do that to kill you, then, yeah, I guess you could worry about it. Down your throat, however, that's all soft tissue. They'd unhinge the jaw, tear muscles, and rupture the esophagus just by solidifying, then when they pulled their arm free, your throat would come with it."

Granuaile swallowed and put a hand up to her neck. "Thanks for the visual."

We were once more on the billowing skirts of Olympus, but this time we were on the western side. There was no reason to search for an appropriate spot; now that Olympia knew of our need, she was only too happy to guide us to an appropriate place to continue Granuaile's binding. Similar to the cave on the eastern slope in that the required thornbushes also provided cover for the entrance, it was situated a good thirty yards or so from a small creek that would provide us with water. The ceiling of the cave was lower, it wasn't so deep or comfortable as the first one, and something small and furry had left pellets of shit scattered about, but it would serve. We scouted patrol routes for Oberon and plotted escapes before we cleaned out the cave as best we could. Connecting with Gaia didn't take quite as long—less than a week, since she'd been expecting us—and soon I was stabbing Granuaile with a thorn as if we'd never been interrupted.

Modern tattoo guns can pierce the skin about eighty to one hundred twenty times per second. I can do it with a thorn about once a second. The tip was sharpened and hardened with a binding, but still it was painful and slow and bloody. And sometimes I'd get a bit distracted.

Because. You know.

Granuaile's bare leg.

Underneath my hands.

There are hosts of mental tricks you can play to keep your libido in check—thinking of baseball is just one—but it's a near-constant battle when there are thighs involved. Smooth, toned thighs that curved and . . . oh, damn. And eventually we progressed far enough up her leg to where she had to take her shorts off.

I know tattoo artists barely notice such things; when they're on the job, flesh is just a canvas to be bloodied and inked. But I wasn't a jaded tattoo artist, and Granuaile's body wasn't simply a canvas to me. It was more like the Holy Grrrail, pronounced with a rolling Scottish rumble.

She wanted to shed her underwear at the same time, but I stopped her.

"Keep those on," I said, silently asking the Dalai Lama to help me give up all earthly desires. She was still my apprentice.

"Why? I'll just have to take them off later."

"No, we'll work around it."

"But it's silly. They'll get all bloody and nasty." She had raised her butt off the floor of the cave and had her thumbs hooked in the sides. The top was already partially down, and there was that beautiful flat expanse between the valley of her hips, leading down to—gods!

"I promise to buy you a new pair. Just. Please. Keep them on."

"Oh. I see." Her voice was toneless as she lay back down and turned away, hiding behind a shoulder. "You're still pretending."

A bit wounded at the accusation, I replied, "I'm not pretending at all. I've always made it clear that our relationship needs to remain strictly professional."

"Right. You go on and keep telling yourself that. You can't hide it anymore, Atticus, so just stop, okay? You know we both have feelings that go beyond that."

"We *can't* go beyond that, Granuaile. I won't."

"And what happens when I'm fully bound? May I do as I please then?"

"Technically, yes. The earth will recognize you as a Druid and answer your call, and you'll be free to go wherever you wish. But new Druids typically remain with their archdruids for a short while to learn how to shape-shift well and to travel the planes properly."

She twisted around to face me, a scowl on her face, and then she punched me hard on the arm.

"Ow!"

"You're being willfully dense! For a man who can see the bonds between all living things, you're remarkably blind to ours. Have you been filtering them out of your vision, seeing only what you want to see?"

Panic filled my frontal lobe and I tensed, though I'm sure all Granuaile saw was my mouth drop open. She was right—I had been filtering quite extensively; I was seeing only what Gaia needed me to see to get the binding done. And then I realized that was a weak excuse.

"Um," I said. The truth was, I could have looked at Granuaile in the magical spectrum anytime I wished in the past twelve years, and I hadn't done so unless I needed to teach her something. When I did, I always filtered out everything extraneous to the objective, just as I was doing now while tattooing her. It was denial, pure and simple.

Once I removed my blinders and looked at the emotional ties between us, I knew precisely what I was looking at. I'd seen knots like this before. Some of them were lust. And some of them, the ones I hadn't dared to confirm for fear that they wouldn't be there, were love.

Granuaile could see them now for herself, and she'd figured out what they meant without my coaching. She was right. I couldn't pretend anymore.

What I could do, however, was feel like a complete dumbass. Again.

I've lost track of how often I've felt that way in relationships. Somehow, despite having more practice than anyone, I've never learned how not to feel like a dumbass. It's like ordering a medium anything at the movie theatre and the teenage employee always, always, asks if you want a large for fifty cents more. Even if you ask them nicely ahead of time not to upsell you, they still do it, because the word *medium* triggers an automatic response in their brains. Falling in love is like that: You always feel like a dumbass at some point, even if you know it's coming—it's unavoidable.

Before I could offer something beyond a helpless monosyllable, Oberon's voice in my head demanded my attention.

<Atticus, three women and a man in white are headed in your direction. They have those thirsty things you told me about.>

You mean a thyrsus?

<Right. They're speaking some other language, and their teeth look really sharp.>

A new panic filled me. Bacchants were on their way.

Chapter 14

Listen, buddy. This is extreme danger. Thanks for the heads-up. Lie down right where you are and keep still. Don't engage them, don't follow, and don't talk to me again until I renew communication. Okay?

<Got it. I'll take a nap.>

Excellent plan. Atticus out.

Granuaile could tell by my faraway expression that something was wrong. "What is it?" she asked.

Before I answered, I sent an urgent plea to Olympia. //Hide Druids / Danger//

//Already hidden//

"Shut down your magical sight right now. Disconnect from Gaia and put on your shorts. We have to stop."

"Again?"

"Yes. Don't draw from the earth in any way. Drop Olympia's marble if you have to. No magic whatsoever."

The marble made a soft scratching noise against the stone floor as she complied. "Okay. Tell me what's happening."

"Oberon's spotted Bacchants. They can smell magic, and they're coming this way."

"How do you smell magic?"

I lowered my voice. "I didn't know it was possible until shortly after we met. Remember that time in Scottsdale, when Laksha was helping me against them? I was standing still at night with camouflage on. I should have been undetectable, right? But one of the Bacchants took a deep breath from across a parking lot and walked right toward me. We had a conversation. Her eyes were unfocused, but she knew I was there. My body odor wasn't *that* bad, so what did she smell? My camouflage."

"So the smell of our binding ritual has led them here."

"Exactly."

We arranged ourselves so that we were lying on our bellies and able to see a severely screened view of the creek and woods below our wee cave. A flicker of bright white from the south caught my eye, and I jerked my head in that direction for Granuaile's benefit, wordlessly directing her gaze.

More white appeared, floating draperies weaving through the foliage, and animals fell silent before their advance. We heard nothing but the soft chuckle of the creek below.

Skin gradually stood out from the searing white. Arms and heads. Dark tangles of hair, groomed by static or maybe playful kittens, provided stark chaotic frames for pale symmetrical faces. They might have been pretty by some standards, except that their eyes were glazed and polluted with madness.

And it was little wonder. Behind the three women strolled Bacchus, the lord of madness himself. Unlike the last time I'd seen him, he appeared calm and in full control of his mental faculties. Indeed, he appeared freshly scrubbed and moisturized, as if he'd emerged from a salon rather than spent the last few hours trekking through the wilderness. His lips were not smiling or even turned up at the corners, but he still radiated a sense of being satiated, drowsy eyelids reveling in Epicurean luxury, an androgynous beauty who'd just gorged himself on full-bodied wine and unpronounceable cheese. As I gazed on him, I realized he had known pleasures that I could never know myself, and a twinge of envy trembled at the hollow of my throat. There were many who would do anything to take the smallest sip of the epic draughts of pleasure he had sampled in his immortal life. And once they had wetted their tongues on it, they were his thralls, for they would endure any abuse to taste it again, and, if withheld from them too long, they would go mad. Either way, Bacchus was worshipped and served.

The allure of unthinking animal bliss is powerful; it always calls to us, in the same way as the edge of a cliff or the waves of the ocean: *Jump*. It is a necessary part of our natures, full of delight and danger in equal measure. Yet to the mind trained in language, taught to spy subtleties and take joy in them, such crude, baser matters can pale after a while. But *there* lies grave peril also: The propensity to empathize with pain expressed in words encourages a poet to avoid the real thing, and a too-passionate love of books can mew one in a cloister, putting up walls where there should be free range. I decided long ago—to keep myself sane amongst the illiterate and unthinking—that there would be poetry in my life. But there would also be fucking. I would have them both, but follow the sage advice of modern beer commercials and enjoy responsibly. There was nothing responsible about the god of the vine.

The Bacchants stopped in front of the cave entrance but did not see it. They raised noses into the air and sniffed, scowling. One of them spoke in Latin, a language both Granuaile and I understood.

"It was here, or near here, but it's gone now."

A second Bacchant observed, "There's something else in the air. Desire. I wonder if it was sex magic."

"That's the best kind."

"Mmm. Lord Bacchus, might we pause to relax? I'm in the mood."

I winced. Her mood, if given rein, would kill us both. My amulet provided absolutely no defense against Bacchanalia, and once they drew us into it, we'd be completely in their power. I fervently hoped that Bacchus had a headache.

He didn't. Instead, he had an agenda. "No. We cannot spend ourselves in sport. Faunus cannot keep him trapped here forever. We must continue to search."

The Bacchants whined. I very nearly mocked them and gave away our position, but I held my tongue until long after they had disappeared to the north and the birds started to chirp again.

Raising a finger to my lips, I whispered to Granuaile, "We're leaving. Bring your ID and your weapon. Leave everything else here. We'll move fast and light but without magic. Don't tap into the earth for any reason."

"Okay," she whispered. "But it'll be dark soon. Can't we cast night vision?"

"No. That spell will linger and give them something to sniff out. I have a different idea."

We slipped out of the cave as quietly as we could, but all our movements felt unnaturally loud now that I knew an Olympian was actively searching for me. My cold iron amulet protected me from divination, and the Olympians probably didn't know enough about Granuaile or Oberon to try to find me through them, but I still felt like the eyes of Jupiter were tracking my every move. I flipped off the sky just in case.

"What was that for?" Granuaile asked.

"General principles," I said. "Let's grab Oberon and go."

We headed south along the creek bed for about a quarter mile before I reached out to Oberon. I didn't think our mental link was especially strong magic, but a form of radio silence had been advisable in case they could smell it.

Oberon? We're near the creek bed heading south. Can you come down and meet us, please?

<Sure thing, Atticus! Are we meeting for dinner?>

Unfortunately not. We have to get out of here, Celtic ninja style. And we shouldn't talk too much in case they're able to detect it.

<Roger that. See you soon.>

Oberon met us shortly thereafter, wagging his tail. I smiled and petted him while I whispered to Granuaile, "You're going to ride out of here bareback."

"On what?"

"On me. When I'm in stag form, I see quite well at night without having to cast night vision."

"But won't shape-shifting draw them to us?"

"It might. But it's a onetime spell, and we're going to literally hoof it out of here as soon as I cast it." I unslung Fragarach and handed it to her, then turned my back and began to strip.

"Do I get to tell you to keep your underwear on?" she said.

"You could if I was wearing any."

I bound myself to the form of a stag as soon as my jeans dropped below my hips. Granuaile climbed onto my back with Fragarach slung over her shoulder and her staff gripped in her right hand. I didn't have any convenient mane for her to hold on to, so she leaned over, wrapped her arm around my neck, and said she was ready.

I turned east and set a pace that I thought I could maintain for a while without tiring too much. Eventually I'd have to draw some energy from the earth to keep going, but I thought that, rather than constantly drawing little sips with every step, it was best to do just one, or even none, if I could manage. Honestly, I doubted they could smell me burning my own draws for energy, but I'd keep it down just to be safe.

The long trek out of the Olympian wilderness gave each of us plenty of time to think. In such situations, I tend to talk with the ghost of my archdruid, whose harsh language and mannerisms live on in my memory. I rationalized that it was better than talking to myself—and, in truth, it was like visiting a different headspace. My archdruid had a way of distilling complicated problems into simple solutions. I didn't always agree with him, but the way he thought occasionally served me well. This time, I shared with him my impossible relationship with Granuaile and the recent evidence—dropped from the lips of Bacchus himself—that this whole setup in Olympus had been a trap after all. A trap, I noted, that we still hadn't escaped.

"If ye escape," the archdruid said, "ye should tup the lass as soon as possible. Ye can't teach her any more, and yer probably going to die anyway."

"I think you're speaking with the desperate voice of my libido right now," I said. "So I'll ignore that. I'm thinking our safest bet is to scamper off and wait this out."

"There ye go again," my archdruid said. "Using your colon instead of yer brain. Ye believe yer thinkin' because yer workin' hard, but all yer doin' is squeezin' out shit. What good would runnin' do, me lad? It'd teach yer apprentice that yer not much of a fighter, for one thing, and that all ye have to do to defeat a Druid is to make his life inconvenient. And, apart from that, ye need to help out the Norse, like ye said ye would. Ye can't go take a few months off to frolic in Mag Mell when ye got Loki runnin' around ready to set the world aflame."

"And what do you suggest I do instead?"

"Stomp on some nuts, boy! Go on the offensive! Find out what's really going on!"

That was advice I couldn't easily ignore. There was certainly more going on here than anyone in Tír na nÓg was willing to admit. Two Roman gods were colluding against me, and they might or might not be working with dark elves, vampires, and someone powerful amongst the Tuatha Dé Danann. Nobody was going to volunteer answers; we were going to have to apply some pressure of our own.

Chapter 15

One of the odd details about sporting goods stores is how incredibly full of steel and straight lines they are. The ambient atmosphere is harsh and fluorescent because, at some point in the planning stages, an executive said, "What, you want windows? Sunlight and moonlight? Fuck *that* noise."

If nature were Little Red Riding Hood and a sporting goods store were the Big Bad Wolf, nature would observe, "My, what orderly rows of synthetic products you have," and the store would say, "The better to dominate you with, my dear."

People go into sporting goods stores ostensibly to prepare themselves to get closer to nature, but, in fact, every time they buy another plastic doodad, they're doing just the opposite.

Still, if you're wanting to go Bronze Age Rambo on some Bacchants and their principal deity, there's some great stuff for booby traps in sporting goods stores. Rope. Twine. Nets. Sharp, pointy tools of all kinds, perfect for throwing and getting stabbity.

But to get the best selection, you have to be in a pretty big city, full of people who are desperate to buy things to get them closer to nature. That's why Granuaile and I were in a store in Thessalonika, a large port city to the north of Olympus, browsing the selection of sharpened instruments designed to kill and gut all the animals people love. My theory was that someone out there had to make knives of bronze or other materials besides steel, and if we picked up enough of them, we'd be able to handle a few Bacchants. We'd emerged from the Olympian wilderness near the tiny village of Petra and hired a car from there to drive us all the way to Thessalonika.

We arrived near dinnertime and got a hotel room, primarily to clean up. I trimmed my beard, which was getting a bit scraggly after weeks of neglect, and felt better without all the hair on my neck. A bit of channel surfing found a station that played old American movies, and Oberon was happy. We left him stretched out on the king bed, watching *When Harry Met Sally*.

You'll love it, I told him before we closed the door. *It will reaffirm your contention that human mating habits are stupid.*

<I think the evidence is pretty overwhelming, Atticus. It's more than a contention; it's an axiom. I could construct proofs with it.>

Is that a fact?

<You watch. Someday I'll have puppies, and I'll sit them down, or sit on them, and I'll say, "Given: Atticus and Clever Girl are humans. Given: Humans have mating habits. Prove: Human mating habits are stupid. Proof: Watch them mate. Q.E.D.">

I think your logic broke down there at the end, buddy, but you keep working on it.

The apprentice and I shared an awkward supper, the unsaid words from the cave remaining unsaid yet hanging in the air between us like little comic book balloons that someone had erased. I cannot speak for her, but my feeling was that our personal drama would have to wait until we had a safe soap opera setting in which to emote. We'd been interrupted twice in getting her bound to the earth, and it was a good bet we'd be interrupted again while those who wanted us dead had a general fix on our location. We needed a change of venue, and she agreed. The only way to do that was to figure out how the Olympians—or Bacchus anyway—had rigged such a trap for us and then dismantle it. We had to go back once more.

To that end, Granuaile and I received a few stares once we visited the sporting goods store. I had Fragarach strapped on but camouflaged, she had her "walking stick" with her, and we were buying more tent stakes and exotic bladed weapons than one could reasonably expect to use on a camping trip.

All the knives were under glass, so we had to have a salesperson help us. Niko—the name on his tag—was a youngish lad in his mid-twenties, handsome enough, and extremely friendly with Granuaile and anxious to help, since I kept quiet. His huge mistake was assuming that Granuaile didn't know anything about knives. Well, maybe that's ungenerous of me. Perhaps he was simply trying to appear competent when he spoke to her about balance and throwing weights and the like, but it came across as patronizing, and I was irritated even though he wasn't talking to me. In truth, Granuaile had surpassed me in throwing a good while back; her aim was naturally better than mine, and she'd been practicing steadily for twelve years.

Evidence that Granuaile found his tone irritating as well came soon enough. She hefted a knife, did a little flourish with it that looked far more complicated than it really was, spun around to the right, and tossed it into the bull's-eye of a dartboard behind Niko's head.

Niko didn't try to explain anything after that.

I turned away, partly to hide my amusement and partly to conduct a routine check of my surroundings. Shoppers in thick-toed boots were milling around. There was a whole lot more flannel on display than you'd see in most places, both on the mannequins and on the shoppers. No one seemed to think this was odd or a bad idea.

There was a pair of clowns in pasty white makeup and bulbous red noses having an animated discussion over two different coils of rope. Their serious expressions didn't match the lurid grins painted on their faces or the enormous colored wigs on their heads. I wasn't sure what they could be discussing. Were some ropes inherently funnier than others?

Their presence was odd too, but it seemed as if Granuaile and I were getting more stares than the clowns were. I could take the Johnny Bravo route and assume we just looked really good in our jeans, but my suspicious nature still thought there was something strange about this crowd. I interrupted Granuaile's perusal to tell her in Old Irish to tap the stored magic in my bear charm if she wished. I formed the binding and showed her how to draw upon it.

"Thanks, sensei." She smiled and touched my arm briefly. I got one of those little sensations where you feel like you need to shiver but in truth you're flushing and damn it why had the Diamondbacks' catchers been so abysmal at the plate last year? Oh, yeah. I had it bad.

Granuaile returned to browsing Niko's wares, and I resumed my attitude of watchfulness. A flash of white near the entrance drew my eye. It was a white flag—depending on the situation, a symbol of peace, parley, or surrender. My eyes trailed down from the flag to a pale hand and from thence to a black sports coat and a pale face framed by straight blond hair, so blond that it was nearly white.

It was Leif Helgarson, hale and whole and healthy as ever a dead guy could be.

I immediately became a twitching bundle of WTF and drew Fragarach right there in the store, dispelling the camouflage on it so that my erstwhile attorney could see it. Granuaile heard this and whirled, staff in her left and a knife in her right.

"Atticus, what—oh, *shit*."

Shit, indeed. Niko had keenly observed that our body language had abruptly switched from customers to combatants, and he squalled for help. I felt a tiny draw on the magic in my bear charm as Granuaile spoke the words for magical sight.

The last time I'd laid eyes on the vampire Leif Helgarson, he was looking smug because he'd just forced me to kill his creator, Zdenik, allowing Leif to retake the territory he'd temporarily lost. He'd very nearly gotten Oberon—not to mention me—killed in the process, and we'd carefully stayed out of each other's way since then. That was because I'd informed Leif through Hal Hauk, my attorney, that I'd unbind him on sight the next time I saw him.

So here he was, in my sight. Twelve years later. Waving a white flag in a sporting goods store in Thessalonika. How the *fuck* did he know I was here, and what did he want? I answered the first question on my own: He'd drunk an awful lot of my blood before we had our falling out. He could probably find me anywhere now. I began to speak the words of unbinding. He saw my lips move and knew what it meant.

"Atticus, please. I am not here by my own will." He stopped twenty feet away, in the middle of an aisle, plainly in sight, both arms raised. His right hand still held the flag. He had a cell phone in his left hand.

A security guard appeared to my left and began shouting at me in Greek to lower my weapon. I didn't take my eyes off Leif. Leif, however, took his off me and addressed the guard in Greek.

"Sir? Sir. Look at me, sir." Eventually the guard looked, and, when he did, Leif charmed him. "You will walk to the farthest corner of the store, face the wall, and piss yourself. You will remain there for one hour before moving."

The guard slunk away. Niko was taking small, panicky breaths behind me, but he'd stopped calling for help. Nearby customers were concluding that this tableau really wasn't their business and remembering that they had moussaka in the oven at home.

Having secured some time to converse without interruption, Leif said, "I have been forced into the service of the vampire Theophilus."

"Since when?" I said.

"Since you made your presence known in Greece by unbinding a vampire in Litochoro." He waggled the cell phone. "This is a single-use phone. He wishes to speak with you."

He began to squat, slowly, and continued to speak. "Do not believe anything he says about me. I am very unwilling. He will call momentarily. Be on your guard, Atticus. You are marked for assassination, because you are the only thing he fears."

Leif scooted the phone across the hard linoleum floor to me. It stopped against the toe of my sandals. I didn't bend down to pick it up.

"I will try to warn you as I can with Shakespeare. Perhaps I can make amends for the past. I must go now, because I'm being watched."

"Watched? By whom? From where?"

He didn't answer. He rose and backed away, his hands up. I watched him go. When he was at the door, the phone at my feet began to ring.

"Granuaile, get behind the counter. All the knives are yours, understand?"

Behind me, I heard my apprentice growl, "All your base are belong to us, Niko." She said this in English, but Niko didn't have any trouble inferring her general meaning.

"Yes! Yes! They are yours!" he cried, apparently some-what fluent in English. Poor guy. He sounded terrified of the girl he'd found so cute a few minutes ago.

"You might want to take the rest of the night off," Granuaile added, back to Greek. "It's a shit job anyway, right?"

I dropped to pick up the phone and then moved to the right, scanning the area around me. Customers were still leaving. Niko was scrambling after them, trying to beat them out the door. A pudgy managerial type was on the phone near the cash registers, presumably calling police. The clowns had managed to miss all this and were still arguing over rope.

I pressed the TALK button on the phone. A male tenor voice of surpassing arrogance flowed out of it, as if the speaker were auditioning for the part of the Douchefa-ther. He spoke in Latin.

"Thank you for taking my call. Am I speaking to the Druid?"

"What do you want?"

"I want to be courteous. Since you have managed to live so long, I assume you attach some value to your life and would appreciate an offer to extend it indefinitely."

"Let me hear the offer in a moment. Since you are in the courteous mood, introduce yourself."

"I am Theophilus. I believe your friend, Mr. Helgar-son, spoke of me."

"He's not my friend."

"Ah. Perhaps that is why he was so eager to help me locate you."

I ignored this; I wasn't going to play their mind games. They were both my enemies. "Tell me about the Ro-mans," I said. "The old ones you used to control."

"Ah! That is ancient history."

"Untold ancient history. Please tell it now. As a courtesy."

Theophilus sighed into my ear, and it reminded me of Leif. He used to like to sigh dramatically too. It must be something vampires did to remember what it was like to breathe.

I was going to take this chance to find out what I could about the Roman campaign to destroy the Druids, since it might be the only one I ever got. Before we'd left for Asgard, Leif had confided to me that Theophilus was the oldest vampire that he knew of. Old as Leif was, he hadn't been born when the Druids were hunted to near extinction, so he couldn't answer any of my questions about that time. Theophilus, though, would have been around when Rome spread north and brought the vampires with them.

"What is there to tell? We vampires wanted to expand our territory, and we did it on the backs of the Caesars."

"But why go after the Druids? They weren't hunting you."

"Not hunting, no, but you have that annoying talent of unbinding us regardless of our strength. It's a bit unfair."

"Unfair is burning all the groves and then stabbing a man with two dozen spears."

"One dozen probably wouldn't have done the job. You're too good at healing."

"So you were behind it all?"

"I cannot take sole credit."

"You mean blame?"

"As you wish. There were many involved. But it was my idea, my pet project, yes: a pogrom against the Druids to ensure that vampires could spread freely around the world. And it worked. Not completely, of course— here we are, talking together—but certainly effective. There are many of us now and only one of you."

"One of you per every hundred thousand humans, is that right?"

A hint of irritation crept into the vampire's smooth Douchetone. "Did Mr. Helgarson tell you that?"

Leif had mentioned the Accords of Rome twelve years ago, but I didn't feel that Theophilus needed to know that.

"Tell me about your courteous offer," I replied.

"The offer is simple: You get to walk out of the store and live. You've certainly earned it, and I appreciate reminders that there are limits to my power."

"No, you don't. If you appreciated that, you wouldn't be threatening me with this courteous offer. What do I have to do to earn it?"

"You must agree not to hunt vampires and to refrain from training more Druids."

"I've never hunted vampires."

"Explain the puddle you left behind in Litochoro, then."

"He attacked me. I don't think he knew what I was. That was simply self-defense."

"Fine. I will accept your word. But you must also stop training Druids."

"That's an unreasonable request. I haven't asked you to stop making new vampires."

"That is because you are in no position to do so."

"And if I say no, which you're assuming I will?"

"Then the old pogrom renews. A very small one, with you and your apprentice the sole targets."

I didn't think his offer was genuine, so I called his bluff. "Okay, sure, Theophilus. You're on."

"I beg your pardon?"

"I agree. I accept your courteous offer."

"You do?"

Granuaile called to me from behind the knife counter. "Sensei, there's a damn clown convention going on in here, have you noticed? There's something strange about their auras, but I don't know what it means."

I blinked and noticed. The two clowns that I thought I'd been seeing over and over were actually more like a dozen. They'd surrounded us. Turning on my magical sight, I saw what was under all the pancake makeup: pointy ears, flattened down and hidden by prosthetic ones. And underneath those rainbow-colored wigs were thick, long queues of black hair. Knives were concealed in the baggy clothing. Over all this was some ice-blue interference—a charm of some kind that had probably befuddled Granuaile's vision. She was still too unpracticed to see through such tricks. These weren't clowns at all. They were Svartálfar—real, live dark elves walking around Midgard.

"You sent in the clowns?" I said into the phone.

Theophilus chuckled and hung up. So much for his offer. The entire call had been meant to distract me while these clowns surrounded us.

"The clowns are dark elves, Granuaile. Kill or be killed. Go!"

Chapter 16

Despite Manannan's warning that the dark elves were after me and the confession of the faery assassin that dark elves had hired his band of rogues, I never thought I'd get to see them in the flesh. I guess if you'd like the dark elves to pay you a visit on good ol' Midgard, spend fifteen centuries blaming them for everything; they'll hear about it eventually.

The dark elves had good reason to bring me some karmic payback. I'd brought them grief with the blame game on my first trip to Asgard twelve years ago. I'd slung some lies in an attempt to distract the Norse pantheon from my true goals, and as a result Odin had briefly believed that the Svartálfar were infiltrating Asgard and were partially responsible for the death of the Norns. I learned later that Odin hadn't been gentle with his rebuke, so the dark elves were justified in seeking to share some of that violence with me.

Too bad they didn't count on my apprentice. While the elves focused on me being all shouty, Granuaile threw three knives, *shik-shik-shik*, and three Svartálfar went down before they even realized the fight was on. I charged to my right, which was also Granuaile's three o'clock, and swung Fragarach at the clown standing there. As expected, he went incorporeal and his clown costume fell to the floor, along with a mess of white face paint and the colorful wig. I didn't stick around to wonder when or where he'd turn solid again but turned clockwise and kept going at full speed.

I felt a draw on my bear charm and shot a glance at Granuaile before I lost sight of her around the partition. I saw that she was taking my advice to heart and moving. She had leapt up on top of the glass display case with her staff in one hand and a knife in the other, and she followed me to the other side of the partition by launching herself backward and flipping over it.

My first thought was, oh, gods, where is she going to land? But then I saw it was a necessary move. She had a whole lot of smoke boiling her way. Empty clown suits competed with flannel for attention on the sales floor.

Granuaile's leap drew the eyes of the Svartálfar creeping around behind the partition; they'd been planning on going smoky and stabbing us from behind. Since one of them was looking at Granuaile instead of me when I turned the corner, he didn't see Fragarach coming and was very solid when I stabbed up through the place where his kidney should be. His death scream attracted the attention of the clown closing in on Granuaile, allowing her to land clumsily but safely between the racks of loud camouflage suits.

"Keep going!" I called. "Flank and ambush!"

I wasn't the only one yelling. The managerial type at the front of the store was no longer trying to control his requests with a tense whisper; he was shouting into the phone for immediate police support, as if gunfire had broken out at Nakatomi Plaza. He needed help *now*, God damn it, *now*!

I charged the clown who was closest to Granuaile even as smoke began to pour over the partition after her. Granuaile fled to the back of the store, out of my sight—especially since I tripped and did a face-plant in the aisle.

I'd been slide-tackled from behind by the clown I'd first swished my sword through; he'd re-formed and pursued me. Now that I was down, he leapt on top of me and plunged his knife into my back—or so he thought. It felt like a rather painful punch, but his black smoky knife was apparently magical, and my cold iron aura refused it entry. Still, I yelled as if I'd been stabbed, then flipped over, bringing Fragarach around as I did so, left to right. He stabbed me again, this time in the gut, and grinned wickedly as he remained solid, clearly willing to take one for the team to ensure that I died. I took his head off instead.

The clown I'd been charging was now trying to slit my throat. In the thespian spirit, I gurgled dramatically and clutched my neck with my left hand, then took a blind swipe over my right shoulder with Fragarach. It connected, and I was rewarded with a tiny gasp. I kicked off the dark elf corpse astride me before it could turn to tar and rose to confront the clown I'd just stabbed. He clutched his arm and hadn't yet turned to mist. He was wincing through face paint already designed to make him look woebegone.

"Aw. Sad clown is sad," I said. Behind him, the boiling clouds of elves were beginning to move off in pursuit of Granuaile. I heard glass shattering in the back of the store and hoped she was all right. I flourished my sword and lunged at the sad clown, expecting him to shift to mist, but he tried to dodge instead and became entangled in a rack of camo suits. I stabbed into his heart easily, somewhat bemused. They must not be able to take their smoke forms when wounded.

This execution earned the especial ire of the Svartálfar who'd been after Granuaile. Three of them solidified out of the coal-black dust and hissed, brandishing their knives. That was fine with me. The more they chased me, the safer Granuaile would be. She didn't have the same magical immunities I did.

I backed up warily and stepped into the remains of the first elf I'd slain.

"Euughh," I said. "Your buddy just turned me into a tar heel."

One of them cursed at me in Old Norse—he called me the dwarf-dicked spawn of Hel's half-dead twat, and I privately gave him props, so few people take the trouble to curse creatively anymore—then they came after me. I turned and ran for the front of the store, back the way I'd come. Once around the partition, I was near the knives and the aisles devoted to outdoor food prep—coolers, hibachi grills, meat smokers, and the occasional flannel-clad mannequin flipping a burger. So intent was I in searching for dark elves at eye level that I didn't see the rope tied between two racks until after it tripped me. I sprawled facedown in front of the charcoal and lighter fluid but held on to Fragarach. The three who'd been pursuing me immediately fell on my back, discovering for themselves that their knives would do nothing more than irritate me.

They were quick, efficient killers, and it wasn't lost on me that if I hadn't been immune to their smoky knives, I would already have died several times. Since we were so close to a rather large supply of standard steel knives, I was in favor of a quick exit.

My escape, however, was not high on their agenda. I struggled to break free, but they redoubled their efforts to weigh me down, not trying to stab me now or do anything much except keep me in place. That meant they were planning something else. I managed to turn my head to see two more Svartálfar behaving oddly down the aisle with the hibachis. One—a female, I noticed—had torn the cap off a tin of lighter fluid and was now pouring it all over her naked partner. As she shook the last few drops onto his shoulders, she gave the drenched dark elf a lighter and told him in Old Norse he was ready.

Ready for what?

The answer was made horribly clear to me in the next few moments. Wearing one of those wicked grins that you never believe can exist outside comics until you see one, the gassed-up dark elf ran straight at me and set himself aflame. The fire didn't get a chance to fully spread across his body, but that was never part of the plan anyway. The plan was to charge me and turn to mist at the last possible instant, showering me with liquid fire. That's precisely what he did, and the bastards holding me down didn't turn into mist until they were sure it had hit me. Oh, and the girl who'd hosed him down in the first place? She followed behind him with a couple more cans of lighter fluid and squirted them at me as if I was her personal barbecue.

Druid's Log, July 15: Dark elves are not only quick and efficient killers but creative and pyrotechnically inclined ones.

During my younger days, some people occasionally got ideas about burning me at the stake—there was a time when tattoos meant you had made a "compack widda debbil"—but I never stuck around long enough for them to try it. I had witnessed a few burnings though. It was usually not a witch at all but some poor person who'd committed no other crime than being born gay or with a third nipple or a birthmark of some kind—and the screams were terrible, unlike any other pain I've heard. This is truth: "Burning alive" is a wholly inadequate phrase to communicate the agony involved in the process. It's every nerve in your skin screaming about the apocalypse, and there's no way you can block that out and find a happy place. This wasn't hellfire or magical in any way; it was simple chemistry, and, as such, my cold iron amulet afforded me no protection.

I rolled onto my right side to smother the flames along my tattoos. I couldn't let my skin melt there or I'd be unable to use magic. I activated my healing charm to start repairing and replacing cells already caving in like Styrofoam; my face and torso were on fire, not my legs. I spat out the words to unbind my shirt even as the elf with lighter fluid poured on more fuel. The whooshing sound a grill makes when the flames are goaded isn't so pleasant when your rib cage is serving as the grill.

I lost my ability to track what was happening. I knew there were four other elves and they would probably finish me, but I couldn't think of anything but putting out the fire. And maybe getting my next breath. The fire on my face was sucking away all available oxygen, and I was gasping for relief.

I wondered if this could be it—surviving nearly 2,100 years, only to be torched by bloody dark elves in a sporting goods store. Nerves screamed despite my efforts to block them, and my left side was entirely aflame; still, I pushed myself up and let the remainder of my shirt fall away. Some of the flames fell with it—but that Svartálf with the lighter fluid kept spraying me down to keep everything alight. A growling noise I'd been hearing for a while was coming from my own throat.

Five closely spaced pops sounded in my ears, and the elves dropped—well, four of them did. The last one managed to go smoky before Granuaile could take him out, but the standard knife he'd been holding clattered to the floor.

"Drop and roll, sensei! We have a few seconds." She ran toward me with a semiautomatic in one hand and her staff in the other. The shattering glass I'd heard earlier had to be my apprentice securing the firearm. Dark elves littered the ground; she'd pulled off a fantastic ambush. I rolled around on the industrial carpet and discovered it wasn't very smothery. It worked to some extent, but I couldn't put out my face and hair, and it hurt so badly I couldn't think what to do about it. Probably because my brain was rather concerned with cerebral hypoxia at the moment. Granuaile fired a couple more times, presumably at the elf she'd missed, and then flannel began to rain from the sky. That smothered the flames admirably, and I realized that Granuaile must have disrobed mannequins to help me put out the fire on my head. I would never scoff at flannel again. Able to suck in a glorious breath or two, I took advantage and tried to return my nervous system to manual control rather than the autopilot of instinct.

"Did we get them all?" I gave a muffled shout through a red-and-black shirt.

"I don't know, still scanning," Granuaile replied. "I did get that one I missed earlier when he became solid."

With the flames extinguished, I could mute the pain enough to think somewhat clearly. "We need to go," I said, tearing the shirt from my head. It felt as if some skin probably came off with it. "Tar stains. Security footage of nonhumans. You know what's going to happen to the building."

Granuaile's eyes widened. "Oh! We need to go." The distant wail of sirens emphasized the necessity.

"Indeed," I said. "Help me up." I extended my right hand and she grabbed it, hauling me to my feet.

"Oh, gods, Atticus, your face . . ." The horror of her expression informed me that I wasn't handsome anymore.

"If it looks half as bad as it feels, I don't want to know. We'll have to find a place where I can replenish."

Turning to the apoplectic manager, I called, "Run for your life!" in Greek. "And don't forget that guard in the corner of the store!" It was now up to him to heed or ignore my warning.

As we moved toward the door, my skin still palpably cooking and every available pore sweating, I said, "I'm running low on magic. I can cast camouflage on us both to get out of the door safely, but I won't try to maintain it. I need to keep healing if I want to come out of this without scarring."

Sirens honked obnoxiously through the streets; the manager's backup was coming, and he'd be giving them a detailed description of us, no doubt. And the security cameras would have the whole thing on tape. The question was whether Theophilus (or Leif) had any intention of letting the police have access to either.

Actually, that wasn't the only question. Why were dark elves working with vampires? The dark elves were supposedly behind the Fae assassination attempt earlier, so did that mean that vampires were also in league with the Fae? And who amongst the dark elves had thought it was a good idea to disguise themselves in Midgard as a bunch of clowns?

These mysteries would have to be solved later. I cast camouflage on us both, and the stored magic in my charm fell to near empty; I kept my pain suppression on but couldn't afford any more magic to heal. The manager squawked when we disappeared.

We motored through the door, flashes of movement with uncertain shapes, and turned left down Kaisareias Street, heading south by southeast, dodging around people who couldn't see us and made no room. Some of them sensed movement—the air went shimmery for a second—and stopped in their tracks, but most were unaware that they were obstacles in a street slalom course. I was running very awkwardly; my left side didn't want to move.

After about a block, I turned off the camouflage to

preserve what little magic I had left. We heard honking that wasn't the annoying sirens of approaching police. It was the sort of honking you hear from horns mounted on bicycles. We also heard bells. Whistles. Kids laughing. I also heard gasps and startled cries as I passed by, a half-melted madman with a sword accompanied by a pretty girl with a staff and a gun.

The source of the happy noises became clear at the intersection of Vizyis Street, where we almost ran right into a whole parade of clowns—evil dark elf clowns, grinning luridly under the streetlights. They were coming from a greenbelt that wound through the city; either purposefully or accidentally, they stood between the nearest source of magical power and us.

At the same time—or close enough as to make no difference—an explosion behind us meant someone had firebombed the sporting goods store with military-grade weaponry. I bet it was Leif, and he knew very well that I had already left the building. I doubted the manager or the security guard Leif had charmed had made it out. There might have even been some other employees and customers left inside, tucked into a corner somewhere.

Most eyes were drawn by the explosion. But some, especially those closest, couldn't miss the burn-scarred man and the athletic woman running across the street. The man was carrying a sword, which was illegal in Greece, and the woman was carrying a firearm, which was turbo-illegal due to Europe's profound lack of a second amendment.

Fingers pointed at us, and I urged Granuaile to keep going.

Some of the clowns peeled off and pursued us on elevated bicycles and unicycles and miniature scooters; some turned the other way, toward the sporting goods store and the approaching police.

The explosion and the dissolution of the clown parade

had confused onlookers and pushed some of them toward the edge of panic. These people didn't know precisely what was going on, but they knew the clowns weren't smiling and it wasn't fun for the whole family anymore.

A couple of clowns took out their black knives, and people started to scream after that—so many people think all clowns are evil anyway, and this only confirmed it. Once the screaming started, there was unbridled pandemonium.

"Pandemonium!" I said. "*That's* what's been going on."

"Tell me about it," Granuaile huffed beside me.

"I will if we can get out of this. We have to get to that greenbelt. Circle this block and head back."

"Where have these guys been hiding?" Granuaile wondered aloud. "They didn't travel directly here from the Norse plane, right? They had to have been staying here?"

"That's a good point. Once the vampires found out where we were—"

"I don't think they did, Atticus. I think it was the dark elves. Remember there were two clowns in the store from the beginning?"

"That's right!" We turned left, heading northeast up Anatolikis Romylias, and a quick glance at our pursuit showed that we had five clowns chasing us. Perhaps more were following in mist form?

"So they must have made some calls, and arrangements got made on the fly."

"That sounds plausible," I agreed. "The vampire on the phone wanted me to think Leif had found us somehow, and that's possible too. He can probably track me because he's had so much of my blood."

"That's really disturbing."

"Yeah. Take the lead; these guys following us can't know yet that I'm immune to their magic knives. If we're gonna get backstabbed, let me take it."

Granuaile lengthened her stride and pulled ahead. I

checked behind us when I heard metallic scrapes and crashing noises. The clown bikes and suits lay strewn at the corner of Atlantidos. They'd gone incorporeal and were chasing us now in smoke form. I'd learned enough about them by now to realize they didn't do that unless they were ready to kill.

"Pour it on," I said. "They're catching up."

We didn't have breath enough to talk after that; we were off the earth's magical grid and had to huff and puff up to Pylaiais, where we turned left, back toward Vizyis. I ran right behind Granuaile to shield her.

It was a wise precaution, for we weren't a third of the way down the block before a wicked thrust plowed into my back and caused me to stumble. I tried to twist as I fell and take a swing at my six, but my injuries were truly debilitating and I couldn't manage anything except a clumsy pratfall. "Granuaile! Go twirly girl!"

There was a proper Mandarin name for the sequence of movements she executed with her staff, but she'd never been able to master the sounds to my satisfaction. Out of frustration, she asked if we could rename the forms with English terms, and I agreed, since she was already working on three other languages. "Twirly girl" simply meant that she twirled her staff rapidly around her in a defensive whirlwind—front, back, both sides. It wasn't impossible to penetrate, but it was damn difficult and would require time to study. I'd use that time to try something I should have tried earlier.

Granuaile halted and began to whip her staff around her so that I was just out of reach. The Svartálfar were bolder than they were wise; one of them tried to solid-ify and get in a quick strike at Granuaile from behind and got clocked in the head for his efforts. He fell un-conscious, as the other four took shape around me and stabbed down quickly. I swiped at them desperately, and one was so surprised that his knife hadn't penetrated that he didn't go incorporeal in time to avoid the blade of Fragarach. The others became smoke, however, and that's precisely what I wished.

Fragarach was blessed with three enchantments, two of which had to be cast; the third, the ability to cut through any armor, was always "on." The first "castable" enchantment gave the sword its name, "the Answerer," because it froze enemies and forced them to answer questions truthfully. The second enchantment, the ability to summon winds, simply didn't have many practical applications, so I rarely used it or even thought of it; the last time I had used it was twelve years ago by Tony Cabin, when I'd blown Aenghus Óg off his feet. Of course, I hadn't had access to Fragarach for much of the past twelve years. Now it would do me yeoman service. I cast the spell and pointed the sword down the street; winds gusted from behind me and blew the dark elves back fifty yards before they remembered they could solidify and stand against the wind. I howled because that had used up the last of my magic, and now I couldn't help but feel every destroyed inch of my burned skin.

Granuaile realized what had happened and yanked me up by my unburned right arm.

"Come on, sensei," she said. "You gave us a bit of a lead. Let's not waste it."

Moving was no fun at all. Neither was staying still; everything hurt. Long after the flames were out, my skin was still cooking and dying, and I couldn't seem to catch my breath. That magic had been the only thing keeping me functioning.

"Move!" Granuaile said, pulling at me, and I staggered after her, much slower than before. The dark elves would have no trouble catching up, I could tell, and they'd have us at their mercy long before we got to that greenbelt.

At least my aura was proof against their knives. Granuaile didn't have any defense against them.

"You go ahead, fast as you can," I said.

"No."

"Get to the trees, buff up your speed, and then you can take them out when they solidify."

"You're coming with me. Let's *go*, sensei!"

"They can't hurt me," I explained, still unable to manage much more than a rolling stagger. The faint breeze this generated against my skin was unspeakably abrasive. "They have nothing but their stupid black knives, and I'm immune. You go and I'll catch up. We'll take them together."

Granuaile was on the verge of objecting again when a gurgling cry behind us demanded our attention. She was quicker to process what was happening than I was.

"Shit. It's him!"

Him again. Leif Helgarson had caught one of our pursuers in the second he turned solid, and then the vampire had simply torn the creature in two. Two seconds later, even as we watched, another dark elf became solid, Leif blurred, and a startled cry was all the death song the Svartálf could manage before one half of his body was forcibly shorn from the other. We stopped trying to run and faced Leif. He waved cheerfully, then tore apart our final tail. I wondered if any of the street's residents were watching this from their windows. Perhaps it was a really good night for Greek television. Leif called to me while standing between still-twitching halves of his last victim.

"May we speak for a spell, Atticus, or will you destroy me now?"

"You know you're safe," I rasped. "I'm out of magic."

"Even so," he said. "I always suspect that you are holding something back."

"That's reasonable," I replied. "Come closer and we won't have to shout."

I turned to walk toward Vizyis. By the time Granuaile spun around to keep pace, Leif had zipped up to walk on my left. He glanced at my ruined features.

"I am sorry," he said. "I did not think they would manage to do you any harm."

"Eleven or twelve smoky bastards against two and you thought we'd walk out without a scratch?"

Leif shrugged a shoulder. "I have seen you lay waste to fields of opponents."

"*Field* is the key word there. There was no field in that store and therefore no magic."

"It is magic I have come to warn you about. You are heading for the greenbelt, yes?"

"Of course."

"Theophilus has seeded it with vampires who are searching for a human with unusual blood."

"Beware the puppet master, eh?"

"Yes, but Theophilus is not the puppet master. He is more of a skilled apprentice, if you wish to extend a metaphor."

"Then who's pulling his strings?"

"Someone from your world."

"Ireland?"

"No. The other one. Tír na nÓg."

"The Fae are behind all this? Someone there is giving orders both to dark elves and vampires?"

"As far as I can tell, yes."

It was no more than I had already suspected, but to have it confirmed was a bit of a shock. But maybe it wasn't confirmed after all. I couldn't trust anything he said.

"I know what you're up to," I growled.

Leif's lips turned up at the corners. "I would be intensely disappointed if you did not."

"You're playing both sides and setting your own odds in Vegas, you conniving bastard. You probably have some Machiavellian shit going down on other planets. Are you expecting me to make a deal with you? An alliance?"

The vampire shrugged again, hands in pockets. "None is needed. For now our interests are the same. That will serve as well as anything else."

"I will never forgive you for using me. For hurting Oberon."

Leif smirked at me. "How fortunate, then, that I do not seek your forgiveness. I will go ahead and dispatch the two at the edge of the greenbelt. After that, you will be on your own. What is it that the young Americans say now? 'Peace out, brah'?"

"No," I said, "not unless they want to get their balls booted into their stomachs," but Leif had already raced ahead, his amused chuckle hanging in the air and fading with distance.

The night settled about us, and for thirty seconds there was no sound except our footfalls, the muffled noise of family arguments, and the wail of emergency vehicles converging on the sporting-goods store.

Granuaile finally asked a question into what passes for silence in the city: "Do vampires have balls?"

"I don't know."

Chapter 17

Once we reached the greenbelt, the elemental of Thessalonika, Macedonia, restored my magic and allowed Granuaile to tap her own. She cast night vision and sped herself up immediately, even though we were crouched underneath a tree. Under the tree behind us, nearest the street, rested the gray corpse of a vampire, courtesy of Leif, head torn from its neck and held between its hands on top of its stomach. Leif had mentioned two, but we didn't see another.

For my part, I filled my bear charm and gave succor to my screaming skin. Now that I had a clear head and plenty of help from Macedonia, I could assess the burn damage and apply my skills to healing it in earnest.

Left alone, I'd wind up looking like Two-Face, because I had deep burns down the majority of my left side and in a few months those would turn into red hypertrophic scars, all the suppleness gone and my ability to scare children increased geometrically. But skin, fortunately, is not that difficult to regenerate. The secret is all in the dermis; maintain a healthy dermis, and cosmetically your epidermis will look just fine. Regenerating the dermis would take more time than the epidermis, of course, but it wasn't going to be like growing bone or muscle tissue either. And if I could get hold of the right herbs, I could even make my special brew for skin health, Elastici-Tea. I'd be a bit scary-looking for a while but hopefully normal-ish in a few weeks; the underlying healing would be finished in three or four days, but the cosmetic side of things would take longer to sort itself out as the dead cells sloughed away and got replaced by fresh ones. I was well aware that I was damn lucky to be here, considering the past hour. The first battle between dark elves and Druids had yielded surprises to both parties, and foremost among them had to be that I had managed to escape. I doubted that I would have if it weren't for Granuaile.

"You were brilliant back there, by the way," I said. "Thank you."

She swallowed audibly before answering. "Welcome." Her voice was quiet.

"How many did you get?"

"Eight. Not that I'm, you know, keeping score or anything."

"I got three. Were there only eleven, or were there twelve?"

She winced. "I thought there were twelve."

"Me too. So that means either the last one got blown up in the firebombing of the store, or it didn't . . ."

"And that means it's either following us or reporting back to its superiors on our skills and tactics."

"It's not following us," I said. "Leif wouldn't have spoken so frankly to us if there were anyone around from the other side to hear it."

"So next time we meet them, they're going to use conventional weapons on us," Granuaile said.

"Yep. And they won't let you flank them again."

She nodded, accepting this, then swallowed again. I realized she was trying to keep from crying. "I didn't get there in time. Are you going to be okay?" she asked.

"Oh, yeah." I tried to smile and realized that, the way my face looked now, it probably wasn't the most reassuring expression I could have made. "I know it looks bad, but I'll be okay given time."

"All right."

"Theophilus and Leif expect us to keep to these woods—maybe the dark elves do too—but I don't see the upside. You can't cast camouflage or unbind vampires yet. I could cast camouflage on you, but if we get attacked by more than one vampire at a time, it's going to be extremely risky. We don't need to fight this battle. The situation's changed. We don't have to go back to Olympus armed to the teeth to make inquiries. We can go back now, as we are, because I know what's happening."

"So just call a cab and go grab Oberon?" she asked.

"Yeah, go ahead. I'll unbind the remains of this vampire first and Theophilus can suck on that."

Granuaile grinned and rose. She jogged the short distance back to the street, put her fingers between her teeth, and whistled.

Chapter 18

"We are about to start some shit we may not be able to finish," I warned Granuaile. "Though we can argue that this is all Bacchus's fault, in order to get around him we're going to have to risk bringing the Greek pantheon into this too. They're probably not going to care who started it."

Oberon said, <Sort of like an NFL referee, then.> He'd taken my injuries in stride once I'd reassured him that I would be good as new eventually.

"I'm not sure what you mean, sensei." We were speaking in the back of a limousine on our way to Olympus. We needed the privacy and the nice bucket full of ice in which to soak my burned left arm. The driver was accommodating and willing to pull over every so often so I could "get some fresh air," but it was really so I could replenish my bear charm and continue healing as we drove. I also didn't mind the luxury after the exertions of Thessalonika.

"We don't have to snag a Bacchant and interrogate her anymore. I know precisely what's going on—what's *been* going on. You heard Bacchus talking outside the cave, right? He said Faunus couldn't keep us trapped there forever."

"Right. Except we weren't trapped. We got away."

"The trap is Olympus itself. It's the only place we can

bind you right now, and twice we've had to interrupt the ritual because of it. We've been operating on Lord Grundlebeard's theory that the entire Eurasian plate was disrupted because Perun's plane got burned up by Loki. I never really bought it—the trembling in North America faded right away and we were able to shift just fine, so why would the trembling last so much longer in Europe?—but I didn't have a better theory to offer. Now I do. It's been a month and a half. If the burning of Perun's plane was the source of the disturbance, wouldn't there have been some fluctuations throughout Europe? Wouldn't the severity of the disturbance vary, being stronger in Russia and less so in Spain and Italy and so on, and shouldn't it have tapered off a bit by now? But it's still going strong. Something is producing the disruption consistently, and it's purposely leaving Olympus alone."

"I thought you agreed the Olympians were protecting their turf."

"They are. But they're also responsible for jacking up everything else, and it's all to catch us in their net. It's Faunus, Granuaile. Faunus and that worthless sot, Bacchus."

"How are they responsible?"

"Pandemonium, you see."

"No, I don't see."

"I didn't see either, because I was thinking of the Roman god's name and not the original Greek. Pandemonium is the disruption of order—it's chaos, in other words. That's what's disrupting all the forests on the Eurasian plate so that we can't shift anywhere else. This is a power that both Pan and Faunus possess—it's explicitly stated in the mythology, and of course it's inherent in the etymology of the word. And none of the Tuatha Dé Danann or the Fae recognize it for what it is. It probably hasn't been used since truly ancient times, and even then it was never on this scale. This might be the first time it's been used outside Greece, so that's why the Fae are fumbling for explanations."

Granuaile got a crinkle between her eyes. "Why would the Olympians have a power that specifically prevents Druids from shifting?"

"That wasn't its original purpose—it's just the purpose they're using it for now, because it's a side effect that gives them an advantage. Originally Pan was a way for people to get in touch with all that's primal in nature and within themselves. He was a great big yang to all the yin of the other gods and the order of Olympus and civilization. Pan wanted to party and fuck and make a lot of noise—and once the monotheists came along and got a load of him—"

<Ha! You said *load*.>

"—he became the very devil himself. He messes with the order of everything. I bet if we took time to pick up a newspaper and look at what's going on in Europe right now, we'd see more than the usual ruckus. And that's because Pan's Roman doppelgänger, Faunus, is screwing up the entire continent. Our tethers to Tír na nÓg are Druidic order laid on top of nature, and he's disrupting them."

"So how do we get to him?"

"If Faunus is out in the world messing with all the forests except around Olympus, we need him to return to Olympus and stay there so we can have all the rest of the forests to work with in the meantime. The way I see it, only one thing will make him come running back."

"What's that?"

"We take away his sex toys."

Chapter 19

Literally and figuratively, the goat-footed god has always been a horny lad. The ancient Greeks provided him with plenty of nymphs and dryads to play with in the forest so he wouldn't be tempted to wander into the cities and fuck around. Fucking around was all well and good to the Greeks, of course, but, you know: "Moderation in all things." The Greeks were trying to lay the foundations for Western civilization as well as one another, so Pan and his worshippers were required to do their unchained frolicking in the woods.

Pan liked a good chase most days. It replaced foreplay. Nymphs were great for providing a chase. But sometimes he felt a bit lazy, so he hunted up dryads on those days, because dryads couldn't run very far from their trees. Dryads who spent more than a couple of days separated from their trees tended to wither and die—and the same was true for the trees. The connection between them was not only symbiotic, it was vital.

I fully planned to take advantage of that to buy Granuaile and me the time we needed. What was true for Pan was also true for his Roman clone, Faunus.

"You know what's cool about a dryad's tree?" I said. We had paid off the limo driver to the south of Olympus and walked into the foothills with nothing but a couple bottles of water and our weapons. I was shirtless because I couldn't stand the feel of fabric on my crispy skin.

"Well, it's an oak tree with an immortal nymph attached. That's pretty cool."

"Agreed. But what's also cool is that a dryad's tree is exactly the same on three planes. It's not only here, but it's on the Roman and Greek planes too, every branch and leaf."

"Each tree is a trinity, then. I dig it." Granuaile was nodding and smiling, but this faded as a question occurred to her. "There aren't three different dryads, are there?"

"No, just one. Pan and Faunus share them, and Artemis and Diana also divide their attentions between them."

"Oh! Right. Dryads are kind of special to the huntresses. Um." Her eyebrows drew together and she frowned, clearly disturbed.

"Yes?"

"Are you sure you want to mess with the dryads?"

"Are you sure you want to be a Druid?"

"Well, of course I am, but isn't there any other way?"

"Sure. We could seek out the Olympians and ask them nicely to stop. But direct confrontation with true immortals will probably not work out in our favor."

"I concur, sensei, which is why I'm questioning the wisdom of pursuing this."

"Would you rather we continue as we have been, knowing that the Bacchants will track us down and interrupt the binding who knows how many more times? There are only so many places around Olympus where we can perform the ritual. No, it's time to act boldly. Better to ask forgiveness than permission and to answer their shenanigans with even better shenanigans. We won't hurt them."

"The Olympians are not renowned for their forgiveness," Granuaile pointed out.

"Well, I'm tired of playing defense. We've been lucky so far in that we've been able to move faster than them, but strategically we've been playing not to lose, if you see what I mean. And the two of us—"

<Hey! Three! Hounds count!>

"—Sorry. The three of us against the world's vampires, the Fae, and the Svartálfar in a confined area are awfully long odds."

"Exactly. So why risk antagonizing more Olympians?"

"It's not about antagonizing anyone; it's about giving us options and restoring our mobility. And shenanigans. But I'm willing to entertain alternatives. Do you have any?"

Granuaile sighed. "No."

<I have an alternative. How about a hundred pounds of quality from Jody Maroni's Sausage Kingdom? A variety pack with the Tequila Chicken, the Toulouse Garlic, and the succulent Polish sausage? I'd forgive anything for a gift like that.>

Not everyone can be bribed with meat, Oberon.

<They can't? Oh! You mean they're vegetarian.>

No, they eat meat. It simply doesn't sway their decision-making process.

<Well, that . . . that's just wrong, Atticus! Are they monsters? It's like they have no moral center!>

"All right. So we need to look for oak trees that are bound to dryads. It's easy. The heart of the tree will be white."

"So it's okay to use magic now?"

"Well, it's not exactly safe. We're taking the calculated risk that we can get this done before the Bacchants or anyone else zeroes in on us. We had a couple of weeks or more to work with the first two times. It's probably okay to scurry around for a few hours."

<Heh! That's what the squirrel said.>

We hiked a quarter mile up the gentle lower slopes of Olympus, until we found a tree with a bright white center in the magical spectrum. Having explained the plan to Granuaile on the way, I created a tether to Tír na nÓg first, and we shifted there to scout a suitable location for our shenanigans along the river of time.

"That will do nicely," I said, pointing to an unoccupied island pretty far upstream. "Time moves so slowly there that they'll spend a century saying, 'Wait,' when they're trying to say, 'Wait, don't leave me here!' "

"How do you use the islands?"

"See the obelisk at the edge of the shore with the Ogham script on it? That's its address. Using that, you open portals to it wherever you are and shove stuff through. We have to use portals instead of trees because we don't want to teleport ourselves into that timestream."

"Nice thinking."

"We learned from someone else's mistake. I think the first person who used a tree on an island to shift is still stuck there. But word is he ought to be able to shift himself out of there in another decade or so."

<So he's been there for centuries?>

He's been there longer than I've been alive.

<Wow. He's missed out on a lot. Where do you think he'll stand on the Kirk vs. Picard question?>

I memorized the Ogham address, and we shifted back to the oak tree with the white center—except we shifted to the one growing on the Roman plane. The dryad was nowhere in sight.

"Where is she?" Granuaile asked as she turned around, scanning the area.

I shrugged. "Nearby. Or maybe on the Greek plane.

She'll let us know where she's at once we start to unbind her from the tree."

"Are you sure this won't hurt her?"

"It'll hurt a little bit. She has to feel it. But it won't be life-threatening the way we're doing it."

"How can you know that?"

"Because while she's frozen in time, her tree will be frozen too. When we bind them back together, it will be as if only a few seconds passed."

Granuaile was unconvinced. "I think we're going to be doomed."

<Alert! Much fear apprentice shows! Adopt Yoda syntax you must!>

"Nonsense. Remember, you're going to speak soothingly in Latin when the Dryad shows up, so I can cast the portal."

"Got it."

Focusing on the white light, I zoomed in my focus to examine the structure of the binding.

It was beautiful stuff. The Greeks approached magic differently than the Celts did, of course, relying on structures reminiscent of their architecture: lots of straight lines, sharp angles, triangles, and mathematical precision; columns of cubes that could be endlessly halved and halved again; and a bloody tesseract at the heart of it all, tying together an oak and a dryad. Funny thing about columns is the lack of redundancy one finds in more organic structures. Knock out a few columns and the integrity is seriously compromised. I unbound a triangle knot and felt a small tremor in the tree. I unraveled a column and felt it shudder more violently.

A cultured voice spoke from behind me in perfect Latin. "Please stop."

I turned and beheld a woman who shone with white around her heart. It was clearly the dryad belonging to the tree, so I dispelled my magical sight and beheld her as she hoped to be seen. She flinched upon seeing my burned features.

She had something akin to a soft-focus filter about her; gazing on her form was like looking at a Waterhouse painting, full of depth and pathos yet suffused with the visual silk of a rose petal, delicate and ethereal and inspiring anxiety in the viewer—I felt I mustn't stare too intently or else I might crush her beauty forever, and I'd pine away until I died of guilt.

Her hair, dark and abundant and festooned with a flowering vine woven throughout, tumbled in a loose braid down her left breast until it ended at her waist. Another flowering vine circled her body, fastening a loose white tunic of thin material about her. Her legs and feet were bare; her eyes implored us to leave in peace.

Hers was the kind of beauty that, once glimpsed, convinced a person that divinity had a hand in it. I have often wondered if this might not be the answer to all of Granuaile's philosophical questions: We are here to create and witness beauty. Gaia creates it every day, and as part of Gaia, it is our task as well. Beethoven saw the truth of it. Van Gogh as well, daffy as he was, and so many others.

"We will stop," Granuaile said. "Thank you for coming to see us."

"Who are you?" the dryad asked.

While my apprentice kept the dryad occupied, I quietly spoke in Old Irish to open a portal to Tír na nÓg directly behind her. Once it shimmered into existence, we didn't even have to force her through. I merely smiled a half-melted smile at her and took a few steps forward, and she backed right into it, fearful of my intentions. I closed the portal once she was through and congratulated Granuaile.

"Well done."

"How much damage did you do?"

"Hardly any. Easy to fix. Let's go do some more."

We kept moving and sent five more dryads away from their customary planes. The Olympians would not be able to divine their presence in Tír na nÓg. They'd worry that the dryads were dying, but both they and their trees were effectively frozen in time. Since the bond between them was only weakened, not broken, what was true for the dryads was also true for the trees.

On the last tree we left two notes—one on the Roman plane and one on earth. We purposely left out the Greek plane, to make it clear we knew who was truly responsible and we didn't wish to involve Dionysus or Pan. With any luck, the Greeks would put pressure on the Romans to resolve the situation in our favor. It read thus:

My lord Bacchus is mad, and his actions have caused some dryads to go on vacation. If you wish them to come back unharmed, Lord Faunus, cease all pandemonium for three months. Rest assured that they will be returned in perfect health if you comply.

I then asked Olympia to relay a simpler message through the European elementals to Faunus, wherever he was: "Some of your dryads seem to have disappeared."

Granuaile, Oberon, and I shifted to Mag Mell, where I spent the night soaking in the healing springs at Cnoc an Óir and doing all I could to revitalize my skin. In the morning, the Fae were abuzz with the news that "Lord Grundlebeard's Curse" had ended, and now they—and we—could shift anywhere in Europe.

Chapter 20

I spent World War II helping Jewish families escape Vichy France by sneaking them into Spain and thence to Portugal. I smuggled them through the Atlantic Pyrenees using one pass or another, and in the process I learned the lay of the land very well. Because of that experience, I knew of the perfect spot to bind Granuaile.

The Pyrenees—pronounced the French way, like *pee-ray-nay*—have some pretty fantastic caves. Cavemen left behind old paintings in some of them, much of it better than contemporary art. Underground streams and rivers flow through others. Some of them shrink down to nothing or to passages that only a banana could slip through, then open again into vast cathedrals of awesome limestone that no human eyes have ever seen—except mine. There was one place that truly belonged to me. I had privately dubbed it Green Man's Retreat, because I was known as the Green Man when the Germans were hunting me.

The Morrigan had told me to keep my magic use to a minimum throughout WWII, because she was going to be damn busy choosing the slain and couldn't shield me from Aenghus Óg. The Pyrenees elemental was sympathetic to this and was anxious to help; who knew when I'd ever make it back if I got chased out of the area?

I needed to keep my draws on the earth to a minimum;

both the Fae and the Tuatha Dé Danann could feel such draws if they were nearby, and thus I could accidentally be discovered. The Pyrenees helped me hide by doing plenty of things for me. If an elemental exercised its own magic, that was just the earth doing its thing, not someone exercising his binding to the earth.

An officer among the Germans had heard tales that someone named the Green Man was helping Jews escape, and he gave them enough credence to send a few squads looking for me. This was in 1941; they had France sewn up and the United States hadn't gotten involved yet, so the soldiers were a bit bored and snipe hunts were a luxury they could indulge. Normally they would not have given me any trouble, but they caught me by surprise when they walked right into my camp while I was sleeping. They had automatic weapons, and I had skin that was fantastically vulnerable to bullets.

I cast camouflage right away and asked the elemental Pyrenees to help somehow. After a few seconds had passed, he caused a minor rockslide south of my position, during which the Germans thankfully did not hose the area with gunfire. They hadn't yet determined I was the Green Man; I was just some crazy bastard sleeping in the woods. They shouted a lot, wondering where I went, and some of them stomped off to investigate the noise to the south. A few stayed in the camp, however, to see what they could turn up. They turned up Fragarach, and I almost broke my silence and begged them not to take it.

Sensing my distress, Pyrenees made me an extraordinary offer. On the other side of the rock wall I crouched against was a cavern with no outside access nearby. He'd grant me access by creating a door in the mountain and would disguise the whole business by massaging the crust underneath the soldiers' feet for a minute. They'd think it was an earthquake.

I agreed and the chaos began. The ground near my campsite was suddenly unsteady, and one soldier squeezed off a round in surprise as he lost his footing. It took out one of his companions, then all the soldiers were falling to the ground on purpose and shooting into the forest, making the admirably paranoid conclusion that they were under attack. Fragarach was carelessly tossed to the ground, useless against machine guns. I created a binding between the leather of the scabbard and the skin on my palm, and it flew to my hand. I ducked into the darkness, and Pyrenees closed the door behind me. Good-bye, cruel world!

The darkness was so complete that casting night vision wouldn't have helped. There was no light inside the mountain. The air wasn't bad, though, so it was ventilated somehow. And it was damp in there—rather chilly too. Since I could not hear or see anything, I settled down to a fitful sleep. Pyrenees informed me when it was dawn.

I emerged from the side of the mountain, squinting, smelling pine, and listening to the morning song of birds. My camp was wiped out; the German soldiers had stolen all my stuff. It took me a week to resupply and get back there, but I had to make the trip; I wanted to see something no one had ever seen before. Pyrenees had kept this secret since before man roamed the mountains, and now he was sharing it with me.

I brought several lanterns and Pyrenees welcomed me back, opening the door for me once again. My breath caught when I saw what was inside.

There was no war and no genocide. No gods to please or offend. Just a cavern decorated by a few geological time periods. Keats wrote the perfect words for it, though he wrote them for something else: It was a *foster-child of silence and slow time,* filled with columns of slowly accreted stone and fingers of future columns stretching toward one another from the ceiling and the floor.

Small pools of dark water reflected my lamplight, and Pyrenees asked that I avoid them. The water was fine to drink, but there were five undiscovered species living in there. As I moved carefully through the cavern, I discovered that air flowed in from several different holes in the back, all of which were too small to admit a human body. Pyrenees explained that these eventually opened up into caves on the Spanish side, and that's why I was able to breathe. I didn't stay in there for long, just an hour or so, admiring the artistry and the patience it took to create such a space. I thanked Pyrenees effusively for showing me.

Almost eighty years later, I still remembered how to get to Green Man's Retreat as if I had made the trip the day before.

Granuaile and I took lanterns and food up there after we shifted to earth from Tír na nÓg. When we arrived, Pyrenees was ready to do his part for Druidry—that is, move some rocks and dirt around.

Thornbushes don't grow in the absence of sunlight, and there weren't any conveniently close by the cave, as we had found on the slopes of Olympus. We had to descend downhill approximately three football fields before we found one. Pyrenees messed with the slope a little bit, building up a berm on the far side of the thornbush, creating a sort of cradle that would keep us completely concealed from anyone looking up the mountain. In order to see us, someone would have to draw even or approach from above. Oberon would be able to watch all approaches and give us plenty of warning during the day, and we'd take breaks at night and stay in Green Man's Retreat to let the "scent of magic" fade, even though I doubted the Pyrenees would be infested with Bacchants anytime soon. I just wanted to ensure we'd be able to finish this time, and if that meant spending a little less time each day, so be it. I still kept healing my burns around the clock and already looked less frightening.

When we reconnected with Gaia and were ready to continue the binding where we left off, Granuaile said nothing about removing her underwear. She pulled up the fabric high on her hip for as long as it was practicable, and then, when it was necessary, she moved it down on top of the raw wounds without comment. She winced but made no sound.

"Thank you," I said quietly, hoping against all my prior experience that she would understand the wealth of meaning behind the two words. A few minutes passed in silence as I slowly filled in the knotwork, one agonizing stab at a time. When she spoke, long after I expected any response, it startled me a bit.

"You're welcome," she murmured. And that did it. I stopped filtering my magical sight and let myself take a good look at the bonds between us. They were rich and complex and numerous, and somehow, without me tutoring her about what they all meant, Granuaile had discerned their meanings.

I sighed and spoke in low tones. "I owe you an apology, Granuaile—no, fuck hedging and weasel words, okay? I apologize," I said. "I just plain apologize. It's been a long time for me—many normal lifetimes— since I haven't had to pretend to be something I'm not. Once you pass fifty and you still look like you're in your twenties, every moment you spend in another person's sight becomes a performance. You never leave the stage, and people notice when you slip out of character. The last woman I loved who knew I was a Druid was my wife, Tahirah. But she never became a Druid, and so she couldn't see what you're seeing. I've never had to deal with that. And she had no idea of the things I could see."

"You must see so much more than I do," Granuaile

said. Her voice was small, as if she feared I'd stop talking if she raised the volume.

"No. If anything, I think it's the other way around. The sight itself is the same for everyone; it's how you filter and interpret what you see that matters, and it's clear that you have an intuitive knack for interpreting what you see, now that you've had time to get used to it. Otherwise you wouldn't have understood everything I meant when I said 'thank you.'"

"It was more than keeping my pants on," she said. "It was more than just us. It had something to do with the past. You're afraid for some reason."

That startled me. She'd seen even more than I suspected—it was akin to telepathy. Was that all it was, interpreting the bindings of consciousness? But I recovered and said, "Yes. I never got to bind my last apprentice, and I know I've told you that before. It's just that we were interrupted and he didn't survive the interruption. I don't want history to repeat itself."

"And you think a romance would be an interruption."

"Wouldn't it?" I smirked at her. "After twelve years of repression and denial, once we began, when would we stop?"

She chuckled softly. "That's a fair point. Two people who can replenish their strength from the earth and heal the ravages of extended friction? It would be Homeric. Three books of *The Iliad* at least."

I laughed at this, and she dissolved into giggles. I rested my forehead for a moment in the crook of her elbow and enjoyed the release of tension. Then, as we both wound down, I planted a soft kiss high up on her shoulder. She quieted and a question formed in her expression.

"Bear with my fears for a while longer?" I asked. "For your sake and mine?"

"Yes," she said. Despite myself, I almost fell into the

green of her eyes. Then she turned away and added, "Sensei," and I shook myself and continued to bind her to the earth.

A month after that talk, unmolested by gods or men, we were past the merely painful part and into the part where a side dish of excitement came along with the pain. I'd faithfully stabbed every point of Gaia's knotwork all the way up Granuaile's side, past the curve of her breast, up to the top of her shoulder like a soldier's braid, and then it began to fall to the shape-shifting loops around the biceps.

A Druid's animal forms are chosen not by the Druid but rather by Gaia. During the process of the binding, Gaia gradually gets to know the Druid and determines for herself which forms would be most suitable. The first band at the very top of the biceps is always the human shape—necessary so that we can shift back to human form. Below that, the Druid gets a hoofed animal, a land-based predator, a flying form, and an aquatic form. Gaia doesn't say ahead of time what the forms will be, so we both had to wait for the tattoos to take shape before we could tell what Granuaile could shift to.

She asked for updates about every three minutes once I began the second band on her arm.

"Can you tell what it is yet?" she asked.

"No, sorry."

"How about now?"

"Not yet. A little anxious, are we?"

"Maybe a little. Can't you at least guess?"

"You'll have hooves."

"I hate you."

I smiled wryly. "No, you don't."

"No, you're right."

Gradually it became clear, the knots resolving into a shape. "It looks like it's a horse," I said.

"A horse! What kind? An Appaloosa? An Arabian?"

"A fast one."

"Probably a red one. Chestnut coat, you know. Super gorgeous."

"Without doubt," I said, and continued my work as Granuaile's eyes lost focus and she dreamed of running faster than she ever could as a human.

The next day began her predator stripe. It was a particularly dark one, requiring lots of ink and time. "I'm not sure what this is yet, but it's going to be a dark coat," I said, and that kept her guessing for the rest of the day. It wasn't until the day after that I could discern with any certainty what the creature represented.

"Huh. It's a black cat," I said.

"A black cat?" Mild outrage colored her tone.

"A big one. Not a kitty cat. Won't know if you're a leopard or a jaguar until you shift."

"Oh! That's better, then."

"I'll say. It's pretty badass."

"What about a panther?"

"Black panthers are really black leopards. They're not a different species. It's just a recessive gene for melanism and a bizarre reluctance on the part of human beings to say the words *black leopard*."

"Hmm. What an interesting choice."

"Gaia wants you to be dangerous in the dark, I suppose. Your flying tattoo will probably leave room for guessing as well. It's tough to differentiate species from these stylized knots."

"I'm not going to be a mosquito or something like that, am I?"

"No. Druids are usually one of the larger birds. Gaia never puts you very far down the food chain."

Once her flying stripe was finished, I could tell Granuaile would be a raptor of some kind, but whether hawk or falcon or eagle I did not know. She wasn't going to be an owl like me.

Granuaile's aquatic form was probably her weakest; it was a sea lion, and while she would be desperately cute, she wouldn't have the manual dexterity I had as a sea otter. She'd be a far better swimmer, however.

It took another week and a half to finish her forearm, which would allow her to shift planes, and the circle on the back of her hand, which would give her control over her own healing. On the last day in mid-afternoon, she sat up to watch me complete the circle, her hand in mine, doing her best to hold back any noises that would betray how thrilled she was. I was pretty thrilled too; I'd healed fully by then and looked like my old self, with the exception of two months' beard growth.

When I inked the final bit and Gaia's glow faded from my sight and from hers, she looked at me expectantly, beaming with excitement.

"Congratulations, Granuaile MacTiernan," I said. "You are the first new Druid on this earth in more than a thousand years." I grinned at her, relieved that it was finally over, and she laughed with wonder and a good measure of her own relief.

I laughed with her and then watched as a strange demolition took place on her expression, as if someone had struck out the supports of the scaffolding holding up her smile. Her lower lip trembled and she sniffled. "I can't believe it's finally done," she said, examining the back of her right hand and wiping away tears with the heel of her left. "Twelve long years."

"Oh, nonsense. They flew by!" I said.

"Yeah, whatever." She sniffed one final time and wiped her cheeks free of tears. Her grin returned, but this time it was mischievous. "So this means you're not my sensei anymore?"

"That's what it means."

"Right. Well, I've waited long enough." She grabbed me by the back of the neck and pulled me to her mouth. "Come here."

I went there.

Chapter 21

<Okay, for the record, what you're doing is nothing like dogs barking, and I object to the whole bow-chicka-bow-wow meme in principle.>

Oberon, please. This is not the time.

<This is the perfect time! It's the first time you and Granuaile have participated in this bow-chicka-bow-wow behavior.>

It's not meant to mimic dogs barking! It's mocking seventies' funk music heard in pornographic videos, specifically the bass line. May we have some privacy, please?

<What? You want me to go away?>

Well, just don't stare at us! I didn't sit and watch and make comments while you were with Fifi, did I, talking about givin' the dog a bone and such?

<Fine. But human mating habits are stupid.>

Chapter 22

We did stop eventually, but only because Oberon threatened to chew off his leg as the sun set for the third time since we'd begun. <I'm desperately bored of being a watchdog, especially since I have to watch you two be grody together.>

Now, hold on! First, you didn't have to watch, because I specifically suggested that you not do so, and, second, it wasn't grody. It was the stuff Al Green sings about.

<You were the one who told me that proverb thingie: "Grody is in the eye of the beholder.">

No, Oberon, that was beauty.

<Whatever. It works for grody too.>

Nothing could ruin my mood right then, so I laughed and admitted he had a point.

How about a hunt, Oberon? Would that suit you?

My hound put his nose in the air. <That depends. What are we hunting?>

Anything you want. Anywhere you want. Granuaile needs to practice shifting planes and shifting shapes.

<I want to hunt dik-diks.>

All right. Tanzania, here we come!

While Granuaile was now a full Druid, she still needed some coaching and practice on what had been theory until this point. She'd memorized the words and the forms of the knotwork admirably, but because we'd been so . . . busy lately, she had yet to cast anything.

We thanked Pyrenees for his hospitality and help before we shifted to eastern Africa. Granuaile and I both placed our hands on a tethered tree, and I showed her amongst the myriad trees where to shift in Tír na nÓg.

"You go first. We'll be right behind you."

"What if I get lost?"

"You won't. I'm going to follow wherever you go."

She took a deep breath, closed her eyes for a moment, and shifted.

<She's going to be talking to me soon, isn't she?> Oberon said.

Yep. Very soon.

<Well, before our conversation gets put on speakerphone, I want you to know that you're my favorite human.>

Aww, thanks, Oberon—

<Even when you're grody.>

That's . . . very generous of you.

Oberon's nose lifted in the air again, but not for the display of any attitude. His nostrils flared. <Atticus, I smell the dead. Lots of them. Coming this way.>

I frowned at my hound. *Vampires?*

<Unless we missed the zombie apocalypse, I'd say so.>

All directions?

<No, from this side of the mountains.>

So they would be French vampires. Perhaps the vampires from the Iberian Peninsula wouldn't be far behind. After my conversation with Theophilus, I could well imagine that he'd given the command worldwide to hunt us—I certainly hadn't ceased to train my apprentice, so I must assume that his promised pogrom had begun and the world's vampires were sniffing us out.

It probably wouldn't be all that difficult to find me, provided I stayed in one place; my ancient blood smelled different from that of modern humans, and if they'd been told by their mysterious Fae connection that I was binding Granuaile to the earth, they'd know to search the wild places in Europe.

I had no desire to remain and take on an unknown number of vampires, so I shifted to Tír na nÓg and found a relieved Granuaile waiting for us. She did a couple of pogo jumps in the dark. "I did it!"

"Indeed. And now let's go to Tanzania. Lead the way again."

We spent some time finding an appropriate place to shift. We chose some acacia woodlands in Lake Manyara National Park, and then we went ahead as before, with Granuaile going first.

<Are you going to tell her about the vampires?> Oberon asked once she'd shifted.

Soon. I need to think about it a little bit. She has enough to worry about at the moment.

When we reached Tanzania, which was humid and warm and full of animals eating one another, we both had our night vision on. Granuaile was giddy.

"Can I shape-shift now?"

"Wait a moment. Bind with Oberon first."

"Oh! Yeah. Duh! I'm sorry, Oberon, I'm just so excited."

<She's dancing like she has to go to the bathroom.>

"He understands," I told her. "Okay. So look at the connection between Oberon and me in the magical spectrum. You need to bind yourself to him in the same way so that you can hear his thoughts and vice versa."

"Will you be able to hear my thoughts too?"

"No. The only person I know capable of human telepathy is the Morrigan, and she doesn't accomplish it through traditional bindings."

"What if we're both in animal form?" Granuaile asked.

"Do we use Oberon as a go-between to speak to each other?"

"I suppose we could."

<If you want to drive me insane.>

"But we should probably try to keep that to a minimum," I added.

Granuaile nodded. "Poor dog would probably go nuts."

<She's a bit more sensitive than you, Atticus.>

Hey!

<Give me two months to work on her and I bet she'll get me a French poodle.>

Do not take advantage of her generous nature!

<Are you serious? You might as well ask me to stop being a hound.>

Granuaile gave a tiny gasp and her eyes widened. "I heard that! Or the end of it. Why would you want him to stop being a hound?"

<Hello, Clever Girl.>

"Hi, Oberon! It's so nice to finally hear your voice! Is 'Clever Girl' your name for me?"

"He's been calling you that ever since that business with the skinwalkers. Watch out. He's buttering you up for something."

"Is that so?" Her eyebrows asked a question of my hound.

<Ignore the surly Druid. I have no shadowy agenda. I am motivated by food.>

"And tonight you're hungry for really tiny antelopes."

<That's right! But I'll settle for whatever we can catch.>

"Okay. I've never hunted before, so you'll need to give me some tips and forgive me if I screw up, all right?"

<Tonight I will cut you infinite slack.>

"Good. Because my predator form is a giant black cat."

<You're a *cat* person?> Oberon whipped his head around to me. <Atticus, you never said anything about that!>

"It wasn't my choice, Oberon!" Granuaile said. "Gaia chose my predator form. If it had been my choice, I would have been a wolfhound like you and Atticus."

That's true, buddy, I said privately. *She didn't have any say in her animal forms. Besides, what does it matter? She's Granuaile no matter what shape she's in.*

<Well, that's a fair point,> Oberon admitted.

"What is?" Granuaile asked.

<He said you'd still be Clever Girl no matter what your shape is.>

"Oh. That's true. Atticus, maybe we should speak aloud to Oberon whenever we can so we don't have to always ask him for clarification when he answers?"

"Yep. Good idea. I'm used to keeping a lid on it, so it will take me some time to break the habit."

<Let's hunt.>

Granuaile and I disrobed and placed our clothes near the tethered tree. We asked the earth to part and conceal our weapons for us.

"One more thing before you shift," I said. "I have to fix your necklace."

"Oh." Granuaile raised her hand to the cold iron amulet dangling at her throat. "Good call. I would have garroted myself."

"Would you mind terribly if I did this for you? Fix it so that it changes sizes with your shape? I could teach you how, but it would take a while."

"No, go ahead," she said.

"You'll have to shift to every form to do it properly, and I know you've been dying to anyway." I moved around her and unfastened her necklace, noting as I did so how much slack and extra chain there was.

Then I stepped away with it in my hand. "So let's take it from the top. Horse first. Go."

Granuaile spoke the words that would bind her spirit to the form of the horse indelibly tattooed on her arm. She shifted to a beautiful copper-colored chestnut, sometimes called sorrel, with her mane slightly lighter than her coat. Her nostrils flared and she sneezed. I told her what she looked like as I adjusted the necklace around her neck and memorized the size and position. She whinnied and stamped on the ground with her hooves, one leg at a time, no doubt marveling that she had four of them. I crafted the first part of the binding that would allow the necklace to shrink back to human size when she shifted.

"Okay, shift back to human. I know you want to run, but this isn't the best place to do it. There are leopards in the trees here and other hungry things."

Granuaile snorted and shifted back to human form. "Atticus, that was amazing! Four legs! Hooves! Incredible!"

"I know. Check your necklace."

She looked down and saw that the necklace was fastened around her neck exactly as it had been before.

"You rock."

<Don't swell his head. It's already the size of a zeppelin.>

I unfastened the necklace again. "Okay, kitty form."

Granuaile shifted and became a sleek black jaguar. I could tell by the shorter, thicker tail and the wider head. She sneezed a couple of times here too.

"Congratulations. You're a jaguar."

Granuaile's joy at this news elicited an extremely loud roar, startling Oberon and me and the surrounding woods into silence.

<I think every creature near enough to hear that just

pooped,> Oberon said, <and then it went into hiding. Hunting tip number one: Stay silent.>

Granuaile lowered her ears and managed to convey a sense of regret. I took measurements for her necklace and had her shift back to human.

"Sorry, Oberon," she said as soon as she got her voice back. "It's Helen Reddy's fault. It was the whole 'I am woman, hear me roar' thing."

<No problem. You still have infinite slack.>

"All right," I said, retrieving the necklace. "Let's see what kind of bird you are. Fly a bit if you want, but don't keep us waiting long."

Granuaile shifted and I whooped. "You're a peregrine falcon! Fastest bird alive! Fly! Be free!"

With a screech of victory, Granuaile took wing; for a moment it was a majestic scene out of *Animal Planet,* and then it wasn't, as she promptly crashed after an awkward banking maneuver. She tried again, crashed again, and then, on her third attempt, climbed toward the moon so she could dive back down at two hundred miles an hour. When she landed in a sort of sprawling skid and shifted back to human form, she groaned and clutched her stomach.

"Oww. Atticus, I don't feel so good inside."

"It's because you've been shifting back and forth so quickly. When you thumb your nose at the laws of physics like you've been doing, the universe tends to get you back through biology."

"I'm not permanently damaging my spleen or anything, am I?"

"Nope. It'll fade. It's just a pain you can't heal or suppress. How was your flight?"

"*So* awesome. The third one, anyway. I can tell I'm going to enjoy that form a lot."

"I'm sure you will. Last one: sea lion."

She shifted and clapped her flippers together. Oberon chuffed at her, and I chuckled as I adjusted her necklace.

"Okay, now hold still in this form awhile. I'm going to make all the forms and sizes recursive so that you can shift directly from horse to falcon or jaguar to sea lion, and the necklace will change properly along with it." A few minutes and it was done. "Okay, shift to jaguar from this form and we'll hunt."

<About time!> Oberon said.

Granuaile shifted to her jaguar form and I shifted to a wolfhound. We both sneezed. My coat was reddish with a white stripe down my right front leg where my tattoos were; I looked like a slightly different dog, since I was in truth one of the old warhounds of the Irish that eventually were bred to become the deerhounds and wolfhounds of today. It made no difference to Oberon, though; to him I was a wolfhound, part of his pack.

<Okay, now take a really deep breath through the nose,> Oberon said to Granuaile. She did and promptly began to sneeze uncontrollably, more violently than she had upon her initial shift. She even tried to cover her mouth with her paw, which was pretty funny.

<Heh! Never knew the world could be so pungent, did you?> Granuaile managed to find some space between sneezes to growl at him. <Aw, you'll get used to it in a few minutes. Okay, we need you to lead us to some dik-diks without running into any baboons, hippos, crocodiles, or other big cats.>

We failed miserably to find any dik-diks, but Oberon wasn't the least bit disappointed. He was highly amused by the entire trip, because Granuaile kept sneezing and didn't get used to her new sense of smell. She'd always been a bit sensitive to odors; her first exposure to demons had caused her to retch miserably for ten minutes. Once we passed near an impressive pile of rhino feces, she gagged and tried to run away from it, but her gagging turned the normally smooth mechanics of a jaguar into a jerky, trembling dance. Oberon chuffed so hard he fell over and pawed helplessly at the sky.

<You know, I've basically been bored for three months while Granuaile was getting bound, but now I'm good. I feel repaid. Never thought I'd see a jaguar brought to its knees by rhino shit. And it probably dumped that here when she roared.>

Granuaile was still gagging and trying to pull herself away from the smell on the ground, her belly on the grass of the savanna. Then she remembered she had other options and shifted to falcon form. She screeched and took wing, elevating herself above the rank odor of the grassland.

<Aw!> Oberon said. <She says she's finished hunting. Wants to meet us back at the tree where you left your stuff.>

All right, we'd better go. We can't keep laughing at her expense.

<But it's fun!>

We'll go to Tír na nÓg and visit Goibhniu. I'll bet he has a snack for you.

We began trotting back to the tethered tree as Granuaile circled high above.

<Does Goibhniu have tasty magical appetizers in his pub? Like, real buffalo wings instead of chicken wings made in Buffalo?>

No, he doesn't have anything like that. He's one of the Three Craftsmen though.

<Sounds like there's a story there!>

Not much of one. They're all sons of Brighid, with skills in various arts.

<Uh-oh. Do they have their mother's temper?>

No, they tend to be jolly lads. Goibhniu is into smithing and brewing. Luchta is a master woodworker. And Creidhne is a master with gold, bronze, or brass.

<So there's no damsel with a tragic history in there? With a name like the Three Craftsmen, they each should build something awesome for a beautiful princess to try to win her favor and then two of them would die.>

You must be thinking of stories from other cultures. Irish women tend to kick ass and do whatever they want. For exhibits A, B, and C, I give you the Morrigan, Brighid, and Flidais.

<Fair enough. So who's the god of cooking among the Tuatha Dé Danann?>

I don't think there is one.

<So the ancient Irish had a god of brewing but not cooking?>

We had our priorities straight.

<Well, then, how do you know Goibhniu will have a snack for me?>

He always has something lying about—pretzels or something to anchor the porter. Allows you to drink more, see. Priorities.

<I'd be more reassured if the priorities had something to do with meat.>

We padded in silence for a while after that, which gave me time to consider the implications of vampires converging on us in the Pyrenees.

Since I hadn't been actively hunted by vampires, ever, this had to be a result of an order issued by Theophilus. That meant I'd need to eliminate him if I wanted it to stop—that was much more logical than attempting to eliminate all vampires. But even then, his successor might issue the same order. Vampires weren't renowned to be live-and-let-live types. To earn myself a modicum of safety, I'd have to make sure Leif Helgarson was the most powerful vampire in the world.

And as soon as I thought of it, I knew that was his plan.

By pretending to act in my interest, he was serving

his. Just as he did back in Arizona, he was manipulating events so that I'd eliminate his rivals and elevate him to the position he desired. And he knew that if he got to that position, he could safely ignore me, unlike every other vampire in the world. The aid he gave us in Thessalonika—tearing apart those last three dark elves—wasn't an act of generosity or concern but pure selfishness. I was his ticket to the top, so he couldn't let me die.

I could hate him all I wanted for it; he still saw that I needed him and was going to take full advantage of it. And he knew that I wouldn't do anything to him as long as there was a chance he could help me eliminate Theophilus.

Granuaile was fairly incensed when she landed and shifted back to human. I shifted as well and called up our weapons from their hiding places in the earth.

"That wasn't very nice, Oberon," she said, yanking on her clothes with irritation.

<I'm sorry, I didn't know it was going to be that bad.>

"You hoped it would be."

<Actually, that was beyond my wildest hopes.>

"What!"

Auggh! That didn't help, buddy.

<I mean I didn't realize how strong your sense of smell would be as a jaguar. I was thinking you'd sneeze a couple of times and that would be it. The rest of it was funny, but it was never my intention to make you suffer or anything. I'm sorry.>

That's better.

"Well, I clearly need to adjust if I'm going to be worth a damn in that shape. I'm sure I disgraced every jaguar on the planet today and deserved to be laughed at. But Gaia chose that form for me, so I need to deal with it if I'm going to serve the earth well. Promise you'll let me try again later?"

<Sure!>

Granuaile petted him and looked over at me. "Where to now?"

"Well, if I'm right, there's a sort of graduation present waiting for you in Tír na nÓg."

"An envelope filled with cash and a card signed by all the Tuatha Dé Danann?"

I snorted. "No, something a bit more epic."

Chapter 23

The proud grin on Goibhniu's face could have lit up Broadway. He placed a work of art into Granuaile's outstretched hands and said, "This is Scáthmhaide."

Granuaile admired it in silence for a few moments, her mouth open and her eyes wide in shock. It was a beautifully wrought staff of oak, carved with knotwork beyond my ken.

Luchta, watching her over Goibhniu's shoulder, asked, "Why doesn't she say anything?"

"Silence is the perfectest herald of joy," I said.

<Perfectest? Can I get a ruling on this?>

I was quoting Shakespeare, Oberon; therefore, it's allowed.

<That guy gets away with everything! Too bad he didn't live long enough to enjoy it. He'd go up to people and say, "You look like your father, and he had a face like a poxy tit! I'm Shakespeare, so that's allowed.">

A giggle blurted out of Granuaile before she could hold it in, and she blushed.

"Sorry. I was laughing at something the hound said."

Goibhniu and Luchta nodded in understanding.

"It's wonderful," she added, and it was. Flush with the wood, the Celtic bindings for strength and speed were carved and inlaid with iron on one end and with silver on the other. The metal was not raised in a ridge or nestled in a valley; it would contact the target at the same time as the wood around it. In this way the craftsmen had created a weapon that would be lethal to Fae, Bacchants, and werewolves, and the bindings meant that Granuaile would enjoy enhanced strength and reflexes while wielding it—even when separated from the earth for a time. It functioned much like my bear charm did: It stored up magic while Granuaile was in contact with the earth and then shared it when she wasn't.

"Unbreakable, o' course," Luchta said. "And waterproof."

"The iron won't rust and the silver won't tarnish," Goibhniu added.

"Amazing," Granuaile said. "But what are all these bindings here along the length of the staff? Atticus, do you recognize them?"

"That's actually Flidais's work," Luchta explained. "Or, rather, it's my work but her bindings. They're the reason for the name: Scáthmhaide means 'shadow staff' in modern Irish. Say the proper words and it'll turn ye invisible. True invisibility, now, not camouflage. There's some fine print, but I don't know it all. I just carved it according to instructions. You'd best talk to Flidais about it."

Granuaile was stunned. "Flidais did this for me?" The craftsmen nodded. "Why?"

"Wish I knew the answer to that meself," Goibhniu said. "She hasn't taught that binding to anyone else, ye know."

"Aye, and everyone from Brighid to brownies a'beggin' fer it," Luchta said.

"But now you know it, right?" Granuaile pointed to the knots.

"Nope. She's got all kinds o' stuff going on there. I don't know which part of it is invisibility and which is pure decoration. I imagine it all accomplishes something, but these aren't standard bindings. They're unique. Ye have something truly special there."

Granuaile remembered not to thank them directly. "You do me great honor. I will do my best to live up to it."

"Attagirl," Luchta said.

"Shall we have a drink to celebrate?" Goibhniu asked. "I happened to bring a few bottles along."

We were at Luchta's studio, one of the most pleasant work spaces I have ever visited: sawdust on the floor, milled wood stacked against one wall along with shelves of burls and knots and branches, and polished finished pieces resting against another. We were near the workbenches, where lathes and chisels and peelers awaited the attention of Luchta's expert hands. The smells of pine and cedar and aged oak filled the space, and these were much more agreeable to everyone's nose than rhino shit.

We had made a brief stop at Manannan Mac Lir's estate to clean up and get a fresh set of clothes. We looked more old-fashioned Irish now than modern American, wearing tunics and pants in his blue-gray color palette. Manannan gave Granuaile a silver belt of cockleshells and sea horses as a sort of graduation gift and made much ado about the strength of her animal forms. Fand gave her some silvery hair-clip thingies and some cookies that may have been magical. Oberon and I got ignored; they didn't remember I was there until I said we had to get going to Luchta's.

Granuaile had her hair all brushed out and shining with silver bits, and I wasn't the only person at Luchta's shop to think she looked like a goddess. A large shadow darkened the doorway and a deep voice called, "Flidais! You are even more fetching than usual today!"

Granuaile turned toward the voice and discovered Ogma there, who blanched once he realized his mistake.

"Oh! I beg your pardon," he said, a flush coloring his cheeks. "I meant no offense."

"No offense taken, sir," Granuaile said, casting her eyes sideways at me with a tiny smirk. "There are worse fates than to be mistaken for a renowned beauty."

Ogma smiled. "I see you are now bound to the earth. Congratulations. And you have a new weapon—congratulations on that also. Are you anxious to try it out?"

"I am, actually," Granuaile replied, casting an admiring glance at Scáthmhaide.

"Shall we have a friendly sparring match, then?"

"How friendly?"

"Say, two falls out of three. Winner takes clothing."

Granuaile raised an eyebrow and replied, "Done," before I could counsel her not to. Ogma was a famed champion of the Tuatha Dé Danann, brother to the Dagda, half-brother to Lugh, and grandfather of the Three Craftsmen. He used to take care of the king's problems; the rumors of his demise in some tales were greatly exaggerated. He was too much of a badass to die. Nuada Silver-Hand, the old king of the Tuatha Dé Danann, used to point at this unbeatable monster or that unstoppable atrocity and tell Ogma to wreck it, and it would be wrecked. One day he said, damn it, Ogma, the Irish need a writing system, and Ogma came up with Ogham script. Granuaile probably knew all this, however, and had decided to accept anyway. The time for me to offer unsolicited advice was over.

Ogma, again dressed only in a kilt, muscles rippling with every movement, asked Luchta if he could borrow a staff. He was much taller than anyone, and his reach far exceeded Granuaile's. Granuaile moved to the far side of the workshop, choosing her spot in the sawdust. She twirled it about experimentally, getting used to its weight and length. These twirls gradually grew faster until the staff blurred like a propeller blade.

Ogma stepped through some of his own warm-up exercises, twirling his staff in one hand at such speeds that Granuaile's hair was blown back a bit. He wasn't one to be psyched out.

Well, not with words, anyway.

As part of Granuaile's training in martial arts, I taught her to take advantage of men's weaknesses prior to the first strike.

If her opponent was a patriarchal, misogynist asshole, she could taunt him into a rash attack by the simple expedient of calling him a bitch; the same man could be set off his guard by feigned displays of fear.

Ogma wasn't that type, and indeed it would have been difficult to find any of that sort amongst the Tuatha Dé Danann, who had comfortably accepted Brighid's dominance for centuries.

If her opponent was a younger, inexperienced man or perhaps unattractive, loud speculation about the diminutive size of his penis would take him out of the cool, quiet place required for martial discipline.

Ogma wasn't that guy either. Ogma was the third kind of guy, like me, who would find Granuaile's skill not uppity or challenging but rather madly attractive.

As long as Ogma didn't check her out in the magical spectrum and discover that Granuaile and I were bound together rather tightly, some part of his brain—perhaps a large part—would fantasize about seducing her, and he wouldn't want to hurt her because of it. Granuaile's job was to make him think he had a chance.

So she smiled at him. She complimented him on his earrings, and then on his six-pack, and stared pointedly at his kilt while she waited for him to respond.

"Thank you," he said, smiling.

"Begin," Granuaile replied, and then she spun and

leapt twice to add gravity and centrifugal force to her first blow, aimed at his head. It was an aggressive attack—perhaps too aggressive. Ogma met it with his staff held crosswise, and, once Scáthmhaide rebounded, he extended his arms to knock it back again, preventing a graceful redirection. She was on the defensive now and off balance. Ogma took long strides, lunging with his staff and forcing Granuaile into a series of desperate parries.

Manannan Mac Lir's instruction about the political situation in Tír na nÓg burst through the door of my frontal lobe and plopped itself down on the couch. Ogma was definitely on Brighid's side, and if he, however erroneously, thought Granuaile was in the Morrigan's camp, this friendly sparring match might not be so friendly. Could Ogma be behind the attacks on us? He certainly had the connections to pursue us if he wished.

I almost dismissed the thought, because it didn't jibe with the perfectly civil and generous behavior of his grandsons, Luchta and Goibhniu—if anyone was on Brighid's side, it was them, and yet they'd been nothing but kind to us.

Still, Ogma could have his own agenda, independent of theirs. There was no monolithic thought police in Tír na nÓg, and nothing was what it seemed. Even combat.

Granuaile anticipated a strike and caught it as it was still coming up; she had the leverage and should have been able to force Ogma's staff down, since she was already over the top. Instead, Ogma's upswing halted and held. He was too strong to be driven down, despite his disadvantage. She lifted and whipped her staff to whack at his head, when the smarter move would have been to shift down and sweep at his legs; he was pretty firmly set, however, his balance impeccable, so perhaps the wild strike at his head was the slightly wiser move to rattle him—it would certainly have rattled him had it connected. However, Ogma leaned back and turned his cheek, avoiding the blow, while extending his arms and striking down with his staff. It cracked painfully against Granuaile's kneecap—it numbed her for a second—and that was all Ogma needed. He pushed, she was off balance and couldn't keep up with the flurry of strikes he unleashed, and he was able to sneak past her guard and buckle her knees from behind.

She knew she was going down and shouted, "Damn it!" as she fell.

"Ha! Excellent." Ogma grinned. "You have been well trained." He shot out his hand to help her up and Granuaile glowered at him. I smiled, recognizing that expression. Oberon recognized it too.

<Oh, now he's done it. Did you see that, Atticus? He's doomed. There's an anvil falling from the sky to crush him, and he has no clue.>

Yes, I saw it, I said, *but careful what you say here. Remember, people can hear you.* Luchta and Goibhniu had cast a couple of amused glances at Oberon when he'd spoken up, but thankfully Ogma hadn't been tuning in.

I'm not sure if Ogma's patronizing tone had been intentional or not—whether he had meant to goad her, in other words—but, regardless, Granuaile was well and truly goaded. She had a fascinating tendency to access another level of ability when she was angry—not rage-fueled barbarism but rather a hyperawareness and clarity that one needs for combat. I had tried to make her access it without the emotion, because the very peak of her abilities should not be dependent on such, but I'd failed miserably. Emotion could motivate her like nothing else; her long-simmering anger at her stepfather had pushed her to become a Druid in the first place.

She was squaring off for round two when Flidais entered the shop. She had abandoned her court apparel and returned to the greens and browns of her leathers.

"What is this?" she asked. "A contest?"

"A friendly one," Ogma answered. Granuaile did not affirm this. Perun lumbered in behind Flidais. He looked pleasantly exhausted, and he had found a tailor somewhere to fashion him a new set of clothes. Apparently Perun had given instructions that his abundant chest hair should be displayed to best advantage, for it was, bursting forth in coppery curls from a deeply cut V-neck tunic of walnut brown.

"Contest is good," he said. "I like to see." He sauntered in my general direction, pulling out a flask of vodka from his belt as he did so.

Flidais raised a hand. "A moment, if you will, Ogma? Our newest Druid is likely unfamiliar with how her weapon works."

"She is familiar," he assured her. "She is quite skilled." He smiled again, and Granuaile scowled. She wasn't trying to flirt with him anymore.

<He's making it worse.>

I know. It's great.

"You won't give her any unfair advantage?" Ogma said. "My staff has no bindings. It's just wood."

This drew a few chuckles, and Flidais elicited a few more when she said, "We know, Ogma."

Flidais reassured Ogma that Granuaile wouldn't turn invisible or anything like that and it would just be a moment, and he relaxed.

Seeing Flidais speak in hushed tones to Granuaile, however, I tensed up.

Flidais was most definitely on Brighid's side of politics. If anything, she was much more Brighid's right hand than Ogma or anyone else. I could never forget that when Aenghus Óg was out to get me, it was Flidais who kidnapped Oberon to force me to confront the god of love directly. She had done so at Brighid's command.

She was also the one who had convinced me to accept the exploded Lord Grundlebeard theory.

And, I realized with a chill, she might also be the one speaking to vampires.

Two events, months apart, that I had not connected until now: Flidais leaping out of my bed, ready to fight because I "consorted" with a vampire named Leif Helgarson; and then Leif Helgarson, on a cold stretch of Siberian tundra, telling me that it was Flidais who had suggested to him centuries ago that he wait for me in some desert, and eventually I would flee there in my attempt to hide from Aenghus Óg and the Fae.

One of them had lied to me about knowing the other. On the one hand, it was far more likely that Flidais would unbind a vampire on sight than give him advice on how to find the world's last Druid, but, then again, if Flidais was truly on speaking terms with vampires, she might do much to hide the fact. She might even give my apprentice an enchanted weapon with bindings no one else could properly read.

That made me wonder. What else was carved into the grain of Granuaile's staff besides a spell for invisibility? Was there a way to trace her, perhaps? A dinner bell for vampires? I know it is rude to question gifts, but this might be of the Trojan horse variety. Even if it were legit, invisibility would not be the devastating advantage that it would be against humans. Vampires could use their other senses to track her movements reliably.

Conspiracies are fun, I've noticed, only when you're the one conspiring. Or if you're one of those guys who live in trailers and believe the government is hiding aliens—they must have fun fantasizing about how badly the nation is being deceived. But to know, for certain, that you are the target of a conspiracy—that's not entertaining. It's a recipe for acid reflux.

I need a TUMS.

<That's not how you spell relief, Atticus.>

It was high time that I did some conspiring of my own. I called to Goibhniu and asked if we could have a quick word. The brewer grinned in good spirits and offered one of those greetings where you grip forearms instead of hands.

"What's on your mind, most ancient Druid?"

"Can you make one of those cone-of-silence thingies so we can't be overheard?" I asked. "I never quite learned that trick."

"Sure," Goibhniu said. "You kind of have to learn it if you're going to have a serious talk in Tír na nÓg. Faeries everywhere." He mumbled a few words in Old Irish and rolled his eyes up and it was done. It was less graceful than the way Manannan had done it, and I didn't quite catch all the words. "There," he said. "I'll teach it to you later if you like."

"Thanks. What's the coin of the realm in Tír na nÓg these days?"

"Gold and silver are still acceptable everywhere."

"Excellent. I was wondering if you had any pods of yewmen frequenting your pub?"

"Yewmen?" Goibhniu's affable expression disappeared. "Who are you wanting to kill, Atticus?"

I shrugged. "No one important here. Just some vampires on earth."

Goibhniu frowned. "That battle was fought long ago, Atticus, and the Druids lost."

"I didn't lose. I just took a very long time-out. The vampires are after me now. Granuaile too. I'm not going to sit back and let them call all the shots this time. I have resources now—the Fae have resources—and we should use them."

Goibhniu considered this and nodded once. "All right, but why yewmen?"

"Vampires can't sense them. No heartbeats. No

blood. But the yewmen do have magical sight, so they can see a vampire's aura and figure out where to stick them, pun intended. They're made of wood, so, duh, a quick branch through the chest and we're done. Cut off the head, bring it to you for bounty, keep a tab running, I'll pay monthly."

"Whoa—bring the heads to me? And a tab?"

"Why not?"

"Because I don't want to be involved when the vampires start wondering who's offing them. They can reach us here, you know. They have contacts, and they can hire yewmen or anyone else."

"Do you know who their contacts are?"

"No."

"Well, I'm sure you have contacts too and can conduct business as cleverly as they can. Don't you have a barfly who conducts such shady doings anyway?"

"Yes," he admitted.

"Employ him, then."

Goibhniu shook his head. "You're asking me to start a war."

"No, it's already started. I'm asking you to help me win it. And honestly it doesn't have to be yewmen only. It could be a standing bounty for anyone seeking fortune. Let the vampires relearn what it feels like to be hunted again. They have had their own way for far too long."

"Any vampire is okay?"

"Yes. As long as it's from Italy. Start with Rome and spread out from there. Follow the path of the Roman conquest, in fact. That will take out the oldest vampires first, and the hunting will get easier as you go." Theophilus was in Greece presently, but so was Leif. I didn't quite want him dead yet, in case he proved useful. The world's vampires marched to orders from Rome, however, and it was time to hit them where it would hurt most. Theophilus would probably have to move to Italy to take over personally if the yewmen were successful.

"How do we know a vampire's head is from Italy?" Goibhniu asked.

"Have them document the proceedings with a cell phone camera equipped with GPS."

"You know they'll just make new vampires to replace the ones they lost."

"I know. But they'll be younger, weaker, stupider, and unclear on why Druids should be feared and hunted if it's a bunch of wee faeries killing them."

Goibhniu's face split in a wide grin, and he laughed. "It's been a merry few months around here now that you're back. No one could call you tedious."

We spoke for a few moments more on bounties and such, and during this time Flidais completed her instructions to Granuaile. I was well pleased and looking forward to the results of my little chat with Goibhniu; when Leif had supposedly died after the Thor business, the news caused vampires from all over the world to fight one another for the right to rule a piece of his territory. Freeing up territory in Rome itself would cause the world's vampires to flail like Muppets in their eagerness to be the next bloodsuckers in chief; and in their wakes, other, smaller power vacuums would open up and consume even more of them. Hunting two Druids would cease to be important. Mwah-ha-ha-ha.

When Ogma and Granuaile set themselves for the second round, I could tell she would win it by following her eyes. She was watching her opponent. She would play the defensive, letting him commit, and then she'd counterattack—decisively. I'd been on the receiving end of it too many times to count. Ogma was watching his opponent as well, but in the wrong way. He was admiring Granuaile's legs and the curve of her breasts, already anticipating what he'd see once he won her clothes. An arrogance had crept into his manner, an overconfidence, and he didn't see that the second round would be much different from the first.

Once it began, Ogma was on the ground in less than thirty seconds, much to the astonishment of everyone but Oberon and me. Granuaile thrust out her hand in his face and said, "Excellent! You are well trained."

The workshop quieted. To have a new Druid, scarcely into her third decade, speak to a god centuries old like that? Throwing his own words back at him? I was so proud.

Ogma, to his credit, did not take offense. He rose without her help, dusted off his kilt, and grinned ruefully. "Okay, I deserved that."

He should have apologized. It would have cooled her down and she would have lost focus; she'd pay attention to the fact that she was sparring with a legend and was being watched by gods. But his admission of guilt without apology kept her focused.

The third round was intense and much longer. It was an outstanding showcase of skill from both combatants. Granuaile wanted to win, and against almost any other opponent she would have, but Ogma was roused now, and he did, after all, have centuries more experience than she.

When Ogma finally got through her defense and dropped her for the second time, he was clearly sweating and his face showed relief. The applause was loud— thunderous, even, thanks to Perun clapping next to me.

"I am liking your peoples more all the times," he bellowed over the noise.

Once it had died down, Ogma leered at Granuaile and said, "Your clothes, please."

"Certainly," she replied, then disappeared.

A few confused noises filled the workshop, then laughter, as everyone realized that she had activated the enchantment on her staff.

"Atticus, will you come hold this for me, please?" her voice called.

"Sure." I walked toward the place where she had been standing and stopped when her hand grabbed my shirt. She pulled me close and then guided my hand to Scáthmhaide. Once I touched it, I could see her.

"I'm invisible to them right now, aren't I?" she whispered.

"Yes. We both should be now."

"Let me try something. Hold this against my belly." She raised her tunic, I touched her belly with the staff, and she let go with her hands. "How about now?"

I checked with Oberon. *Can you see us?*

<Nope.>

"Okay," Granuaile said. "Keep it there." She quickly took off her clothes, always keeping contact with the staff, and tossed her tunic and pants toward Ogma. They became visible as soon as they left her hand. There was much laughter at Ogma's disappointed face. I saw that this could not have turned out any better; though Ogma had technically won, Granuaile had lost nothing and had, in a sense, outmaneuvered him. And no one would patronize her after this.

A familiar faery in Brighid's livery appeared in the doorway to the shop and cleared his throat pompously. Recognizing the herald, everyone stopped and stared at him. His voice, like a foghorn, projected certain doom.

"All of the Tuatha Dé Danann are called to the Court immediately to hear a message from the Olympians."

Luchta frowned at the herald. "From the Greeks or the Romans?"

"From both. Hermes and Mercury have come together to deliver the message."

Granuaile tilted her head toward me and whispered, "How did they get here?"

"As messengers of the gods, they have the ability to walk the planes like we do," I explained. "Just not in the same way."

"Any idea what they're on about?" Goibhniu asked the herald.

The faery coughed softly into his fist and paused, as if considering his answer deeply. "While I cannot say for sure, my speculation would be that it has something to do with the Iron Druid."

Several heads started to turn in our direction, but they caught themselves and none spoke a word about our silent, invisible presence.

"We'd best go, then," Ogma said. Everyone nodded and murmured agreement and began to file out of the shop. Granuaile and I followed; we asked Oberon to wait for us in the workshop. I gave her my tunic so that she'd be covered up in case we were forced to show ourselves, but I fully intended to behave like the proverbial fly on the wall—the one that always gets away and never gets swatted.

When we got to the great wide meadow of the Fae Court, Granuaile found it interesting that there were far fewer Fae assembled to witness the audience of the Olympians. There were hardly any, in fact, aside from the assembled lords, and even they were not fully in attendance. All the Tuatha Dé Danann appeared, however, shifting themselves on short notice to the Court on Brighid's command.

The Olympian messenger gods floated three feet above the ground, perhaps ten yards from the small hillock on which sat Brighid's throne. She was dressed far more formally for this occasion, draped in flat silken panels of royal and powder blue. She affected boredom as she waited for the Tuatha Dé Danann to assemble. When all seats had been filled, she turned her head to the gods in a dilatory manner and said, "All are present. You may proceed, sirs."

There are teachers out there who like to tell their students that the only difference between the Greek and the Roman gods is their names. This is patently untrue. Apart from the wings on their ankles, Hermes and Mercury have very little in common—and the same is true of every Olympian pair. The Greeks and Romans were different people, after all, and imagined their gods differently.

Hermes lacked body fat to a rather indiscreet degree, and I desperately wanted to lob a cheeseburger in his general direction to see if he'd let it fall. There were ribs and veins showing, and some of the veins also appeared to have whipcord muscles of their own. His eyes were red-rimmed, haunted, and supported by baggage that wouldn't fit easily in the overhead bin, but they were fixed professionally on Brighid's defenses, unless I missed my guess. If the shit went down, Hermes would be ready. His hands were large, with square-cut, chunky fingers, like those in Frank Miller sketches, and his bare feet were also oversize. He had the skin tone of a mime and spoke like one too—that is, he let Mercury do all the talking. He held his caduceus in his right hand as if ready to brain someone with it.

Mercury looked as if he'd just been shat out of a Milanese day spa. In modern popular imagination, his was the silhouette that delivered flowers quickly to your loved ones. Bronzed skin and whitened teeth made me suspect abnormally high levels of asshattery. His feet were sandaled, and he steepled his fingers together in front of his stomach before he spoke.

"The gods Pan and Faunus and the goddesses Artemis and Diana demand the immediate return of the dryads kidnapped from the slopes of Mount Olympus."

Holy shit. I'd thought that Brighid's herald was pompous, but Mercury was schooling him on that with every word. Oil and contempt practically dripped from his lips.

"If they are harmed," Mercury continued, "the life of the Druid Siodhachan Ó Suileabháin is forfeit, and blood price will be required of the Tuatha Dé Danann for not controlling him. His life may be forfeit anyway," he added, "because the god Bacchus has sworn to slay him."

"Your gods and goddesses address their suit to the wrong party," Brighid replied, "for we are not the Druid of whom you speak. Nor do we have any control over him. He is not our subject and we cannot be held responsible for his actions." She turned to her assembled kin. "Do any of you have any knowledge whatsoever about these kidnapped dryads?"

She let the silence linger for the space of ten heartbeats, then regarded the Olympians again. "There is your answer."

"We hear you and will deliver your message even so to Olympus."

"Before you go, a question," Brighid said. "In case I am able to contact the Druid, is there any guarantee of his safe conduct if he returns the dryads?"

The Olympians exchanged a glance, and Hermes gave Mercury the barest of nods.

"He will be safe from all save Bacchus if he returns the dryads within the night," Mercury said.

Hermes finally chose to speak after all. His voice was a melodic aria struggling to break free of base speech, as if someone had shoved a wee creative genius into a gray suit and a grayer cubicle and told him to just fucking *stay there* forever. It was odd how the impeccably groomed Mercury could say "hello" and inspire visions of a quick strike to the sack, yet when Hermes spoke—

the much rougher-looking of the pair—it was beautiful and sad and I wanted to buy him a beer so I could help him weep into it. "All the members of my pantheon are willing to forgive the trespass if the dryads are returned immediately," he said.

Well, that was it for me. I wanted to return the dryads immediately. So did Granuaile.

"Atticus, let's go," she whispered.

"Yeah, let's."

We turned our backs on the Court as Brighid exchanged farewells with the Olympian messengers. We had a mission.

"The faster we do this, the better off we'll be," I said to Granuaile once we were out of earshot. "While all the Olympians wait around for Hermes and Mercury to talk things over and send messages back and forth, we'll get this done."

"I'm all for it," Granuaile said, "but I'd like a fresh set of clothes first."

"Oh. Right."

We returned first to the workshop to pick up Oberon, then we shifted to a safe house of sorts in the Uncompahgre Wilderness in southwestern Colorado. It was a cabin located near the old Camp Bird Mine, some ten miles west of Ouray, and I had bought it under an alias six years ago to conduct some business with Odin. Surrounded by a forest tethered to Tír na nÓg, it was an ideal rendezvous point and a place to store changes of clothes for times like these. It was also out of Coyote's territory and a safe place for Oberon to spend some time by himself if necessary, since it was equipped with a large doggie door and plenty of food and water—not to mention squirrels and deer galore.

Granuaile and I changed clothes quickly and told Oberon he'd be on his own for a while.

<How long?>

"Hopefully only a few hours. Less than three months. You are terrible with time anyway. Now, listen, you are absolutely forbidden to go into any mine shafts around here. They're off limits, you understand? If a squirrel runs inside, you count him dead; you don't go after him. And you don't get to pretend that they are Batcaves either. You can't save Gotham from here."

<Okay. I remember the rules.>

"Have fun hunting, buddy." I petted him and he wagged his tail. Granuaile finished strapping on a replacement set of throwing knives and kissed his head.

"I hope we'll get to go hunting with you soon," she said.

<Yeah! Maybe we'll try for caribou. There are fewer pungent aromas in the tundra.>

"That's very considerate of you," she said, smiling.

<Hey, will you put in disc two of *The Fellowship of the Ring* before you go? I need a refresher on the mines of Moria.>

Chapter 24

We shifted to the first dryad's tree in Olympus and cautiously scanned the area. Seeing no one, I opened a portal to the island of slow time, with the admonition to Granuaile that she should watch. "I'm going to have you do the later ones."

"Okay. Why don't we just open portals wherever we want?"

"You can't open them at all if you're not in an area that's been bound to Tír na nÓg. But we avoid them because it takes longer to open one and uses far more energy. We shift via trees because it requires the least amount of the earth's power. That's why Aenghus Óg's huge portal to hell drained the earth and killed it."

Parts of the dead land around Tony Cabin were functioning on a basic level again, but large patches were still dead, and it had taken us years of toil to bring it back even to weak levels of life.

The first dryad we'd separated from her tree stared uncertainly back at us, suspended in midair a few feet above the ground of the Time Island. Her arms were splayed out toward us in a final, desperate bid to grab hold of this plane. I held on to Granuaile's left hand and told her to reach through and pull the dryad back with her other.

"I don't need some kind of long pole or something?"

"No, as long as half of you stays here, you won't get pulled into that timestream."

"What about pulling her out, though? Won't that cause whiplash or something?"

"No, in that timestream she's only begun to fall. Gravity just figured out she's in the air above the island, but she hasn't even had a full second to fall five yards or so. Look at her. She's hardly moved, and it's been almost two months for us. So yanking her back right now would be no worse than one of those tango moves where you extend your arm and then pull your partner back to you. Grab her gently. Remember, to her we're a blur in the sky."

"All right." Granuaile reached through the portal and took her time wrapping her fingers around the dryad's wrist. "Ready?"

"Yep. Do it."

Granuaile pulled, the dryad found her feet on solid ground again, then reeled as soon as Granuaile let her go. The dryad blinked and sat down heavily underneath the canopy of her tree.

"What happened? My head spins."

"Sorry about that," I said in Latin.

She peered at me and her eyes widened. "Your face. Wasn't half of it scarred and melted a moment ago?" She noticed that Granuaile looked different too. "And now you have strange markings on your arm. What magic is this?"

"It is the magic of the earth and of the Fae," I replied. "I apologize for the inconvenience and whatever pain you might have felt. I was forced to use you to get the attention of Faunus. He wasn't allowing me to bind my apprentice to the earth, you see. But all is well now, or will be shortly. I'm going to mend the broken bonds with your tree."

"How?"

"The same way I unbound them, except backward. Are you capable of seeing your bond with the tree?"

"No. I just feel it."

"Please tell me if you feel better, then. This shouldn't take long."

Granuaile offered to help the dryad to her feet, but she shied away. "No, thank you," the dryad said. "I'll manage by myself."

"Okay," Granuaile said, backing away with a friendly grin on her face. She continued chatting and apologizing while I turned my attention to the magical spectrum and sought to restore order to the small bit of chaos I'd brought to the tree's binding with the dryad. It took a little longer than unbinding, for creation is always more difficult than destruction, but it wasn't like visiting a modern doctor's office either, where patients must learn the true meaning of patience before they can get treated. The dryad admitted she felt whole again once I was finished.

"Excellent. Again, I'm sorry for the necessity, but I'm very relieved we could restore you completely. We have to perform this same operation on five more of your sisters and need the time and space to do it in. If you would refrain from calling to Faunus or any other god for two hours, that would give us sufficient time to rebind all dryads to their trees without interference, and then, when everyone's safe, you can call to Faunus and receive an enthusiastic welcome back, which will no doubt include several erotic terms for which the Latin language is still renowned today."

The dryad's jaw dropped. Granuaile flashed her a Spock salute and wished her long life and prosperity.

"Who are you?" the dryad asked. "I'm so confused."

"I've had many names throughout the centuries," I began, but Granuaile was reminded of one in particular and jumped in.

"In Toronto they called him Nigel," she said.

"Ugh. You never want to be Nigel in Toronto," I told her. "Trust me."

"I don't know where Toronto is," the dryad said, looking lost.

"It's a place across the ocean with a great film festival and a bad hockey team," I explained, but she still looked bewildered. "Their ticket prices are sky-high, but they haven't hefted the Stanley Cup since 1967. I know there's always next year, but, *damn*, you know?" None of this helped. The dryad looked ready to go fetal, so I thought it best to leave her alone and move on to the next one. I gestured to Granuaile, and we shifted to the next dryad's tree and repeated the procedure. We tried to keep the chitchat to a minimum but were unfailingly polite and very apologetic. I let Granuaile do the last two, portal and all. She left the portals open while she was binding the dryads back to their trees, but I'd speak to her about it later.

The last dryad was a bit more miffed at us than the others, who had been more bemused than anything else. She wasn't afraid of us, and neither was she above threatening us a little bit. After I finished mending her bond to her oak, she said, "You'll suffer as no mortal has suffered in an age."

"But I fixed everything," I protested.

"It was arrogance from beginning to end," she replied, slipping into her tree. Her voice changed once she was inside. "Suffer," she said, or rather the leaves seemed to say it, no more than a husky whisper and rustle on a windless day.

I looked at Granuaile and she shrugged. "It's done," she said in English.

"I don't know. That was weird. You'd think that she'd be nicer to us, since I've already demonstrated that I can destroy her bond to the oak."

"It's because she has friends here," a voice said from behind.

Granuaile and I turned around and saw no one at first. But then a large group of women draped in white shimmered into view, with a single smirking figure in the center of them.

"I swore I'd tear you apart with my own hands, Druid," Bacchus said. "I may be mad, but I tend to remember things like that."

Chapter 25

Usually I treasure new experiences. I still remember my very first Sno-Cone, for example: It was Highly Artificial Raspberry and turned my tongue blue. My first time in Madagascar was awesome because lemurs are kind of funny; they throw fruit at the back of your head when you're not looking and then point at one another when you turn around. But there are times when you don't appreciate novelty, such as when you're trying to run for your life, and this was one of those times: I couldn't shift away from Bacchus, because the damn tree slapped my hand away every time I tried to touch it, thanks to the dryad inside. New experience, but not cool.

"Should we go invisible?" Granuaile asked.

"No, they'd smell the magic and chase us."

"The man is mine," Bacchus said to his horde of maenads, "but you can entertain yourselves with the woman." And then he charged me with all the confidence of the truly immortal.

"Don't grapple," I advised Granuaile quickly. "Keep them at a distance. They're stronger than you are but not as quick."

It might have been better to advise her to run, but she was already moving toward them. There were close to a hundred of them and only one of her, but since the

Bacchants were half stupid with liquor and secure in their numbers, they had difficulty processing the fact that Granuaile was attacking *them*. Nor would they be immune to wood. I caught a flash of her lunging forward and flipping Scáthmhaide down hard on a skull just to set the proper tone. The Bacchant crumpled and Granuaile sprang away, content now to lead the drunken savages on a merry chase. I loved how she always struck first when threatened; she appreciated the value of surprise and wielded it with often deadly results.

I didn't get to watch her much after that; Bacchus was in my face. Like his followers, he was immune to iron, so Fragarach was useless and I left it in its sheath. We had never tangled personally, and I'd rather hoped we never would. But I'd seen him fight before against Leif, and he wasn't terribly skilled, just terribly strong. I leapt about eight feet straight up, and he bull-rushed headfirst into the dryad's tree, which cracked and groaned.

"Ow, watch it!" the dryad said.

I'd tucked my legs underneath me for the leap but kicked out with my right as I fell, to take advantage of Bacchus's rebound. He took it on the chin and flopped backward after staggering a couple of paces. His skin was changing before my eyes: The baby-faced libertine was being replaced by the wine-mad monster. Where a soft blue tracery of veins might show beneath a pink blush of skin in his contentment, now they throbbed green and stood out like vines, and the whites of his eyes flooded with a deep burgundy. If he got hold of me, I'd be in trouble. Goading him would work in my favor though, since he would lose even more discipline the crazier he got. And since I knew *exactly* what kind of guy he was, I employed the advice I'd given to Granuaile and said, "Come on, bitch. Charge me again and see what happens."

He lost his mind completely after that. He purpled and drooled as he roared and gave not a single shit about it. He rose and quivered and just yelled inchoately in a roid rage, until his lungs gave out. I bore this display with patience and used the time to figure out how to beat him. Unlike the Norse or the Tuatha Dé Danann—or me—the bloody Olympians couldn't be killed. They could be harmed, but they could heal from anything; even if they were disintegrated or blown to tiny bits, they simply regenerated on Olympus and put on a fresh toga. There had to be a solution to him, or else the Morrigan would be here fighting him for me, fulfilling her oath.

The best solution would be to run and use some other tree to shift away. In fact, I hoped Granuaile would do exactly that. But the cries of pain I heard in the forest weren't hers; in battle, as in charity, it is better to give than to receive.

Bacchus finished emoting and charged me again. I crouched, ready to jump, and then it was a simple matter to fake the leap and watch Bacchus launch himself over my head. His face met the tree for the second time, and while he was in the air above me, I punched him in the groin as hard as I could. In my mind's eye, he was supposed to curl up and cradle his crushed grapes, but that's not what happened. It toppled him so that he fell headfirst down my back, and he grabbed clumsily at my legs as he hit the ground. It wasn't a move or a punch or anything more than a desperate flail on his part, but it knocked me off my feet and sent me sprawling.

Before I could scramble away, he managed to clap a hand around my ankle and haul me toward him. I twisted around and aimed a kick at his head. It rocked his neck back and he lost teeth, but he shook it off and grinned bloodily.

"No, you're not getting away now that I have you."

He aimed a vengeful punch at my groin, but I turned in time to take it on the thigh instead. That would be a nice bruise. I kicked him in the face again, and the fucker laughed. Apparently he could turn off pain much like I could, but, unlike me, he found physical punishment amusing. I tried to make him laugh harder by kicking him some more.

Bacchus tired of it after all and slapped my leg down on the next kick, then leapfrogged on top of my knees, pinning them. I bucked, crunched up, and landed a solid blow on his temple, but this failed to dislodge him. He grabbed my shoulders and slammed me back to the ground. Against a normal opponent, that would have been a stupid move because I could still deliver rib-cracking blows to his body, but Bacchus simply didn't care. He wanted to taunt me and he was saying something in Latin, but I ignored this and crafted a binding in Old Irish between his toga and the dryad's tree. The binding worked, but this also failed to dislodge Bacchus. He lunged forward, bore down, and let the toga tear away from him rather than let me go. His strength was such that I began to doubt I could match him. I reached for power, felt that it was abnormally low, and remembered that Granuaile had left the portal open. I was going to need her help to get out of this—though she might very well be thinking she'd need my help to escape the Bacchants at this point.

I shouted for help in Russian and added that she should break the wine god's elbow. I kept shouting it in a loop.

"What is it you say?" Bacchus said. "Some pithy insult?"

His fingers dug into my shoulders painfully, until

his thumbs ground into bone. My blows were having no effect. He merely pushed down on my right shoulder and began to pull on my left one, and soon enough he had torn my arm loose from its socket. He kept pulling; he really did mean to tear me apart, limb from limb.

He never saw what hit him, and neither did I. But I saw—and he definitely felt—his left arm bending the wrong way, heard the crack and tearing of tissue, marveled at the white bone splinters shredding the inside of his arm. He collapsed on top of me in shock, and I was finally able to dislodge him; a few Bacchants trailed by, seeking an invisible Granuaile.

I got to my feet and put a bit of distance between Bacchus and me. We both had useless left arms, but only one of us now had a clear plan of how to proceed. Bacchus was howling over his shredded arm and spurting what passed for blood among the Olympians—ichor, I think they called it. He'd heal up far faster than I would with a similar injury, but he was seriously jacked up for the present and kneeling only ten feet or so in front of the still-open portal. He'd probably never even seen it, since he'd originally approached me perpendicular to it. I walked toward him coolly, right side first, and he staggered to his feet once he saw this. He backed up as he did so, putting himself closer to the portal. Bacchants streamed between us, still pursuing Granuaile, mindlessly obeying the last order they were given when they could have easily taken me out. Bacchus roared and waved me forward with his right hand, daring me to charge. I chose my spot carefully, waiting for two Bacchants to pass between us before I shot toward him with juiced speed and planted a swift kick to his chest. He tried to grab my foot with his right hand, but he wasn't quick enough. He staggered back and through the portal, realizing too late that there was no ground underneath him anymore.

I grinned as I closed the portal on his bellow of rage. "It's going to take him a thousand years to finish falling on his ass," I said.

Chapter 26

Abruptly cut off from Bacchus, the maenads stopped caring about Granuaile and began wondering where the hell they were and why they were wearing white nighties.

"Oh, my God, what happened to your teeth?" one said.

"*My* teeth? What's up with *yours*?"

"My teeth are fine! Wait." She put fingers with torn nails up to her lips and discovered she had a mouthful of fangs. "Oh, Jesus, they're all pointy and shit!"

The screams, once they began, were contagious. Part of it was the terror of sheer confusion; part of it was terror at their future dental bills. I actually was happy for them: We'd discovered a way to free them from their thrall, and they could be human again.

Granuaile appeared, Scáthmhaide in hand, and looked worried about my dangling left arm.

"Yes, you do get to shove it back in," I said.

"I was afraid of that," she said.

"Thanks for the assist. Normally I would chew you out for leaving open a portal that long, but this time I'll let it slide."

She grinned and gave me a quick kiss. "Thanks."

Letting an amateur shove your arm back into its socket is unpleasant, but when you have magic at your disposal, it's better than getting insurance and waiting five hours for a professional to do it. Jogging north together until we found a tethered tree without an annoyed dryad inside, we shifted to our cabin near Camp Bird Mine to greet our happy hound.

<Great news, Atticus!> Oberon said as he bounded toward us, fresh from getting a drink in the Uncompahgre River. <I have independently verified that there are no Balrogs in this mine. And no goblins or cave trolls either. Only rats. I don't know what they're eating though. It makes you wonder about those rats in *First Blood*, remember them? They were hanging out, no visible nests, just waiting deep in this abandoned mine for a tortured Vietnam veteran to pass by in his attempt to escape a brutal small-town sheriff with the ability to boss around the state police and the National Guard.>

"Oberon, did you go into the mine?"

<No, I just listened at the entrance and sniffed around a bit, honest!>

"Oberon?"

<Okay, I might have set foot across the threshold. I was only trying to ditch those two ravens.>

"What two ravens?"

<The two that have been following me around for a while now. See them on the roof over there?>

Casting my eyes toward the mine foreman's house, I saw the ravens he was talking about. They weren't the normal kind. They were a bit bigger than usual, and each had one eye that gleamed white.

"That's Hugin and Munin," I said.

Granuaile tensed. "Odin's ravens?"

"Yep."

She began to scan the area. "He's here somewhere?"

"I doubt it. He won't get within striking distance of me again if he can help it. He probably has backup ravens and everything. I bet this is a call to arms from

Frigg. She'll be wanting me to kill Fenris now that you're bound to the earth. But stay on your guard in case I'm wrong."

We began walking toward the foreman's house, our eyes never resting but searching for threats. None appeared, though Hugin and Munin did their best to serve us up some turbo-grim *memento mori* action.

As we neared the front porch, Frigg floated from the backyard to meet us. She was wearing another of her Dalek dresses, but this one was blue and green with white swirls reminiscent of marshmallows melting in chocolate. She smiled and greeted us, the very picture of hospitality, her sour expression from months ago now gone. An arm appeared from underneath her hair and waved gracefully at the door to the abandoned house. "Shall we go in?"

I winced. "It's probably not a good idea," I said. "It's been vacant for years, and the last time I was in there it was full of rodent droppings."

"Oh, I am well aware. But that is no longer true." She lowered her voice conspiratorially. "A dwarf owed me a favor, and I permitted him to clean the place for our use. He has been very industrious; I am sure you won't recognize it. But I should warn you—he is in mourning."

"I'm sorry to hear," Granuaile said. "But why does that require warning?"

"Well." Frigg pulled at imaginary tufts of hair on her chin—or else it was a sign language of some sort. "He's . . . you know. In mourning."

"No, we don't know," I said. "We've never seen a real Norse dwarf before."

<I'll bet he doesn't have a Scottish accent. He won't be calling you laddie.>

"Oh. Well, you're probably expecting the beard, but it won't be there, you see. They shave them off to express their grief."

"Instead of crying?"

"Precisely."

"Would it be rude to ask why he's in mourning?" Granuaile asked.

Frigg smiled. "You won't have to ask. He will tell you all about it. That's part of their process. And in truth, Druids, his story is why I'm here. If this doesn't convince you to help us against Fenris, nothing will. Oh, one more word of caution," she said, pausing before the door. "He is a Runeskald, so please forgive his unusual speech. Even in English, he tends to wax poetic."

She preceded us into the house, understanding that we'd want to have no one at our backs, and waited for us to enter. The interior had been utterly transformed.

Where an old chewed-up beige carpet had rested, riddled with the piss and shit of untold numbers of rats, a gleaming hardwood floor awaited instead. The peeling wallpaper had been replaced with something new and warm.

Well, that was probably a lie. The colors were actually cool, but I had once spent a purgatorial week forced to watch HGTV, and during that time I noticed that the hosts and designers described everything they wanted to do as "warm." Even if they were working with ice blues, they were *warm* ice blues. I learned that *warm* was the best possible all-purpose adjective to use when remodeling; home owners couldn't hear the word enough. A designer could tell a couple that she was going to place a warm steel sculpture of Beira's frigid tits on top of a white marble pedestal in a walk-in freezer and the couple would nod enthusiastically, blocking out everything except the warm. Let it be known, therefore, that the entire miraculous remodel of the foreman's manse was warm. Even the dwarf responsible for it, who was introduced to us as Fjalar, greeted us warmly.

Fjalar was very clearly in mourning. His red-rimmed

eyes regarded us tragically, and I did my best not to laugh at his sad little chin, a white pocked moonlet gleaming underneath a pouting lower lip and the cantilevered overhang of his epic mustache. The reason dwarfs grow beards became obvious as he spoke: Their chins are too emotionally expressive, capable of quivering and frowning and lending the dwarf an air of vulnerability that they no doubt feel would attract unwelcome advances.

His voice was a lusty, sonorous baritone, bereft of Scottish accent and thick with a Norse one, and he used it to invite us to a place at the table. I noticed that all his dark hair was braided into multiple lengths, not like dreadlocks but not like any fashion I had seen before on males. Each length had something clasped or tied around it, usually gold or silver, but I saw colored strips of ribbon as well. He saw that I was curious about it and pointed to his braids with a thick finger.

"You spy my braids, to be worn for a year and a day. Signs of mourning, brother-memories, friendship flags, and rings of clan and craft."

"Yes, Frigg told us. I'm very sorry."

"All will I tell you, speaking fulsome, time in hand," he said. "For now, bread and mead call us, appetites whetted, to witness what I have been nursing, encased in iron, licked by flame, and tended with relish."

He waved grandly to a cook pot over a fire. The hearth looked good as new, and in front of it was a long wooden table with benches and candles. Pitchers of mead waited to be poured into drinking horns, and loaves of crusty bread waited in wooden bowls. Crossed axes and shields hung on the walls. Fjalar had done his best to turn the living room into a mead hall. A warm one.

He ladled out a bowl for each of us, including Oberon once we requested it. Fjalar looked to Frigg first to see if she was okay with it, and she shrugged her shoulders and said, "Druids." Fjalar shrugged back and filled up a bowl for the hound.

Oberon had nothing but praise for his meal. <Atticus, you really need to find out how he made this. If this is how Norse dwarfs cook every day, you need to make friends with them. Really. Seriously. I mean, really.>

Okay, Oberon, I hear you.

<But you're just sitting there! Clever Girl, tell the dwarf he's awesome.>

"This is fabulous, Fjalar. I wish we could enjoy the hospitality of dwarfs more often," she said.

<Thanks, Granuaile! It's about time somebody listened to the hound! Now tell him his chin looks like a dimpled golf ball.>

Oberon made this last comment as Granuaile was taking a sip of mead, listening to Fjalar's gracious reply. She managed both to spit mead and choke at the same time.

Fjalar and Frigg looked alarmed, and I looked like an ass because I laughed. Oberon chuffed.

"You'd better get used to it," I said, pounding her on the back a couple of times, "because that's the way it's going to be. He's like that all the time."

"Thanks for the timely heads-up," she wheezed. We then had to spend a few moments apologizing to our hosts for our terrible manners.

After dinner was finished and we had showered Fjalar with another round of compliments and thanks, he cleared away the dishes and brought us cups of Irish coffee.

"Many thanks, Fjalar," I said. "You've researched your guests' preferences well."

"Glad I am that I could so satiate you, for I have a tale long in the telling to share, if your leisure serves."

"No doubt this has something to do with Loki," I said.

The dwarf nodded. "It does."

"We know some of it," I said. "We saved Perun from Loki in Arizona."

Frigg's brows rose in surprise, and so did the impressive hedgerows above Fjalar's eyes.

"Perun lives?" Frigg asked.

"Aye, but his realm is indeed destroyed. He is now a guest of the Tuatha Dé Danann."

Frigg leaned closer. "Did he say why Loki pursued him?"

"He said Loki had wanted to kill Thor, and since that option had been taken away from him, Perun would have to do."

Frigg made no comment but shook her head to communicate her disapproval. Fjalar turned to her. "Then why in the nine realms did he come to us, fire-wreathed, rash, and wanton, screaming after someone named Eldhár?"

<Atticus, wait! SHUT UP!>

"Um, that would be my fault," I said.

<Damn it, you never listen!>

"Your fault?" Fjalar said. His eyes widened. "You sent Loki Truthslayer to Nidavellir?"

<Clever Girl, quick! Choke him!>

Granuaile twitched but didn't follow through. "I'm afraid so," I said. "Sorry."

<Auugh! Is the dwarf ever going to make tasty nom-noms for us again? NO. You've ruined everything!>

"*You* are responsible!" Fjalar began to rise from the table and Frigg placed a soothing hand on his shoulder.

"Fjalar, he is our guest," Frigg said.

"He is our enemy!" the dwarf roared. Despite her attempt to make him sit, he rose, pointing at me. "Thoughtless tongue of a tiny mind! Seven times seven hundred Shield Brothers dead—"

"What?" I said.

"Have patience, you see he is unaware!" Frigg said. "He could not have known what Loki and Hel would do."

"What did they do?" I asked. "Fjalar, please, I do not know what happened. Tell me what they did."

The dwarf glared at me, his fingers itching for an axe. Frigg never removed her hand from his shoulder. He took several deep breaths, his chin mottled with blood-lust, until he finally mustered the will to take his seat calmly.

"I suppose it is meet and proper," he said, "that you should hear first why I mourn, beardless and braided. And then your woman and hound will know I have just cause, am truly honor-bound, to cut you down."

Oberon growled at his words.

Stop that this instant!

"Please," I said to him. "Say on."

Perhaps if we had warning, horns sounded with alarm, we could have mustered a stronger defense, offered tapestries of wards and fire-tested stone. As it was, our defense faltered, heat-ravaged, and our stone doors melted, slagged to ruin by the sulfur breath of volcanoes, Loki's fury unchained. Nidavellir opened to him, he gave vent to his spleen, gall and bitterness churning in his eyes, madness made plain, spewing the venom he had choked down for so long in his bondage, deep in the darkness of that sepulchral cave. Our guards he set aflame and then bellowed above their screaming, demanding that we produce the wretched construct, dwarf-crafted, known as Eldhár. He paused for our answer, and we bore him honest tidings that nothing did we know of such a construct, but this he refused to believe, heart hardened against the truth, he who trades in lies like the winds trade in rumors of storms. Awash in fire, orange and yellow, he shot through tunnels and the noble caverns of Nidavellir, ancient dwarf-home, solid sanctuary until that day. Deeper and deeper he delved, past our cities and into rough-hewn mines, and even past these until he burned the raw, untouched rock, the virgin flesh of the earth. We lost him somewhere in the dark, his flames extinguished, his shrill demands for Eldhár fallen silent, grave-still, not even a whisper of misplaced anger in the abyss.

Then we wondered, and we sent out queries to Asgard, Vanaheim, and elsewhere: How had Loki won free? Was Ragnarok begun? Who was Eldhár? There are many dwarfs who hold that name, but none of the king's smiths had crafted a construct of that calling.

We heard first from Odin Allfather, far-seeing, wise-ruling. He warned us to beware of Hel, cold and cunning, and to look for her spies in our realm; she must not learn that Loki was in Nidavellir. Straightaway we searched, seized, and questioned; her minions, death rattlers, stringy shadows of the eternal forlorn, we found in abundance, and held them captive. But our prudence came too late, availed us not!

Too open had we been about Loki's arrival, too free with our questions and messages. Hel could not fail to hear that Loki Giantborn had come to Nidavellir, losing flame and voice and pain-racked visage in the black of some pit, far beyond where we feast and work and dwell.

To my shoulders fell the weight of the mountain, for such is the weight of my king's command. King Aurvang, son of Vestri, golden-maned, mighty-thewed, many-wived, bold in battle, spake unto the king's smith, who in turn spake unto me, and my task was made plain: The Stonearms, the king's own hammers, needed armor to withstand Loki, proof against fire, wards against his wrath.

I am a Runeskald, one of seven, seniormost and filled with lore, who emblazons armor with the truth of runes, elemental forms, matched to thought and deed and purpose; weapons too, carved with kennings both old and new that I sing betwixt my workshop walls, always imbuing steel and stone with the poetry of life, the songs of war.

It had never been done before, warding armor so well against fire that a dwarf could withstand the implacable malice of Loki Kinslayer, flame-haired cruelty, molten-tempered mischief. But I was not asked if it could be done; I was told to make it so.

I sang to the steel and struggled with the runes for a sevenday, yet could not find the form and song that would keep steel cool in fire. In perversity, desperation driven, I plied my craft on leather and surprisingly found a measure of success. Pursuing it further, doubly determined, I sang of skin-sealed moisture, sinews hardened with courage, tanned hide of taut resolve that deflects danger, and of surfaces chapped instead of burned. And the runes I crafted were oblong and rounded, heat-shedding shapes of domed protection, sigils of steadiness in the face of fury, waves of quenching water to drown licking fingers of fire.

Into the smithy's flames I tossed two shields of leather, one of my skaldic craft and one bereft of my attention. The standard shield burned, while the skaldic shield only charred and blackened around the edges. Heart-swollen and pride-puffed, I applied my hard-won skills to a set of armor, and it was during this time that Hel's army came to Nidavellir.

News of her father had reached her pestilent ears, cold with patient malice. Swiftly, she assembled legions of *draugar* to invade our mountain, defile our homes, stain the beauty of our axe-hewn halls. They came with weapons drawn, modern rifles like our smiths now make, shooting into our tunnels but never spreading out, always marching deeper, past our treasures and warrens of riches. Many thousands were they, yet so were we and determined to stop them, for now we thought Ragnarok had begun.

The hammer horn sounded throughout Nidavellir, and the Stonearms assembled, and with them the Black Axes, the Shield Brothers, the Maidens of Wrath, and the Guardians of Lore. Miners and craftsmen, merchants and millers, all were called to martial arms, all of them answered, abandoning the day's cares for the defense of the realm, save for myself and the Runeskalds by especial command of King Aurvang. "You must remain in your workshops, ever diligent," he said, "and continue crafting the armor to slay the father of lies, whensoever we find him."

And so battle was joined without my hammer, and the king's skalds will never sing of my valor around the hearths of my people.

Here is what they sing instead:

Grim-visaged and stouthearted, dwarfs young and old, yet Shield Brothers all, marched to meet the shambling blue *draugar* of Hel, detested queen of frosted twilight. Her army, unbreathing, steeped in the attar of woe, unleashed a hail of bullets, stolen weapons from the mines of Midgard. Deafening thunder roared through Nidavellir that day, rattling teeth and rifle fire and ringing shields and battle cries. Forearmed, skaldic runes on shields and helmets, the front line advanced undaunted, metal pieces flying back at the foe, ragged soldiers who knew no honor in life. They, heedless of any harm below the neck, bore the ricochets in silence.

The Shield Brothers pressed forward, unwitting of their coming doom.

Cunning Hel, bride of ice and despair, gave commands in tombstone whispers to her soldiers, who raised their

weapons and fired at the ceiling above the Shield Brothers, bullets whipping off rocks, tearing through flesh
from above, felling many who never struck a blow for
their clans, never hewed a head from its shoulders.

The front line marched on, and behind them quick-
witted Shield Brothers raised their skaldic wards, redi-
rected ricochets, foiled the efforts of Hel. And finally,
when the armies met, the *draugar* learned of the strength
of dwarfs! Rotted skulls flew from rotted bodies as axes
swept the air over shields, while others were trampled
under the vanguard and hewn apart by subsequent
ranks.

The *draugar* shrank back at first, their orderly advance exploded, but then they swelled as corpses will
with blowflies and maggots, filled the tunnel with their
unholy bodies, halted our advance and held their line,
while their back ranks emptied magazines above the
Shield Brothers' heads, ceaseless ammunition thrown
up to tear us down, and some found targets after two,
three, or four ricochets.

Slowly, by attrition, the *draugar* took their toll, slaying noble dwarfs in heat and noise and close rock walls
with cowardly attacks. The dead soldiers of Hel pushed
back, advanced again despite the best efforts of the val-
iant Shield Brothers, courageous warriors to the last.

Bodies of their dwarven brethren, slick with blood,
impeded both retreat and advance. The wounded, no
matter how they cried for help, could not be tended in
that close tunnel with so many enemies to fight; naught
but enduring agony, desperate breaths, and despair was
their lot, until their honorable deaths brought them
peace and immortal glory.

Back, back, beneath the onslaught, the Shield Brothers gave ground, slowly yet inexorably, pushed by
the juggernaut of Hel's army. Yet every footstep was
dearly won, for it took hours for the *draugar* to travel

the distance a dwarf may walk in five minutes, crawling over the massed dead.

And in that time, assembling in the Grand Cavern, a mighty force of Shield Brothers awaited, ready to protect the market and residences and streets there. Ricochets would not be so effective in the Grand Cavern, and the Shield Brothers had firearms of their own. So when the tunnel forces were pushed back to the cavern, they abruptly retreated on a signal from their general, fell behind the lines, and allowed the *draugar* to walk into an ambush.

Thousands of shambling soldiers were mown down by a fusillade from dwarf-made guns, and a furious cry of victory echoed in the cavern! Blue and twitching, heads shattered by bullets, the *draugar* fell in ranks, turned to foul dust, leaving their weapons behind.

Yet still they came, innumerable as ants or the swarms of summer bees, and after we had slain a thousand with unremitting fire, they paused, and we entertained hopes that our resolve had taught Hel to reconsider her rash invasion of Nidavellir. But then they flooded once again through the opening, yet with this cruel difference: They held the bulletproof skaldic shields of our fallen brothers in front of their heads, and thus we could not slay them, only poke holes in their rotted flesh, slow them for a time with a shattered thighbone, a pulverized ankle, nothing more. And then the chill craft of Hel manifested itself, and we shuddered in horror at her plan, for every piece of it represented the death of a Shield Brother in the tunnel: The *draugar* began to make a wall of shields, three high, linking them together and then creating another column, by which method they created a corridor that would allow them to maneuver in safety.

And it was, indeed, a corridor. Strangely, the *draugar* made no attempt to advance in the cavern, to advance on our treasures, to reach for our lives or destroy our homes.

Putting aside their modern weapons, the Shield Brothers charged with axes and hammers to break the wall, and the resultant clash of arms thundered in the great cavern, as *draugar* were beheaded and dwarfs were shot by the defiant minions of Hel. Reports came back that the *draugar* were advancing through and past the cavern as fast as they could move, their objective elsewhere, their purpose unclear.

And then in the court of King Aurvang a Svartálf bowed, ambassador of the dark elves, longtime resident of our realm, and announced he brought a message from Hel, she having no other way to speak to us in safety.

"Speak," King Aurvang said, his fury palpable, "and then begone from my realm! We will have no traffic with Svartálfheim henceforth for this betrayal!"

"My people should not be punished for bearing you a message," the ambassador said, "especially since it may save the lives of many dwarfs. Will you hear me in patience, rashness reined, ire checked with prudence?"

Our king made no promises. "Speak your part, Svartálf," he said.

The dark elf simpered and bowed again. "Hel wishes me to say she has no designs on your realm and wishes no more harm to the noble dwarfs of Nidavellir. She simply searches for her father, Loki, whom she has heard is currently visiting. Her army will not attack dwarfs except in self-defense or if their progress is impeded."

"And when she finds her father, what then?" King Aurvang roared, wrath awakened, patience fled. "Will she reduce my tunnels to rubble, set my caverns aflame, slaughter my people?"

"Nay, noble king," the Svartálf replied. "She will leave with him if she can, containing his madness so far as she is able. Her quarrel is with Asgard and Vanaheim, not the honorable people of Nidavellir."

"Have you aught else to say?" the king asked.

"My message is complete, sire."

"Then remove yourself from my presence and my realm! I never wish to see you more!"

When the Svartálf had gone, chastised yet unrepentant, the king sent for me. I rushed to answer his summons on bended knee.

"Runeskald Fjalar," he said, "long have you labored for our greater good as a poet and enchanter of armor. Now I must ask of you a service befitting a hero. Retrieve the Deadman's Shroud and wear it yourself. Follow Hel's hordes and discover what they intend, then report back to me. Slay none except in the utmost extremity. You must live to return the shroud and speak of her plans."

"It shall be done, sire," I said, and wept as I bowed deeply to him. Never had I been asked for so weighty a service.

The Deadman's Shroud was crafted centuries before my time by the greatest of all Runeskalds, Mjotvangir son of Rathsvith, nimble-fingered, honey-throated, unmatched scion of clever craft. The shroud may be worn only by Runeskalds, but, once worn, it convinces the dead that the wearer is also dead. There is no copy, for none have ever duplicated the skald of Mjotvangir; his runes exist for all to see, but the dread words he sang while crafting the shroud are forever lost.

Orders given, I was led to the king's treasury and presented the Deadman's Shroud, sacred relic of my forebear's skill. I collected my skaldic shield, fire-tested, then was ushered to the front lines of the Shield Brothers, where battle still raged. Rather than try to break through the wall, where I would be exposed to gunfire, I was vaulted bodily over it on the premise that I would draw no fire once I landed, shroud-wrapped, disguised from dead eyes.

I landed heavily but intact, drew stares but no fire.

Identity concealed, purpose hidden, I joined the stream of dead forward through my own realm, an invader of my own home.

What a wonder Runeskald Mjotvangir had made! I marched unremarked in the midst of putrefaction, cold malice, and unknown intention. Past warrens and neighborhoods and then past mines and pockets of wealth, I followed the stream of dead ever downward. And then, after seemingly interminable hours of this journey, so far down I knew not where I was, the *draugar* before and behind me stopped and pressed themselves against the wall of the tunnel we traversed. I did likewise, waiting, breath heaving in a passage where no other breath heaved, until a giant of a dog rushed past: Hel's own hound, named Garm, of yellow eyes and unmatched determination, nose following a trail I could not smell, doubtless made of malignance and the acrid trace of sulfur.

The dead, and I as well, continued after him, always coursing down, into the unlit depths where no dwarf had roamed for years. When the darkness became too much for my eyes to pierce, the shroud did me a service and lit my way, alarming none in the process.

After another hour of peregrination, I entered a vast chamber already full of *draugar*. There, high up on a ledge, glowed the resting form of Loki Firebreath, supine on the rocks, slumbering in peace, only his bare skin revealing a blue aura of simmering flames.

Garm sat beside him, stalwart sentinel, ever vigilant. The legions of Hel made no move to wake him but rather faced outward, ready to face any threat, and there they still wait at this very moment, protecting the sleep of Loki, Hel's father, lord of mischief.

I hurried back to tell my king of this news, and grimly he sent word to Asgard of Hel's doings in Nidavellir.

Her father found, Hel's goal was accomplished, and the dead stopped flowing into Nidavellir, but still they wait silently far below our cities for Loki, robed in wrath, to waken again.

More than ten thousand *draugar* fell that day to dwarf weapons. Seven times seven hundred Shield Brothers fell defending their homes, their children left fatherless, their women widowed. And for what? For a selfish god's nap in the deep! For a Druid's foolish tongue! You see me here, beardless and braided, for the loss of an uncle and a nephew in that battle! Why should I not now, in justice draped, exact a measure of the blood shed for a careless word three months ago? My fallen family demands it, as do the families of all the dwarfs who died that day!

"You will not move," Frigg said to Fjalar, her voice as cold as his was hot with rage. "Do not stir to shepherd violence here. These are your guests and mine."

The dwarf looked apoplexed. "But my honor—"

"Will restrain itself for a while longer," Frigg finished. "Odin has a plan that will pay your people properly and tax the Druid heavily."

"What plan is that?" I asked.

"You already know it well. Now is the time," Frigg said, "while Loki and Hel are occupied, while Garm is stationed elsewhere, to cripple their efforts to bring about Ragnarok. Hel's realm is half empty. There you must go to slay Loki's spawn, Fenris, Odin's bane, devourer of gods."

"You want me to go to Hel and kill Fenris?"

"Yes."

"I thought he was supposed to be tied up on an island in the middle of a black lake."

Frigg rolled her eyes and waved this away. "Snorri Sturluson made that up. He was bound in Hel and there he remains, tended by her minions."

"I can't get into Hel." I knew the shift points to get to the planes of Nidavellir and Jötunheim—the first was in Iceland and the other in Siberia—but I'd never tracked down the shift point that would take me to the third root of Yggdrasil, which would lead me all the way down to the spring of Hvergelmir and the lower realms of the Norse.

"Untrue. None other than the goddess Freyja will lead you there. She is your guide and your surety of return."

I snorted. "Forgive me, Frigg, but Freyja is no surety of my return. Not after what happened in Oslo six years ago. Say rather that you're holding a shotgun to my head and Freyja will pull the trigger."

"She besmirched the honor of the Æsir that day, but none more so than her own. This is her penance. Only by your safe return can she restore her good name."

"And once I'm returned from Hel? Will she attack me then, her oath fulfilled?"

"No, of course not. But you are not going alone. In addition, good King Aurvang has already promised the services of the Black Axes."

"The Black Axes!" Fjalar exclaimed. "How many of them?"

"All of them. You will lead an army to kill a single wolf."

"He's not an average wolf, and you know it," I said. "What is Loki up to?"

"It is something akin to the Odinsleep," Frigg said. "He is healing. He has not had a decent night's rest in centuries. He is drained, and now he heals for an indeterminate time."

"So he'll be even stronger when he wakes?"

"Yes."

"Will he still be batshit insane?"

"His sanity has always been doubtful. He once tied a rope to the beard of a nanny goat and the other end to his testicles just to make Skadi laugh. It was an extremely high-pitched tug-o'-war, and his idea of kindness. If you are wondering if he will be less likely to pursue malevolent impulses than in the past, my guess would be no."

"Can Freyja get us into Hel without having to fight through legions of *draugar*?"

"Yes. You will take the path that the Æsir use."

For a while, no one spoke. Eyes shifted around the table, measuring expressions, and wood popped and crackled in the hearth.

This was precisely the sort of thing that Odin had requested of me some years before. Since I had been directly or indirectly responsible for the deaths of many of those tasked to fight in Ragnarok, I had to take on some of their responsibilities. Fenris had to be slain, and we would find no better opportunity than this, while he was still bound in Hel and many of her forces were absent.

"My hound stays here," I said, "safe and unmolested."

<No, I want to go with you!>

No. We are not arguing about this. I need you to be safe.

<But I'm always safe with you.>

You wouldn't be in Hel.

"And your apprentice?" Frigg asked.

"She's not my apprentice anymore. She is a full Druid and may make her own decisions," I said. I turned to Granuaile and spoke softly: "You are not under any obligation to accompany me. You should remain here and do something heinous to your stepfather's oil business. Take Oberon with you."

Granuaile's green eyes bored into mine. Her head shook minutely and she brought up her left hand to caress my beard. "Idiot. I'm going with you. My decision."

"Okay."

<Can I go if I call you an idiot and stroke your face with my paw?>

No.

Oberon whined. <This isn't fair!>

One of us has to live through this. I always want you to be the one who lives.

<What if you don't come back?>

Go down to Ouray and find someone there who likes big friendly dogs.

<They wouldn't call me Oberon. They'd call me Max. You know how many big dogs are named Max? Like, *all of them*. Atticus, don't go. Just send a poisoned box of doggie treats to this wolf and forget about it. He hasn't seen any heist movies.>

That's actually not a bad idea.

<Well, I've always been smarter than you.>

Chapter 27

I understand the attraction of forgiving gods. There are times, like this one, during which I wish for nothing so much as forgiveness for my trespasses, and if I could truly feel such forgiveness, I would cling to the source of it like a newborn to his mother's breast. But Odin doesn't forgive. Nor do the Tuatha Dé Danann. The attitude of both parties is to make whatever restitution is possible and, in the words of my old archdruid, "stop looking at the entire world as a hole to put your cock in."

There was no pardon in the face of Frigg either, who amongst the Norse was most likely to offer succor to those who sought it. Her eyes were cold. She would never say to me, "Go now, you are forgiven."

To seek absolution from humanity would be to seek my own folly. One may speak of forgiveness here, and another may actually mean it there, but legions remain who would condemn a starving man to amputation for pinching a crust of bread. We are petty creatures who seek to aggrandize ourselves by feasting on the dignity of our fellows.

There was nothing to be done; weeping would not mend it, nor would raging. I could only strive to live so that my merit outweighed my discredit. To pay for the lives of nearly five thousand dwarfs slain by my careless words, I had to kill the biggest, baddest wolf in all the world's stories.

Fenris wouldn't fall for a bowl of poisoned kibble. He'd probably turn up his nose at a poisoned steak too; he was too smart to be tricked. Had Týr not been willing to sacrifice his arm, he never would have allowed himself to be bound by Gleipnir, the masterwork of Fjalar's ancestors, the unbreakable dwarven fetter made of six impossible things. Fenris was a wolf that could reason and speak like a man—like an Old Norse man, anyway. He'd trust nothing from the hand of the Norse anymore. But that didn't mean we couldn't poison him.

"Give us time to prepare?" I said to Frigg. "Where and when shall we meet Freyja and the Black Axes?"

"On the very tip of the peninsula southeast of Skoghall in Sweden. Östra Takene. You know it?"

"North end of Vänern Lake?"

"Precisely. Say, midnight, Swedish time. Will that be sufficient for your purposes?"

"I think so."

"Then Freyja will see you there." Frigg rose, and, belatedly, so did the rest of us. Oberon recognized that our visit was finished.

<Guess there won't be any dessert, then.>

Fjalar glowered at me from underneath his impressive brows, but the effect was ruined by his comically bald chin. Frigg nodded to us and we thanked her and Fjalar for their hospitality. The dwarf growled at us, which I supposed was the best I could expect from him right then.

<Can you at least ask for the recipe before we go?>

I think he'd rather put us in his next recipe.

We showed ourselves out of the foreman's manse and walked up the hill to our own cabin.

"So we're going to Hel, eh? How do we prepare for that?"

"We're going to yet another sporting goods store—one here in the States, preferably without dark elves or vampires inside, where we can get ourselves some bows and arrows. Then we're going to cook us up a big heaping batch of poison."

"Let me guess: wolfsbane?"

"Yep. Why should we wear rubber gloves?"

"Because the aconite in the leaves will seep through our skin."

"Ogma was right," I said. "You are well trained." I was expecting a well-deserved punch on the arm, but Granuaile instead sank down and swept my feet out from under me and dropped me on my back. She kept walking and spoke over her shoulder.

"Trained by the best," she said. I was about to declare that I loved her when she added, "It's not going to work."

"What isn't?"

She stopped and turned around, waiting for me to get up. "Picking him off safely from a distance using poisoned arrows."

"Why not?"

"Because somebody else would have done it by now if it were that easy. Freyja could go down there by herself with a sniper rifle and put a bullet in his brain if it were that easy. Odin could have used his spear. A hobbit could have chucked a rock at him with such accuracy and velocity that it beggars belief."

<I'm going to do a Rick James parody in your honor, Granuaile. "She's a very clever girl, the kind you don't take home to Ogma. She will never give you Brussels sprouts when she could give you steak.">

Granuaile petted Oberon and complimented him on his singing voice, while I rose from the ground, brushed myself off, and sighed. "You're right. It's wishful thinking on my part. But I still think we should make the poison. I'll put it on Fragarach's blade. You can put it on your throwing knives if you get a chance to use them. Maybe we should get you a bowie knife or something while we're at it. Your staff won't be able to do much damage to him."

"It'll get me close to him," she said, referring to the invisibility spell.

"True. But you still can't do it all by yourself. His hearing and sense of smell will be excellent. We'll need to provide a distraction for you if you're going to sneak up on him."

"An army should prove sufficiently distracting, shouldn't it?"

"Let's hope."

"Let's also hope this goes better than the last time you tried using poison."

"Definitely." She was alluding to an unfortunate encounter with skinwalkers in Arizona.

We ran errands after bidding farewell to Oberon. We grabbed some gloves and some bags and shifted to a forest in Germany with plenty of wolfsbane—also known as monkshood and myriad other names. There were species of it in the United States—even in Colorado near our cabin—but this species contained the most concentrated poison.

After a trip to one of those giant retailers that sells luxury camping gear and slippers lined with sheepskin, along with more practical wares, we each had two knives of sufficient size to earn the notice of a wolf like Fenris. We returned to our cabin in Colorado to distill the poison and prepare our blades. Oberon was out hunting for his dinner, so we left him to it and enjoyed a shower together, which included auxiliary exercises that occurred to us along the way. Afterward, I decided I had endured the beard long enough. It had been something of a necessity during Granuaile's training and even more so during her binding, but now I should be able to keep myself trimmed on a regular basis, so it was back to the goatee.

It was near midnight in Sweden after that. We decided to dress in black to pretend to be Celtic ninjas. Comfy black jeans and black long-sleeved shirts, even black gloves. We both had our iron amulets tucked underneath our shirts. Strapped to our thighs on either side were newly poisoned knives; I had also poisoned Fragarach.

"Ready?" I asked.

"I don't know. Should we take some bottled water or something?"

"I don't think so. Frigg made no mention of such preparation. It should be a quick operation. We'll mooch off the dwarfs if we have to."

"What if they won't give us any?"

"Then we'll steal from the dwarfs if we have to."

"Gods, Atticus. I'm in charge of logistics from now on."

"That reminds me. We're going somewhere cold. Let me show you this binding the Morrigan taught me to raise your core temperature. You can hang out in the snow in jeans and a T-shirt and not get all shivery."

"Sweet!"

We shifted to the northern shore of Vänern Lake, or rather close by it. We were underneath the canopy of an evergreen forest, facing south, where the smell of the lake wafted to us on the night air. A minute's walk toward the shore revealed a large fire with silhouetted figures nearby. Casting night vision, we saw many more waiting on the beach in the darkness, armed and helmeted figures, all dwarfs. There was an army, all right—but only the one fire, presumably serving as a signal.

I startled as I turned my head. Right next to me, painted so black I hadn't seen it in the dark, was a strange, massive vehicle bristling with weapons. It wasn't of human manufacture. I had almost run into it; thankfully, no one was inside to train one of its many weapons on me.

I crouched down at the edge of the trees and cast camouflage. I couldn't see Granuaile, so she had probably already cast her own camouflage or else her invisibility spell.

"Do you see Freyja?" I whispered. Her voice answered from my left.

"I don't know what she looks like."

"She'll be the tall one in this crowd."

"Ah. Yes, she's near the fire but not directly next to it. A few ranks back. Standing in a chariot."

I scanned near the fire until I found her. "Okay. Let's sneak up and hail her. If she betrays us, we take her hostage, go back to the trees, and shift away. Stay invisible until we know it's safe."

"Got it."

I wished I could cast Coyote's spell that he called "clever stalking," which would muffle our footfalls, but we had to simply move as quietly as possible through the crunchy sand, depending on wind and conversation and the clank of armor to disguise our passage.

The Black Axes were impressively armed—I mean, their arms were bloody huge. Their shoulders and biceps were larger than those of most bodybuilders, with enough hair on them to earn Perun's respect. Those arms hung out from broad golden breastplates, sans armor, allowing maximum freedom when they took a swing at anything. The Black Axes didn't have shields but rather skaldic armor; their breastplates and helmets bore runes on them that most likely made them bulletproof. Instead of a shield, they carried a sort of parrying axe in the left hand, with a small hooked blade at the top and a guard to cover their fingers. The axe in the right hand had a large black scything blade, also inlaid with telltale skaldic sigils. My money was on armor piercing. It was an army of Fragarachs.

Aside from the skaldic golden design of their breast-plates and helmets, the Black Axes covered the rest of their bodies with black lamellar armor. Here, they said, shoot your guns and arrows at the shiny protected parts. Ignore all the rest of us that you can't see clearly anyway. It was a heavy mobile infantry designed to run at night.

A few of the Black Axes had beards spilling out from underneath their helmets onto their breastplates, but the majority of them did not. That meant their hair was probably braided as well, and they would be no fans of ours if Fjalar had spread word of my role in sending Loki to Nidavellir.

Granuaile and I were able to sidle up to Freyja only half detected. We made occasional noises that caused a few curious helmets to turn in our direction, but they never saw us and dismissed the noise as made by an-other dwarf behind us.

The Black Axes were packed pretty tightly around Freyja and her chariot, and we could get no closer than two ranks away. It would make taking her hostage problematic if she wanted us seized. Having no choice, I hailed her. Heads whipped around toward my voice, and grips tightened on axe handles.

"Where are you?" the goddess demanded. Firelight flashed off the long blond braid that fell down to her waist. She was beautiful, though a bit mannish in the jaw. She was proud and had reason to be. She had killed more frost giants than any of the Æsir on the day I in-vaded Asgard.

"First, do I have your word of honor that you mean us no harm?" I asked. "Frigg assured me that you do not, but I would rather hear it from your own lips."

"On my honor, I mean you no harm," Freyja said. "Wishing is another matter."

"Good enough," I said, and dissolved my camouflage. "I neither mean nor wish you harm."

Once Freyja had located me, her eyes searched beyond my back. "Were you not to bring another Druid?"

"She is here. She'll reveal herself when she feels safe."

"The two of you are to ride along in my chariot. The Black Axes are to follow in their own conveyance. Are you ready?"

"Aye."

Freyja dropped her eyes to an especially hulkalicious dwarf next to her chariot. "Axemaster, we'll see you at the Spring of Hvergelmir."

"Aye, lady." He bellowed orders, and these were re-bellowed up and down the beach. The horde of dwarfs moved toward the trees, where their looming gunships waited. As the space cleared around Freyja, Granuaile revealed herself and nodded.

"Lady Freyja, it is my honor to meet you. I am Granuaile."

Freyja did not return the honor, but she did nod back. "Join me. We follow the root of Yggdrasil to the Spring of Hvergelmir. There we will see the gates and walls of Hel. Some of the Black Axes will assault one end of the wall, drawing attention, and our party will fly over the other, sparsely defended end to find Fenris."

We climbed into her chariot, and I experienced a moment's disorientation before I remembered that it wasn't pulled by horses or oxen or any other beast of burden but rather by a few gray domestic house cats. Freyja made an odd purring noise and we lurched forward, jerking at first but then smoothing out as we left the ground and ascended, flying briefly over water before banking around and flying back toward the forest. We skimmed above trees that looked like green pipe cleaners, then reached a wee pond and dove straight for it. I knew what was going to happen, but Granuaile didn't. Her fingers clutched the edge of the chariot and she said, "Um," but made no other sound.

That water, it turned out, wasn't very wet. It was a portal to the Norse plane. I recognized it because there was a large fir with roots in the pond, just like the pond in Russia that led to the spring at Jötunheim. We didn't have to splash through it: The air pressure just changed, our ears popped, and we were following the root of Yggdrasil, the World Tree, down to Niflheim. It was clear for a time, then we plunged into the mists for which the plane is named.

The journey made me miss Ratatosk. Though Oberon might have disagreed—his nature bent to dislike squirrels as a rule—I thought Ratatosk had been a splendid creature and wholly undeserving of the death he found at the hands of the Norns. His death had been my fault, of course. I was beginning to think I'd never balance the scales I'd tipped twelve years ago.

The root of Yggdrasil disappeared into dark, bubbling waters ringed by an epic stone wall with eleven different arches for egress, from whence eleven rivers flowed. One of them, Gjöll, flowed near the gates of Hel and must be crossed. But now that the dwarfs had crafted flying machines, there would be no bargaining with a bridge keeper. Even the massive wall was no obstacle, but Freyja wished to preserve the fiction that it was. Once the dwarven gunships landed on the banks of Gjöll, half of them split off and went to bombard the walls of Hel, hoping to draw fighters to the walls and distract those inside from our true purpose.

As they flew off with Freyja's blessing, I took the opportunity to look around at the alien landscape of Niflheim. I sort of wished Freyja had a digital camera on her so Granuaile and I could pose like tourists on top of the stone wall encircling the spring. We'd point east with huge smiles on our faces, and then the caption would read, *Nidhogg is over there!*

In Niflheim, even under weak starlight filtered through mists, there are blues and hints of soft pinks reflected in the ice. They hint at comfort and reflections of a brighter world; they whisper of the fires raging in their primordial opposite, Muspellheim. In certain light and with a little imagination, great crags of ice could be mistaken for those old red-white-and-blue bomb pops sold from the backs of square white trucks.

Once we circled up into the sky and headed for Hel, above the mists, I saw distant purple crags with black hash marks sparsely distributed about them, lonesome trees howling of their isolation in the chill winds. Still, even with that icy anguish for a backdrop, the swirling mists offered colors and hopes that something inside them might not be so cold. All that ended once we sailed over the wall into Hel.

In Hel, there are no blues or any other suggestions that somewhere there might be a sun or an ice cream man. The color palette is confined to that of a Gustave Doré engraving, grays and blacks and subtle shadings of these rendered in harrowing crosshatches and highlighted with sudden, glaring areas of nothingness, like splotches of vitiligo sent to haunt the dead with memories of what real light did to the eyes. The clear air is redolent of dishwater and mildew, and the mist is formed from the moist, clammy exhalations of snuffed dreams and hopeless sighs, which collect in the lungs like clotted cream.

Freyja drove us into the mists at some predetermined point, but I saw nothing to indicate that this stretch of sickly mist was a waypoint of some kind. It was, to me, an unkind plunge into air that felt like spiderwebs and snot.

Behind us, the black dwarven ships followed, eerily

silent, running on compressed rage, I suppose, or some other inventive fuel.

Granuaile started to choke and cough a whole second before I did. The mists crawled up our noses and into our lungs and settled about our brachia like wet snow. We both looked at Freyja, who appeared undisturbed—but also appeared to be holding her breath. I guess she just "forgot" to suggest that we do the same. I turned around, letting my back serve as a breaker through the mist, and was able to take a couple of clear breaths that way, enough to hold for a while. Granuaile followed my example.

I was tempted to "accidentally" jostle Freyja and cause her to expel her breath, but I decided to let her have her petty revenge. I had killed her twin brother, after all; this was a small fraction of the grief I deserved.

Until we landed on the icy rocks of Hel, we didn't get clear of the mist. It hung over us at a low ceiling of ten feet, depressing the horizon and swirling slowly like dead leaves in a current. Nothing moved nearby. Behind us, the dwarf gunships landed single file, forming a wall in the process. Their guns all swiveled to face behind us.

"It would be no use turning all those guns on Fenris, would it?" Granuaile asked.

"Hel loves her beastly brother," Freyja practically snarled, yanking a spear out of a slot in her chariot. "She surrounded him with a kinetic ward long ago. Not arrows nor bullets nor Odin's spear can reach him now. We have to kill him up close."

Granuaile's green eyes found mine. She smirked and put up her fist. I bumped it.

"So where is he?" I said.

Freyja pointed with her spear into the mist in front of us. "That way. Not far."

"Why can't we see anything?"

"The mist is like that. Though you think you can see

the horizon, you can't. Your functional visibility is less than twenty yards."

"Great. Can he hear and smell us now?"

"Most likely."

"Do you have a plan?"

"Yes. Go that way and kill him."

I waited patiently for more detail.

"Preferably," she added, "before Hel finds out we're inside the walls and sends everything she has against the Black Axes. Once they start firing, it's going to draw a horde. Some of them will get through and over the ships, and then our army of five thousand won't stand a chance against her hundreds of thousands."

Freyja's sentence was punctuated by a shuddering hiss, followed by more all along the wall of gunships.

"What kind of guns are those?" Granuaile asked.

"Circular-saw launchers," Freyja said, grinning at us for the first time. "Aimed at the neck, but they take off arms and legs too. Don't you love the dwarfs?"

"They're charming, yes," Granuaile said.

"Let us go," Freyja said. "Time escapes us. I'll speak to Fenris and front him. You attack from the flanks. Beware: He is very fast and can change his size."

"How do you mean?" I asked.

"He is a son of Loki Shape-shifter, giant-born. Like Hel and Jörmungandr, he can grow or shrink as he sees fit."

"Lovely. So if we run across a wolf puppy, don't believe it."

"Precisely."

I cast camouflage on myself and drew Fragarach, plus the knife hanging out on my right thigh. I carried that in my left hand, and once I used it I would have another waiting on my left thigh. Granuaile held her staff in her left hand and spoke the words for invisibility as she drew a large knife in her right. She disappeared from view.

"I'll take the left and Granuaile will flank right," I said.

"Forward, then," Freyja said.

I padded into the mist on bare rock and checked my connection to the earth. As in Asgard, the magic was still there but strained and weak, like getting only a single bar of wireless signal. If I needed a surge of power, I'd have to draw it from my bear charm. I quietly boosted my strength and speed as I walked, knowing I'd need both against a monster like Fenris.

Behind us, the sounds of the gunships swelled as they brought heavier firepower online. There must be a whole lot of *draugar* coming our way. Hel was not a master strategist, but she didn't need to be with the type and number of soldiers she had at her disposal. When your army is truly disposable, there are no letters to write home to loved ones, no veterans' benefits to pay, no logistics to worry about, then there's no need to be clever in battle. Just drown your opponent in bodies. Freyja was right: We had no time to be cute. We had to finish quickly if we wanted to get out of there.

I failed to find him after twenty yards. Nor did I find him in the next twenty. But I heard Freyja's voice call out to my right and behind me shortly afterward and a rumbling reply directly to my right. I turned but saw nothing in the thrice-damned mist. Still I moved toward the husky voice.

"Freyja, is it? I have heard from my sister that you lost your brother some time ago. Such a shame. I forgot to send my condolences, did I not? Please accept them now."

Freyja told Fenris what he could do with his condolences. The wry chuckle fell from above. I looked up and to my right again, following the noise, and spied two massive legs stretching up into the mist. Poking out beyond them was half a snout—the nose and open maw of Fenris. Clearly he had decided to confront us in the Economy Size. Much larger than Garm, who was a monster at six feet at the shoulders, Fenris was at least twice that, maybe more. With jaws that size, he could handle us like large Milk-Bones, except we would be much more squishy. Quietly and quickly as I could, I minced my steps to the left in search of his rear legs. Freyja kept talking to distract him—that was excellent work. Still, he sensed us.

"Who do you bring with you?" he rumbled. "I smell others."

"There are dwarfs fighting the *draugar* behind us," the goddess replied. "Slaying them all, I imagine."

"I rather doubt it," Fenris said after a couple of loud sniffles. "This isn't the stench of dwarfs. This is something else. Humans. Living ones. Where are they?"

Granuaile had beaten me to the rear legs, for at that moment Fenris yelped and the muzzle disappeared from the ceiling as he whipped around to snap at something painful on his left side. His right rear leg shot forward for balance, planting itself right in front of me. There was a red ribbon tied around it, which I recognized as the fabled Gleipnir, so I swung Fragarach with all my enhanced might just above it, hoping to hobble the beast and turn his attention my way. It worked! Sort of.

Fragarach cut cleanly through his entire leg, amputating it with one strike, but I had now freed him. Instead of turning around to his right, where he could no longer rest any weight, he kept turning left and down, circling around so that his giant tail caught me smack in the chest and sent me flying backward. I dropped Fragarach and the knife and stretched my hands beneath me to make sure my head didn't hit the rocks first. It didn't, but it wasn't a happy landing either. My left hand took the brunt of it and I sprained my wrist. I also banged my elbow hard enough to make me cry out; it was a taste of what Bacchus must have felt under Granuaile's staff. My left arm would be useless for the near future; sprains don't mend themselves in seconds, even magically assisted. My tailbone would no doubt give me a bit of pain later on as well. For now it was a dull ache underneath the adrenaline.

My ears pounded with the sound of cannon fire and the howls of a giant wolf, but I longed to hear something from Granuaile, anything that meant she was still alive. I hadn't heard her since we moved forward.

I clambered to my feet and retrieved Fragarach from where it lay, then looked up to see Freyja charging a much-reduced wolf, as he was still spinning counterclockwise, snapping at something . . . invisible. Granuaile lived! I charged too, though a bit awkwardly without the free use of my left arm.

Unlike Granuaile, Freyja was fully visible and making noise. She obviously wanted to get the wolf's attention, and she managed to—but not the way she would have liked, perhaps. As I charged, she leapt at him, spear cocked in her hand. She thrust it at his head as he lunged at her, letting Granuaile go for the moment. He saw the spear and shrank, twisting his head at the same time, so that her thrust overshot her target and grazed along the side of his head. Fenris caught Freyja's legs between his jaws, she screamed, and he tossed her away into the mist so that he could return his attention to the invisible demon pestering his left side. Granuaile was probably chucking all of her throwing knives into his ribs and driving him crazy. He lunged around to his left, snapping at something he couldn't see, but thankfully his teeth sank into nothingness. I made my own leap at Fenris—which he didn't see coming—but he was still shrinking in an effort to spin around faster to catch Granuaile, and he shrank faster than I expected. I'd put quite a bit of force behind my jump, and now I was going to overshoot him entirely. I swiped at his head and just scratched the top of it between his ears, doing no lasting damage beyond whatever the poison could do to him. Thus far, despite having been wounded repeatedly with poisoned blades, he'd shown no ill effects.

My scratch secured his attention, however. His jaws whooshed closed, with an audible clap of jowls and teeth, where my legs had been a split second before. I landed safely if a bit unsteadily on the other side of him, and he barked in frustration before speaking.

"Who strikes? Who hides like a coward from my eyes? Show yourself!"

Yeah, right. I had made sure Granuaile was of my mind on this matter: When in a fight for your life, you never, ever fight fairly. Honor and sportsmanship are wonderful in games that don't matter, but it's the honorable guys who always die in real battles. "When there's blood involved," I'd told her, "you always use every advantage you have to make sure it's theirs that spills and not yours. If you want to feel guilty about taking unfair advantage afterward, you go ahead and feel that shit. But live to feel it."

In this situation, though, showing myself might make Granuaile safer. It might give her another free shot to finish Fenris for good. Blood was still squirting out of his leg, and I could see now that he had several throwing knives lodged in his bleeding skin, plus a larger one stuck in his left leg. Between that wound and his missing right leg, he wouldn't be making any astounding leaps my way. It could work out.

I dissolved my camouflage and whistled at him. "Here, boy. Nice doggie."

His eyes flashed at me and his lips peeled back into a snarl.

"Who are you?" the wolf growled. "Some new god?"

He spoke in Old Norse, so I replied in kind. "Not quite. I'm the guy who kills gods when they piss me off. Freyr, for example."

Fenris flinched as if I'd slapped him.

"You killed Freyr? And you come here with Freyja?"

"You're the blood price, see? How's that leg, by the way?"

"About the same as Freyja's, I imagine." He did his best to lunge at me with just his front legs and his jacked-up rear left, but it was an awkward move and bereft of speed. Using her second large knife, Granuaile employed the wolf's momentum to open up his right side. Fenris yelped and tried to pivot right, but that put weight on his bleeding stump, and he yowled louder as he lost his balance and crashed down onto his leaking guts.

I cast camouflage again and sprinted at him, thinking of little else besides a prayer to the Morrigan that Granuaile wasn't trapped underneath him. Even though Fenris had shrunk significantly, he was still bigger than Garm. If Granuaile's head was underneath all that weight, she wouldn't be able to breathe.

Fenris struggled to get up but flailed messily instead. Without his back leg to lift him, he couldn't stand again, and his wounds were finally taking their toll. He realized it was over as his eyes searched for me.

"You have my curse upon you, godslayer," he said between bared teeth. "You and all your—"

I hacked through the back of his neck and cut through his spine. "Shut up," I said.

Wiping Fragarach hastily against the wolf's fur, I called for Granuaile. She appeared on the other side of the great wolf's neck, grinning at me. Her left arm was a sleeve of blood.

"Made you nervous, didn't I?"

My shoulders slumped in relief. "A bit, yes."

"Nice kill shot."

"Thanks. What's all that?" I chucked my chin at her arm.

"He got a tooth or two into me at one point. It's all good. No rabies."

An especially loud explosion from the vicinity of the dwarf ships reminded us that we needed to get out of there.

"Did you see where Freyja landed?" I asked.

"No. Too busy running for my life."

"I think she flew off that way," I said, pointing vaguely behind me.

We jogged together in the direction I thought she'd flown, keeping about ten yards between us. I was giving some panicked thought to how we'd get out of Hel without Freyja's help if she turned up dead. I was reasonably sure I could use the root of Yggdrasil to shift back to that nice wee pond in Sweden, but getting past the walls and gates of Hel was another matter entirely. I doubted the dwarfs would give us a ride over the wall if we told them one of their favorite goddesses was a chew toy, and I was positive the cats would listen to no one but Freyja.

Granuaile found her first.

"Atticus, she's here! Bad shape, though."

Freyja's spear was lying some distance from her awkward form. Her legs were twisted at odd angles and sheathed in red.

"Okay, you stimulate skin repair, and only that, hear me? No adrenaline. I'll stop the bleeding."

We laid on hands and got to work. The wounds Fenris had made would have killed her from blood loss had we arrived much later. She'd already lost consciousness, and soon her brain would be starved entirely for oxygen. She needed a transfusion, but she wouldn't get it here.

"Gods, what a mess," Granuaile said. "Wish we could put some of it back in."

"You and every field surgeon who ever lived."

Freyja's right leg and right arm both had breaks, probably from the way she landed. She most likely had a concussion as well, though I thankfully saw no blood pooling underneath her head. I couldn't set her bones here.

"We'll have to carry her to the chariot," I said. "Think we can do it invisibly?"

Granuaile nodded. "Once the spell is cast, skin contact with the staff is all you need. We could support her under either shoulder, hold the staff across the back of our necks with our outside hands, and sort of drag her that way."

"Make it so."

"Aye, Cap'n."

I took a few more seconds to stabilize Freyja's circulation, then we hefted her up between us as planned. Before we had taken three steps, we heard an anguished cry erupt near the body of Fenris. We recognized the gravelly source of it and hurried: That was Hel's voice. If she'd burst through the Black Axes, there was no telling what kind of reception awaited us.

Hel's unseen wailing continued as we dragged Freyja closer to the sounds of fighting, and it was difficult not to cringe at the noises Hel made. Half her throat was dead and rotting, after all, so normal cries were impossible for her. The addition of tears, mucus, and genuine emotion on her part made it unbearably animal.

Thinking of the stages of grief, I wondered if Odin had counted on what would happen when Hel reached rage. Could this be the trigger for Ragnarok, right here? Or would she stay her hand until Loki wakened from his sleep?

Knowing I was caught between Hel herself and Hel's

army, every step seemed unnecessarily long. I wanted to
be in the chariot and flying already—but who knew if
Freyja's flying kitties were still alive at this point?

The mist brought us nothing but the sounds of battle, dwarfs dying and *draugar* falling for the final time.
When the combatants finally hove into view, I knew I
never wanted to face off against one of the Black Axes.

Hel must have pushed through the lines on an unstoppable wave of *draugar*, but most of these now littered
the rocks ahead, and the remaining few were falling in
hand-to-hand combat with the dwarfs. The axemen were
closing the breach one swing at a time, toppling heads
and sometimes even torsos with their blades, such was
the force generated by their muscles. My earlier suppo-
sition that their blades were armor-piercing was borne
out before my eyes; I saw a dwarf's axe cut through the
steel-plate helmet of one undead soldier with no more re-
sistance than that of wet cardboard.

A cluster of them facing outward drew my attention:
They were guarding Freyja's chariot.

"There's our ride home," I said to Granuaile. "You
see it?"

"Yep." The ground between the chariot and us was
clear of *draugar*, except for the remaining pieces of
them.

"If we suddenly appear amongst them, they'll cut us
down without thinking. Drop the enchantment now and
I'll hail them."

"Done."

I shouted in Old Norse and hoped that Hel wouldn't
hear it over the sounds of war and her own sorrow.
"Black Axes! To me! To Freyja! Defend the goddess!"
A dozen wee warriors swarmed around us and escorted
us to the chariot.

"Is she alive?" a gruff voice asked.

"Aye, but barely. The wolf is dead."

"We figured Hel wouldn't make that noise if he lived."

"Right you are. It's time to run."

"I'll tell the axemaster," the dwarf said, seeing us safely into the chariot. "Don't wait for us. Go!"

He made it sound so simple. But when I looked over the front of the chariot, the cats' eyes staring back at me did not seem anxious to leave.

"Hey, cats," I said. "Let's go. Let's boogie. Come on." I pointed up at the ceiling of mist. "Back over the wall. Let's do this." They stared at me. One began to lick his nether region. "Giddy-up!" I cried. "Heaahh! Move 'em out! Shoo!" This earned me more stares and more licking but no movement. "Go, damn it!"

"Atticus, that's not going to work," Granuaile said.

"Yeah? Well, you try it."

Granuaile faced Freyja forward so the cats could see her face. "Listen," she said. "Freyja is hurt." The cats took sudden interest. Their eyes, indifferent before, were now clearly focused on Granuaile and Freyja. "Your mistress needs help. We need to leave now. Over the wall, back the way we came. Take us to Frigg. Take us to Frigg, and I'll buy you some tuna."

At least, I think she said *tuna*. Her words were drowned out by a roar from Hel, who appeared in her half-hot, half-rot form to demand an explanation, her hair touching the ceiling of snotlike mist. Though she was twenty yards away, we could already smell her. "Who killed him?" she wanted to know, the great knife Famine clutched in her skeletal left hand. "Was it Freyja?"

The chariot jerked and we lifted off the ground; Freyja's cats were suddenly anxious to escape.

"Nope. That was me!" I shouted.

Hel's eyes focused and then narrowed in recognition. "You! You're supposed to be dead!"

"You should have learned from the mistakes of the Æsir," I said. "Never fuck with a Druid!"

I shouldn't have said that.

As we rose into the clouds of mist, all sounds of battle and rage below muffled by its close stickiness, Hel's giant right hand followed us in and closed on the open back of the chariot, halting our progress in midair. Granuaile and I yelped, and the cats protested with a noise primarily composed of vowels.

Freyja's kitties were powerful, and thanks to them Hel couldn't drag us back down, but neither could we escape. Hel's right hand was on the "hot" side, and thus it looked lovely and cultured and gave no hint that it belonged to something hideous. Granuaile slapped at her thighs, searching for a knife, but she had thrown them all at Fenris and slammed her bowie knife into his leg. I handed her mine.

She snatched it, cocked it over her shoulder, and threw it directly into the back of that giant lovely hand—not hard enough to pin it to the chariot floor, but hard enough to stick in there. A bellow from below and we shot skyward as the hand disappeared. I think the cats were in a hurry, because we didn't seem to spend so long in the snot this time. More likely Freyja had taken us through it a bit slower than necessary.

"You poisoned that blade, right?" Granuaile asked.

"Yep. We can always hope. I doubt it will take her out, though."

I held much more hope that the Black Axes would make it out okay; I'd had no time to assess the state of their forces. I rather feared that the dwarfs in Nidavellir would have to bear a counterattack now. It would be better if Hel were somewhat cowed by this affair and rediscovered caution.

"Hey, Granuaile," I said once we got clear of the mist and were sailing back to the wall. "Will you ask the cats to keep the portal to Midgard open for the dwarfs?"

"Sure. I don't know if that's something they can do, but I'll try."

"Thanks. I'd hate to think we were stranding all the dwarfs in Niflheim."

Red hair streaming behind her in the cold wind, Granuaile asked our transportation to keep the door open for the dwarfs. I distinctly heard a *meow* in reply.

"Oberon was right about you," I said. "You really are a cat person."

Chapter 28

Sound and light returned to normal once we crossed over the wall. Colors came back, and the thundering of artillery coming from the other side of the wall echoed in our ears. Once we got an angle, I could see that it was significantly damaged and Hel had made absolutely no return fire. She'd never upgraded her own defenses, assuming that she would be the one to make an attack. Perhaps that would keep her busy also.

Someone must have been watching for us, or else the dwarfs used radio or something, for the attack broke off and the ships began to rise to follow our chariot. Looking behind us, I saw more dwarf ships sailing silently over the wall, following us back. I had no way of knowing how many returned, but I knew that honor was important to them and that the dwarfs would feel better for dealing Hel this defeat.

We swerved up the root at a ninety-degree angle but thankfully did not fall out the back of the chariot. There was, instead, just a slight sense of vertigo as we completely ignored gravity.

"I could get used to cat chariots like this," I said.

We splashed up through the pond and the night sky was full of different stars—earth's stars—then we banked around until we found a rainbow in the dark. It was on this occasion that I discovered that Granuaile had never heard of Ronnie James Dio. My shock at this news was such that I almost completely missed the fact that we were traveling on Bifrost, the rainbow bridge to Asgard. Only when we reached Asgard and got a serious frowning from an unknown keeper of the bridge—Heimdall being dead—did I notice that we weren't on earth anymore. The cats meowed at the frowning man and the rainbow pointed elsewhere; Freyja's cats promptly followed it back down to Midgard, where it led to the foreman's manse in the mountains near Ouray.

Granuaile couldn't believe it. "You mean Frigg never left here?"

"Well, Fjalar went to such trouble to decorate it warmly."

Outside on the porch, we delivered Freyja into Frigg's care and reported with great satisfaction that Fenris was dead, Hel's walls were heavily damaged, and that at least half of the Black Axes, at minimum, would be returning to Nidavellir. Frigg turned her head to a patch of shadow under the roof of the front porch: "Tell him." Two ravens took flight into the darkness.

Before Fjalar could ask us a question or issue a challenge, Frigg asked him to fix some broth for Freyja. He gave us a dire eye but obeyed without a word.

"Thank you, Druids," Frigg said. "You have dealt a serious blow to Hel's plans. We will keep you informed of any developments."

She bent her head to Freyja then, in clear dismissal, and we made our farewells.

We walked in silence back to our cabin, where Oberon waited, full of something he'd killed and therefore drowsy and uninterested in what we'd been doing.

<Rah-rah, the humans return,> he said with a yawn and a halfhearted wag of his tail. <You know, it's cold way up here in the mountains, even though summer's

barely over. Come, humans, fulfill your evolutionary purpose and build your hound a fire.>

We laughed at him, and Granuaile rubbed his belly while I built a small fire for him in the hearth. Once he was satisfied, I made hot chocolate with marshmallows while Granuaile changed out of her blood-soaked shirt. We clinked our cups together in the kitchen and kissed.

"So what now?" Granuaile asked.

"Well, we could go figure out who's trying to get us killed in Tír na nÓg," I said, "or start binding your iron amulet to your aura, or find out whether all the evil clowns in the world have been dark elves all along."

Granuaile poked me in the chest. "I have a better idea. How about introducing me to all the elementals one by one? I've only met a few so far."

"A sort of Druid World Tour? We could make T-shirts with a list of all the elementals on the back."

"Yeah. But first let's go somewhere with a name I can't pronounce that has a really nice hotel with a giant bed in it."

"Gods below, you are brilliant."

Oberon roused himself to full wakefulness in the living room. <Oh, no! Wait! Drop me off at a poodle ranch!>

Epilogue

The giant bed we found in Tlalpujahua, Mexico, had been sufficient for our purposes, and it was not long after that we picked up Oberon from his guest stay at a poodle ranch in Vermont and embarked on the Druid World Tour. I was showing Granuaile some of the Old World doorways to Tír na nÓg that humans could walk. Occasionally, humans discovered them by accident and found themselves in Tír na nÓg, and if they were extraordinarily lucky they managed to find their way back.

The old doors were good to know, I argued, because even though they were sparsely distributed, they functioned even when the trees did not. They were constructed in caves, which were not subject to the same whims and forces that trees were.

Part of the exercise was just damn cool, because caves are like that, and I emphasized this to Granuaile. But, in truth, I had another agenda: I wanted Granuaile to be impossible to catch. Strategically speaking, falling in love with her was a mistake, the sort of thing that Machiavellian types would exploit, for my enemies—vampires, dark elves, you name it—would always view Granuaile as a lever to use against me. She was quite the badass in her own right now, capable of feats I couldn't match, but during our connubial sequestration in Mexico it occurred to me that we would have precious little chance to lay low going forward. She'd never get an opportunity to truly enjoy her powers and nurture a sense of harmony in the world as it stood. I kept thinking back to that conversation with Jesus where he said if I'd remained meek, I would have inherited the earth. But there was no going back to that idyllic time when only *one* god wanted to kill me. Now I just wanted the earth to stick around so someone meek could inherit it. And I hoped that we two Druids would manage to stick around as well. I wasn't nearly through staring at her yet.

We emerged from a cavern in the Apuseni Mountains in Romania; the range—in the western part of the Carpathians, in the old province of Transylvania—was famous for its hundreds of caves. The vista we beheld at the cave's mouth smacked of the bucolic rather than the vampiric. Sheep and cattle competed contentedly for their share of abundant grassland directly below, a friendly forest waved at us a short distance beyond, and zero stone edifices loomed over the landscape with palpable auras of ickiness.

<Didn't you say this was supposed to be Transylvania?> Oberon asked.

"Yes, I did. It is."

<I was expecting to see a road lined with impaled victims leading up to Vlad's castle. And plumes of smoke— that's key. Because if you're evil, your neighborhood is supposed to be on fire most of the time.>

"Vampires are a bit more discreet than that these days, Oberon."

<Well, I hope we at least find someone who will laugh loudly and inappropriately at other people's pain, preferably before a commercial break and accompanied by a sinister crescendo in the shrill soundtrack. Hey. You feel that?>

"Feel what?"

No sooner had I asked him than I felt it: a trembling in the earth—a building one. I shot a hello and query to the Apuseni elemental. //Greetings / Harmony / Query: Plate event?//

//Greetings / Druids welcome / Advice: Run / Not plate event / God event through me//

"We need to get out of here," I said, as the ground bucked beneath us. We heard loud cracking reports of stone shattering to our rear: The cavern from which we had just emerged was crumbling and filling in with stone that had been stable for centuries. We scrambled down the hill, across boulders and shale, into the forest below. A minor landslide followed us.

"Someone's after us," I explained to Granuaile, who probably hadn't heard my quick conversation with Apuseni. "Some god is causing this through the elemental. Let's shift to Colorado."

"Got it," she said.

Once down to the friendly forest we'd spied from above, we put our hands to a tethered tree, but it wouldn't respond; the paths to Tír na nÓg were cut off somehow.

"Pandemonium," a voice croaked from the branches above. We sought the source and found it: A crow with red eyes stared back at us. It was the Morrigan.

"You won't find anyplace on the continent that will let you shift away," she said, and I shuddered involuntarily. It was always disconcerting to hear the crow speak English. "They've trapped you here. That earthquake was Neptune's work, and Faunus will deny you every tether to the Summer Lands. You'll find the old ways collapsed or guarded. You're going to need to run for the British Isles, Siodhachan—and I mean literally run all the way there. It's the only path I've seen where you live through this."

"Live through what?"

"You'll see. The ankle-winged boys are coming to tell you now." The crow tossed its beak at something behind us. We turned and looked up.

Hermes and Mercury descended from the sky, pale savage beauty paired with golden pomposity, and the Roman demanded to know what I had done with Bacchus.

"Ask the Fates," I said, shrugging.

A bolt of lightning lanced down from the heavens to strike Oberon, who first yelped, then barked at the sky.

<Hey! Who did that? Mother clucking chicken!>

Oberon was unharmed because of Perun's fulgurite on his collar, but one of the Olympian sky gods had clearly intended for him to die. It was a message meant to put me in my place, to reduce me to quivering obeisance.

I looked up and spoke loudly: "That was damn rude, Jupiter. The last god of Olympus who was rude to me was Bacchus."

"Where is he?" Mercury demanded again.

"Why do you wish to know? Have the Roman wine cellars run dry?"

"You will return him or suffer the consequences."

I shifted my gaze to Hermes and asked, "What is the Greek interest in this?"

Hermes shrugged and spoke in his taut melodious tones: "Olympian solidarity, officially. But, in truth, Artemis was extremely vexed about the kidnapping of the dryads. As was Diana. All nymphs of the wood are sacred to them. This Bacchus affair is their chance to exact revenge for what they promised to forgive."

I could almost hear Granuaile saying, "I told you we shouldn't have touched the dryads." I carefully kept my gaze on the Olympians so I wouldn't have to see it in her face.

"Well, Bacchus and Faunus should be blamed for it, not I. They forced me to do it, and, besides, I returned the dryads unharmed as promised."

Mercury said, "We won't let you do to the Olympians what you did to the Norse, Druid. Return Bacchus or die."

"Return him or die? That's not much of a choice. If I bring Bacchus back, he will kill me."

The messenger gods didn't even bother to shrug. They merely raised their eyebrows as if to say, "So?"

"Haven't you ever heard of *Catch-22*? Throw me a bone here, guys. If I'm going to die either way, what's the point of giving Bacchus back?"

They ignored my question completely and Mercury said, "Choose, mortal. Will you return Bacchus or no?"

Fuck these guys. "No," I said. "He's a dick."

"Then so be it." They flew straight up and away, revealing two floating chariots behind them in the distance, almost hidden against the hillside. Two helmeted figures with bows released arrows at us—Artemis and Diana. They knew I would say no. They'd planned for it.

The Morrigan crunched down in front of us in her human form, now fully armored, and took the arrows in a massive ebony shield. I had never seen her bother with armor before.

"I am here to fulfill my oath to you, Siodhachan Ó Suileabháin. Run now," she said, "for England. You have two immortal goddesses of the hunt on your trail. I shall hold them as long as I can, but it won't be forever." She drew a sword from a scabbard at her waist.

"Morrigan?"

Artemis and Diana goaded their chariots forward. The Morrigan turned and pointed west, her red eyes blazing through an ebony helmet. "Go, Siodhachan! They come!"

I grabbed Granuaile's arm to pull her away and we ran, Oberon at our side, into a forest we suddenly found foreboding rather than friendly.

Acknowledgments

To my family, friends, and all my wonderful readers: Much love and a raised flagon to you!

As always, the keen insights of my alpha reader, Alan O'Bryan, helped me tremendously in the process of writing. He also got me playing Magic: The Gathering again and smooshed me with a Boneyard Wurm. Friends are rad like that.

I am so blessed to have editors at Del Rey who are capable of both geeking out and rocking out—often at the same time. Thanks to Tricia Narwani and Mike Braff for throwin' up the horns and encouraging all the world-building.

I recently discovered that my agent, Evan Goldfried, knows more about beer than I do. In my eyes, this makes him An Authority on Just About Everything. I respect his authori-tah!

Amalia Dillin (@AmaliaTD) knows more about Norse mythology than most humans. I've enjoyed chatting with her, bouncing ideas off her, and occasionally pleading for her help. If you find my representation of Norse mythology heinous, please don't blame her; I'm the guy who wrote the heinous stuff.

For those who may be interested, the *Poetic Edda* in its entirety can be found online for free. You'll see where all the dwarf names come from, discover the circumstances of Loki's binding, and so much more. If you keep reading different sources of Norse mythology, you'll also discover that they contradict one another in myriad ways. (And that is nothing to be ashamed of; it's an endearing feature of most belief systems.) One point of confusion is naming the Nine Realms of Yggdrasil and deciding where they're located. The map I've included at the front of the book (drawn by Priscilla Spencer) is organized according to various sources and a few core beliefs o' mine regarding Norse mythology: 1) Three is a magic number, so there are three realms on each of three levels; 2) dwarfs and elves are not the same thing. No, they are not the same thing at all, and as for all those sources that say they are, well, I think the dark elves must have gotten to them; and 3) given number 2, the dwarfs live in Nidavellir, and the Svartálfs live in Svartálfheim, and they're not the same place either.

Thanks again for reading! You can find me on Twitter @kevinhearne or on Facebook if you'd like to say hello.

extras

orbit

www.orbitbooks.net

about the author

Kevin Hearne is a native of Arizona and really appreciates whoever invented air-conditioning. He graduated from Northern Arizona University in Flagstaff and now teaches high school English. When he's not grading essays or writing novels, he tends to his basil plants and paints landscapes with his daughter. He has been known to obsess over fonts, frolic unreservedly with dogs and stop whatever he's doing in the rare event of rain to commune with the precipitation. He enjoys hiking, the guilty pleasure of comic books and living with his wife and daughter in a wee, snug cottage.

Find out more about Kevin Hearne and other Orbit authors by registering for the free monthly newsletter at www.orbitbooks.net

if you enjoyed

TRAPPED

look out for

FADE TO BLACK

by

Francis Knight

Chapter One

I forced the door, nice and quiet, with my ever-so-slightly-illegal pulse pistol at the ready. Magic wasn't usually on the agenda for runaways, but this little madam was exceptional: booby traps a speciality – I'd almost gone up in flames this morning. Twice. If it wasn't for the obscene amount of money her parents had offered me to find her, I'd have given it up as a bad job.

The room beyond the door was even more dingy and rubbish-strewn than the corridor, and that was saying something. Rainwater had driven through a broken window and the faint stench of synth drifted up from where it pooled. I sidestepped around it. You could catch a fatal dose and never know until it was too late. Residents hurried away behind me with a mutter of footfalls. One sight of me, a burly man in a subtly armoured, close-fitting all over with a flapping black coat, and the scavenge-rat teens that called this place home took to their heels. I dare say it looked too much like a Ministry Special's uniform with an added coat. Living this far down, a nose for trouble was essential.

I checked around carefully, trying to listen past the far rumble and thump of factories above us. A flash of movement off to my left, a hint of bright blue shirt. Lise, the girl I was after. With nothing to alarm me – yet – I made my careful way in. There it was again: a flicker of blue, floating in the gloom. I slid my fingers round the pistol's trigger and pointed it. It wouldn't kill her, but it would give me just enough of an edge. I didn't understand it myself because it's not my kind of magic, but the man who sold it to me had explained it as a way of interrupting thought processes, quite abruptly. An almost painless magical cosh, if you will. It would shut her down, at least for long enough for me to restrain her. Killing people wasn't my line of work, or my style. If I'd had a taste for it I'd have stayed with the guards or, Goddess forbid, gone into the Ministry Specials, but I hadn't liked the amount of paperwork, or the restrictions. I preferred the more freeform business I was in, where responsibility wasn't something I needed to worry about.

I slid forwards, making sure there were no nasty surprises waiting in the rubbish at my feet. She moved again and black hair whirled out as she ran down a short corridor. I followed with exaggerated care, in case she had any more tricks in store for me. She wasn't stupid. There had been those booby traps. Plus, she'd covered her tracks like a professional. It had taken me a week to find her, a length of time almost unheard of. I'd nearly had to resort to magic, and I never like to do that.

The information from her parents had shown me she was book-smart at least, a high-ranking fifteen-year-old student in alchemy. Bright enough to cover her tracks almost seamlessly; and ruthless, or desperate, enough to defend her retreat. Clever enough to come down here, on the border of Namrat's Armpit and Boundary, right where the people she normally mixed with wouldn't dream of coming. Where people minded their own business or else, and she had a hope of hiding without falling into the black hole we knew as Namrat's Armpit, or the 'Pit for short. I tried not to think of the alchemist's brew of toxic chemicals, residue of the synth disaster, just below the floor.

Rain rattled a broken window and a door snicked closed ahead of me. The little brat had led me a merry chase, but I had her now and the fat pay-purse was all but in my hand. She knew I was there though, and she'd proved resourceful so far. I decided not to trust the door, or the girl. Trust wasn't a luxury I could afford in this line of work. I had a small wooden baton attached to my belt and used it to push the handle down.

As I pushed, fat sparks bloomed from somewhere above and dripped down the doorframe. I leapt back just in time to avoid the blast. Heat seared the exposed skin of my face and hands and the stench of burning clothes choked me. I rolled until I was sure the flames were out.

Electricity was a new development, and not more than two or three of the really good alchemists had got a grip on it yet. Luckily. Yet she'd learned from my earlier care with her traps, wired the whole damn thing and rigged it up to black powder just as an added bonus in case I avoided the electricity. I was reluctantly impressed.

Runaways had never given me this much trouble before; it was the bounties that did that. This girl had a powerful desire not to go home. Having met her parents, I could sympathise, but a paying job is a paying job, and once I took one on it was hard not to follow through.

I slipped through the door with the pulse pistol held out in front of me. The room was dank and gloomy, lit with fifth-hand light bounced down from better areas far above. Among heaps of rubbish, a parade of small puddles rippled on the bare stone floor where rain leaked through two broken windows. The water gleamed with an oily glint – synth, almost certainly. A thin, filthy mattress contaminated the end of the room. A small light, a rend-nut-oil lamp with a glass cover, scented the air as it glowed next to the makeshift bed, casting a pool of warm light on the sodden blanket that was littered with food wrappers – pretend meat, fake gravy, the tarted-up processed vegetarian shit that was the only kind of tasteless junk available down here. Or pretty much anywhere under Trade.

The wavering light of the lamp made the room behind seem black as Namrat's heart. Namrat: tiger, stalker, winner in the end. Death. If I was a religious man, I would have prayed to the nice Goddess that he wasn't stalking me today. As it was, I kept still and kept looking. She had to be in there somewhere.

My finger tightened on the trigger at a shadowy movement in the dark beyond the mattress, and something flew towards me. I leapt away, but not in time to completely avoid it. It smashed on the stone and let loose a rush of greenish gas. Streamers of it ballooned like smoke, sticking in my throat and blinding my stinging eyes. Oh, she was good, more than good. She was making me work for my money. That's nearly as bad as using magic.

Footsteps pattered on the concrete as she passed me and I aimed the pistol blindly. Pain leapt through me where the blade on the trigger bit my skin, not much but enough to give me some power to fire. The pistol let loose a buzzing pulse in a wild trajectory and I was rewarded with a snatch of a scream that ended with a heavy thump as she fell to the floor.

I took a few moments to drag myself away from the gas, wiping my streaming eyes and coughing it up. Finally it began to clear, helped by the breeze from the broken windows, and I could see her. She was stretched out in an ungainly pile, face-down in a puddle. Before I did anything else I cuffed her. She'd given me too much trouble already; I wasn't taking the chance of her escaping now, or maybe pulling something else out of her bag of tricks. I rolled her out of the puddle, saw to my bleeding thumb with a quick bandage from the stash in my coat, and had a look around as she came to.

It was, quite simply, a shithole. Walls crumbling where they hadn't been strengthened against the ravages of prolonged synth contact. No window intact. No direct light, not ever, not down this far, yet no Glow tubes to light the room. No nothing really, except that mattress and the oil lamp, something only the poorest of the poor ever used, because of the rancid smell. Even the people who lived in Boundary didn't live in this sort of place, unless they were seriously desperate. The rats weren't keen either, which was its only plus.

I had to wonder why she thought this was preferable to living with her very well-off parents, albeit an arrogant bully of a father, and a mother sneaky where he was blunt. Another three months, her sixteenth nameday, and she could have left them to themselves.

They were made for each other. He'd been a big man, fifty perhaps, had once been muscular by the looks but running a little to fat. Two streaks of grey sliced through his black hair like arrows and he had a way of walking as though he owned anywhere he was – or, perhaps, anyone. He'd given me the creeps, especially as there had been something so oddly familiar about him. Not the face as such – bland in a fleshy kind of way – but the way he held himself, the gestures of his hands. It had brought back long-buried memories, but I'd shrugged off that creepiness, told myself I was imagining the familiarity, when I'd seen how much he was willing to pay. I'll forget a lot for that much cash.

As he'd shouted and railed, threatening to have my licence withdrawn if I should even dare to think about refusing the job, his wife had winked and flirted and hinted at other methods of payment. She was perhaps ten years younger than him, carefully trim to the point of being haggard, with a shrewish mouth and watchful eyes. I'd been tempted to refuse them, just to see what would happen, but the money was good and I preferred the runaways to the bounties. They were easier to find, less likely to try to kill me, and I could pretend I was doing something towards setting the world right rather than souring my underdeveloped conscience by condemning some small-time fraudster or petty thief to twenty years or, worse, a one way trip to the 'Pit.

Well, runaways *had* been easier, until this one.

She groaned as she came back to herself and I stopped looking in the tatty cloth bag that probably held all her possessions. There was little enough in there, except for a large stack of money. I was a good boy for once, and kept my fingers away from shiny temptation. Daddy probably knew how much she had, down to the last copper penny.

"Come on, Lise, time to stop playing house and go home. For some reason your parents are looking forward to seeing you."

I hauled her up to her feet, not as gently as I could have; the wired door could have caused me a lot of pain, or worse, and she'd burned a hole in my best coat. She obviously hadn't been thinking clearly, didn't know I was a mage or didn't know that pain is a very good source of power for magic. Not many people do, because there aren't supposed to be any pain-mages any more, not since the Ministry took over. My pistol isn't the only possession of mine that is ever-so-slightly-illegal.

She wasn't very steady but I grabbed her bag and half pulled, half carried her back to the carriage. On the way she regained the use of her voice and I was treated to a stream of language I was sure a girl of her age and privileged background shouldn't know. By the time we reached the carriage and I had the door open ready to throw her in, she was kicking and biting and doing everything in her power to get me to let go. I was tempted once or twice to dump her as hard as I could on the floor, or maybe use the pistol on her again, but I held on to myself with all the restraint I could muster. Her screeches brought a gaggle of spectators to see us off, and I had a reputation to keep clean. In public anyway.

I dumped her in the back of the carriage, behind the metal grille I'd had installed for just this sort of thing. She tried to bite my hand when I threw in her bag and slammed the door in her face. I suppressed a smile as she shrieked with rage, and used my spare juice for a little more magic. If you know what you're about you can store it, for a while anyway. It didn't take much to mould my face into an approximation of her father's – one of my talents, my Minor, to change the way I look. Not for long, or very much, which makes it fairly useless most of the time, but handy for getting a rise out of people when I'm feeling, shall we say, less than well disposed towards them?

She spat through the grille. "You bloody bastard!"

"Technically, no. But I can understand why you might think so." I wiped the spit off my cheek and her father's face off mine. Moulding my features like that always gave me a banging headache, and I soon regretted using it to satisfy my little urge for revenge.

I fiddled with the valves and flicked the glass vial with the Glow in it. Should be enough left to get her home, and me home after without going to the expense of getting another. That wouldn't stop me charging her father for a new vial. I started up the engine with a yank on the frayed cord, wincing at the grind of metal as the gears mashed. I'd never quite got the hang of carriages, or getting them started anyway.

The Glow doesn't work as well as the synth did, not on carriage engines. The synth had been engineered for this sort of thing, brewed up in an alchemist's tubes to power the city, the factories, carriages, everything. Cheap and easy to make. A glorious achievement for Mahala and the Ministry which ran Alchemical Research along with everything else. Also a handy way to get rid of the mages who'd powered everything before, and had thus had way too much power for the Ministry's liking. Shame synth turned out to poison people too. Glow was the replacement: clean, just as cheap and not given to killing anyone. They said.

The newer carriages managed the switch from synth to Glow better of course, but this one was old when they stopped the synth, and the conversion from one fuel to another had been a rush job. It made for a clunky ride, not helped by the fact I was too stingy to sort out the springs in the suspension; the upholstery, which had long since got ripped out in the back there; and the general dents, gouges and what-not from unhappy passengers. Not much of a ride, my carriage, but at least there *was* a ride. I took us out into the choking flow of rattling, creaking traffic that surged through Boundary and on towards the more exalted areas where her parents lived.

"Why are you taking me back?" She'd settled down into a morose, accepting huddle.

"Because I was paid to." I thought about the electrified doorway. "Not for fun, I can assure you."

"I'll pay you," she said, and I wasn't surprised. It was a usual tactic.

I shook my head. "They're paying me more than a young girl with no income could afford to match."

"I'm shocked they even noticed I wasn't there." Her voice was quiet, suddenly sullen. All the fight had gone out of her. It usually did when they realised it was a lost cause, but the look on her face as I glanced backwards before I overtook a lumbering beer wagon made me pause in my standard responses. There was a panicked look to her, a thoughtful desperation behind her eyes. She turned away, maybe angry that she'd been caught feeling something.

"Your father was very concerned," I managed to lie; though I was pretty sure it was the fact that he wanted to avoid any gossip or scandal that had prompted his concern. I'd half expected him to say, "What will the neighbours think?", though he'd fallen just short of that.

"Concerned he won't have anyone to blame now," Lise said. "Concerned he's lost his personal punchbag and scapegoat. Concerned he's lost the money he paid to you."

It took a tricky bit of manoeuvring to get us on to the road through the slaughterhouse district, which these days had nothing much to slaughter, and on to the ramp that led up to No-Hope and beyond, past the thundering factories of Trade, up to where the sun actually shone on people, to Heights and Clouds and beyond. The slaughterhouse was almost empty of any animals, and full of people making use of the space anyway. You could no longer tell where you were from the waft of blood and the stench of the tannery's main consumable as you headed down Pigeon Shit Lane. Nothing much to slaughter meant nothing much to tan either.

Once we turned the corner on to the Spine, the twisting road that led from the rarefied heights of Top of the World right down to the sunless depths of Boundary, adverts shrieked from every shop, the little blinking Glow lights that powered them shining red and yellow against the planking. We got caught up in a snarl of wagons, carriages and walkers so I was pushed to find a way through. I managed by not caring about scraping the shit out of my carriage – it was too screwed to worry about, with every last scrap of decorative brass rubbed or gouged off years ago. Other people did care, and when they saw I wouldn't give way they usually made a hasty swerve to save their paintwork and the little brass icons of the Goddess, saints and martyrs that were so in fashion in these days. I took particular pleasure in knocking them off.

Glancing in the mirror, I saw what should have been obvious from the start. The fading yellow bruise, a sallower counterpoint to her dusky skin, all along the whole of the left side of her face, half covered by her dark swing of hair. She fiddled with her sleeves, ensuring they were pulled well down over her wrists, making me wonder what could be worse to see under the cloth than was apparent on her face. "Your mother?"

She laughed, a short snatch of cynical wretchedness. "She wouldn't notice if the world ended, as long as she could keep finding new boy toys to play with. She doesn't notice half the things *he* does, or if she does she doesn't care."

Somehow that didn't surprise me. These days, not much does. I miss it sometimes. "So, just wait three months, till you're sixteen, and then go. There won't be a damn thing they can do."

"I won't last that long. It was only luck that I managed to get away this time. He can make me stay, if he doesn't finish me off by then. There's a lot he can do. He's in the Ministry. If I don't stay, I'll end up in the 'Pit, dead first or not."

That made me suppress a shudder. The Ministry were sticklers for appearances, that everything should be seen to be perfect. They ran the guards, were experts in making people disappear, usually sending their corpses to the 'Pit to save their precious crime statistics, or so rumour had it. It would never be common knowledge: they ran the news-sheets too and guarded that privilege jealously. The Ministry ran *everything*, and had done since well before I was born, though Dendal says they didn't used to be as paranoid. That had started around the same time as the synthtox, when they began slowly and subtly drawing the strings ever tighter round us, till now you hardly dared breathe without permission.

I wasn't surprised that my background check into her father hadn't turned this Ministry connection up. It was standard practice among Ministry men to hide who they were, even when someone probed as thoroughly as I did. Secrecy was almost like a second religion for them.

I should take her home. My personal motto runs: Mine is not to do and die, mine is to find the warm body and take the money. Motto number two is: Don't mess with the Ministry, it's bad for your health.

We all have our off-days.

Maybe it was the soft pinging noise inside my head – Dendal trying to get hold of me. Maybe it was the name that accompanied the pinging, one I never wanted to hear again. Or maybe I have a rebellious streak a mile wide. Never fails to get me into trouble. I swung the carriage round with a crunch of gears and headed back down the ramp, making a dray almost crash into the back of me in a welter of swearing and skid marks. We headed for some of the less salubrious addresses, like mine. I liked the lower-rent places; it meant I could save more money for when I got out of this trade. Plus, people in those areas tended to mind their own business, if they liked their ears where they were. I wasn't about to lose the cash for this job, but, contrary to popular opinion, I'm not completely heartless – provided it doesn't cost me anything.

I glanced in the mirror again; Lise's eyes were wide and wet with surprise. I coaxed the Glow to churn faster, skittering the carriage round corners, turning always downwards, towards the workshop of the little man who had made my pulse pistol. Dwarf ran a business making outlandish, and ever-so-slightly-illegal, instruments for a hefty price. He could use an alchemy-student apprentice with a talent for booby traps. I slowed the carriage to a crawl as we passed his workshop. I couldn't afford to give up the cash for this job, and I really didn't want to piss off her Ministry dad by not taking her back, but I could make sure she had somewhere safe to run to next time.

"I've got no choice but to take you home. I don't mess with the Ministry, they don't break my door down and drag me off to the 'Pit. But a girl with your talents should be able to blow a damn big hole in her father's house to escape, right?"

She looked thoughtful, and I detected a hint of deviousness about the quick smile. Good – she was going to need it, but I reckoned she had the brains to figure it out.

"Next time you run away," I said. "Come here."

Chapter Two

By the time I reached the shabby little rooms in No-Hope that Dendal laughably called his offices, it was mid-afternoon. The brief minutes when real, actual daylight shone through the windows were long gone, and the tatty signs proclaiming our business looked forlorn in the almost perpetual half-light of dim Glow globes that had seen better days. Dendal's sign said MESSAGES SENT IN MAHALA, 6M. MESSAGES FURTHER AFIELD, 6M + 1M PER MILE. OTHER SERVICES ON REQUEST. He'd left out the part about magical services only after a long and detailed argument. Mainly about how I didn't want to be arrested for being a mage. It's the only argument I've ever won against him. My sign said simply, PEOPLE FOUND, REASONABLE DAILY RATES, DISCRETION GUARANTEED. Both the signs were rather incongruous, as Dendal had never got round to replacing the bright red flashing sign over the door that stated brazenly, MA'S KNOCKING SHOP,

CHEAP BUT CHEERFUL. We still got the occasional confused customer.

Still, in my rather shady line of work, an address to work from got you out of hired-thug territory and into the licensed-bounty-hunter area. There isn't much difference, I'll grant, except you tend not to get arrested so much in the second category. Being arrested was a somewhat permanent position in this city. Basically, it often meant you were dead. I didn't want to be dead. I still don't.

Dendal was happily absorbed in his work, surrounded by candles of every size and colour. Not to mention a few shapes that would make an acolyte blush. If he'd used his magic he could have lit the room up brighter than noon at Top of the World, that rarefied place at the pinnacle of the city that soaked up sunlight and blocked it for us lesser mortals. Unfortunately for him, and me, our magic wasn't something you spent lightly. Unless you were kinky that way. Instead, he was busy writing, probably a missive for someone who'd not learned their letters, which was most people down here. That's how he earns most of his cash. The magic is a sideline, and one we have to be both discreet and careful about using.

I handed the pay-purse to our secretary, Lastri, and considered asking her to make me some tea, but changed my mind. Lastri always answered the request with a look that seemed to intimate she'd rather stab me.

She raised a cool, dark eyebrow my way and the corner of her mouth slid up in that superior smile that always made me wonder why Dendal kept her on. She must be one of the few attractive women I've met that I've never tried to talk into bed. She'd eat me alive and spit out the bones to use as toothpicks.

"You have a message," she said with a pleased purr that I didn't like one little bit. "Several, actually."

I waited for her to carry on, but she pinched her lips together and wrinkled her nose. Not out of reluctance to share bad news, of that I was sure. Lastri had never quite approved of me. I felt a need to twist her a bit, make her say it when she so obviously wanted to string it out and make me squirm. "If you'd care to share?"

"Message number one is from Val." Ah, yes, the delectable but not exactly bright Val. Nice line in massages, great pair of legs and tonight's lucky lady. I had the whole thing planned, the food specially smuggled in from the takeaway down the road, the wine that was stronger than it appeared, even had a scented candle I'd pilfered from Dendal's collection. Not that I'd need those things, but you had to make it look right.

"It reads, 'Screw you'."

Ah. Well, not entirely unexpected. At least there was still Nirma—

"Message number two is from Nirmala." Lastri was trying hard not to grin by now. "It also reads, 'Screw you'."

Sela wouldn't let me down. Long-term girlfriend, for me that is: must be at least two weeks. Only Lastri looked insufferably smug. She calls me the Kiss of Death, and I am that to any fledgling relationship. Any hint of it taking wing, I kill it. Not intentionally, not even consciously, but I manage it just the same. My trouble isn't that I dislike women or enjoy messing them around. It's just I like them *all*, and the chance to flirt is one I can never pass up. Except with Lastri. I'm not irretrievably stupid or suicidal. "Message number three?"

"Message from Sela reads, 'Screw you sideways'. The PS reads, 'Hope you like how we decorated your rooms. I'm sure you'll like the abstract art. Blobs of red paint are very in this season, but may clash with the curtains'. Seems like your diary is suddenly free, Rojan." Lastri was openly grinning now.

"Anything else?" I kept myself as still as I could, given the circumstances. One hint of weakness and Lastri would never let me forget it. Besides, no point dwelling on it. Only I would, if I didn't do something to take my mind off them. All of them. How the fuck did they find out about each other? It didn't matter. What mattered was that my rooms were splattered in paint and lonely time stretched ahead with little to fill it but work. I was going to miss them. All of them.

I threw myself into my shabby chair behind the desk with no two legs the same length and a complicated system of books and pieces of folded paper trying to keep it level. I'd long since come to the secret conclusion that the desk was alive. I'd get it level, go home, come in the next day and it would be more uneven than ever. We'd come to an uneasy truce, me and desk. I stopped trying to make it flatter than a flatbread, and desk made sure it wasn't so tilted that my cup slid off when I wasn't looking. I'd taken to taping my pens to the surface, none the less.

I reached into one of the drawers, gingerly: we had yet to come to a truce about the springs that made the drawers snap back shut on unsuspecting fingers. My hand darted in, grabbed the bandage and was out again before desk knew what I was about. A small but satisfying victory.

I laid my right hand on the desk, palm up, and undid the hasty bandage from earlier. My finger throbbed with the release of pressure and a runnel of blood oozed out. Luckily, I was used to this sort of thing. It still hurt though. I used the old bandage to clean the wound up as much as I could and got a dollop of the thick green salve that Dendal swore by poised and ready. This was going to sting something chronic. You could etch steel with that salve, I was sure.

"Told you, shouldn't use the pistol."

Dendal's papery voice startled me and the salve dropped from my fingers and splatted on to the floor.

"Namrat's bloody balls, Dendal, you almost gave me an apoplexy."

He grinned at me in an absent-minded way, his thin, grey hair flying about him haphazardly. A spare sort of figure, quite a bit older than me, though I've no idea how much. He'd just always been around. He had thin, fleshless cheeks, a shy smile that could transform his face into a kindly grandfather's, and a sort of air that he should be meditating, or was. His thoughts were probably a thousand miles away, playing with fairies. He wasn't always very *here*, if you see what I mean. Too obsessed with his work. Lastri made sure he ate occasionally and didn't fall out of the window thinking it was the door or something. But Dendal wasn't just another absent-minded idiot with fly-away hair. When he managed to get his head out of his books he was sharper than the blade on my pistol and shrewder than ten rich traders. When he spoke, I listened. Well, mostly.

"Pistol's clumsy for someone like you, Rojan."

I looked up sharply. It wasn't often he could recall my name. "No, it's a pretty efficient way of producing pain. I promise you that."

Dendal hummed a tune under his breath and rocked back and forth on the balls of his feet. My thumb was forgotten as his eyes detached from the now. He linked his hands together and *twisted*, bringing a great crack from his hand and a breathless cry. Shit, I hated it when he did that.

His eyes flew wide and he began to babble, nonsense things at first, gradually becoming more coherent. One of his fingers stuck out at an odd angle. Dislocated. Double shit.

Lastri stood behind him, her usually bland face looking worried now as she mouthed something over his shoulder. Something about Dendal trying to contact me all morning. That explained the pinging noise in the carriage – I'd been too distracted by Lise at that point to answer.

The quality of Dendal's voice changed, became deeper, younger. A voice I knew and never wanted to hear again, channelled through Dendal, who would take any pain for his magic, to fulfil his gift and communicate.

"Rojan, at last!" Perak's voice was rasping and weak and I wondered what trouble I'd have to get him out of now. We hadn't spoken in almost eight years, and that was how I liked it.

"Perak." I tried to keep my voice steady as I swore in my head. My brother was trouble, always had been, and if I got involved I knew the trouble would end up being all mine while he waltzed off into another daydream, unaffected. He didn't have his head in the sand about life; it was so far down he could see bedrock.

"Rojan, you have to come." There was that rasping again, and a bubbling sound in his voice. He spoke so low I could barely hear him, but the panic was obvious as he rambled. He'd always seemed to float through life, never seeing or hearing any dangers, and this fear seemed so unlike him I sat up and really listened.

"I'm in the Sacred Goddess Hospital. They took her. They shot us and took her. You have to come, you have to help find her. That's what you do, isn't it? Find people? Please, you have to come." He trailed off and it was only then that I realised he was crying.

My teeth became islands in a mouth as dry as desert. "Find who?"

"Elsa's dead," he said, as though I hadn't spoken. "They killed my wife, they almost killed me, and they took my daughter. You'll come, won't you?"

I didn't hesitate. He'd caused me enough grief to last a lifetime while he sailed through every calamity without scratch or punishment, left all of it for me, but I couldn't leave him with this. I hadn't even known he was married, never mind a father. Yet now his wife was dead and his daughter was missing. The years, and with them the animosity, rolled away. No matter how much I hated it, I was always going to be big brother. "I'll be there as soon as I can."

Dendal staggered to a chair and began the painful business of putting his finger back. At least he'd have enough power from that for a spell or two later, storing the pain, the power, in his muscles for a time until it leaked slowly away. One advantage of the dislocation over the cut, as he often told me, at infinite and tedious length. Pain dislocating and pain putting it back. Twice the pain, twice the power. Which is all very well, but I'd rather have as little pain as possible.

Seeing Perak again was going to be a different sort of painful. On my own personal scale of bad days, this was shaping up to be at least an 8.4.